ALSO BY KEVIN GUILFOILE

My First Presidentiary (with John Warner)

Cast of Shadows

Cast of Shadows

KEVIN GUILFOILE

Alfred A. Knopf New York 2005

THIS IS A BORZOI BOOK
PUBLISHED BY ALFRED A. KNOPF

Grateful acknowledgment is made to Jon Langford for permission to reprint an excerpt from
the song lyric "Last Night on Earth" by Jon Langford. Copyright © 2000 by Jon Langford.
Reprinted by permission of the author.

Library of Congress Cataloging-in-Publication Data
Guilfoile, Kevin.
Cast of shadows / by Kevin Guilfoile.—1st ed.
p.   cm.
ISBN 1-4000-4308-5 — ISBN 1-4000-7826-1 (trade pbk.)
1. Murder victims' families—Fiction.   2. Identity (Psychology)—Fiction.
3. Chicago (Ill.)—Fiction.   4. Physicians—Fiction.
5. Murderers—Fiction.   6. Cloning—Fiction.   I. Title.
PS3607.U48C37 2005
813'.6--dc22   2004048983

Printed in the United States of America
First Edition

For Mo, who said everything would turn out exactly the way it did

The opinions which naturally spring from the character and the situation of the hero are by no means to be conceived as existing always in my own conviction; nor is any inference justly to be drawn from the following pages as prejudicing any philosophical doctrine of whatever kind.

Mary Shelley, from the preface to *Frankenstein*

Part One

Anna Kat at Rest

This wasn't grief Davis felt, staring at her so-still feet pointing at impossible angles to the tight synthetic weave of charcoal carpet. Grief is born. Grief matures. Grief passes. Despair, on the other hand, which arrives in an instant, ferments into depression. And although depression was months away, at least, already he felt himself not caring. About his life, his wife, his practice, his patients, his new home, near the golf course, and his second home, by the lake. He imagined everything—people, property, possessions—in flames while he stood before it all, impassive, not caring.

The fluorescent lights exposed the room from the ceiling straight down, a glow so bright and perpendicular that Davis couldn't find a shadow in the entire place. From the inside, the broad windows to the street looked covered in black paint, and from the outside, beyond the police cars and oily snow-drifts and yellow tape, the store was as white and naked as a nighttime portrait of a home by Mies.

There were cops on the sales floor and they were talking, but Davis's mind registered only the broken echoes of their whispers: *"What's he doing here... he'll tramp all over the crime scene, for Chrissakes..."* The cop standing next to Davis was named Ortega and had been his patient once. Tonight, Ortega had let him in the back door of the Gap—led him through the stockroom and out onto the floor and inside the rectangular checkout island where he now stood—and Ortega was getting his ass reamed by a detective for it. Anna Kat's feet went in and out of focus, but Davis's eyes never left them. From the ankles down they looked like tan plastic, rigid enough to have been severed from one of the mannequin torsos dressed in ribbed sweaters against the wall, and he began thinking about Ortega's lifeless semen and the day he, Dr. Davis Moore, had delivered the bad news to the cop and his pretty wife. Catholics, he remembered; they decided against in vitro. They clucked their tongues at the anonymous DNA and all those extra embryos, the routine runoff of his work. He wondered if they had ever adopted, if the cop, now a parent, might understand that the sorrow Davis now felt was incurable.

Back the way he came, jacketless in the dark and snow. A different cop would drive him home to the big Prairie-style house on Stone Avenue, where Anna Kat's mother, Jackie, would be sobbing into the consoling collars of their neighbors. He would prescribe something for her and pour the Macallan all around and hope they could manage a numbing, dreamless sleep. The first morning after would be the worst of all, when he would wake having forgotten, and then, in the daylight, remember that his only child was dead.

Anna Kat at Sixteen

— 1 —

These women were older than his wife. More desperate maybe, Terry thought. They were around his age, late thirties, and that embarrassed him. In front of men, he was never uncomfortable talking about Martha's age. In fact, he liked to show her off with hand-holding and impromptu snuggling and by sharing the same side of the table at restaurants. He was certain he could give up drinking or smoking pot, and he planned to when the child was born. Pot, anyway (if there ever was a child). But there was no high like the ability to inspire jealousy, and his marriage to young, smart, sexy Martha could turn other men a sickly pale green. That high he could never quit cold turkey.

The other women were stealing curious looks at Martha, her face tilted at a month-old issue of *Newsweek*. Of course, they were wondering what a woman so young was doing here. There was both envy and pity in the creased corners of their eyes when they glimpsed her and then looked away. Their husbands noticed her, too, Terry figured. The first look gauged the size of her breasts. The second, the shape. The third lingered long enough to measure her youth, her weight, her curves, her face against the standard of other men's wives.

Whatever sexual electricity her husband imagined throughout the room, Martha Finn was oblivious. She was nervous, though, for reasons that had nothing to do with jealousy or fantasy or lust. Unlike many of these women, her eggs and ovaries functioned as designed. And unlike many of these men, Terry's sperm were frisky and numerous, which accounted for the self-satisfied grin on his face now, she figured with a wince.

A nurse led them from the white leather chairs, past several examining rooms and unmarked doors, and into Dr. Moore's office. From the clean lines of the windows to the custom couch and desk, Davis Moore could have been any successful professional. There was a disconnect, a deliberate one, between the spare, monochromatic environs of the waiting room and the warm mahogany of Dr. Moore's office.

"It still seems so strange," Terry Finn said, his fear concealed beneath an anxious snicker. Martha touched his knee.

At work Terry was used to being the alpha male in the room, but Dr. Moore—tall and thin with a long torso and a tight weave of brown hair (a politician's head of hair, Terry thought)—was an impressive figure. He wore a white clinician's jacket over an expensive cotton shirt and a red silk tie. His voice was a gentle but commanding baritone, as steady as his hands, which amplified relevant words with confident gestures. His desk was free of clutter, suggesting a man who solved problems as he encountered them and immediately disposed of the paperwork. He was also modestly famous: *Chicago* magazine had named him one of the city's "Top Docs," stating in a caption under his picture (which Martha had carried in her purse since they had made the appointment) that Davis Moore was one of the nation's leading experts in cloning and cloning ethics.

"Some couples have doubts about the procedure," Davis said. "Some have moral questions science can't answer. And there's quite a bit of opposition from some of the organized religions, of course. Do you go to church?"

"On Christmas." Martha reddened.

"If it makes a difference to you, I believe in God myself, and I'm at peace with the science at work here," Davis said. "We can't clone a soul, you know. Actually, I've found that some religious people find cloning a less troubling option than conventional in vitro, with sperm and egg." He had been through countless of these preliminary meetings and could predict the questions, and even the order in which they would be asked. He barely listened to them before answering anymore.

"You don't need to create as many embryos, is that right?" Martha said.

"That's right. In many cases now, we need only one."

"I know there are some legal issues," she said. "I've been doing some searching on the Internet. A little reading here and there. Only enough to make me realize how little I understand." She giggled, and when she smiled Davis realized how it changed her, as if her unsmiling face were a masquerade disguise, and her grin like an unveiling. "I know some doctors out east got in trouble last year."

"We are bound by strict guidelines—rules and laws both—and there are severe penalties for violating any of them. They range from loss of a doctor's medical license to jail time. For instance, the donor must be dead. That's to make sure your child doesn't run into his double in line at Jewel." Terry and Martha and Davis laughed.

Martha said, "It seems incredible to me—well, the whole process is still incredible to me—but amazing that you can clone someone after they're dead."

"DNA isn't as fragile as we once thought, and although we have sophisticated methods for storage and preservation, they really aren't even necessary," Davis said. "With current technology we can recover viable DNA even from long-dead tissue. Once an individual is cloned, however, his remaining DNA is destroyed. We never make multiple clones from the same individual. Your child would be the only person alive with his genetic markers. Unless the procedure results in twins, of course."

"Exactly who are the donors?" Martha asked, her voice becoming more assured.

"Sperm and egg donors, mostly. When they go through the donation process they indicate whether or not they want to make their DNA available for cloning after they pass on. If the answer is yes, they also contribute blood—it's ironic, but we can't clone from reproductive cells alone—and are paid about three times as much. If they're egg donors, the fee could be a multiple of ten."

"Women donate their DNA less frequently," Martha said, recalling a fact from her research. "That's why most cloned children are boys."

"Correct. Sperm donation is much more common than egg donation, and there are still very few people who donate cells specifically for the purpose of having them cloned. For most donors, it's an afterthought, a way to make a few extra bucks just for rolling up your sleeve and signing your name on one more line. Some people do it for ego: the thrill of knowing their DNA will live on, something like a quest for immortality, although that's a lot of nonsense, of course. A lot of people, particularly women, still find the idea of their genetic duplicate to be a little unsettling. An old classmate of mine wrote an article in the *New England Journal of Medicine* last year claiming some relationship between this phenomenon and female self-image. I don't know if I believe that, but who knows? There are control issues, too. Regulations. We don't want people being cloned without their permission. Laws and ethics say we can't just take nail clippings out of a wastepaper basket and clone a person without his knowledge. And as you're aware, there have been multiple privacy laws enacted by Congress over the last five years. It's illegal even to keep a record of someone's DNA unless they've been charged with a serious crime."

"How does implantation work?" Martha asked. Husbands are never worried about implantation, Davis thought, only extraction.

"When we're ready to move ahead, we will take one of your eggs and remove the nucleus, leaving us with just a shell. Then we add a cell nucleus from the donor—usually DNA from a white blood cell—and stimulate it to behave as if it were an egg fertilized naturally. After that, the implantation is identical to in vitro."

"I understand there are more applicants than donors." For some reason, Martha tried to hide the tiny piece of fringed notebook paper on which she'd written her questions. "If we decide to put our name on the waiting list, how long should we expect before DNA becomes available?"

"Some people will wait three or four years, but it's not just first come, first served. Martha, you said in your pre-interview that Huntington's disease runs in your family?"

An impolite question from anyone but a physician. "Yes," she said. "I had myself tested. I'm a carrier."

"That makes you a priority candidate. You'd go to the top of the list. Any child you would have through natural conception or through a conventional insemination or in vitro process—that is, a technique that uses your own genetic material—would be at high risk for Huntington's. The cloned embryo you would receive will be screened for any known hereditary disease, so you could still carry the child without passing on any propensity for illness. In essence, with cloning, you're adopting a child in the embryonic stage. And while he is not, technically, your natural child, neither is he somebody else's. From that perspective, I think in vitro cloning is superior to other techniques. There are few gray areas in cloning law. You never have to worry about the natural mother or father showing up one day, demanding their rights to your child."

"What about the parents of the donor?" Terry asked.

A good question, but a telling one, Davis thought. He's more interested in potential liability than in the procedure itself. "Well, if they're still alive, the clone is not their offspring, legally or ethically. He'll be a different person, with different likes and dislikes. He will have a personality all his own. A soul of his own, if you believe in that sort of thing, which, as I've said, I do."

"You said 'he.'" Martha squinted, like she was preparing for a gust of bad news. "So there's no chance it might be a girl?"

Davis sucked in a chestful of air. Three times in the last year his answer to this question had been countered with indignant and uninformed lectures on eugenics from angry would-be parents. He was pretty sure at least one of those was a setup, though. The couple showed up on the local news that very same night to register their "shock" about what they learned during their visit to a "clone clinic."

He said, "As much as we'd like the odds to be roughly the same as they are in nature, about fifty-one percent in favor of girls, the present reality of our donor profiles means you're more likely to have a boy. Within that framework,

Congress says gender selection must be random. We do have some choices, however. While I am limited in what I can tell you about the donor, we do try to match some superficial physical characteristics with the parents. You're both fair, so we'll try to find a rough match for hair color. Many people who go through this process don't want to raise a lot of eyebrows among their friends and neighbors over the provenance of their child."

The Finns appeared neither surprised nor upset. Terry said, "That's another question I had. How much of this information is public?"

"Yes. Good. That's important," Davis said. "As the parents of a cloned child, you'll be required to have him checked every six months by a pediatrician, at least until his sixteenth birthday. We have a doctor on staff here, Dr. Burton, and she is excellent, but you won't be required to use her if you're more comfortable with someone else. Whomever you choose, however, you will need to notify your child's pediatrician that he is treating a clone, and that doctor will file regular reports to this office. It's all for the sake of ongoing research, as well as to safeguard the integrity of the procedure, and it's all protected by the doctor-patient privilege. By the way, we perform many different kinds of procedures here, and Dr. Burton sees other patients, not just cloned children, so no one will be suspicious if they spot you in her waiting room."

"What about the child?" Martha asked. "Would we tell him?" She added hopefully, "Him or her."

"That's up to you, of course. I think most therapists agree you should wait until they're in their teens, at least. It's a lot for a kid to handle, existentially speaking. Of course, in fifteen years, it's not going to seem as strange or new as it does now." After a silent moment Davis looked at the clock, but patiently, the way they'd taught him seventeen years ago at the University of Minnesota. "I have another appointment waiting, but do you have any other questions? We can stay here until they're answered."

They didn't. Not at this point. Cloning was still so new. Just to be talking about it in a comfortable, old-fashioned room like this, surrounded by wood paneling and books and maps on the wall—it was weird, like something out of H. G. Wells. Davis intended it that way. Get them accustomed to the idea over time, and over time weed out the ones who aren't ready. The initial meeting, he always said, was the first of many trials.

He walked them to his office door and then returned to his desk and made notes in a newly created file on his computer. *Martha and Terry Finn. High-priority candidates. Wife wants child more than husband does. Will probably return for another consultation, or seek second opinion. Don't expect to schedule this quarter.*

In their Acura, suffering the stop-and-go traffic along the circumferences of look-alike suburban malls, Martha read aloud random half sentences from the New Tech Fertility Clinic brochure as Terry tried to keep both her and sotto voce sports radio playing on separate channels inside his head.

Terry wanted a child, he supposed. He knew Martha wanted a child, and they had discussed the many options and consequences before deciding to go this route. Before deciding to enter a DNA lottery. Reproduction the historical way, the God-conceived and Darwin-endorsed way that begins with prodigious or precisely timed coupling, results in children of a certain kind. Before birth you didn't know anything about them, of course, except maybe the gender, but the things you learned as they grew up were not so much surprises as they were the winnowing of potentialities. He thought of the Sunday after he and Martha returned from their honeymoon. They had opened their wedding presents in front of a small gathering of family. Each wrapped parcel was a mystery of sorts, but contained a gift checked off from their registry. Unwrapped, the appliances and silver and china were pleasing and familiar. Your own child must be a little like that. A gift to you from yourself.

But a clone. A clone is not the same. A clone is a gift from a stranger. A clone could be loved as much as your own flesh and blood, he was sure, but the light and darkness inside a clone child is not the light and darkness inside your own soul. Unlike a natural child, evolution has not sorted through the genes of two people and made something new and better. In a clone, the mistakes of the last generation's DNA are repeated. Their child would be an old model, and who knows what kind of glitches he'd suffer?

But Terry could tell by Martha's tone that the prospect excited her. According to the literature and the videos they'd explored, it would be a long year or more of testing and counseling and schooling, harder on her than it would be on him. Over the last ten months, as they'd seesawed back and forth over the idea of being parents, he found himself just as happy when she was leaning toward yes as when she was leaning toward no. A little boy, a stranger, would start his life by profoundly changing theirs. He knew it was the right thing.

He reached over to touch her left knee, but the seat belt and windshield glare had positioned her body so that he couldn't reach it with his hand, and so he rubbed his knuckles against the blue cotton covering her hip and with his thumb made cuneiform shapes on the top of her thigh that he hoped would translate as affection.

Martha smiled and closed her eyes, leaning back against the headrest. She set the brochure on her lap and with her own thumb tickled her flat belly and imagined herself as host to a new life for a man now dead. She knew it wasn't like that exactly, but she believed in people, loved all people, loved even their mistakes, and believed that every person, even saintly ones, wanted and deserved a second chance.

— 2 —

From the passenger seat of his twenty-year-old Cutlass Supreme, Mickey Fanning watched the door of the New Tech Fertility Clinic for most of three days. Each morning he arrived at 7 a.m. and claimed the best of spot of all, on the opposite side of the street and just south. This morning he shifted into park, freed himself from the fraying shoulder harness, and scooted across the bench seat. It had occurred to him the night before that he would be less conspicuous if he weren't behind the wheel.

At eleven, exactly eleven according to his old watch, which he checked and adjusted whenever time and traffic were given on talk radio, he slid back to the driver's side and pulled out, circling the block until he could find a less good but still adequate surveillance position. At 3 p.m. he did it again, settling even farther down the street. He left for his motel only after the last doctor locked up, noting the exact times of the physicians' arrivals and departures in a perfect-bound pocket notebook, the cover of which he had decorated with blue ballpoint crosses and the letters JESUS across the top and JUSTICE down the left margin, with each word sharing the adorned initial *J*.

His cleverest friends called him Mickey the Gerund back in the days when he had clever friends. Since he was nineteen or so, Mickey had been suspicious of clever people. Clever people were very nearly intellectuals, and intellectuals were the reason—one reason, anyway—that the world was going to hell soon, starting with the Arab nations, followed shortly thereafter by atheist China, pagan India, and then, probably, the United States, from the coasts inland (although the heartland was rotten with sin, too, a fact to which he was about to testify). Intellectuals, in his experience, didn't believe in right and wrong. Mickey the Gerund believed in nothing but. Not just the practical right and wrong of deeds as revealed to the apostles by the example of Jesus Christ (although that, too), but right and wrong as it has existed from the beginning (and ever shall be, world without end. Amen). God did not arbitrarily decide what was right and what was wrong; God was right and wrong incarnate. What else did Jesus mean when he said, "No one is good but God alone"? The Lord did not invent righteousness, but instead was made up of it. If Mickey were ever called to account by the laws of man for what he had done and what he was about to do, he would calmly produce his four-hundred-page typed manifesto, in which he explained this and other truths. Few would understand it, but those few would have a chance, just a chance, of passing through the needle-eyed gates of His Kingdom.

He watched a couple exit through the tinted doors. The man was older than the woman and they were holding hands. She was young and fit and wholesomely pretty. He watched her, was aroused by her. He prayed in a distracted whisper, but the words spilled out in an unexamined, rote chain. Mickey the Gerund did not believe that sex was evil in itself (and procreation was, of course, preferable to the reproductive perversions that took place in jars inside the clinic), but he was certain that his sudden covetous lust for this woman was proof she was trapped in the clutches of a demon. Would it not distort the bigger picture, disrupt the master plan, he could extract some measure of justice through her. He wasn't going to fall for such wicked temptation, however. The devil would no doubt sacrifice a common siren to maintain control over the hell soldiers still inside the building. Mickey had sworn off many sins on the day he decided to give himself to Jesus, women being one of them, and women had been the hardest of all to give up. In many ways celibacy had been the most rewarding, however. He saw things clearly. So long as a man thinks he might again know woman, his mind will always be fogged with desire, and Mickey was reminded of this by every unclean thought and every painful erection.

Mickey pointed his first and second fingers at the couple as they paused beside their parked Acura down the street, cocked his thumb hammer, and let it fire, first at her, and then at him.

— 3 —

"Here. I got you a present."

Anna Kat placed in front of Davis a thin, square package, about as long on a side as one of her slender fingers. Then she reached back and found a chair with her hand and pulled it forward so she could sit opposite him, across his desk.

"What's this for?" he asked, pleased. Anna Kat's visits to his office were often inconvenient but they always cheered him. Surely it was not unusual for a man to be proud of his daughter, to feel bettered by her, but Davis dared to consider his relationship with Anna Kat especially close. In spite of his dedication to work, he had raised the kind of young woman a teenaged Davis Moore would have admired, would have befriended, would have pursued with all his energy and charm. More important, he had raised the kind of young woman who would have seen through teenaged Davis Moore's unflappable, swaggering bullshit.

"It was supposed to be for your birthday," she said. "But then I figured you could use it before then, and anyways, once I get a gift for someone, I pretty much want to give it to them right that second, so I guess you could say this is really a thanks-for-the-impatience-I-inherited-from-*you* gift."

"From *me?*" Davis pretended to be offended as he lifted the tiny-bowed present and began picking at the wrapping. "Your mother's the impatient one. Always was."

She laughed. It was so easy to make her laugh. When she was small he could get her started, and the giggling recharged her like an alternator, until minutes had gone by and she became incapacitated by a delirious aerobic seizure. That would get Davis started, too. Countless times, Jackie discovered them together in the family room, turned on their backs like turtles inverted on their shells, at the mercy of spasms of laughter.

The tape unstuck and the paper unfolded to reveal a small, reflective disc in a black plastic case. "What's this?"

"Newly uncovered birth and death records: Arkansas, Missouri, Texas, Oklahoma, New Mexico, and Nevada. Eighteen hundred through 1833, although not all the states are complete."

Davis turned it over. It had no label, or even printing. "Where did you buy this, exactly?"

"Buy?" AK fingered through a bowl of candy on his desk for something chocolate, no crunch. She pinched a tiny Hershey bar, unwrapped it in a manner that was unconsciously similar to the technique just used by her father to unwrap his gift (picking at the ends, first the left side and then the right). "No buy," she said with candy in cheek. "Download. Copy. Burn."

Davis reproached her with a severe stare.

"Yeah. So," she said. "There was a certain amount of hacking involved." A remorseless confession.

Davis shook his head.

"You can *possess* information, but no one can *own* information, Dad," she said. "These are allegedly public records just sitting on a server in Dallas, and they weren't going to release them for another two years. Even then they were going to charge an astronomical fee for the privilege. That's fascism."

"Uh-huh."

"This isn't just an early birthday gift, it's an act of nonviolent protest."

"Well, thanks," he said, and he meant it.

"Speaking of violence"—in the bowl she found a peanut butter cup she had missed on her last pass—"heard anything from the religious wrong lately?"

Davis shrugged. "Eh. Letters. Notes. Barely literate stuff. A lot of quoting and misquoting from the New Testament."

"Anything from the Hog?"

From the credenza behind him Davis pulled an inch-thick stack of erratically lettered envelopes, bound by a rubber band. The letters inside were all signed "HoG," and accompanying each signature was a crude drawing of a hand with the index finger extended upward. Davis had once joked to Gregor, one of his partners at the clinic, that the person who sent them must be a University of Arkansas Razorbacks football fan. *Go, Hogs!* Davis joked. *We're number one!*

"Threats?"

"Sure. Or warnings, anyway."

"You're so casual about it. I hate that."

"Do you want me to look more nervous?"

"Yeah," she said and then smiled. "I just think about it a lot. I don't want anything to happen to my dad."

"Nothing's going to happen to me, AK." He knew this had been on her mind lately. "That . . . *the incident* last month with the clinic in Memphis, that was a freak thing. And they caught the guy. Or he's dead, anyway."

"He had an accomplice."

That was probably true. Police suspected the bombing had been instigated by the infamous Byron Bonavita, and they might have blown their best chance yet of capturing him. An investigation of the dead conspirator had been little help so far. "Maybe. Maybe not. I won't lie. There are a lot of insane, angry people and it's going to happen again sometime. Somewhere. But you want to worry, worry about me when I'm driving up the Tri-State Tollway. I'm much more likely to get myself killed in merging traffic than I am in some explosion here at the office."

"Yeah, yeah, I know. We already had that talk in driver's ed. A state trooper came and he had gory slides of car wrecks and everything. It was gross."

"Besides, if you're so certain something's going to happen to the clinic, why are *you* here today?"

"Money." Anna Kat turned her head sideways and dropped her hand, palm-up, on the desk. She wiggled her fingers. "Besides, I'm too young and pretty to die. Stick with me at all times, Dad, and you'll be perfectly safe."

God, Davis thought. How often since the day she was born had he silently expressed the same notion in reverse? If he could only be with her all the time, nothing could happen to her. To them. He pulled his wallet out of the desk and placed two twenty-dollar bills in her hand.

"Speaking of young and pretty, I saw Dr. Burton in the hall," she said.

"Did you say hello?"

"I did," she said, then, "Mom hates her."

Davis froze his hand above the drawer as he was about to return the wallet there. "What are you talking about?"

"She says she doesn't like having someone that pretty around you all day. She says Dr. Burton's just your type." Her voice was singsongy in the last few syllables, in imitation of her mother.

"She said that to *you?*"

AK shook her head. "To Aunt Patty. She was kidding. I think. Sort of. Little bit."

"That's crazy."

"We don't use that word, Dad. Remember?"

Davis frowned. Yes, he knew better. Jackie's family had a history of mental illness and a tradition of suicide going back four generations that they knew about. She could be eccentric at times (a trait that he had found alluring once), and Davis and AK monitored her odd behavior for signs of true irrationality. Occasionally, father or daughter would worry when they caught Jackie talking to herself, or when she began one of her obsessive weeks of top-to-bottom housecleaning, but the other would usually counsel patience. The advice always proved to be sound when Jackie returned to normal.

And, AK might remind him, Davis had been through a stretch of odd behavior himself: an embarrassingly clichéd midlife crisis in which he purchased an impractical performance car and even took seven weeks of skydiving lessons, although he quit before his first solo jump. Davis never cheated on Jackie, never even considered it, but over several late nights at the office he confided his concerns about Jackie's health to Joan Burton, and that established an intimacy between them that his wife could no doubt sense. He wasn't sleeping with Joan but they were keeping a different kind of secret.

"It would help Mom if you were around the house more. Heck, maybe I'd like it, too." She stretched across his desk and punched him collegially in the arm. "Especially the weekends. Of course, I'm going to be working Saturdays soon, but you could still hang with Mom. Work with her in the garden."

Davis's hours at work had long been a point of contention with the Moore women. In one of her less subtle moments, Anna Kat had framed for him a *New Yorker* cartoon that labeled one of the caricatures a "Stay at Work Dad."

Typically, Davis didn't commit. "You looking forward to your job?"

"It's just the Gap," she said. "I spend half my time there, anyway. And now that Tina works there it'll be like regular Saturdays, only with an employee discount."

Davis laughed.

"Let's do something," Anna Kat proposed. "The three of us. This Saturday. Before I start. How about we go into the city? Eat at Berghoff's. Maybe do the architecture tour."

He had appointments on Saturday. Three of them. In his periphery, he could see them on his computer screen, highlighted in blue. Many of his patients couldn't take time off during the week to see him. He'd explained it to Anna Kat a hundred times.

"All right," he said. "That sounds like fun."

"I'll make the reservations." AK jumped to the flat treads of her tennis shoes and walked around his desk and drew his cheek next to hers. When she pulled away Davis could see red scratches on her cheek, already fading, transferred from his half-day stubble. He was lucky to have a teenaged daughter who wanted to spend any time with him at all. "I'm gonna hit the Beast for an hour before Old Orchard. Then I'll be at Libby's. Don't wait up."

AK walked down the hall and Davis could hear her call good-bye to Ellen, the receptionist. He turned toward the window and a half minute later he saw her bike accelerate into frame as it turned from the sidewalk onto the street. Her hair had grown about six inches below her helmet and it flared above her shoulders as the air drafted past.

"I love you," he said quietly, which he often did in those days, just to hear the words said.

— 4 —

In the parking lot outside a football stadium some years ago, Mickey the Gerund saw a friend (this one a like-minded friend, a friend to the cause) pull down the backseat to give him access to a cooler of soda pop in the trunk. Mickey's Cutlass didn't have such a feature, but he immediately saw its usefulness, and constructed one of his own. With a hacksaw, he cut a piece from the middle of the backseat about the size of a box you'd buy boots in, and he cut a slightly smaller piece from the metal frame behind it. When reassembled, it looked like an armrest recessed into the back of the seat, although if somebody sat against it, the odd piece would probably come loose. Fortunately, no one ever sat back there anymore.

His sons used to sit there in the days when he so arrogantly put himself and his family before God. We are all born sinners, he realized now. Specifically, we are born with the animal instincts to survive, to seek pleasure, and to reproduce. If you are a God-fearing, God-loving man, you are obligated to act on the last of these urges and to sublimate the first two. This is a paradox of sorts: God wants us to live and to procreate in order to spread His gospel on earth. But ultimately, life here in this bodily dimension means very little to the Lord or to His truest followers. Death here means nothing. What did John Lennon say about dying? "It's like getting out of one car and into another." Something like that. John Lennon was an agnostic or a Buddhist or a Hare Krishna or some crazy damn thing, but that part he got right. Too bad he didn't know Jesus so he could find out just how right he was.

Mickey's guns had never bothered his wife, Bev. Her father had been a hunter and she grew up in a house full of rifles and bows. Oddly enough, she became alarmed only when Mickey wanted to learn how to use them right. He joined a gun club and went there for target practice three days a week. When Jim, their oldest, turned ten, Mickey started to bring him along. Before he'd let Jim shoot, he taught the boy how to carry a gun and how to store it safely. How to check to see if it's loaded, and how to clean it. He taught Jimmy *respect* for guns. Bev didn't see it that way.

"I don't like having all these weapons around," she said. "I don't like you getting Jimmy all excited about them. He buys the magazines now. And the catalogs. I want him to have other interests. I want him to play sports and have hobbies he can share with his friends at school, not just his daddy."

"It's just target practice," Mickey told her. "It's a sport he can enjoy all his life. Like golf."

At the recommendation of a friend at the beer distributor where he worked, Mickey started meeting Tuesday nights with a special group. He called it Bible study, and Bev assumed it was a male-bonding thing somehow related to Promise Keepers and didn't ask too much about it. It didn't have anything to do with Promise Keepers.

They numbered thirteen and called themselves "The Hands of God." They usually met in the kitchen of Phillip Hemley, who worked a white-collar job in Morgantown somewhere. Insurance. They talked about how modern-day religious institutions obscured the true word of God under a fog of politically correct bullshit. They talked about what God *really* said in the Bible, and what He preached in the non-canonical texts that the Catholics originally (and the Protestants since) have hidden from the flock. They talked about the words of God that the selfish and the weak didn't want to hear.

Until one day when Mickey the Gerund suggested they stop complaining and do something about it.

A few weeks later, Mickey the Gerund came home to Bev and their sons and announced that he had quit his job. He sold their house, too (and put a down payment on a smaller place in another town), and had withdrawn about a third of their savings. I'll be gone for a while, he told them. He'd return if he could, but then he'd be gone again soon after. Bev would have to support the boys on the few thousand he left them and on the money she made cutting hair.

The other members of the Hands of God had taken secretly from their own savings and given Mickey about $80,000 in cash. Phil, the insurance guy, said they were his "backers," and they talked about it as if it was an investment, but they weren't going to get their money back. They were sponsoring Mickey the way the kings and queens of Europe supported explorers to the New World, but for the Hands of God, the return would be everlasting life.

Two months later, Mickey returned to the smaller house as a new man, called into God's army. He announced that he couldn't love them anymore, that he was giving all his love, every bit of it, to God. To seal the covenant, Mickey explained, he had taken a razor blade and circumcised himself in a motel bathroom. Bev left with the kids that night, and the following week she took out a restraining order against him, which was insane. He told her he would never hurt them. In fact, he was sacrificing himself *for* them. He had answered God's call, as Abraham did, and hadn't God said to Abraham, *I will bless you abundantly and make your descendants as countless as the stars and the sands of the seashore; your descendants shall take possession of the gates of their enemies and in your descendants all the nations of the earth shall find blessing—all this because you obeyed my command?* His family would be rewarded for Mickey's service. They had nothing to fear.

He stayed for another month or so, his split-level becoming the new head-quarters (a church even) for the Hands of God, who made plans and studied maps and prayed together. They agreed on the details of the next expedition, and Mickey left in his Cutlass Supreme to make it all happen.

They made one mistake. In Memphis. One of the Hands insisted he had a friend down there—a like-minded friend—who could help with the opera-tion. Reluctantly, Mickey agreed because the friend offered him a place to crash and the Memphis mission was going to take at least two weeks, which would devour a large chunk of his hotel budget.

After the two weeks were up, and the mission had just been completed, the friend ended up getting himself killed—shot in the chest by Memphis cops—and Mickey was nearly caught fleeing the scene. In a meeting, the Hands of God agreed that on the next job, in Chicago, and on every job after, Mickey would work alone.

At exactly four-thirty in the afternoon on his third day of surveillance out-side the New Tech Fertility Clinic, he climbed over the front bench and crouched in the backseat. His windows weren't tinted, but they were dirty, covered in dust and white water spots, and the rear dash was piled high with mystery paperbacks and magazines and maps and fast-food containers, all of which acted like military camouflage netting, protecting the inside of the car from curious eyes. He opened the pass-through and retrieved a narrow black plastic storage container from the trunk. He recalled the combination, and the box creaked apart in halves. Wedged in the foot well, he began assembling its contents.

— 5 —

Davis stood inside the desk at reception and opened the patient's folder in his hands. He had his back to the waiting area, and when he looked up he could just see inside Joan Burton's examining room.

In her white smock, with her back to him, talking to a young boy and his mother, Joan displayed none of her sensual curves. He couldn't see any part of her perfectly oval face with its impossibly deep dimples or her long, elegant fingers or her thick ebony hair, which, when not restrained by pins and spray as it was now, sprung from her head in exciting, unpredictable ways. At a holiday party last year, Joan drew stares from every man and woman in the restaurant, with her hair framing her face like an ornate ceremonial headdress. Davis had stolen long, chaste looks at her all night.

He wrote down a list of prescription medications this patient was currently taking and returned to his office with the information, which he relayed to a pharmacist holding on the phone. Then he input the information into a computer file (where it belonged) and tossed the notepaper away.

Davis reached across the desk to his phone and dialed home. His wife picked up on a digital extension, and from the thinness of her voice Davis could tell she was outside in the garden.

"Hi," she said.

"I'm coming home early," Davis said. "Do you want me to grab something on the way?"

"Like what?"

"I dunno. Italian."

"AK's not here. And she's eating over at Libby's."

"She told me. Is she sleeping over there?"

"Probably."

"Perfect," Davis said. "I'll pick up something at Rossini's for the two of us. You grab a nice bottle from downstairs. We haven't had a date in a long time."

"A very long time," Jackie said.

"I'll see you in half an hour," he said. "I love you."

"Bye," she said.

Davis grabbed his sport coat and walked down the hall. He knocked on Joan's open door—she was still consulting with a patient—but didn't stop or say anything as he passed.

"Good night, Davis," she called after him.

He waved to Ellen and she smiled back. The waiting room was empty, and he casually stooped to snatch some magazines from the couch and return them to the coffee table. He turned out a light that, to his irritation, others usually forgot to turn off. He detoured into a corner conference room and opened the vertical window blinds on a pair of adjacent exterior walls.

Outside, it was warm and humid, and the air stuck to his face like a plastic Halloween mask. There was an easy breeze from the lake, which did little more than push the heat around. There were no protesters at the curb, at least. The heat and the rain often kept them away.

In his head, he calculated the quickest route to Rossini's this time of day. He kept an ever-updated table of driving instructions in his short-term memory, convinced he could add days or even weeks of productivity to his life simply by avoiding traffic. His wife always had the frutti del mare, and tonight he'd have the shrimp tortellini. If he called them by York Street and ordered before the light at Hillman, it should be ready shortly after he arrived. You didn't want it to be ready before you got there. You wanted it to come off the stove just after.

His new Volvo was parked near the back of the building (he left the most convenient spots open as a courtesy to his patients) and he was still experimenting with his keyless remote, getting a feel for its range. Standing at an angle to the front of the clinic, looking through the conference room, he could just make out his car around the corner. He pointed the remote at the conference room window, wondering if he could unlock his car from here, through the double panes of windows.

Later, he'd say it sounded like a cork popping, although he couldn't say for sure if that was the sound of the gun or the sound of metal striking bone.

He knew it was a bullet the instant it entered, just below the left shoulder blade, exploding a rib before exiting his abdomen. It felt like someone had struck him with a baseball bat in the left side while a second attacker stabbed him in the gut with a knife. His knees buckled, and he hung there for an instant, suspended by God knows what, before collapsing onto the walk.

He could hear shouting and pointing (yes, he would later claim in a tired, confused discursive that he could hear people pointing) and he definitely heard a mistuned car speed away, although it didn't occur to him at the time the vehicle might be carrying his assailant. He scratched his head against the pavement looking for blood and couldn't see any. He moved his hand, which had instinctively covered the pain in his belly, and when he held it in front of his face it looked like a flat brush dipped in red paint. Someone approached and tried to turn him from his left side onto his back. He resisted. Then he blacked out.

— 6 —

The Beast was a device invented by Anna Kat's coach, Miss Hannity, from parts of old Nautilus equipment and an even older Universal weight machine. It was designed to increase stamina and also to work muscle groups in the order that a volleyball player would use them. There was a spike exercise and a dig exercise and a serve exercise, and each consisted of a combination of repetitions involving the legs and then the arms. Always the legs and then the arms. Miss Hannity had begun the process to have the Beast patented (she had a lawyer and everything), and once, after a game, she had even asked Anna Kat's father if he would give a medical endorsement of the workout. For marketing purposes. Davis looked it over and said he was impressed but he gave Miss Hannity the names of an orthopedist and a physical therapist. *My word won't carry much authority,* he told her. *And anyway, with some buyers, it would probably be better if you were not associated with me at all.*

AK rode her bike up to a gazebo-like structure behind the school gym. She turned at the last minute and backed up with her sneakers paddling against the pavement, walking it into a narrow stall. She readjusted the bag over her shoulder and jogged to the locker room door.

The fall semester wouldn't begin for another month, but there was sporadic activity at the school throughout July and August. Changing into long, baggy basketball shorts and a size-too-small T-shirt over a black sports bra, she heard other voices and lockers slamming shut, but the showers were mostly empty, which raised her hopes. When she opened the door to the weight room she saw a handful of football players around the bench press, but none of her teammates were working out this afternoon. The Beast was all hers.

She slid into the device on her back and raised her legs in a recumbent bicycle position, with her feet resting on a pair of levers positioned on either side of a tall weight stack. She inserted her arms underneath a padded bar behind her head. One of Miss Hannity's innovations allowed the user to change the resistance without leaving the chair. AK set the weights at a warm-up level and began her workout.

In her headphones was an unfamiliar song, part of a mix given to her by a friend. The singer sounded British. Or maybe Scottish. Definitely rakish. He sang:

> *Last night on earth*
> *Don't pick up that pen*
> *We're so ill-equipped to deal with all*
> *The pressure, risk, and stress*
> *They can't hurt you now*
> *It doesn't matter what they say*
> *You can still feel anger across the grave*
> *But it was fun anyway*

As she marked the repetitions with exhales, the weights behind the bench press stopped chiming on the other side of the room. Through the forest of machines, the boys would be able to make out only parts of her body—her calves, her hips, her shoulders maybe—and AK smiled to herself as she pushed her legs against the weight and extended her arms. They thought they were being so quiet, but their stealth was giving them away.

Only in the last two years had Anna Kat begun to think of herself as pretty. In junior high she had been skinny and bookish and so self-conscious about her height she wore sexless flats and carried herself bent forward, as if her shoulders were made of concrete. Oddly, the girls in her class noticed her potential before the boys did. Pretty girls—popular girls—began inviting her to Starbucks, to the mall after school, to parties. She developed an interest in clothes. Her skin cleared. Volleyball straightened her posture. Her freak- ishly high hips were now the delta of tanned and toned legs that stretched endlessly to her new black pumps.

She felt desired in amounts equal to her desire.

When her workout was finished (three sets each, serves, spikes, and digs), AK grabbed a towel from the shelf and walked out, pretending cool indiffer- ence to the warm, admiring stares on the backs of her legs as the frosted Plexi- glas door slid shut behind her.

Between the weight room and the girls' shower, three pairs of glass doors looked out to the practice fields behind the school. Two of them opened with a sucking sound and AK felt the thick heat balloon in the hallway before the cool, forced air of the school pushed it back. Two runners in tank tops and bil- lowing weightless nylon shorts walked past to the boys' locker room. A third, whom she knew from chemistry, mumbled a bashful "Hey, 'K" and hurried on. A fourth, trailing the others, paused and smiled at her. She waited for the locker room door to shut behind the last of the other runners before say- ing hello, but she couldn't get the greeting out of her throat before the boy ducked into the wrestling room.

Anna Kat followed.

In announcements and on bulletin boards the wrestling room was called the auxiliary gym, but aside from certain PE classes, hardly anyone other than wrestlers used it for practice. It was a small room relative to the main gym— maybe forty feet square—and thick green-and-yellow mats were rolled against the walls. The boy sat on one of these with his palms next to his hips, grinning.

"Hey," he said.

"Hey," she said.

AK sat beside him. The windowless room smelled like hot vinegar from fifteen years of adolescent sweat and poor ventilation. No place Anna Kat knew smelled just like it. It smelled like the worst of boys in close quarters. Like prison, she imagined. The odor depressed her.

"What's going on?" she said.

"Nothing," he said. "I got another disc for you in my locker. Some classic stuff. The Clash. Dire Straits. The Mekons."

She said, "I've been listening to that Mekons disc you gave me last month."

"And?"

"It's growing on me." She stared at the blank wall on the other side of the room.

He said, "Are you okay?"

AK didn't want to talk about her dad. Well, she did, but not with him. She tried to dispose of the matter quickly. "I was at the clinic this afternoon. It's just sometimes I think I'm competing with all those little embryos in test tubes. Other people's kids. I know he cares about me, but he spends more time with them than he does with me. This will really be my last year at home. It's frustrating, that's all."

The round of mat beneath her felt spongy and sticky to Anna Kat's nervous hands, but she remembered how much like concrete it had seemed against her back during a karate elective her freshman year. When the mats were up like this, the wrestling room was floored with thin, sandpapery carpet, and AK removed her right shoe and scratched her toes against it through her sock. It wasn't meant as an advance, necessarily, but in a few seconds the boy had kicked off his left Nike and pinned her shin against the curve of the mat with his calf.

He leaned over and kissed her and she kissed him back, draping an arm over his shoulder and touching the wet fade of his sweaty crew cut. In an instant, he had a hand on her breast.

"Sam," she said, pulling away.

"Hmmph," he said, reattaching his lips to hers.

"Sam," she said, disengaging again. "Let's see a movie tomorrow."

"Like a date." It was a clarification more than a question.

"No," she said. "Just . . . just *something*."

Sam slid his hand up the inside of her thigh and snapped the elastic of her panties with his thumb. "This isn't something?"

She pushed his arm away and laughed. "It is. It's just weird."

"Dating is complicated, AK," Sam said. "This is *un*."

"Un?"

"Complicated." He looked for a smile and didn't get one. "Look, you go to the movies or even Starbucks together and people are talking. You're seeing Daniel—"

"Sort of."

"You're sort of seeing Daniel. I'm seeing Chrissy—"

"And Tanya. And Sue."

"You know about them?"

"What's the matter? More complicated than you thought?"

"Nah." He looked at his feet. "Is that what this is about? I mess around with other girls?"

"No." She shook her head. That wasn't it. The problem she didn't want to admit to was guilt. She felt a bit used. She felt a bit like a user. No one was forcing her to meet Sam, of course. She liked being with him. They did things together that seemed grown-up. They did things together that frightened her. Things that excited her. *That* was the problem. She liked the way he could thrill her, the dangerous feeling she had when they were together. When she thought about it, though, she didn't much like *him*. Although he was intelligent, Sam could be cruel to people he didn't like, and he treated his friends only marginally better. To get laughs he said mean things to people's faces (instead of following the widely accepted high school policy that called for saying mean things behind people's backs). He was indifferent and selfish and cynical, and while these things made him cool and even a kind of popular, that didn't mean that anybody really liked him. If they were dating, she would have to defend him, and Anna Kat didn't know how she would do that.

Sam's hand was inside her shirt and flat against her bare back, pushing her toward him. They were sweaty and gritty and aroused. Sam's teeth closed around her right earring and pulled just the right amount too hard. "Did you lock the door?" he whispered.

"No . . . ," she said, as if an apology were coming.

"Good," Sam said, and he pulled her down on top of him in the narrow space between the rolled-up mat and the wall.

In her locker, several walls and halls away, Anna Kat's cell phone was ringing.

— 7 —

There was no place she knew where Dr. Joan Burton felt more useless than in a hospital emergency waiting room. In a building filled with sick people, sick people she had been trained to help, she could do nothing but sit and do triage helplessly in her head. That boy, twelve or so, has a broken finger. The young man—newly minted from college, she suspected—folded into a chair across from the television like a passenger waiting for his plane to crash, possibly appendicitis. An older woman, escorted irritably by a husband of too many years, most likely psychosomatic something or other; she becomes ill to force him to pay attention to her, Joan quietly diagnosed.

Gregor and Pete, the other partners in New Tech, sat in chairs equidistant from her, the three of them facing different directions. No one spoke. They were worried about Davis (although, secretly, Joan suspected that she cared for his health more than they did, even if they'd known him longer), but there was another element to their concern: it could be any one of them bleeding out in the operating room just now.

The clinic building was on the television, monitored by a rerouted traffic helicopter. From the air it looked institutional and generic, which is what Gregor and Pete and Davis had in mind when they moved in, Joan guessed. The building was nonthreatening, its cube shape unobjectionable to anyone but an architecture critic. Deliberate police paced the lawn in front. She could see yellow evidence flags stuck in the ground at varying radii to the spot where Davis fell. Curious bystanders assembled at a safe distance. A banner of text across the bottom titled the events "Clone Clinic Terror."

Frantic nurses had led Davis's sobbing wife and daughter to another room inside. Joan was thankful for that, mostly because she wouldn't know what to say to them. She had always been uncomfortable around Jackie Moore. Even under these circumstances, every glance between them would be loaded with subtext in Joan's mind.

Davis had confided their occasional troubles to her in intimate detail. Ever attracted to older men (Joan's graduate school relationships consisted of a series of affairs with professors and residents), she reciprocated in an empty, flirtatious way, knowing the aspects of his character that made Davis most desirable—loyalty, confidence, empathy—were the very traits that would keep him tethered to home, even (or rather, especially) if home was making him miserable.

Joan had had three sexual relationships with married men in the past, and she eventually regretted them all. Two of those men were now divorced, and that assuaged and compounded her guilt in equal amounts. The third was still married, and when she was reminded of their affair—by a photograph, or a printed reference to the Garfield Park Conservatory (which he had admired), or by the exit to his home on the Edens Expressway—an icy shiver consumed her. Never again, she thought.

The status quo in her relations with Davis suited her fine. He liked her and she liked him, and except for a touch on the arm that lasted two seconds too long when he was helping her with her coat at last year's Christmas party, it remained unphysical. She could enjoy the vicarious attentions of a smart and handsome and fit older man, and she could sneak looks at him in the office and imagine, in the car on the way home or alone in bed at night, what might have been possible between them had they met at another time, in some other place.

When Gregor appeared through the swinging doors to the trauma center, Joan realized she hadn't noticed he'd been gone.

"It looks good," Gregor said. "He's going to be fine."

"Thank God. Lord. Christ," Pete said. "Are you sure? Can we see him? Can I call that reporter?"

"What reporter?" Joan frowned.

"Channel seven. I'd have to look up her name. She promised me she'd keep the cameras away from the hospital if I called her as soon as we knew something."

Gregor nodded. "Yeah. Call her. In a minute." He looked at the TV. "Any news? Have they caught the guy?"

Pete said they hadn't.

"Bonavita!" Gregor growled. "Fucking Bonavita for sure. He's going cross-country. Memphis, Chicago, probably Saint Louis next."

"I have to call my wife," Pete said. "She's at her cousin's house in Barrington." He slid a hand flush to his forehead, under his short bangs. "Can we go home, do you think?"

Joan said, "We can't hide."

Her partners gave no indication they agreed.

An hour or so later, after Pete and Gregor had made their calls and they had waited again in silence for a nurse to tell them it was okay to come back, they walked through emergency to an elevator that took them to the third floor and Davis's private room.

Davis was unconscious, tubes pushing out of his nose and mouth like the legs of an oversized translucent insect. His thin, taut blond wife, her almost comically round blue eyes tethered to the dressing on his wound, leaned over his bed with the weightless control of an ex-gymnast.

"He needed a lot of blood," Jackie said. "He needed a lot of blood, but he's going to be all right."

Joan suggested New Tech set up a temporary Red Cross donation center at the clinic, and all three doctors agreed to give blood the next day. Joan gave red-eyed Anna Kat a stiff squeeze with one arm, which she answered with a wet, worried stare.

At home, in the dark morning, alone in bed, Joan relived her own years-ago encounter with unchecked evil and told herself, as she would say again in a few months' time when evil would come again, for Anna Kat, that at least the stuff it took from Davis could be replaced.

— 8 —

Mickey the Gerund was over three hundred miles away, in a forty-dollar-a-night highway motel room near Alexandria, Minnesota, before he knew Davis Moore had survived.

Moore had left the office a little earlier than he had the past few days, but Mickey was ready, barrel pointed, scope tuned to the proper focal length. He recognized Moore in the shadows of the foyer, disappearing momentarily into a conference room, where, for some reason, he opened the vertical blinds. Mickey thought about taking him out at the window, and even tensed on the trigger when he knew he had the shot, but decided it was better to be patient. They wouldn't let photographers inside the clinic to see the body, and this was, after all, a media event. He wanted every mad scientist in the world to see Davis Moore bleed out on the ground, and for that he needed to drop the body where the helicopters would have an unobstructed view.

Of the four doctors at New Tech, he'd picked Moore because he was the worst sinner. He was one of the country's most vocal advocates of reproductive cloning, testifying before Congress and writing papers for the journals, and newspaper editorials. He was handsome and eloquent and he helped give the procedure respectability. One of his colleagues had said, after one heated battle in Congress, that if it hadn't been for the advocacy of Davis Moore, the cloning procedure would be unavailable to the thousands of parents who needed it. Somewhere in the backseat of the Cutlass was a torn photo from a magazine, mailed to the Hands of God by a sympathetic acquaintance, that celebrated the smiling physician as if he were a movie star. Davis Moore was near the top of the Hands of God hit list.

"Shit," Mickey spat when the woman on the news said Moore was in stable condition, recovering. The sinner would live to ridicule God another day, and the Gerund's pride was hurt on top of it. He considered himself a good shot at that distance. Still, Mickey had fired a bullet, the bullet had struck flesh, and news of the event was right now on televisions in Minnesota and California and Washington and probably even Hong Kong. Cameras were showing the yellow-bordered crime scene and reporters were describing to the world the diabolical things Davis Moore did for money and how his assailant clearly wanted him and doctors like him dead. That was the point, after all. There wouldn't be many "fertility" doctors or researchers or even drug manufacturers getting good, sound sleep tonight.

Mickey liked to be philosophical at moments like this. It might be a while, years even, but someday he'd get another crack at Dr. Davis Moore, God willing.

A twenty-four-hour news network, one of only eight channels beamed into this cheap motel, interviewed a pair of advocates, one pro-cloning and one anti-cloning. Mickey sat at the edge of the queen-sized bed holding a bowl underneath his chin and spooning oatmeal he'd made on a hot plate. The ugly pro-cloning woman was ranting about the radical right wing and terrorism and how even her life had been threatened recently by these fanatics. It sounded like an empty, pathetic cry for sympathy but Mickey knew the claim was true because he had done the threatening, plucking her name and dozens of others off the screen during interviews just like this one.

Mickey had seen the anti-clone pansy before, as well. The liberal networks always brought him out to speak for the opposition because they wanted to make anti-cloners look ineffectual. He had a red beard that covered a weak chin, and he wore bad makeup and sweated a lot. He sent his best wishes to the Moore family and said his organization condemned violence and wished the police would bring the criminals responsible for this shooting to justice. Mickey hated this fellow, who cared more about politics than morality. Mickey wasn't anti-cloning, he was pro-God, and he wanted to show the world that God's warriors were strong. He didn't believe that might made right, but rather that the righteous were mighty and the scientists and the feminists and other soldiers of sin would need more than the backing of the Supreme Court and the complicity of the news media to force the surrender of good people. Mickey had a gun and goodwill and a visa stamped by God's hand that would allow him free passage anywhere the Lord's work called him.

Phil and the others would be watching the news back at the church now. Mickey wanted to call them, but they had a rule against that. The feds knew about the Hands of God. They'd be watching the phone traffic. Mickey the Gerund didn't make stupid mistakes.

He opened an atlas on the bed and began charting his way toward the next target. He'd driven miles out of his way tonight, but that was part of his strategy. Mickey had steered to the expressway, pulled on in a random direction, and driven until he was too tired to stay on the road. If he didn't plan his getaway ahead of time, it would be harder for any fed profiler who tried to get inside his mind to catch up with him, impossible to predict his next move.

He'd stay another day in Minnesota to relax. Do some reading. Maybe find a place in the woods where he could take some unscheduled target practice. Obviously he needed it.

Then on to Denver.

Davis at Forty-one

— 9 —

LOCAL WOMAN SLAIN AT OAK STREET STORE
Staff report, Northwood Life

Police are investigating the brutal rape and strangulation of a woman found slain at the Gap store on Oak Street in downtown Northwood late Wednesday.

Anna Katherine Moore, 17, was found dead shortly after 12 a.m. at the clothing store, where she worked as assistant manager.

Sgt. L. C. Clayton of the Northwood Police Department confirmed Thursday that Moore's body was discovered by the store manager, Lisa Stephens, after she received a call from the victim's parents, who became concerned when their daughter didn't return home from work. Moore had been beaten and strangled and there was possible evidence of sexual assault, sources say.

Investigators believe the attack occurred shortly after 8:45 p.m., when Moore sent two other clerks home in advance of a coming snowstorm.

"She had told these individuals that she was going to lock up and head straight home," Clayton said. "Obviously someone stopped her."

Police hope to be able to say more over the next few days as to who might be responsible. "Our detectives are continuing to interview people in an attempt to identify suspects," police spokeswoman Donna Bartlett said.

Moore, who would have graduated in June from Northwood East High School, had worked part time at the store for less than a year. She was planning to attend the University of Illinois in the fall, where she hoped to major in psychology, Stephens said.

Moore was the only daughter of Dr. Davis and Jacqueline Moore of Northwood. Her father, a partner at the New Tech Fertility Clinic on Sheridan Road, was wounded in a shooting incident last year. Police say there is no evidence of a connection between the incidents.

On Thursday, the store remained closed, the sidewalks and entrances fenced in with crime scene tape, as police searched for clues. Individuals who had been to the Gap store on Wednesday, or who might have information regarding this crime, are being asked to contact police.

As news of Moore's death spread through town, residents expressed a range of emotions.

"She was so beautiful and so kind. Who would want to hurt her like this?" Stephens said.

"It makes me real nervous," said a female resident who asked not to be identified. "I've never thought twice about coming down here at night. Nothing ever goes on in this town.

"It's scary," she added, staring at the police tape across the front door.

By Thursday afternoon, a makeshift memorial of flowers and signs had appeared by the main entrance to Northwood East High School. Within hours, friends of the victim had added stuffed animals, photographs, poems, and other notes of remembrance.

"I can't believe it," said one student who described himself as a friend of the deceased. "She loved everybody. And everybody loved her."

— 10 —

The detective was polite each morning when he called, and Davis feigned patience each morning when the detective, after small talk, confessed to having no leads. Well, not zero leads, exactly: a profile had been made of the attacker. The police believed he was white and fair-skinned. They had some general idea about his size, based on the placement of the bruises and the force exerted on her arm, breaking it in two, but that ruled out only the unusually short and the freakishly tall. They did not think he was obese, according to their reconstruction of the rape itself. He may or may not have been someone Anna Kat knew—probably not, because if she had been expecting someone that night, she might have told somebody, but then again, who can say? The medical examiner said the injuries were consistent with rape, but could not comment on whether the state's attorney would include sexual assault along with the murder charge when police apprehended a suspect. When Davis expressed outrage after that information had appeared in the paper, the detective settled him down and assured him that when a beaten, broken, strangled girl has fresh semen inside her, that's a rape in the cops' book, no matter what the M.E. says; and then he apologized for putting it that way, for being so goddamn insensitive, and then Davis had to reassure the detective. That's all right. He didn't want them to be sensitive. He wanted the police to be as angry and raw as he was. The detective understood that the Moores wanted a resolution. "We know you want closure, Dr. Moore, and so do we," he said. "Some of these cases take time."

Often, the police told the Moores, a friend of the victim will think aloud during questioning: *It's probably nothing, you know, but there's this strange guy who was always hanging around* . . . This time, none of Anna Kat's friends could offer even a cynical theory. Fingerprints were too plentiful to be useful ("Everyone in town has had their palms on that countertop," the detective said), and the police were sure the perpetrator had worn gloves anyway, by the thickness of the bruises on her wrists and neck. Daniel Kinney, Anna Kat's off-again boyfriend, was questioned three times. He was appropriately distraught and cooperative, submitting to a blood test and bringing his parents, but never a lawyer. Interviews with Northwood students continued.

Blond hairs were found at the scene, and police had determined they belonged to the killer by comparing the DNA to his semen. With no suspect sharing those same microscopic markers, however, the evidence was an answer to an unasked question. A proof without hypothesis. Before or during the rape, she had been beaten. During or possibly after the rape, she had been strangled. One arm and both legs were broken. Seven hundred forty-nine dollars were missing from a pair of registers, and there might have been some clothes gone from the racks. (The embarrassed store manager wasn't sure about that, inventory being something of a mess, but it's possible that a few pocket tees were taken. Extra large. The police noted this in their profile.)

Northwood panicked for a few weeks. The bakery, True Value, Coffee Nook, the fruit stand, two ice cream parlors, six restaurants, three hairdressers, and two dozen or so other shops, including the Gap, of course (but not the White Hen), began closing at sundown. More spouses met their partners at the train, their cars in long queues parallel to the tracks each night. The cops put in for overtime, and the town borrowed officers from Glencoe. If you were under eighteen, you were home before curfew. The Chicago and Milwaukee TV stations made camp for a while on Main Street (news producers determined that Oak Street, where the Gap shared the block with a carpet store, a parking lot, and a funeral home, didn't provide enough "visual interest" and chose to shoot stand-ups around the corner, where there was more pedestrian traffic and overall "quaintness"), but there turns out to be a limit to the number of nights you can report that there is, as yet, nothing to report, and TV crews disappeared as a group the day a Northwestern basketball player collapsed and died of an aneurysm during practice.

The old routine returned in time. By spring, Anna Kat might not have been forgotten—what with the softball team wearing the "AK" patch, the special appointment of Debbie Fuller to fill the vacancy of student council secretary, and the three-page, full-color yearbook dedication all keeping her top of mind around campus—but Northwood became unafraid again. A horrible alien had killed on its streets; Northwood had been shattered, and the people made repairs. The town grieved and, like the alien, moved on.

— 11 —

Davis prescribed his wife too many pills. When he felt like taking some himself, which was often, he would remove a few capsules from the brown bottle in her bathroom, rub the scar on his belly, and chase the pills with scotch. The bottle's cap boasted cruelly of a mechanism that could keep his child safe. Sometimes he'd sit on the toilet, rolling a crystal rocks glass between his hands, and wonder if he and Jackie were addicts yet, one day deciding it was okay if they were.

Jackie hardly laughed these days. Davis, always reticent, was noticeably more so. "We never make love anymore," Jackie said one night across a cold chicken dinner and supermarket wine (the good stuff from their cellar having been depleted and never replaced). Davis agreed.

Old and strictly observed habits enabled them to go days without talking: Davis locked the doors at night and rose from bed first in the morning; Jackie paid the household bills; Davis curbed the garbage and recyclables early Monday before work; Jackie shopped for groceries on Wednesday; Davis kept the tanks in both cars more than a quarter full; Jackie picked up the laundry and dry cleaning twice a week and changed the sheets every Thursday.

Sometimes when they did speak, frequently drunk or numbed, the words came out in cruel, irretrievable bunches:

God, Jackie, is that really a lot to ask? Do I ever ask you for anything? I expect so goddamn little and you can't even give me that!

You don't ask for a thing, Davis. You don't ask for anything, and you don't give me anything. Honestly, it's not human to live this way!

Northwood's senior class president, a thinnish boy named Mark Campagna, came to the house with Anna Kat's yearbook, or the yearbook she'd ordered anyway, with her name embossed on the cover in gold. Mark explained how he'd passed it around to every kid in the class, and they'd all signed, every single one. He'd made sure of that, even sat at a folding table outside the cafeteria every fifth period for a week and hunted down the kids he'd missed in the hallways between classes. Davis and Jackie thanked him and meant it, but Davis wasn't ready to read a book filled with sentimental teen angst and melodrama, so he put it on the shelf next to her underclassman yearbooks and they promised each other they'd read it on her birthday next year. Jackie read every word the following day.

Then, just as the winter was ending, Jackie's behavior went off-axle. No doubt there were many factors besides Anna Kat's death that snapped her, including her family history and the long, cold winter. These didn't help, in any case. Returning from work one evening, walking from the garage in the lengthening daylight, Davis noticed her digging in the backyard. After watching a minute, he saw she had already turned over most of the sod in the back, leaving two large rectangles of soil with a narrow walkway of grass separating them. She had to have been up to this for days.

"What are you doing?" he asked.

"Digging," Jackie said, not unpleasantly.

Over the next month, she planted obsessively. Flowers and vegetables and even small trees filled the rectangles. To Davis, there seemed no order to it, but clearly there was in her mind. She had an electrician install a floodlight over the back deck, and before bed she would sit at the window in their room and stare down attentively, hand at her chin, as if the backyard were a giant chessboard. Sometimes she seemed pleased, but more often it made her despondent. "No! No! No! No! No! No! No! No!" she'd cry, punching herself just above the knee. Davis would ask her what was wrong and she'd be unable to say. He'd suggest, gently, that she should see a therapist if the garden was causing her so much stress. Then she'd seem all right for a couple of days, hardly mentioning the garden. Then she'd be back in the mud, in her black, knee-high pullover boots and her thick, striped gloves and her sunglasses and baseball cap.

In May, she dug it all up and started over, transferring the plants she could save and basically creating a mirror image of the original, flipping the entire thing on the axis of grass in the middle. Ultimately, she found this configuration even more offensive, and she dug it up again in July and again in September, and on the morning of the first, unexpected frost in early November, Davis found her on the kitchen floor, arms around her knees, sobbing.

The psychiatrist (too late for a psychologist, Davis said) prescribed antidepressants and they seemed to help through the winter. She still seemed cold to Davis, but of course she could have been exacting retribution for the weeks and months he had ignored her when she was calling out to him in the semaphore of odd behavior.

Just before Christmas, almost a year after Anna Kat had been taken from them, Davis asked the detective if the police would return their daughter's things when they no longer needed them for evidence. Later, wondering why he asked, he supposed he felt helpless, maddened by the investigative inertia.

For God's sake, somebody, do something! Pull Anna Kat's clothes from the evidence room! Examine the bloodstains. Maybe for ten minutes, you'll be thinking about her.

Jackie's therapist suggested she return to the garden in the spring. Her attitude toward it would be some measure of her improvement, a yardstick by which the doctor could adjust the dose as well as the combinations of medicine, psychiatric pharmacology being an inexact science, she told them (Davis managed to hold back a sarcastic reply). Jackie still spent most of her days there, but she seemed to enjoy it. June came and went and she hadn't replanted even a single bulb.

In his basement office, Davis kept binders and files with notes about his family history. At the Kane County flea market he bought an old library card catalog for $325 (haggled down from $380), and he flipped over the yellowed bibliographic three-by-fives, filling the blank backs of the cards with information about twenty-seven hundred close and distant relatives. Davis had ancestors fighting in every war back to the Revolution, and long-ago uncles who farmed six of the thirteen colonies. He had a grandfather's grandparents who traveled the world by chartered sail, and great-great-great-greats who never dared a day's walk from the pile of dirty blankets in which they'd been born. He had relations in silent movies, aunts who'd written children's books, and in this room he made connections between them—lines drawn from every twice-removed to every in-law to every stepdaughter and illegitimate son. Six different branches of his family tree grew like ivy across the blue walls, and in their comforting shade he trapped himself for hours and hours and hours. More than that since AK's murder.

Davis had a distant cousin (for lack of a more descriptive phrase) who had been an outlaw in Missouri. None of his dead relatives fascinated him more, although information on Will Denny's life was hard to come by, and what there was of it was at best half legend. Even his exact position on the Moore family tree was in doubt. Denny sardonically referred to himself in letters as a *filius populi*, a legal euphemism literally meaning "son of the people," and used by courts and churches and genealogists in place of the more colloquial "bastard." Denny's mother was Davis's great-aunt several times over, but the name of his father was a mystery, and Davis had long conceded that the statute of limitations had run out on the solution.

Through persistence and the Internet, Davis found a collector in Saint Louis who owned a photo of Denny, taken toward the end of his life. The collector allowed Davis to copy it, and the grainy, glossy reproduction hung in a frame by the door in the basement office. Silver-haired Will Denny grinned out from his daguerreotype. He wore an expensive high-collared suit, a carefree old-timer of sixty years or so with plenty of money and the freedom to spend it on stud poker and liquor and whores. His hands were thick, and his face used and pale and friendly. Davis always imagined a boisterous crew of associates just outside the frame that day—hangers-on, apostles, some drunk. Denny posed with a black tie, a long rifle, a muscular dog, and a new hat hanging on the high back of his chair.

Staring at it these days, Davis found it difficult to embrace the romantic myths he once held about his outlaw cousin. Denny, a fugitive for most of his life, seemed to have too much in common now with the faceless beast who had swallowed Davis's daughter.

He had often wondered what people in Will Denny's time—good, moral people, not criminals—would think of the work Davis did at the clinic, if you could make them even imagine it.

But now he wondered what Denny would do, if a devil had done to his daughter what a devil had done to Anna Kat.

If you could make Denny even imagine it.

— 12 —

Eighteen months after the murder, the detective told Davis (still calling twice a week) that he could pick up Anna Kat's things. "This doesn't mean we're giving up," he said. "We have the evidence photographed, the DNA scanned. Phone ahead and we'll have them ready." Like a pizza, Davis thought.

"I don't want to see them," Jackie said.

"You don't have to," he told her.

"Will you burn the clothes?" He promised he would.

"Will they ever find him, Dave?" He shook his head, shrugged, and shook his head again.

He imagined a big room with rows of shelves holding boxes of carpet fibers and photos and handwriting samples and taped confessions, evidence enough to convict half the North Shore of something or other. He thought there would be a window and, behind it, a chunky and gray flatfoot who would spin a clipboard in front of him and bark, "Shine heah. By numbah fouwa." Instead, he sat at the detective's desk and the parcel was brought to him with condolences, wrapped in brown paper and tied with fraying twine.

He took it to his office at the clinic, closed the door, and cut the string with a pair of long-handled stainless steel surgical scissors. The brown postal paper flattened into a square in the center of his desk, and he put his hands on top of the pile of clothes, folded but unwashed. He picked up her blouse and examined the dried stains, both blood and the other kind. Her jeans had been knifed and torn from her body, ripped from the zipper through the crotch and halfway down the seams. Her panties were torn. Watch, ring, earrings, gold chain (broken), anklet. There were shoes, black and low-heeled, which they must have found near the body. With a shudder, Davis remembered those bare mannequin feet.

There was something else, too.

Inside one of the shoes: a small plastic vial, rubber-stoppered and sealed with tape. A narrow sticker ran down the side with Anna Kat's name and a bar code and the letters UNSUB written in blue marker, along with numbers and notations Davis couldn't decipher. "UNSUB," he knew, stood for "unidenti- fied subject," which was the closest thing he had to a name for his enemy.

He recognized the contents, however, even in such a small quantity.

It was the milky-white fuel of his practice, swabbed and suctioned from inside his daughter's body. A portion had been tested, no doubt—DNA mapped—and the excess stored here with the rest of the meager evidence. Surely they didn't intend this to be mixed up in Anna Kat's possessions. This stuff, for certain, did not belong to her.

"Fuckups," Davis muttered.

He planned for a moment on returning to the police station and erupting at the detective. *This is why you haven't found him! You useless shits! He's still out there while you fumble around your desk, wrapping up tubes of rapist left-behind and handing them out to the fathers of dead girls like Secret Santa presents!*

The stuff in this tube, ordinarily in his workday so benign, had been a bludgeon used to attack his daughter, and his stomach could not have been more knotted if Davis had discovered a knife used to slit her throat. He had often thought of sperm and eggs—so carefully carted about the clinic, stored and cooled in antiseptic canisters—as being like plutonium: with power to be finessed and harnessed. The stuff in this tube, though, was weapons grade, and the monster that had wielded it remained smug and carefree.

There was more. A plastic Baggie with several short blond hairs torn out by the roots. These were also labeled UNSUB, presumably by a lab technician who had matched the DNA from the follicles to genetic markers in the semen. There were enough hairs to give Davis hope that AK had at least inflicted some pain, that she had ripped these from his scrotum with a violent yank of her fist.

Rubbing the Baggie between his fingers, Davis conjured a diabolical thought. And once the thought had been invented, once his contemplation had made such an awful thing possible, he understood his choices were not between acting and doing nothing, but between acting and *intervening*. By even imagining it, Davis had set the process in motion. Toppled the first domino.

He opened a heavy drawer in his credenza and tucked the vial and the plastic bag into the narrow space between the letter-sized hanging folders and the back wall of the cabinet.

In his head, the dominoes fell away from him, out of reach, collapsing into divergent branches with an accelerated *tap-tap-tap-tap-tap-tap.*

— 13 —

Justin Finn, nine pounds six ounces, was born on March 2 of the following year. Davis monitored the pregnancy with special care, and everything had gone almost as described in Martha's worn copy of *What to Expect When You're Expecting.* There was a scary moment, in month six, when the child was thought to be having seizures, but they never recurred. It was the only time between fertilization and birth that Davis thought he might be exposed. Baby Justin showed no evidence of brain damage or epilepsy, and after the Finns took their healthy child home, they sent Davis a box of cigars and a bottle of twenty-five-year-old Macallan.

The house on Stone fell into predictable measures of hostility and calm. Davis and Jackie were frequently cruel to each other, but never violent. They were often kind, but never loving. An appointment was made with a counselor but the day came and went and they both pretended it had slipped their minds.

"I'll reschedule it," said Jackie.

"I'll do it," said Davis, generously relieving her of responsibility when the phone call was never made.

In the third month of the Finn pregnancy, Jackie had left to spend time with her sister in Seattle. "Just for a visit," she said. Davis wondered if it was possible their marriage could end this way, without a declaration, but with Jackie on a holiday from which she never returned. He didn't always send the things she asked for—clothes and shoes, mostly—and she hardly ever asked for them twice. Jackie continued to fill the prescriptions he sent each month, along with a generous check.

In Jackie's absence, Davis avoided social, or even casual, conversation with Joan Burton. It had been fine for him to admire Dr. Burton, even to fantasize about her when he could be certain nothing would happen. Throughout his marriage, especially when Anna Kat was alive, Davis knew he was no more likely to enter into an affair than he was apt to find himself training for a moon mission, or playing fiddle in a bluegrass band. He wasn't a cheater, therefore it was not possible that he could cheat. With Jackie away and their marriage undergoing an unstated dissolution, he could no longer say a relationship with Joan was impossible. He feared the moment, perhaps during a weekday lunch at Rossini's, when their pupils might fix and the dominoes in his head would start toppling again: *tap-tap-tap-tap-tap-tap-tap-tap-tap.*

Jackie returned just before Christmas as if that had been her intention all along. She and Davis fell back into their marriage of few words. Davis restarted the small talk with Joan, even buying her a weekday lunch at Rossini's.

Anna Kat had been dead for three years.

Justin at One

— 14 —

Every spring on the Northwood Garden Walk, a guide from the historical society described the process contractors followed when building a new home within town limits. An ordinance prohibited construction of any new house if a computer in the assessor's office found it to be "in excess of fifteen percent similar" to an existing house. To gain approval, the architect's drawings were scanned and the locations of rooms, sizes of door frames, and placements of stairs were checked against every home in town. Minutes later, a number emerged with recommended changes ensuring the unique nature of each Northwood residence.

The Finns' gigantic Victorian-style home had scored 1.3 percent on the assessor's scale. No alterations necessary. Spanning two generous lots, it was much larger than it looked from the sidewalk, with much of the interior space hidden in turns and angles not visible on the outside unless seen from overhead. Terry hired a pilot and a photographer to fly over the neighborhood and snap such a picture so he could show it to befuddled friends who marveled at the roominess inside. "It's like Dr. Who's Tardis," Terry liked to say. Martha still didn't know what he meant by that, despite his attempts to explain. She laughed and called him "geek."

Davis parked across the street, having passed by it once, lost in thought, wondering if this was a good idea, to violate the see-without-being-seen policy he had maintained since Justin's birth. He palmed the toy, which Jackie had been kind enough to intercept and wrap when she saw him heading out the door with it.

"What's so special about this boy?" she asked.

"They're all special," he replied, and she casually added this to the list of secrets he kept from her.

"Dr. Moore," Martha Finn said when the door was open only a crack. "What a surprise! We must have the healthiest house on the block today between the two of you."

"The two of us?" Davis wondered quietly before noticing Dr. Burton in the living room across the foyer. He took a long, stiff step inside and Martha shut the door. "Hello, Joan," he said.

Joan tilted her head and her new black bob angled away from her face as if the part in her hair were a hinge. "Davis!" she said. "What are you doing here?" She recognized right away how condescending that was and regretted it. "I mean . . ."

"I always like to pay our kids a visit on their first birthday," he lied. He had made such calls occasionally over the years, but never since Joan had joined the practice. She let it pass.

"Thank you so much." Martha, short and thin, all residual signs of pregnancy burned away power-walking, took the toy truck (a little advanced for Justin, she'd tell her husband later, but nice) wrapped in shiny red paper. "Can I get you something to drink? Terry's at the store getting some things for the party later."

"Party?" Joan asked, kneeling down to watch Justin pick at the wrapping of her gift, a developmental contraption of letters and cubes and zoo animals and plastic rings, each deliberately too big for a trachea. "How fun."

"Mostly *our* friends, of course, not his," Martha said. "Wine and mimosas. Fruit and cheese platters. Too much talk about work and baseball."

"He looks good." Joan grinned and shook her hair in his face. "Robust."

Standing at the edge of the carpet, Davis studied the boy. He had watched him several times from his car, following Martha discreetly when she took Justin to Costco or the park. He looked like any other kid then, and like any other kid now, his red overalls stenciled with birthday pudding handprints. Justin lifted a giraffe to his forehead and made a curious, grown-up face. When Joan and his mom laughed, he did it again.

Davis tried to imagine AK's killer at one year—a different house, a different mom, a different time, a different toy—making a face exactly like this. He thought about AK at that age, already having acquired the big green eyes and high cheekbones she would keep through adolescence. Her laugh on the old videos was a close relation to her teenage giggle, and her polite stubbornness was hardwired in the womb. Now he tried, but couldn't extrapolate a killer from these pudgy little hands and thin blond hair.

Minutes later, outside, at the door to Joan's Spyder, she asked, "Do you have an hour?"

"Jackie's got dinner at five."

"That's more than an hour."

"I suppose it is."

Marty's was close to the train, and did a fair six o'clock business during the week. The Sunday crowd, lined up around the bar, heads angled at a spring training Cubs game, was sparser. Over whiskeys on the rocks and a table tent advertising hot-and-spicy chicken wings, Joan asked Davis how he was doing.

"How am I? Fine."

"What's with the birthday visit?"

"Just a whim."

"Uh-huh. How's Jackie?"

"She's fine."

"That's not what I've heard."

Goddamn, Joan. Subtle like a frying pan to the temple.

"What have you heard?"

"Are you having an affair with Martha Finn?"

Davis coughed a half-swallowed sip of whiskey into his glass. "What?"

"It fits. You show up at her house on the kid's birthday, conveniently when her husband is out of the house. I ran into Gregor exactly the same way a few years back when he was diddling that one, you know, Sante Gramatica. Remember?" She started whispering, one sentence too late. "Anyway, it's okay with me if you are. I just wanted to make sure you were discreet." She paused to assess how her speech was coming off and might have decided it sounded thick with ulterior motives because she added, "For the sake of the practice."

He laughed, and it looked natural to her. She relaxed.

"Sorry. I thought I had to ask. Professionally."

"If I had a nickel for every time someone thought I was having an affair . . . ," Davis said.

Without even a grin, Joan put a dime on the table and slid it in front of him. "So things with Jackie are good?"

"I didn't say that." He shrugged, surprised at his own candor, having been put on edge by Joan's directness. "AK would have graduated from Illinois this June."

"I know."

"With the exception of her—episode—a few years back, Jackie's handled it better than me, and that's put a strain on things at home. She's been able to move on in many ways, but I just can't stop thinking about Anna Kat. Every day, I remember a new thing. By the time I'm sixty, I'll have replayed every second of AK's life in my head. Reincarnated her in carbon copy. Repeated every move she made right up to the end."

"Do you think that's healthy?"

"I'm sure it's not. It's like I have to live her life for her because she's not here to do it herself. And it's not just her. I spend more time in the basement with my dead relatives than I do upstairs with my own wife. I'm an asshole."

Joan frowned for a long moment, then ordered two more drinks with a gesture. "Can I tell you a story?" she asked.

Passing through the revolving doors of the medical center into the Houston night, Joan felt like she was swimming in steaming black liquid. Hair went limp across her scalp. Blouse adhered to her skin. She didn't sweat; the city sweated on her.

When she arrived from the Bay Area for her residency in January, she found Houston more hospitable than she expected. There were decent bookstores and an active theater community and a good symphony (not that she ever attended). The people were friendly (although most folks she met were, like her, from elsewhere) and the winter days pleasant when it wasn't pouring rain. The summer nights were something else, however. In the summer, it was like breathing coffee.

This neighborhood on the southwest side of the nation's fourth-largest city was the site of a de facto evacuation every night at six. It was empty now except for the hospital and a few gated apartment complexes and the Taco Cabana down the street, where insomniacs and night-shifters sat at tiny, unbalanced Formica squares and paired hastily made fajitas with cold bottles of Dos Equis. Right now she was more tired than hungry.

Across the street, into the parking garage, Joan took long, swift steps with locked knees. Sleepiness aside, she felt hyperaware in the lonely fluorescent-lit concrete cavern.

When she'd parked here, seventeen hours ago, there were minivans so tight to either side that it strained muscles in her thighs just to climb out of the car. Now her used Taurus was an orphan, almost completely alone on level eight.

Joan didn't pick the man up until he was twenty yards from her and closing. He might have crossed over from level seven, heading up. He looked to be in his thirties, but might have been a hard-living twentysomething. He wore a wedding ring—or a ring on that finger anyway—and he had a hoop in his left ear.

"Miss? Miss? I'm really embarrassed about this, but my car got towed and I'm just three dollars and seventy-five cents short of the fee. Is there any way you can help me out?"

Joan's hand went into her purse, where her thumb found a folded-up five and her pinky sought out a lighter-sized canister of pepper spray. She watched him walk toward her. He wore an open blue windbreaker, presumably to ward off a sudden shower, and his striped shirt was tucked into acid-washed jeans. Low on his forehead he had an Astros cap, but not one with the current logo. His auburn facial hair reflected a few days of neglect, but wasn't organized into anything you could call beard or mustache.

In his left hand he had a thick ring of keys. Among them, she glimpsed one of those frequent-shopper discount cards from a large chain grocery. Later, she'd wonder why she found that detail so benign.

She grabbed the five.

The fist with the keys struck Joan across the cheek and she yelped as she fell into the car door. He grabbed her by the hair and twisted her head back and forth while ripping the purse off her shoulder. He pulled a gun from the rear of his waistband and pressed it above her ear like he wanted it to stick there by itself.

"Get in the fucking car and drive," he growled, pushing her into the driver's seat and throwing her own keys on the floor mat, where she had to grope for them. As he hurried to the passenger side, she never thought about running, never presumed she could outpace him.

He directed her down, out of the unmanned garage, and east on Bellaire, then northeast on Main, away from the med center toward downtown.

"Do you have a family?" His voice was cold and hard to understand, like a robot mumbling.

She nodded, trying to keep the tremble in her hands away from her voice. "Parents. Brothers. Not around here."

"I mean kids," he said testily, waving the gun at her in a hammer motion.

She shook her head. He didn't say why he wanted to know, exactly. "You have to take care of your own," he said.

"What?" She wondered right away why she was asking him questions that could encourage or antagonize him, or both.

"No one else matters," he said in a dreamy, drunken octave one register higher than he likely intended. "Your son. Your mom. Your goddamned fucking wife." He ordered her east on Memorial. "Where do you live?" he asked.

"Sugarland," she said.

He bisected her purse, opened her wallet, and lifted her license to read it in the passing streetlights. "Liar," he said, and leaned his head indifferently against the window.

They didn't drive far, to an empty lot surrounded by office buildings. In six hours there would be five thousand people within screaming radius. Just now, there was no one.

He grabbed her hair again. "Get in back."

Pinning her to the bench seat with his knees and the barrel of his gun, he searched casually through the rest of her purse, filling his pockets with cash, a cell phone, and gum. Then he doused her face with her own pepper spray—mercifully, in a way, she thought, as it allowed her to focus on the pain in her eyes, instead of the horror below.

And it gave her an excuse to cry, which, in those dark, awful, vulnerable moments when she imagined that such a thing as this could happen, she had sworn she would never do.

"Jesus. Joan. I didn't know."

"Because I didn't want you to know."

"Why?"

"Because you'd look at me like that."

"Sorry."

"Stop it."

"So why are you telling me now?"

"Because I think you need someone to talk to. I thought it might help open you up if you knew I was a"—she started to say *survivor*—"that I had been through it. I don't pretend to know what Anna Kat went through. But in the moments before it happened, behind the wheel of that car, I imagined the worst happening to me. Imagined my life ending with a bullet, or a knife. In just a few instants I became resigned to it. But I survived it. Like you. The way you survived an assassin's gun. And you survived Anna Kat's attack. Or you will. But you need to talk about it, Davis. It's been a long time."

"I just don't think it's fair," Davis said, reaching his hand inside his jacket to finger the old wound through his cotton dress shirt. "For different reasons—insane reasons—people wanted us both dead, but somehow I lived and she died."

Joan tilted her glass against her lips and let a piece of ice slide inside her mouth. It melted there while she waited for the sentimental tone of the conversation to dissipate. "You've been sleepwalking at work ever since it happened. That's why I was so surprised to see you at the Finns' today. That's the sort of gesture I'd expect from the old Dr. Moore."

"Maybe I'm coming around," Davis said. He forced a smile.

"Maybe. Have you ever talked to anybody? A professional?"

"Jackie and I have seen a marriage counselor off and on."

"Has it helped?"

"Hard to say. We're still married, sort of."

"Well, you can always call me, you know, if you're still having trouble. Especially at work. I have a sympathetic ear regarding matters of the office."

"Has Gregor or Pete said anything to you? About me?"

"Not in four years. They asked how I thought you might be holding up, between the shooting and AK. Nothing since."

Davis peered into his glass. "The guy who attacked you. Why did he say that?"

"Why did he say what?"

"That bit about 'your son, your mom, your wife.' What was the point of that, you think?"

"My shrink told me he was trying to explain himself. Apologize. Make excuses. He knew what he was doing was wrong, and he was trying to put blame somewhere. Maybe that's right. I don't know."

"Did they ever catch him?"

"Nope."

"Do you think you'd know him if you saw him again?"

"I used to think so. It's been ten years now. He's changed. My memory of him has changed. I think I've aged him in my head, so he's always that much older than me. I'm not sure the guy up here"—she tapped her head—"looks much like the real asshole anymore."

"Do you still feel helpless? Like you just have to do something, anything?"

"Do anything? For what?"

"To find this guy. To make him feel what you felt."

"That's exactly the rapist's point, Davis. I *can't* make him feel what I felt. I could shoot him dead and he'd still have me trumped. You know the movies where there's this really evil bad guy, who does horrible, unspeakable shit? And in the end, the good guy, the cop or whoever, turns the tables on him at the last minute and kills him? Pushes him out a window, or chops him up in a boat propeller, or whatever? I hate that. I hate it when the bad guy dies. I think it's much worse to have to live with what you've done."

"Yeah," Davis said. "Well, *I* live every day with what he's done." The "he" Davis meant, of course, was Anna Kat's killer, but to Joan that man and the Houston rapist were the same: faceless, nameless evil.

"Evil takes up space," she said. "When the men who commit it—and it's mostly men, you know; we can have that discussion another day—when the men who commit evil die, it creates a vacuum, and somebody else gets sucked into it. Killing the evildoer doesn't kill the evil. Another takes his place. Evil is a physical constant. Like gravity. The best we can do is to try to keep ourselves and the ones we love on the right side."

"Our moms, our sons, our wives," Davis repeated. "You know what I really struggle with? Not *who* so much as *why*. I mean, I want AK's killer to be punished, but he could be one of thousands of interchangeable punks and monsters and assholes. I hate the thought that there was no reason for it. No motive. That AK died just because some ex-con passing through town needed to scratch an itch. I wouldn't even need to know his name if I could just see into his eyes and try to understand why he did it. Why it had to happen."

"Would that really be enough?" Joan asked skeptically.

"I don't know," Davis said. "What if you really could fight it? Fight evil. Wouldn't you? Wouldn't you have to? At any cost?"

She reached out and touched his arm between his elbow and wrist. "Some prices are too high, Davis."

He said nothing, but didn't agree.

— 15 —

Mississippi was just about his least favorite place in the world, yet it was also the place he felt the safest. That was just another one of those contradictions that Mickey felt proved the existence of God. The natural order was continua and spectra, with extremes at either pole and graduation in between. Everything changed by degrees and everything in the universe could be said to be mostly one thing or the other—hot or cold, black or white, right or wrong. Only omnipotent God had the power to make it both things at once: hot *and* cold, black *and* white, right *and* wrong. Killing people was always wrong, but couldn't God, on occasion, make it right as well? The same way he made Mickey both miserable and content here in Mississippi? At least it was springtime and not so hot. It was wet, though. Before this afternoon Mickey doubted that three hours had passed since he'd arrived without a heavy shower replenishing the mud and mosquitoes.

The farm was large and neglected, 150 acres of knobby land and rocks and rotting barns and stables. It had been a cotton plantation years ago and that made Mickey a little uncomfortable—he admired African-Americans who had persevered through slavery and prejudice and who, having been rejected by the mainstream culture, had developed a culture of their own, a culture that espoused solidly conservative social values. Didn't polls show that blacks were against cloning for any purpose, even research, by a margin of more than two to one? Harold's family hadn't owned this land during the days of slavery, at least, but Harold was undeniably a bigot, if an old-fashioned one, occasionally letting slip an almost quaint Southern slur like "nay-gra." Mickey scribbled a mental note to have a talk with Harold one of these evenings, sipping lemonade on the big porch, about ways to bring more African-Americans to the cause. That would really freak out the West Coast liberals, wouldn't it?

Three years ago, Mickey wouldn't have risked coming here. Harold was too well known, and the feds were always watching his property, raiding it twice a year with warrants drawn on suspicion of harassment, or solicitation to commit murder, or violation of the RICO statutes. They never got a conviction, however. Harold had an ACLU lawyer who counterattacked with the First Amendment, once even taking his case to the United States Supreme Court, which found seven-to-two in Harold's favor, igniting the editorial pages in New York and San Francisco with white-hot outrage. In the last twelve months, Harold said, the feds had grown bored with him, or frustrated that they couldn't make anything stick, and so they mostly left him alone. "You can stay here as long as you like," Harold told Mickey. "But I wouldn't use the phone."

Harold Devereaux wasn't even an official member of the Hands of God, although HoG probably wouldn't have survived the last few years without him. Harold called himself an "independent contractor serving one client only: the Lord God Almighty." He was a prolific writer and anti-cloning pundit, but most famously (and this was what had brought him before the Supreme Court) he was the proprietor of a Web site identifying clinics, doctors, and researchers who advocated or practiced the cloning of human beings. Occasionally, when one of these individuals would die or retire, Harold would put a red line through his or her name. Sometimes the doctor would only be wounded, and Harold would change the color of his name from black to gray. Many people, specifically the individuals named on the site, didn't like this. They called it a hit list. Harold's ACLU lawyer disagreed, and seven justices happened to agree with Harold's lawyer.

Out of 357 names, there were twenty-four red cross-outs on Harold's site. Mickey was responsible for nine of them. Six had died of natural causes, six more had retired or quit out of fear for their lives or the lives of their families, and three had been shot in the head by an unknown person or persons. The police suspected the same killer might have perpetrated all twelve, Mickey's nine plus the other three. They even had a name for him: Byron Blakey Bonavita. Two years ago Byron disappeared into the Kentucky woods with the FBI on his trail, and since then, every time Mickey offed a doctor, some witness claimed they'd seen Byron Bonavita in the area. He was like Elvis. Mickey didn't know if Byron had committed the other three killings or not, but he was glad to have the FBI looking for someone else's face every time he finished a job. That was probably why he was still in business.

There weren't many targets in the small towns surrounding Harold's ranch. Mickey was here on a social visit. Through his Web site, Byron collected donations for anti-clone "lobbying," and he quietly dispersed much of it to several individuals and churches that spread the word about the evils of modern science. The Hands of God was one of them. This had brought the Hands of God to the attention of the FBI, which had already seen the group's name on several threats to fertility clinics around the country. Phil and the others denied they had ever threatened anyone, and none of the threats bore an Ohio postmark. The feds didn't know about Mickey the Gerund and the long box in the back of his Cutlass Supreme.

"I can't tell you how happy I am to have you here for a few days, Mickey," Harold said. "You are a true instrument of the Lord."

"Thank you, Harold," Mickey said. "It's nice to have a place to lie low and to get some genuine rest. When I went to bed last night I was sure I could have slept long into this evening."

Harold was an odd-shaped man, with narrow shoulders and legs as yellow and brittle-looking as dried straw. In between, he had a large round belly that looked like an errant pregnancy or a gym ball. In the yard, Harold's children played on an expensive mahogany swing set. Mickey had been here three days and wasn't even sure how many kids the man had. At least four. Harold's third wife was in the kitchen someplace. She was young and pretty because Harold was wealthy and famous, having once been on the cover of *The New York Times Magazine*. Mickey didn't like to imagine them having sex, but he couldn't help himself—another of God's contradictions, and a cruel one. Through the window blinds looking into Harold's office from the porch, Mickey could see a counter that kept track of the visitors to Harold's Web site. The number was in the millions (Mickey didn't know when Harold had started counting) and it clicked off another every few seconds. People were buying Harold's message at the same rate they were buying hamburgers, Mickey thought.

"What's the latest in Washington?" Mickey asked Harold, who kept pace with such things.

"Nothing," Harold said. When he lifted his glass to his lips, a ring of condensation remained on his T-shirt at the summit of his belly. "Cloning's not even on Congress's agenda this session. They don't want to touch it. The less they have to acknowledge the issue, the better, as far as they're concerned."

"Same old same old, huh?" Mickey said.

Harold's blue-gray beard pinched the area around his lips as he puckered them. "Don't get me wrong. I love this country and I believe in democracy. But there are some issues, *hard* issues, that elected representatives are ill-equipped to deal with. They are controversy-averse, and our enemies use that to their advantage. There's an old axiom in the Capitol: *That which is legal tends to stay legal; that which is outlawed tends to stay outlawed.* Once something like cloning is legal, the government is likely to keep it that way just so they don't have to talk about it ahead of the election. Whatever they say is going to piss off half the people."

"More than half the people agree with us, Harold," Mickey said. "I saw a poll the other day—"

"I don't need to see the polls," Harold said. "I just talk to my friends and neighbors. There's nobody divided on the issue around here. If our sonofa-bitch congressman had to vote on the cloning amendment, and he voted against it, we'd kick his ass out and he knows it. But the other side votes with dollars, and all they need to do is keep the amendment off the schedule. Cloning interests are happy, congressmen are happy, and now it's two against one, with the American people getting the shaft."

"It's a shame all right."

"You know I have a standing offer to debate any senator or representative on the other side, and do you know how many have taken me up on it? Zero. Sure, I go on the talk shows every now and again, but they put me up against people who don't matter: college professors and feminists. What does being a feminist have to do with making clones? Can you tell me that?"

Mickey sucked some tart residue from an oblong ice cube in his glass. "Reproductive freedom. They say cloning is a necessary part of a woman's right to choose. It frees them from the shackles of their uteri, blah, blah, blah."

"That proves my point!" Harold was excited now. "Cloning was discovered and perfected by man just a few years ago. How can it be necessary? These lib-erals have been ridiculing the Bible for years, but then science figures out how to make a human being from a man's rib—literally!—and they claim it as a momentous and necessary advance in the evolution of species. Ridiculous. It's dangerous, is what it is. It's not even man *playing* God—it's man *taunting* God. But God has the last word because man might be able to make man in man's image, but only God can make man in God's image. Only God can forge a soul."

"Amen," Mickey said, clutching a few mixed nuts from a bowl between them.

Harold breathed loudly through his mask of hair. "So where are you headed next?"

The children shouted something and whinnied and chased each other around the back of the house. "I don't think you want to know the answer to that."

Harold laughed. "You're right, I don't. Just do me a favor and keep your business out of this county. There aren't many legitimate targets here anyway, except for the university, I guess, but if some shit goes down in my backyard the feds will be up my ass again in a heartbeat."

Mickey nodded. "Harold, you got a three-hundred-mile halo around you as far as I'm concerned. Don't you worry about it."

"A three-hundred-mile halo." Harold tried to picture such a thing. "Who was that preacher out West that tried to build the nine-hundred-foot Jesus?"

"Oral Roberts."

"Yeah, Roberts. A nine-hundred-foot Jesus and a three-hundred-mile halo." He laughed.

That was the last they said for a long while, until Harold's wife called them for supper. Four days later, outside a private research facility in Arkansas, Mickey shot a laboratory technician in the back of the head as he went to lunch. The technician died on the scene.

The Little Rock police passed around a sketch of Byron Bonavita.

Justin at Three

⋈⊐⋈⊐⋈⊐⋈

— 16 —

On a hot private Michigan beach no bigger than a city driveway, Terry and Martha Finn made attentive barriers of themselves as Justin played between them. Up a steep and uneven staircase of railroad ties was the cottage—or what they called the cottage, anyway. Most would call it a damn nice second home, with three big bedrooms and all new appliances and ceiling fans mounted up high, in silent rotation—more for psychological effect than anything else. In an hour, Gary and Jennifer Hogan and their daughter, Mary Ann, would arrive for the holiday weekend. Saturday and Sunday would pass on the boat and on the mahogany deck with adult conversation and lots of drinking, the grown-ups periodically rescuing the kids from boredom with a story or a game or a silly face.

"So who do you think the guy was?" Terry asked his wife, sticking his lower lip out at a blue plastic dinosaur, which Justin had lifted in front of his face.

"Who?"

Terry nodded at their son. "Him. The guy."

"Oh, stop it."

"Seriously."

"They can't tell us. It's against the law. No use worrying about it."

"It's against the law for New Tech to tell us. It's not against the law for us to find out. You know. Hire a private detective or something."

"Stop." She laughed.

"There's gotta be a paper trail somewhere. Once he grows up, hell, you could throw his picture out there and somebody might recognize him. The donor was alive after cloning became legal, so he could only be dead a couple years."

"Right."

"There's this, too." Terry lifted the back of Justin's T-shirt, exposing a birthmark near his left hip that looked a little like West Virginia, or a long-spouted teapot. Without looking, Justin absently swatted at his father's hand and Terry let go.

Martha smiled and, tired of squinting at the sun reflecting off the lake, closed her eyes.

"He swears a lot."

"Who?"

"Justin."

"Don't be silly."

"He does. Don't you think? For a three-year-old."

"Well, stop swearing around him," Martha said.

"I don't."

"You just did."

"When?"

"Ten seconds ago. You said *h-e-l-l*."

"That's not swearing. I'm talking about a real potty mouth."

"They're just words to him. Funny sounds."

Terry watched his son dig trenches in the sand with the tail of a tyrannosaur. "Do you ever wonder if some of the guy's memories—the donor I'm talking about now—if some of his memories might be in Justin's genes?"

"What? Like Jung?"

"Who's that?"

"Carl Jung. The collective unconscious."

Terry molded his face into a half-serious sneer, the way he often did when Martha's total recall of her college notebooks threatened him with a tangent. "This morning, Justin got hold of this knife—"

"A *knife?*"

"A plastic one. It was in the bag with the bagels."

"Oh."

"Anyway, he was pretending to cut with it, against the tablecloth, and he looked sort of like he knew what he was doing."

"From watching you cut the bagels, probably."

"No, he was holding it like a scalpel. Long, smooth incisions. Like a surgeon."

"Give me a break."

"I know. It's silly. I'm just saying. Suppose we found out he had been a doctor. That would be a kick, wouldn't it?"

"I suppose he learned to swear on the golf course, then." Martha grinned.

The joke was funny, but Terry didn't laugh. Martha was always dismissing him, tossing aside every decent idea he proposed. He had once admired her because she was smart, but he didn't realize that with intelligence would come condescension. He was the one who worked, the one who paid for the two homes and the two cars and the expensive vacations with his fat commissions as a futures trader, but he hadn't been a great student, and Martha, who thought smarts were an end in themselves, never offered him the respect he deserved. Now they had a child together and the child was obviously bright and she acted like Justin got that from her side, even though she hadn't passed a single one of her supersmart genes to him. If for no other reason, he wanted to find out where the boy came from to remind her that Justin's brains didn't come from her.

"So what do you think?"

"About what?"

"About having a guy check into Justin's past."

"He's three, Terry. He doesn't have a past."

"Okay. The other guy. The other him."

"They're completely different people. He'll get more of his personality from us than he will from some mystery man."

"Dr. Moore said they were like twins, didn't he?"

"Yeah. So?"

"You know how twins sometimes have, like, ESP? What if Justin's still got some memory of his twin? Through ESP."

"You got all of this because Justin said the S-word last night?"

"Not just that."

She tossed her strawberry highlights away from her mouth and grinned at him. Her skin glistened and her teeth shined. She looked out-of-the-package new. "Go ahead. I don't care. You've still got your own credit card. I'd rather have you spend it on this than a girlfriend or something."

"Cheat on you? Never."

With Justin between them, they shared a sandy kiss.

"Ass-word! Ass-word! Ass-word!" Justin chanted.

Their faces stretched into grins and, lips never parting, they started the kiss again from the beginning.

— 17 —

There were piles of M&M's in little dishes, and lace patterns pressed for display under the glass coffee tabletop. There were yards and yards of bookshelves along the walls, but on them no books. The room was surrounded instead by ceramic animals, porcelain figures, wood frames, acrylic doodads, glass vases, scented candles, and assorted whatnots. Facing east, the room was bright, and Barwick had chosen a chair—a green one with high arms and a buttoned back, upholstered in unidentifiable fabric—that pointed her away from the window. Mrs. Lundquist sat directly in the sun's light, causing Barwick to be curious about the older woman's fair, preserved skin, which contrasted so drastically with her own mocha complexion.

"You were telling me about this oral history you were doing," she said.

"Right, right," Barwick said. "For the university."

"Syracuse?" she asked. "SU?"

"No," Barwick said. "University of"—she thought she might be giving something away, but then decided what the hell—"Chicago."

"Hmmm," she said. "I see."

"We're going around the country, selecting people at random, and getting them to tell us their stories. These tapes will be transcribed and filed for the benefit of—you know—future generations."

"Sounds like interesting work."

"Oh, it is. It is. I get to meet a lot of nice people. Like you." She smiled abruptly, charmingly. "You see, history has always been told through the lives of extraordinary people. Presidents and world leaders, generals, what have you. But the really good stuff, the genuine article, is in the everyday. Did you know that we don't have a good first-person account of what it was like for an average person who lived in ancient Rome?"

"No, I certainly didn't," she said.

Neither did Barwick. She was making it up. "Oh, we know what the battles were like, and what went on in the Senate. And we have their myths. And plays." Were there Roman playwrights? There were Greek ones, for sure. She should have used the Greeks as an example. "But we don't have the everyday stuff."

"Well, what can I do for you?"

"If it's not too big an imposition, I'd just like to have a chat. Ask a few questions. Have a conversation. Then I'll go, and you'll never see me again. Although you *will* get a fifty-dollar check from the university." She wondered how she would get a University of Chicago check. "Or from our grant office, anyway." That sounded easier to fake.

"Sounds lovely," Mrs. Lundquist said, and it occurred to Barwick that this could be a case study of why old people made such easy marks for scam artists and grifters. She wasn't here to con the lady, though. Not really. This was legitimate business.

Barwick burned the first disc discussing life in Watertown, New York. Mrs. Lundquist liked to walk when the weather was fair, so every evening she wrote a letter to a friend or a relative and the next morning she walked it to the post office. She'd sometimes stop by Great American and pick up groceries, just a bagful, but in six days or so, she'd accumulate two weeks' worth. On Wednesdays, a man from the store named Harvey delivered bags too heavy for her to carry.

By disc two, they were on to family.

Her husband died last year of heart disease. She had three sons, one who had moved west to Buffalo, another who'd settled south in Atlanta, and the youngest was killed in a skiing accident about nine years ago. That was the one Barwick had come to hear about. But she was patient. There wasn't any reason to rush her.

"What happened to Eric was a horrible thing," Mrs. Lundquist said. "But it was an accident. Eric was a fantastic skier. Fantastic."

"What did Eric do?"

"What did he do? When he died, he was still a student. A senior at Cornell. He was interested in social service. He was always trying to save people, involved in those campus protests, peaceful ones. He thought about the Peace Corps, or teaching in the inner city. Don and I thought he'd end up a guidance counselor. He was a very good listener. So smart."

"Do you have any pictures of Eric?" Barwick asked. "Any of your kids, I mean. Just to put names to faces."

Mrs. Lundquist's face glowed like filament. "Of course."

The Finns hadn't asked for pictures. In fact, they'd specifically told Big Rob they didn't want to see any photos of Eric Lundquist, and that was passed on when the assignment was handed off to Barwick. They didn't want to know what Justin would look like as a teen, or as an adult. But Barwick wanted to see. She had never met a clone before. She wanted the thrill of looking into a photograph and seeing the grown-up face of this baby boy, photos of whom she had in the glove compartment of her rental car out front.

Mrs. Lundquist, still spry, was up the stairs and down in less than a minute. On her return, she had three faux-leather-bound three-ring albums in her hands. Barwick moved to the couch and they propped the albums open across their laps. The Lundquist boys were all handsome—tall, blond, broad-shouldered, thin-waisted, with beautiful hands and sculpted legs. She particularly noticed Eric's softball-sized calves. Even from photos, she could see that Eric was special. Barwick tried to recall her high school days (not so long ago, she told herself), and yeah, she'd have had a crush on Eric. Her friends and she would have made him the stuff of phone gossip. They would have memorized his class schedule. They would have secretly hated his girlfriend.

"Did Eric have a girlfriend?"

Mrs. Lundquist smiled. "He was shy, but very popular with girls. Did you know he was a lifeguard at Lynde Lake? I'm sorry. Of course you didn't. In high school, he dated the student council president. She was a lovely girl, Glynnis. I still have lunch with her mother once a week. Do you know that Glynnis is a broker on Wall Street now?"

"That's unusual," Barwick said.

"For a girl? It sure is. Eric saw one or two girls in college. No one serious enough to bring home. Don and I met a gal down in Ithaca once, when we picked him up. She was Indian—you know, from Asia. I can't remember her name. It was hard to pronounce."

"That's okay."

The photos preserved the boys' lives in more or less equal amounts. For the older ones, however, there were recent pics with their current families, posed shots with the wife and kids in their living rooms and nearby parks. Eric's gallery ended the summer before his senior year, when he was about twenty.

One of the pictures showed Eric sitting high in his white painted chair at Lynde Lake. His head was turned over his right shoulder, toward the camera, and he was making a saluting gesture with his hand. Barwick guessed he was about eighteen here. Happy. Invincible.

"Hunh," Barwick said, accidentally out loud.

"What's that?" Mrs. Lundquist asked.

"Oh. Well. Hmm. Did Eric ever have any surgery?"

"You mean was he hurt? No. Never before his accident. Not a day in the hospital."

"Not even elective work?"

"You mean plastic surgery?" Mrs. Lundquist looked amused. "Gosh, no."

"Hunh," Barwick said again.

"Why do you ask?"

"No reason," she said. "He was a beautiful son."

"You're a dear," Mrs. Lundquist said, and after eating a single M&M, she started to tell Barwick about the time in sixth grade when Eric slept all night in a closet to hide from 7 a.m. clarinet lessons.

— 18 —

Years ago, Davis had tried to get Jackie interested in her own family history, but even talking about it bored her. "I'm much more interested in my family *present,*" she said, one of thousands of unsubtle jabs she had leveled over the years at his eighty-hour office schedule.

Working from some old photographs and letters Jackie inherited from her mother, Davis constructed an incomplete chart of her clan going back five generations, and presented it to her in a frame one Mother's Day. Jackie said she liked it and hung it in a spare bedroom where she kept her treadmill and her sewing and craft supplies. When Anna Kat assembled a seventh-grade project on her ancestors (basically cribbing years of her father's work inside a slim decorative binder), she used her mother's chart as a demonstration piece to explain the terms and techniques of genealogy and received an A from her teacher. Shortly after AK died, perhaps as soon as the day after, Jackie took the chart down and Davis hadn't seen or asked about it since. He understood why looking at it was so difficult; he felt pain as well as pleasure these days when he sorted through his own family files. Those manila folders and index cards represented real lives to him, just as the files in his office, with the names of cloned boys and girls, represented children who were now loving and being loved. The difference with the files at home was that many of his relatives no longer existed outside of his little blue room. When he pulled a card on his great-great-uncle Vic and updated his date of birth or his social security number, he was certain to be the only living person who thought about long-dead Vic that day. There was sadness to that—bittersweetness—but such simple and melancholy tributes to the dead were also satisfying. He didn't look forward to the day when he could think about Anna Kat and not be hurt by her memory.

"Did you ever consider it?" she asked him. It was late and they had been drinking wine and reading to themselves. Jackie had started a conversation and Davis had faked his way through it but now realized he didn't know what they were talking about.

"Consider what?"

"Cloning her."

"AK?"

"Of course, AK."

Davis gave her a crazed look. "No. Absolutely not. It's illegal, for one thing." That was an absurd comment, a *cruel* thing to say, given the secret he kept from her, and he knew that, now that he had made such an excuse, she would never forgive him if she discovered the truth.

"Not seriously, I guess," Jackie said. "It's just, I wonder what it would be like to have her back. Even as a baby. To give her another shot at life. To give us another shot at keeping her safe."

"It wouldn't be her," Davis said.

"Would that matter?"

"Yes," Davis said.

Jackie closed her book, and her voice became softer, which it did when she was angry or sad or nervous. "You act like a cloned child isn't real. That would surprise a lot of people if they heard you say it."

"She's real to the new family. To people who knew the original, she wouldn't be real at all. To them, she's a doppelgänger. A smudged copy. A ghost with no memory. Would AK be AK without that scar across her knuckles? The one she got learning to ride a bike? If she had fillings in different teeth? If she were a swimmer instead of a setter? Afraid of heights instead of spiders? If she liked English better than math?" Jackie turned flush and Davis held out his arm, but he couldn't reach her chair and so he suspended his hand, palm up, in the air between them. "I know what you're thinking. That all these years later there's still this . . . this absence, and the desire to fill it with something can be overwhelming. But to certain people clones can be like projections of the originals—abstract figures, actors on film, a cast of shadows. If we had another little girl walking around this house inside a shell that looked like AK, wouldn't that only make the void blacker?"

Jackie started to cry and Davis joined her, but he didn't go to her and she didn't come to him.

— 19 —

Big Rob's office was so tiny he couldn't clear the space between either side of his desk and the wall without sliding through hip-first. Sally Barwick sat in a foam-padded aluminum chair with torn vinyl upholstery. If she stretched a muscled leg out in front of her, her red shoe would have hit Big Rob's metal desk before it straightened. She could tilt her head back on her long brown neck and knock on the wall behind her, and Big Rob, from his chair, could do the same to the opposite wall. Phil Canella's lanky body was wedged between a filing cabinet and the wall, the only other human-sized space in the room. Philly, like Big Rob a former cop turned private investigator, had driven down from the northern suburbs on a case. *Just dropped in to say hi.*

Barwick held up a three-sided section of sandwich from the Ogden Avenue Deli, one flight down. The thick, striated layers of meat and lettuce and tomato and toast made it difficult to bite no matter how many angles she tried.

"It's not him," she said after managing a mouthful of bread with some mayo and turkey.

"How do you know?" Big Rob asked.

"The Finn kid has a birthmark. Eric Lundquist did not."

"So what does that prove?"

"They're clones, Biggie. Genetic duplicates."

"What do you know about clones, Barwick? I mean really. You some kind of expert all of a sudden?"

"It's common knowledge. Read *Time* magazine. Go hire a doctor, an expert or whatever, and ask him if you want."

"I'm not hiring a doctor, Barwick. The Finns are already paid up. I'm not going back to them to get money for an opinion, and I'm not paying some doc out of my pocket."

"Take my word for it, then."

His cheeks filled with corned beef, Big Rob waved an inch-thick red folder over his head. "I don't need your word for it. I got eight months of diligence here that says Lundquist's the guy, and I'm not going back to the Finns and telling them that it's suddenly a whodunit."

"Okay. So what do you want?"

"I want you to give me the discs and sign off on your interview with the old lady. Based on the work we've done just following the paper (solid detective work, by the way—congratulations), the Finns already think Eric Lundquist's their guy, and if we hand over the interview they'll get exactly what they want: a biography of their son's cell donor."

"Except Eric Lundquist's *not* their son's cell donor."

"Says you. These people are chasing a phantom, anyway. This Lundquist fellow, the clone donor or whatever, no matter what, he ain't the same person as their kid. You got your nature, and then you got your nurture, and so forth. So what if you're right? Whatever curiosity they got, you've got the stuff that can satisfy them."

Sally said, "If Lundquist's not the donor, don't you want to know who is? Something stinks here, Biggie. We might be on to a huge scandal here. Woodward and Bernstein shit. Don't you want to know why all the paperwork, all the medical records, point to Lundquist as the cell donor, but the two kids don't look alike? Why the Finn kid has a birthmark that Eric Lundquist never had?"

"I want to know everything my customer wants to know. No more. Right, Philly?" His friend nodded. "The customer wants to know about Eric Lundquist."

Barwick took a pair of audio discs from her bag and slid them across Big Rob's immaculate desk. "I've already transcribed the relevant sections."

Big Rob tagged Canella with a frustrated look. "Let me tell you something, Sals," Philly said. "We're in the business of providing answers, not truth. When a woman hires us to follow her no-good husband, we follow him and take pictures. If her man's got a good reason for being with his personal assistant at a Lincoln Avenue motel, that's not our say-so."

Biggie added, "In the Finn case, we followed the evidence and we did good work. The client will be happy. *We* should be happy."

Barwick stuffed the check in the pocket of her denim shirt. "You'll call me with the next job?"

"Yeah, Sally. Next week. I got a rich geezer on the Gold Coast maybe messing with his grandson's babysitter. Evening surveillance. Real sick stuff. You'll like it."

"Yeah."

"Don't get down on yourself. You're just starting out, but you did terrific work here. That 'oral history' thing is classic. And crap, how many times do we get a chance to make a client happy? Most of our jobs end in divorce or a lawsuit."

"You're a wide man, Biggie."

"You mean *wise* man, hon." But he knew what she meant.

Home in Andersonville, north of Wrigley, by the lake, Barwick cooled off by rinsing her shallow Afro in the sink and read the same page of a paperback novel six times before going to bed. Asleep, she dreamed she was sitting on the beach at Lynde Lake with Justin Finn, grown to a man of eighteen or so. His face looked like Eric Lundquist's. On his back was the kettle-shaped birthmark. He took her hand and let her slide it up and down the sides of his hairless, powerful legs.

"No worries," Justin said. "You've got a job. But I've got a job, too."

"Can I help?" Sally asked him.

"Shhh," Justin said, and then they were off the beach and in the front room of Mrs. Lundquist's house with the knickknacks and the M&M's. Justin touched her cheek, and he walked out the door into the snow.

Justin at Five

— 20 —

Before Jackie stopped pretending she knew her husband well enough to properly shop for him, she bought him a new home computer for his birthday (the one he had, obsolete three times over, was hardly used). She thought it might help Davis with his hobby, which devoured nearly all his free time now. At least she *assumed* he was still working on his family project down there; she passed by the blue room only on the way to the laundry and back or into the unfinished crawl space where she stored many of her gardening tools.

Davis connected the wires, plugged in the peripherals, and started to input the history of his dead family, but it felt like starting over to him. The special reports and hyperlinked organization offered by the computer seemed redundant, and not better than the paper system he'd spent years refining. However, he found it useful for research on the Internet (research he had been doing previously in spare moments at work), and for an occasional hand of virtual bridge. He and Jackie used to play two Saturdays a month with Walter and Nancy Hirschberg, but they'd fazed out the regular game around the time of Jackie's breakdown, and Davis hadn't partnered with his wife over an actual deck of cards in more than seven years.

On a Sunday afternoon, while he was listening to the Cubs and Cards on WGN and skimming Internet message boards for info about an elusive great-uncle on his mother's side, a software advertisement snared his attention.

THINK IT'S FUN LOOKING INTO YOUR FAMILY'S PAST?
NOW TRY GAZING INTO YOUR FAMILY'S FUTURE
WITH SIX BRIDGES SOFTWARE'S
NEW FACEFORGER 6.0!

He clicked through to the Six Bridges Web site and read only a few paragraphs on the product before confessing his Visa number to the company's secure server. He was given a password and downloaded the program and manual to his computer.

He installed the software and experimented with scans of Anna Kat as a baby. He ran the program through trial after trial, aging her to seventeen after entering dozens of variables: *Will the subject be a drinker? A smoker? How much? Will the subject spend time outdoors? In the sun? Unprotected? How much?* In one week, he had a result good enough to print. Davis held the paper next to a photo taken of AK the Christmas before she was killed. It wasn't perfect—the eyes weren't quite right—but it was pretty damn close. Any friend of hers would recognize it as AK for certain.

The following day he purchased a digital camera at an electronics store and rescheduled two appointments to free up the afternoon. The street where the Finns lived curved east of their home, and Davis parked his car on the other side of the bend, where he still had a good view of the front door and driveway. He waited there, the engine running, listening to public radio. Hours passed with no sign of Martha or Justin. He dozed briefly. Around five-thirty, a Mercedes sedan pulled into the driveway. Terry Finn, home from the office. Alone.

In the past year Davis had started to feel foolish and guilty about Justin, and if it hadn't been for the boy's regular checkups with Joan, he'd have tried to forget about him altogether. What had he been thinking? Temporary insanity was the only way he could rationalize it, and in doing so he actually felt some empathy for his wife's history of emotional illness. It would be another ten or more years before Justin even remotely resembled AK's killer, and her killer would be ten or more years older as well. Possibly even an old man. In all likelihood, they'd be impossible to match by sight, even if he could get them in the same room. He was playing a game of catch-up he would never win. And what if the Finns moved away? How had he planned to keep track of the boy then? It shamed him to think that he had started such a radical experiment without giving two serious thoughts to any of it.

Of course, logic had never been a constant in his equation. Only in his most dreamlike fantasies had he expected to use Justin as a means to *capture* AK's murderer. Even if Justin grew up, and Davis or someone else recognized the face, how would he explain it to the police? What would he have to offer as proof? Certainly not his reputation as a respected physician, which would be shattered the instant he confessed to such an insane plot.

All Davis longed for on the day he exchanged the stuff in his credenza with Eric Lundquist's DNA was a chance to look into the eyes of his daughter's murderer. Or, in Justin's case, a simulacrum of his daughter's murderer. Over the past year, the day when he could satisfy that desire had begun to seem more and more remote. The new software had fanned those smoldering embers again. If he could just get a good photo of the kid, he could plug a dozen variables into the machine, find the face he'd been searching for, and extinguish this latent compulsion once and for all. Davis could finally accept Anna Kat's murder, Justin Finn could live a healthy life unaware of the machinations that had created him, and Jackie could have her husband back whole. Their marriage had been strained since AK's death and hyperextended since Jackie's breakdown. Their latest bout of conjoined misery had been the result of his neglect, not her instability, and Davis was convinced he could make her happy again. Once he stopped torturing himself, he could stop torturing his wife.

When it became clear the Finns had retired for the evening, however, he realized none of this would happen tonight.

He waited until Saturday morning to try again. After half an hour Terry, Martha, and Justin pulled away in a Chevy minivan and he followed at a conservative distance. They drove less than a mile, parking the car in the moderate bustle of downtown Northwood, and Davis found an angled spot on the street about half a block away. He followed them into Starbucks.

The coffee shop was packed from rear to window, and when the door shut it trapped Davis inside with the fresh-brewed aromas. There were half a dozen people here he knew. He should have set up across the street and tried to sneak a picture from there when the family walked out, but now that he was in, he couldn't turn around and leave.

"Hi, Dr. Moore," Libby Carlisle said to him. Libby had a stout athlete's build with thick, strong legs, and her hair was kinky and rust-colored. She wasn't pretty, but her toothy smile reminded Davis of a famous actress and so he found her looks compelling by association. Libby had been a friend of AK's. At one time, maybe her best friend. Davis hadn't seen her since the funeral.

"Hi, Libby," said Davis. Positioned by the only exit, he was certain the Finns couldn't escape. "What are you doing home?"

"I'm married now, in case you didn't know," she said, patting the handle of the baby stroller at her side. "Thom and I moved back here about six months ago. Weird, isn't it? When you're in high school all you want to do is get the heck out of town. Then something always pulls you back." She wasn't at all self-conscious about the loss they both shared and Davis appreciated that. Talking with AK's old friends was usually an exhausting chore.

"Yeah. Funny," Davis said.

"Say hi to Mrs. Moore," said Libby, backing out the door, pulling her child behind her.

Davis stood in line and practiced his order, *tall skim latte*. The Finns were three customers in front of him. Terry had picked Justin up into his arms to keep track of him in the crowded shop, and the boy was staring back in Davis's direction, running a toy car across his father's shoulder. His blond hair had thickened, and his parents had let it grow long in back, probably the result of a tantrum he'd thrown at the barber. His face had thinned. His nose was red from a bug; his eyes were royal blue. He giggled at something his father whispered in his ear, and Justin whispered something back and giggled some more. Davis tapped the bulge of camera in his pocket. How strange would it look for a local (and somewhat renowned) doctor to be taking photographs of customers at Starbucks?

When it was Davis's turn to order, he got change from his five and joined the waiting crowd at the end of the counter.

"Dr. Moore!" Martha Finn said. "How are you?"

"I'm fine, Martha, thanks."

"Terry, you remember Dr. Moore."

"Of course," Terry said. He shifted Justin in his arms so he could extend a hand for shaking. This would be almost the last time Justin could be held this way. In a few months he would be too big for his father's thin arms to handle. "Good to see you."

"How's Justin doing?" Davis asked.

Terry turned the boy around, and Justin pressed his chin to his father's chest, shyly.

"Just great. He's getting over a little sniffle now, but he's been terrific." Martha wiped Justin's nose with a paper napkin like a housewife tidying the living room in front of unexpected guests.

"Glad to hear it."

A teenager called the Finns' order and Martha tucked the cups into round cardboard insulators. "He has an appointment with Dr. Burton in a few weeks. Maybe I'll see you then."

"I'll try to peek in while you're there, if I can."

"Wonderful. Good-bye now."

"Good-bye."

"Justin, say good-bye to Dr. Moore."

"Bye."

"Good-bye, Justin."

By the time Davis's latte arrived, the Finns had backed out from their parking space and gone. To the zoo or the mall or the club.

He drove home and, after a quick search of the kitchen, asked Jackie where she kept the Yellow Pages.

— 21 —

Barwick was in bed but not asleep when Big Rob called. Her mother had phoned from New Orleans around seven and they had talked for over two hours. Or it had resembled a conversation, anyway.

"Did you know your sister is getting married?" Mrs. Barwick asked.

"Of course I know, Mom. They've been engaged almost a month."

On the other end of the line, Mrs. Barwick was performing some task in the kitchen, the clanking of plates audible under her train of thought. "Oh, I didn't know if she'd told you."

"She told me. You and I have already talked about the registry. And I know you know I know because you haven't asked me about boys since it happened. I figured I'd won a reprieve."

"Fine," Mrs. Barwick said. "Have you been looking for a job?"

The first syllables of Sally's response came out so loud, the cute guy upstairs must have heard them, even with the TV and the vacuum on. "*Jesus, Mother.* I *have* a job."

Mrs. Barwick said, "Yes, but I only tolerated this spy stuff you do because I figured you'd give it up when you got married. Now I want you to have a career. The way modern science is going, maybe I don't need you or your sister. Maybe I can clone myself a grandson."

"Investigation is a perfectly good career, Mom."

"What is? Chasing cheating husbands and taking dirty pictures through the soiled windows of cheap motels? It's no wonder you hate men."

"I don't hate men. I had a date on Thursday."

"Tell me everything about him."

And so on.

When the phone rang again twenty minutes later Sally figured her mother had been unsatisfied with her choice of last words and wanted to take another stab at it. She tossed the *Tribune* crossword puzzle off her lap, sending the cat running, and turned down the radio before reaching for the phone.

"This is a weird one, Barwick," Big Rob said.

"What have you got?"

"I just had a beer with Phil Canella. Seriously, I oughta move this operation to the burbs. He's got more business than he can handle. The closer you get to the Wisconsin border, the more suspicious the spouses, I guess."

"What's up?"

"Remember the Finn case? The parents of that clone boy who wanted the scoop on the cell donor?"

"Yeah, sure." Truth was, she hadn't stopped thinking about Justin Finn.

"Well, there was another private eye at the bar with us, a friend of Philly's. Scott Colleran of Gold Badge Investigators. You heard of him?"

"No."

"His office is way up north. By Six Flags in Gurnee. Anyway, we met up for happy hour at the Toad, swappin' stories and whatnot, and it turns out Scott's got a client who wants pictures of the Finn kid."

"What? No! Who?"

"Come on. Scotty's not gonna give up his client. We're in the confidentiality business, remember?"

"Confidentiality doesn't apply inside the Ten Toad Saloon, apparently."

Big Rob laughed. "We were just talkin'. Anyway, that case got you so worked up when we were on it, I thought you'd think that was funny."

Yeah, some crazy old man looking for snapshots of five-year-old boys. Hilarious. "This Colleran guy isn't serious about taking the case, is he?"

"Sure he is. Why wouldn't he?"

"What if somebody's casing a kidnapping? What if the client's a child molester?"

"Nah, pedophiles take their own pictures. Or they buy them on the Internet. Besides, Scott checked him out. Says it's on the up-and-up."

"Good. Scott Colleran checked him out. I guess the children of Chicago can walk the streets safely." This was the sort of sarcasm Sally's mother hated.

"Come on. Colleran's all right. Like I said, he vouches for the guy."

"I told you there was something unholy about that Finn case, Biggie," Barwick said. "This is all related."

"Relax. It's probably just a run-of-the-mill custody deal." He paused and Sally could hear him take a bite of something crunchy over the phone. "So do you want the job, or what?"

"What do you mean?"

"Same as Philly, Gold Badge has more work than they can handle. This is what I've been talkin' about: an office in the burbs. Anyway, I knew you had a hard-on for the Finn case so I told Colleran you were a first-rate shooter and looking for some extra work. The job's worth four hundred to you, minus my commission. Four-fifty, if you can get it done without turning it into a conspiracy. Or worse, a moral dilemma."

Sally knew this was a horrible idea. She also knew she couldn't say no to a chance to snoop around the Finn case. "What sort of pics are they looking for?"

"Close-up. Face only. Nothing for the raincoat crowd. Front and side. Mug shot deal, or as best you can get without being noticed. You'll need a telephoto."

"I've got a bad feeling about this, Biggie."

"That offer of four-fifty is for a limited time, hon."

This was a test of sorts, she realized. Big Rob was alternately encouraging and skeptical about her long-term prospects as a private investigator. He was clearly fond of her, but he also wondered if she (or any woman) had the constitution to do competent work for questionable clients. *Information is morally neutral,* he'd say. *You have to be as well.* "Yeah, yeah. You know I'll do it. You'll get me the address?"

"Got it right here."

Three mornings later, Barwick sat on a man-made slope overlooking a soccer field, casually snapping photos through a long lens. The sky was Chagall blue with a single Magritte cloud. The air was comfortably cool and dry. Below, boys and girls chased one another across a truncated field. There were nets and lots of uncalled hand balls and, occasionally, even goals, but no one kept score. It was difficult to tell who was on what team, with kids in both jerseys tending to gang up on the one closest to the ball. First-year players, teenies they were called, were still finding their way in the game.

Through the lens, Barwick found and lost Justin a dozen times, snapping the shutter when she could catch him between the back-and-forth and the up-and-down. She recalled Eric Lundquist's face, kept fresh in her memory by a recurring dream, and tried to match it against the boy's, almost two years older than when she took on the earlier case. She supposed Big Rob might have been right. Lundquist could be the donor. There might be an explanation for the birthmark. Maybe the old woman had forgotten. Maybe she was lying. Maybe it was some sort of genetic quirk. Sally had known identical twins in high school and she could always tell them apart. Their ears were a little bit different. Maybe one had a birthmark and the other didn't. What did she really know about genetics, anyway?

On the job, Barwick wished she could be more like Big Rob, wished she could keep her curiosity on a leash. But how could she watch this kid through the camera, violating him with each exposure, and not wonder who was paying for this and why? She'd been trying to think of an explanation that didn't churn her stomach, and to this point she'd come up with nothing.

"Which one is yours?"

Barwick brought the camera down between her knees and turned toward the voice. She was sitting about six feet to Sally's left: petite, pretty, not as old as most of the other moms. She'd brought a picnic basket, a cardboard carton of juice with a straw, and a home magazine.

"Oh, no," Barwick said. "I mean, none of them are mine. I'm a student at the Art Institute. This is for midterms. Big show. You know—*Innocence of Youth.*" She laughed. "It's a whole big theme or something."

"I *thought* you were a little young for the mom thing."

Barwick waved her hand. "I'm not as young as you, am I?" The woman blushed. "I'm Sally."

The mother put her juice down and stretched her body close enough to extend a hand. "Martha Finn," she said.

Barwick thought immediately of the different ways Big Rob might tell her she'd blown the case. Sarcasm was the most likely approach, but he could just as well choose a violent tantrum. He could decide she was unreliable. A flake. He could stop calling with work.

Still, have a spaz now and she'd no doubt make things worse.

"Nice to meet you," Barwick said.

"Do you mind?" Martha asked, lifting her basket and making a motion with her shoulders in Barwick's direction.

"Please," Barwick said and the two scooched closer together.

"You're a photographer?"

"A student. Someday I'd like to call myself a photographer."

"Are you getting anything good?"

"Yeah," Barwick said. "The sun's a little bright. There's such a thing as too nice a day when you're taking snaps. Lots of shadows."

"Taking snaps," Martha said. "I like that."

They watched the game and chatted for a while until Barwick realized that Martha probably expected her to take pictures, so she pointed the camera toward the field and took a few hastily focused pics of the other kids.

"Hmmm," Martha said. "Could I ask you a favor?"

"Sure."

Martha pulled a cheap digital camera from her bag. "You can't get a decent shot from the sidelines with one of these. Would it be too much to ask you to take a few photos of my son? I'll pay for all your film."

Barwick giggled and Martha joined her. Everyone friendly. She hadn't blown the case after all.

"Of course," Barwick said and raised the camera to her eye. Another critical mistake, almost. She pulled it back down and smiled. "Which one is yours?"

— 22 —

It took about ninety seconds for a nurse to inform Dr. Burton that Dr. Moore's black Volvo had pulled into its spot, and another minute or so for Joan to say good-bye to her contractor, who had called with a few questions regarding the tiling she'd selected for her new bathroom. Following that, it was a ten-second walk from her office to his.

"Can I talk to you, Davis?"

Davis looped his collared jacket over the top of the wooden coat stand, caught the whole thing as it toppled, and then wrestled coat and rack until they were in balance. Joan Burton looked fantastic. Under her smock, the silk shirt she wore billowed in the right places. Her hair was pulled back today, and the elastic at the back of her neck strained to contain it. He imagined the band snapping and waves of dark hair crashing around her face, hiding and revealing it like a dance of veils. At first, he didn't even notice she was upset.

"Sure, Joan. What's up?"

"You know Justin Finn?"

Davis was certain his face didn't betray panic, but he quickly slid into his chair, where his knees trembled unseen. "Sure. Something wrong?"

"Yeah, I'd say so." Joan shut the door and perched on the edge of the chair nearest his desk. In one hand, she held a large gray binder with a white sticker running down its spine. The label said *XLT-4197*, which was the office code for Justin Finn. Of the dozens of clones who had been conceived in his clinic, it was the only code number Davis had memorized. "Is he okay?"

"The kid's fine. It's our control that's gone to hell."

"What's the matter?"

"I just did his five-year checkup," Joan said. "There's been a colossal screwup, and when I report it, you're gonna take the heat. We all will, actually, the whole clinic, but mostly you."

Christ. The five-year. Davis knew this was coming; Martha Finn had even mentioned the appointment when he saw her at Starbucks. Somehow, this morning, he hadn't been ready for it. "Tell me," he said. He hoped something would occur to him. Sometimes solutions make themselves. Not often in Davis's case, unfortunately. He was a plotter. A plan-aheader.

Voice lowered, Joan said, "This kid isn't who we claimed he is. His DNA doesn't match the donor. Hell, he doesn't match any donor on file. I don't have the slightest idea where he came from."

Davis said nothing. She'll keep talking, he thought. Joan hates silence. Since the day she had joined the staff at the clinic, Davis had often counted on her to answer her own questions when others were slow to respond.

"This is a nightmare. How do you think it could have happened?" she asked. "I have a theory, and the disciplinary committee might let us off with a slap and a fine, but who knows what the parents might do? If they decide to sue . . . Do you remember that couple in Virginia last year? Jesus Christ. Anyway, I was looking back through the files, and around the time the Finns were being prepped for implantation, we fired this young admin after a long list of screwups." She turned pages on a legal pad. "Tardiness, bad reviews, poor attitude, complaints from the nurses, complaints from patients. About six months later he was brought up on drug charges in McHenry County, dealing designer drugs to teenagers or some shit. I don't remember him that well, but I recall Pete having to testify at his trial. Do you remember that?"

"I remember, yeah." Davis did remember the kid. That had seemed like a big deal at the time. There were lots of nervous meetings between the partners. New Tech's reputation was on the line. Their license had been threatened. But Joan was right. That was nothing compared to this.

"Anyway, I can't prove he had anything to do with it—not yet—but if we dig around a little bit, we might find he had access to the samples, and that might be enough to build a case against the guy. I have a feeling."

Davis stared at her, thinking, trying to forge a blank look that would hold the silence but also provide emphasis no matter what he said next. Joan was offering an answer of sorts. She had tried to solve the mystery with a story that turned out to be more plausible than the truth, and now that he'd been caught, Davis felt stupid and lazy for not leaving a trail of lies to a likelier culprit than himself. Now he was tempted by the opportunity to put the blame on a punk kid who was already in prison. The repercussions for a doctor found guilty of illegal cloning could be devastating: loss of license, possible jail time, shame. To a convicted drug dealer, however, the consequences of the sort of negligence Joan was suggesting would be, well, negligible.

There would be an investigation, though. Perhaps a trial. Testimony. Controversy. This story made sense to Joan, and others might believe it, as well. Still, the last thing Davis needed was scrutiny, and this had the low rumbling of a rolling snowball gathering size.

"Joan," Davis said, his hand on the back of his neck.

"What?"

"It wasn't any admin with access to the samples."

Joan's face twitched as her fragile denial shattered like blown glass and fell away. "Oh, God, Davis. Do not tell me. Do not tell me you've known about this."

Davis nodded.

"Goddammit!" she screamed. The legal pad bounced off his desk and landed sprawled on the floor. "Do you want us all to lose our goddamned licenses?"

"Let me explain."

"Can you? Really? Can you explain how a fuckup like this happens and you don't tell anybody? How long have you known?"

"I've always known, Joan."

She glared.

"There wasn't any fuckup. Justin was born of the same DNA I had scheduled for the procedure."

Joan's voice dropped to a croaking whisper, the result of nausea, he supposed, acid reflux. "What are you saying? This is some sort of experiment? If you've been conducting live trials on your own, there's going to be a shit storm, and the disciplinary committee is just the start of it."

Davis hoped Joan would be able to read his lack of expression.

"Well, who's the donor, then?" Joan asked.

"I don't know. I cloned him to find out."

Davis explained it more like a lawyer than a doctor, beginning with Joan's own assault and her frustration with the law. He told her that on his daughter's seventeenth birthday, AK had taken him aside and apologized for years thirteen through fifteen, inclusive. They had laughed over that and sat on the cedar steps of the deck behind their house, leaning on each other and staring out into the yard. He told Joan about the providence in a vial the cops had delivered by accident, and about the Finns and their healthy baby boy. About the paperwork he faked and the sample from the donor of record, Eric Lundquist, he destroyed.

"This is insane, Davis," Joan said quietly. "Insane. What did you think you were going to do with this child?"

"I'm not going to do a thing with him, Joan. He's going to enjoy his life and I'm going to wait for him to grow up."

"And then?"

"And then I'll be able to look into the face of AK's killer."

"He won't be her killer," Joan said.

"No, no, he won't. But I'll know what he looks like."

"Is that important?"

"It was," he said. "Yeah, it still is."

"You'll be arrested, if they find out what you did."

"Maybe."

"*I'll* be arrested, unless I go to the committee with this right now."

Davis made a quarter turn in his chair. From the beginning this was the part that had troubled him most. Of course, he had hoped Martha Finn would choose Dr. Burton as her son's pediatrician because he wanted to keep the boy close. It was always likely he'd have to involve Joan down the line and he had never come to terms with it, even now, as he was about to bully her into keeping her mouth shut. "You never wondered what you'd be capable of if you ever again came face-to-face with the asshole who attacked you?"

"I can't even believe we're having this conversation."

"Have you told anybody about this? Pete? Gregor? Anyone?" He meant the source of Justin's DNA, and he was sure she hadn't. "You can't, Joan. You know you can't. Forget about you and me for a second. Forget about the horrible thing you think I've done, about the breach of ethics and the lack of controls and all that bullshit. Think about Justin."

"I *am* thinking about Justin," she said. "I'm thinking about this poor little boy you just decided one day to carve out of a monster."

That was a little melodramatic, Davis thought, although he might have put it the same way if the situation were reversed. "Fine. So you turn me in and Justin's parents find out who their son really is? What will that do? To him? To the Finn family? Let's say they prosecute me and the story makes the news— *Mad doctor clones daughter's killer!*—and that guy, that monster, whoever he is, out there, that guy realizes there's a living, growing, three-dimensional composite of himself that could, eventually, point the finger at him. You don't think he's going to do something about that? Christ, you might as well kill Justin yourself."

That was unfair, Davis thought, but necessary. He watched the helplessness inside her build like steam in a kettle. Her face looked pressurized, her insides rusted shut like a forgotten metal box at the bottom of the ocean. Flush. She began to shake.

"We can protect him, Joan. *The two of us.* We can protect him with a secret."

They sat together for a half hour or more, saying little, a contract between them drafted in the silence. When a nurse knocked on the door to alert Joan to an arrived patient, she nodded at her, nodded at Davis, and loped toward the exam room.

— 23 —

This spot was probably too close but Mickey was tired, tired of years on the road, of napping in his car and sleeping in cheap motels and crashing in the homes of strange "friends of the cause" whom he didn't entirely trust. When you're tired you get careless, and he supposed sitting in this chair was exactly that, but screw it. He'd earned the right to take a few chances. Earned the right by accomplishing so much and not getting caught. He and Byron Bonavita.

Byron was probably dead, rotting away peacefully and undetected high in some Blue Ridge Mountain tree house, Mickey supposed, although only he and a few others in the Hands of God guessed as much. The FBI now suspected Byron in twenty-six clone-clinic killings, but Mickey had done all but five of them. Byron Bonavita might have been famous, but in truth he wasn't prolific. He was a bogeyman made out of government incompetence and fed like a casserole to the starving and witless media.

Mickey the Gerund enjoyed his freedom, but in the moments when he was most honest with himself, he resented the credit Byron got for his work. Of course, the victims were the point here, not the perpetrator, but wouldn't it be better for the cause if the public weren't able to pin the killings on a single lone-wolf radical? If they thought there was more than one Byron Blakely Bonavita out there taking a courageous stand against the evils of humanism and science and technology, wouldn't they be forced to confront the issue of cloning, to take a stand, to say I'm for this or against it and here's why? Wouldn't some senator or congressman or even president have to stand before the people and say, *While I deplore the tactics used by groups like the Hands of God, their actions represent a strong popular sentiment in this country that something must be done about immoral acts being committed in our name by doctors and scientists all across this great land of ours,* et cetera, and then democracy could do much faster what Mickey and, at one time, Byron were doing oh-so-slowly, on a case-by-case basis.

That's why Mickey started mixing things up. He still shot the occasional doctor when the situation called for it, but more and more he was using other tactics. He cut the brake line on a Lexus once, and poisoned a bottle of water with arsenic and slipped it into a clinic fridge. Neither of those were kills, but the point was the same. There had been a few that had been even more personal. In addition to the twenty-one dead, Mickey had wounded more than thirty, many of them patients and secretaries and support staff. He took credit for eleven retirement cross-outs on Harold Devereaux's Web site, and in some ways those were better than kills. There was something extremely satisfying when a clone doctor cried uncle. It was like a man repenting, although the doctors were never contrite, always issuing a statement instead that claimed they were doing it for the safety and security of their family, et cetera. That was part of Mickey's job, too—intimidating the wife or husband and their kids with threatening letters and e-mails and phone calls. Occasionally he'd get close enough to whisper in some kid's ear. No one appreciated how diverse and effective his tactics had been. That was the price of success for a covert soldier, he told himself.

This coffee shop, named Gimbel's, had the best little chocolate pastries, airy French ones, which was why he was sitting at this window counter for the third straight day. No one thinks anything about it now, but later, when the girl behind the counter is being asked by the cops if she saw anyone or anything unusual lately, she'll tell them, *There was this guy in here for the last couple days and I'd never seen him before,* and then they'll show her a picture of Byron Bonavita and ask her if it could have been him, keeping in mind that this photo is over seven years old now, and she'll say, *Yeah it could have been this guy, maybe a couple years older and heavier,* and the papers will run the Bonavita manhunt on its front page again tomorrow. It was all becoming so predictable.

An hour ago he had walked into the clinic across the street and asked for some literature. It was a cool northern California day and he could see why people paid a fortune in rent to live here. If it weren't for the earthquakes and the fact that his job didn't permit him to take a permanent address, he might think about moving here himself to enjoy the temperate bay climate and the French pastries. There would be other things to consider, however. Like his neighbors. There were like-minded folks in this part of the country, but you had to look hard to find them.

After the receptionist handed him a stack of information (*disinformation,* he would prefer to call it), Mickey asked to use the rest room. Security was unusually lax here, probably because he'd never been to northern California before. They probably thought they were off Byron Bonavita's radar. The bathroom smelled like alcohol and oranges. When he finished his business he washed his hands and walked out of the men's room and across the street and ordered a coffee and a pastry and read some of the clinic literature. The brochures pictured happy families, unburdened of recent stresses, which might have included infertility or hereditary disease or just the unpredictable timing of bearing children the natural way or the inconvenience of adoption or all of the above.

Fifteen minutes ago, a nurse from the clinic had entered the shop and picked up an order of six coffees, which she must have phoned in. She did a double take when his eyes met hers. Maybe she had seen him in the clinic, or maybe she saw that he was reading the clinic's brochures. It couldn't have been so unusual for prospective patients to stop in the coffee shop after a visit to the clinic. The only way it might have gone pear-shaped, really, would have been if the nurse had conferred with the girl behind the counter and they had lumped their private observations together to make a suspicion, but the nurse didn't do that. She gathered up her coffees in a cardboard box, checked the integrity of the lids, and rushed back to the clinic, crossing the four lanes ladder-style, one at a time, in stops and starts. Mickey's carelessness wasn't really carelessness after all, when you considered the remote chance that any person might put her two together with someone else's two and come up with a conspiratorial four.

When Mickey finished his coffee he looked at his watch. It was later than he thought and he wished every town with a fertility clinic also had a place as nice as this coffee shop, where the pastry was so good and the time passed so quickly. He gathered up the brochures and folded them into the pocket of his green windbreaker. With a wave to the girl behind the counter—*Holy shit, Officer, I sure do remember Byron Bonavita. He sat right there by the window, looking across at the clinic, and he even waved at me friendly-like when he left!*—Mickey passed through the glass door into the sea-seasoned air that was just the right temperature and began the walk to his car, which he'd parked far enough away that he wouldn't have any problems with fire engines and black-and-white traffic.

When the clinic men's room exploded he was half a mile on, his back to the concussion, which sounded like a steel drum being struck inside a giant pillow. He turned with the others on the sidewalk, exchanged with them puzzled glances and *What on earths?* Then after a pause he continued on to his car, where he looked like just another guy rushing home to the evening news to find out the source of that nasty black smoke in the distance.

— 24 —

After three weeks with the new software and the soccer-field photographs of Justin, Davis had produced fifty-four different composite sketches, each using a different set of variables. Working from the police profile of the perpetrator, Davis assumed the killer had been younger than thirty-five, so he made a series that imagined Justin at twenty, another at thirty, and another group at forty. The oldest ones were grotesquely unreal, with features more appropriate to Australopithecus, so he discarded them.

The others he taped to the walls of his basement room, over and between the names of his relatives. There was nothing here he could be sure of yet. No reason to choose any of these faces over the others. There were a few patterns emerging, however, in the shape of the eyelids, in the width of the mouth, and in the curves about the lobes of the ears. Davis had very little confidence in the hair. He had no way to know how long the killer kept it, how he styled it, or even if he still had it on his head at all.

He spent nights in this room memorizing these faces, and in his thoughts they were a team, a gang, a mob, a cult. Thirty-six individuals each responsible for his daughter's death. The devil goes by different names, and this monster had many heads.

This was a problem. How could he know which of these faces to hate? How could he feel anything like a catharsis when he wasn't sure at which countenance he should be directing his rage? He hadn't closed a chapter of his life the way he'd hoped; he'd opened the file on another mystery. The name of AK's killer was still an unanswerable fill-in-the-blank, but his face was now a maddening multiple choice.

As he studied them, conversed with them, spent time inside their imaginary heads, he found one that seemed especially cruel. Especially soulless. He threw the others in a drawer and consulted only this one, spending long hours in the blue room with it, imagining the sketch to be real. For three weeks, as the autumn turned gray and cold, Davis tried to convince himself it was the face of his enemy. Tried to converse with it. To understand it. To accept it. That was the long-sought goal, after all, wasn't it? Acceptance?

He couldn't do it. Not with so many doubts. This couldn't be why he risked his career. Why he now risked Joan's career. For a few dozen lines drawn and colored and shaded by a computer program and chosen by him arbitrarily—for what reason? Because this is how Davis expected him to look? Bald. Snarling. Empty inside. Odds were good the guy didn't look like that at all. Joan had been raped because her attacker didn't look like the sort of guy who would attack her. AK wasn't naïve. Some nut had tried to kill her own father, after all. Her deranged murderer most likely didn't look so deranged.

Davis sorted again through the three dozen sketches, this time pulling out not the ones that looked evil, but the ones that looked real. Familiar. Unthreatening. He narrowed them down to four.

He exported the pictures to Web-friendly files and then uploaded them to a list of crime-fighting Internet sites. Without revealing his name, he pleaded for any information about these men, or any man who resembled them. He was counting on a break from a stranger.

He didn't offer too many details, not his name or the town where he lived or the specifics of the case. Using the handle JusticeForAK, he said he was a loving father and that he believed one of these men was his daughter's killer, a man he was anxious to meet face-to-face. His open call sounded anguished and menacing and hinted at vigilantism, which was the tone he hoped to set. The people who would recognize a murderer might not be on speaking terms with the law, he reasoned, and if he ever found the man he was looking for, Davis couldn't go to the cops, anyway.

He had been foolish to believe otherwise, but he understood now that the only way he could ever know the face of Anna Kat's killer would be to put himself in the same room with him.

What he would do then, he couldn't even guess.

— 25 —

Joan had to stop watching the television police dramas she loved. She found herself empathizing with the bad guys.

Or feeling as guilty as them, anyway. She felt guilty all the time. And warm. Hot. She sweated through her days. Her nights were sleepless, her mornings unbearable. How she hated the mornings when the scenarios in her head all seemed so bleak. Public shame. Loss of her practice. Prison. Sure, on the cop shows, women's prison didn't seem as frightening as men's prison. But still . . . she was a *criminal* now. There was no changing that. Even if she were never a suspect, she would always be a fugitive.

A seven-minute walk from her condo to the beach. It wasn't *getting* cold anymore, it *was* cold, especially after dark, but people were still here, walking north and south along the waterline. Older couples—empty-nesters—and because it was Friday, teens. Underdressed high school kids with their hands in each other's back pockets. Rollerbladers. Desperate dogs and their owners, home late. Northwestern students up the shore a few miles from campus for who knows why, sneaking beers, tossing Frisbees.

Sitting in the hard, damp sand in a pair of old jeans and a heavy Cal Bears sweatshirt to pull over her knees, Joan felt safe here. Anonymous. No one could call her with bad news or knock on her door. When she was here, alone as far as the rest of the world was concerned—the police, Davis Moore, the Congressional Board of Oversight—Joan Burton didn't exist.

She was angry with Davis for keeping the truth about Justin from her, and then she was mad at him for telling her. For involving her. But she was doing the right thing, she knew. Davis should never have done what he did—it was an inexcusable breach of ethics, honestly—but she could only deal with the situation as it was. What did the army call it? *The facts on the ground.* That's what she was working with, the facts on the ground. Nothing would be served by sending Davis to prison and endangering Justin's life. What else could she do but look after the welfare of the child? Her *patient.*

Joan had another reason to do everything she could to find AK's killer: she might have been able to prevent her murder.

"Hey."

A pair of guys, boys actually, were standing over her, but at a respectful distance. She guessed they were college kids, but it was getting harder to tell. They looked so young. They could be in high school for all she knew.

"Hey," she said.

One of the boys said, "I dropped my keys. We were just looking for them."

They were good-looking, broad-shouldered, and square-jawed—athletes, she guessed. But they hadn't lost their keys. They were flirting.

"You haven't seen them anywhere, have you?"

She laughed. "In the sand? In the dark?"

"We're pretty much screwed, aren't we?"

She nodded. They paused. She wondered if they knew how old she was. If they were as bad at gauging her age as she was at guessing theirs. If in the dark she looked good enough to be a student. A hot college girl. Maybe. In the dark. Joan didn't say anything.

"We'll see you around," one of the boys said finally, and they moved on down the beach, pushing each other, joshing with each other, not looking for their keys.

As brief as it had been, as inconsequential, the attention should have made her feel better. It would have before all this. It didn't.

A few months before she died, Anna Kat had come to see Joan at the office. Her father was away at a conference, preaching to the converted on the virtues of new fertility techniques.

"I have a problem," AK said. "About a boy."

She didn't call him by name, although Joan knew AK had been seeing a kid named Dan. He'd dropped by with her one day to see her dad, and Joan, never missing a vicarious opportunity to relive her mostly enjoyable high school days, snuck a peek and found him, well, okay, she supposed. He was a little on the thin side, a little bit smug, a little heavy-lidded, a little *ordinary.* Joan didn't know what the selection was like at Northwood East, but she was pretty sure AK should have been out of Dan's league.

"He hurts me," Anna Kat told her. "And I'm afraid I like it."

"Like it?" Joan asked.

AK put her hands over her eyes. "No. Not exactly. God, this is embarrassing. I mean, I don't enjoy it. But the fact that I don't enjoy it doesn't keep me away."

"Is he really such a prize?" Joan asked.

"That's just the thing. No. I don't even like him, really. It's so hard to explain." When Joan at last looked into AK's red eyes she understood how desperate she really felt. "It's like, a few months ago I went to this party and got pretty smashed—"

Joan painted her a requisite but unconvincing frown.

"Whatever. I don't even drink that much," AK said. "In fact, the morning after that party I swore I was never going to drink again. Two weeks later, though . . . somebody offered me a beer and it was as if I forgot it ever happened. Things with . . . with this guy, it's kind of like that. I tell him things have to change, they don't change, but I act like I don't care."

Joan had wondered why AK had come to her, given all the things her mother had no doubt been saying about her around their house. Jackie had made it very clear to Joan's face that she didn't like her. She could only imagine what was said behind her back. Joan supposed she was younger than a lot of adults AK knew. And she was single. And a doctor. Maybe that still counted for something with some people.

And maybe, just maybe, someone else in the Moore house had been painting a different picture of her. One could hope.

On the beach, nine years later, she was disappointed in her advice to Anna Kat. She hadn't had the guts to tell her own story of sexual assault, and since the day AK was killed, Joan had wished that she had. Instead, she told her to be true to herself. The fact that AK was coming to her at all was evidence that something wasn't right about her relationship with D—with this guy. More than anything, Joan said, think about what your dad would want for you. He loves you so much, AK. And even if this isn't something you can talk to him about—and no, I don't suppose it is—keep his counsel close. Keep his love in your heart always.

"But you won't tell him?"

"No, I won't tell him."

"No matter what happens?"

More than any other, that remark had haunted Joan. *No matter what happens?* From the moment she said it, Joan wondered what AK could have meant, and when she heard the news of her murder, Anna Kat's plaintive voice came tumbling back into the fore of her mind and she was sick, just sick about it. Had AK really known she was in danger? Was she begging Joan to rescue her? Joan didn't see Davis in the days after the murder and was going to tell him about their conversation as soon as she could, but then she heard the police had cleared Dan, the ordinary boyfriend, with a DNA test, and she decided to keep her pact of silence. For almost a decade, AK's words had been a mystery, and Joan still wondered if there wasn't something she could have done to protect her. If only she hadn't kept the promise she'd made to Anna Kat that day.

"No matter what happens," Joan had said.

So there was more than one kind of guilt gnawing away at Joan as she sat on the dark, wet beach, indifferent to coy come-ons from college boys feeling out a North Shore Friday night.

Of course, there might have been an explanation other than guilt for her sleeplessness, her nervousness, her uneasiness, her *sweatiness.*

She was in love.

Justin at Seven

— 26 —

Justin let himself in with the key the Barkers had given his parents before leaving for Spain. The Barkers' dog, Austin, three quarters as high as Justin was tall, padded silently to him, and Justin consumed a few minutes petting him in a gentle, repetitive motion between his neck and the curve of his back, with the hand that was not holding the gray plastic bucket. Austin probably spent as much time in Justin's yard as he did in his own, and although this was the third time the boy had been in the house when the Barkers were away, it never occurred to the dog to bark suspiciously or growl or hide under a bed. His mother had fed Austin that morning, and she would again this evening, but Justin wasn't here to serve meals. He was here to experiment.

And also to get out of the house. His parents didn't notice Justin's presence when they were fighting, so it was no surprise that his absence went right past them as well. Shouting now seemed their preferred form of communication. They began with low-decibel snapping in the morning and slowly pushed the volume up over the course of the day—as if somewhere in the house there were a master knob, like the one controlling the intercom system, that turned itself up and up and up—until they finally sent Justin to bed and began reproaching each other in hateful whispers, so as not to keep the boy awake.

He didn't understand all of it, but Justin was smart enough, even at seven, to know that the things they were yelling about weren't always the things they were mad at. On Monday his dad might come home from work and ask him to pick up his GI Joes from the living room carpet and put them in the toy box in the den. On Wednesday, however, he might say, *Jesus Christ, pick up your goddamn dolls!* You didn't have to be ten to know that something besides GI Joes was pissing his dad off.

It had something to do, he figured out, with a woman named Denise. Justin didn't know why, but his dad liked Denise and his mom didn't. His mom was always calling Denise names and telling his dad that she didn't want him to see her anymore. His dad said she was being "ridiculous" and that Denise was a nice girl and of course he *liked* her, he never would have hired Denise if he didn't *like* her, but they weren't having an *affair,* for crying out loud, if that was what she thought. On the other hand, by the looks of these credit card bills, his mom had gone off the budget again, whatever that was, but his mom said the budget was no good and they had to redo it because they hadn't realized how much they'd need for Justin's clothes this year, he was growing out of them so fast, and his dad said, *Justin's clothes? Really? Justin's clothes? You weren't shopping for Justin's clothes at Ultimo,* but he never said what she was actually shopping for there.

Following an incident at a comic book store, his mother told Justin she didn't want him hanging around Danny Shubert anymore, because he was a "bad influence." Trying a little bit of his dad's logic, Justin replied, "I *like* Danny, but we're not having an affair, if that's what you think." His mom fell to her knees and hugged him around the neck and cried into his T-shirt and said she was sorry and forgot to punish him, so it worked as far as that went.

Boy and dog crept to the living room and Justin pulled a bundle of dry sticks and a wad of newspaper from the bucket and placed them in the brick fireplace. Austin curled himself on the couch around a chewed tennis ball that had found its way in from the backyard. On his knees, Justin produced a book of matches and lit one on the third try, hurling it immediately at the pile of kindling. The match expired and he lit two more in the same way before the paper took the flame.

In quick succession, he added the following fuels to the pyre: army man (in kneeling position), worn paperback mystery (Dean Koontz), old CD (sound track to *Grease*), dead flies (tweezered with an entomologist's care from his bedroom windowsill), Lincoln Log (short connector), Lego brick (blue). When each item was added he allowed the results to hold him trancelike, the memory of each reaction recorded for future consideration.

When the bucket was empty, Justin searched the room on hands and knees for something local, something belonging to the Barkers, but something that had already been forgotten, that wouldn't be missed. Under the coffee table he found a drawer and, inside it, a cardboard pocket of photographs awaiting their appropriate place in albums or desk frames. Flipping through them he came across one he thought particularly dull, a shot of Mrs. Barker on the patio stooped next to an older woman who was smiling but shriveled like a sun-dried insect in her wheelchair. He carted it back to the fire and tossed it in with the rest. He watched the paper and plastic and chemicals warp and fold and shrink the image, the old woman and her wheelchair becoming smaller and smaller and smaller and then disappearing altogether into smelly chars.

Not until then did he notice how much smoke filled the room. Austin left the couch with a moan and trotted around the corner and up the stairs. Still unaware of the existence of dampers, Justin climbed up the back of an uphol-stered chair and cracked a window at the top. He would return tomorrow to collect the half-burned, half-melted mound he had made, hide it, preserve it, and then start one anew.

— 27 —

Clutching her big camera with one hand, like a pistol, in a park near Lake Michigan, Barwick found an old tree with thick and twisted leafless limbs. Martha and Justin had been following by a dozen thoroughbred lengths and when they caught up with her she was already framing the shot through her eyepiece.

"Here," Sally said. "Here is perfect."

Every few months, Martha Finn would call Barwick and have her drive up Sheridan Road to Northwood so she could take photos of growing and chang-ing Justin, often posed in idyllic settings in the yard or here in the park or on some decorated impromptu stage in the Finn home. Once, he was dressed in a red bow tie and black shorts; another time he wore the orange and white of Terry's alma mater, the University of Tennessee. Today, Martha called his look *young, casual chic:* new blue jeans, white dress shirt, clean deck shoes, brushed hair, face scrubbed to an ivory matte finish with pink accents.

Every fall, Scott Colleran would call Big Rob and ask for a recent photo of Justin for his anonymous client, which Barwick would reluctantly provide from the digital backup of her one-on-one photo sessions with the boy. She'd get paid twice for the same job, and in her dreams, Justin would allay her guilt.

"We are just instruments," he'd say.

Barwick had the dreams about three times a month. They were set in dif-ferent places: her high school, her apartment, Mrs. Lundquist's parlor, Big Rob's office (or at least in locales she understood to be those places, even if they didn't physically resemble them). One took place at a departure gate at O'Hare. In most of them, Justin, in Eric Lundquist's grown body, wearing Eric Lundquist's face, wanted to talk about duty.

"Fulfilling responsibility," he'd say, "is the most important thing."

"You sound like Big Rob," she'd say.

"Big Rob is a wide man," Justin would say.

"But what if those responsibilities are in service of a cause that's unjust?" Even while she was saying things like that in her dreams, she recognized it wasn't anything like the manner in which she—or probably anybody—really talked.

"You and I are instruments," Justin would say. "Instruments don't have causes."

"Who has causes, then?"

Justin didn't seem to care. "Other people."

When she handed over the photos, Big Rob would always say to her, "You're like a double agent," which only deepened her ambivalence. She had betrayed one friend to earn the trust of another. *This is what it takes,* she told herself. *You need to be willing to go where other detectives are not.* Her angst was mitigated by the satisfaction Big Rob and Scott Colleran expressed in her work. The client was very pleased, Colleran said. *Very pleased.*

"Hop up in the tree, Justin," Sally said. He surveyed the waist-high place where the old trunk separated, forming a flat area like the palm of an upturned, three-fingered hand. He obeyed and, turning toward the camera, froze his expression in a broad grin. When he realized the photo was some minutes from being snapped, he relaxed his face and stared at some kids, kids with fewer obligations, playing on a jungle gym in the distance.

Martha stood at Sally's side, trying to approximate the shot in her mind. "I like this."

Remotely, Sally arranged Justin's posture and put the camera to her eye. "Smile," she said, and he did. She clicked the shutter seven or eight times, producing that many identical exposures. Justin's expression never changed even slightly—sunny and adorable in every one. When she pulled the camera away the real Justin seemed like a portrait, as well—an idealized version of a little boy. Even the surface of the lake in the distance seemed not to be moving.

"Stay there," Barwick said. She adjusted the lens and took several close-ups of Justin's face. She would offer these to Martha, but they were really for Gold Badge's client. Through the lens, Justin looked surreal, hyperfocused. The horizon fell away around his blond curls. His smile was unwavering. His eyes, active and blue and deep, were like galaxies.

His eyes.

She pushed the camera aside. Justin was maybe fifteen feet away. Without the camera his eyes were like many others—heavy-lidded dots in a boy's tiny head. Through the lens, though, they were intimate. Seductive. *Familiar.*

They were the eyes that romanced her in dreams. The eyes Eric Lundquist wore when he came to her as Justin. She looked through the eyepiece again, turning the zoom until only Justin's jewel-like right iris filled the frame. These were not a seven-year-old's eyes.

She took a picture of his eye. This one for herself.

Hours later, with Justin on a playdate, across a wrought-iron table at a Northwood wine bar, Martha said, "It's lovely having a friend I can call for this."

"I like coming up here," Barwick said. Noting that this was a nice place in a wealthy town, not the Wild Hare, a reggae bar on Clark Street where she spent most of her free evenings, she tried not to gulp the twelve-dollar glass of Oregon Pinot Noir Martha had ordered for her, and measured the meniscus of her glass against Martha's every few minutes. "Justin's a great kid."

Martha demurred with a gracious smile and an uncertain squint. "Yeah. Gosh. Yeah, he is. I think he's got a crush on you." Sally flushed. "He's got a good heart, you know. Last week, I was making dinner and he just, you know, he just started setting the table. All by himself. Without me asking. It was so cute. At this age, he wants my approval so much."

"That's great," Barwick said.

"And he's so smart. Ninety-ninth percentile on all the tests." She blushed, the percentile scale being such an inflated and meaningless cliché (but irresistible nonetheless). "He has little moments, of course."

"Yeah? Like all kids, I imagine."

"Like all kids. Right. That's what I mean. You know, he uses bad language sometimes."

Barwick grunted. "Oh. Well. *Shit.*"

Martha spasmed, choking wine back into her glass. "God, Sally, you make me laugh. I don't have friends like you up here. I mean, I have friends, but not like I used to. Not the kind of friends I used to have in the city."

"What happened to your old friends?"

"Eh. You move. You get married. You have a kid." Martha took a long sip. "You have a kid and it becomes hard. When you're single you can drop everything. You're flexible. If you live in the city, even after you're married, you can still make dinner or a play or a last-minute happy hour on a whim. When you have a child it's harder. Impossible, in fact. Most of the time friends don't even call, and you know what? You're glad when they don't 'cause you're so goddamn tired."

"Yeah," Barwick said, although she really had no idea. She curled her fingers around the thin crystal stem—her smallest opposite the others, it and her ring finger forming a dull scissors. A pretty young couple about her age sat at a nearby table and leaned their heads close above their glasses, whispering things too private for Sally to hear. Barwick usually felt superior to twenty-somethings who lived in the suburbs. Not today.

"And kids. Lordy." Martha took another sip, bringing the level in her glass below Barwick's. "Were you ever in trouble, Sally? When you were little?"

"Oh God, yes," Sally said. "I was a terrible kid. Really drawn to the bad boys, you know? In tenth grade, I was suspended for six weeks. I was almost expelled, but my parents got me back in somehow."

Martha made a shocked circle with her lips, indicating that she found this gossip both delightful and scandalous. "Really? What did you do?"

"It was stupid. Some friends of mine and I had sat at the same table at lunch for two years and we were determined that no one else would sit at it when we moved to the other campus as juniors. So we broke into the school on a Saturday, stole it, and drove it in this guy's truck to the Indiana Dunes, where we got drunk and smashed it to bits with shovels and hammers. The cops showed up and we were arrested and because the theft was committed on school property, they weren't going to let us come back."

"Doesn't sound like such a big deal."

"Like I said. Stupid."

"I was such a Goody Two-Shoes," Martha said. "Never in trouble. Student council. Yearbook." She rolled her eyes. "That's why I'm so nervous about Justin, I'm sure. When people don't follow the rules, it makes me very anxious." She paused. "Justin's been setting fires. Nothing big. No damage yet. He keeps finding matches. Lighting candles. He lit a bunch of newspapers in the fireplace."

"A little scary."

"He's been stealing from me, too. I find jewelry in his room. You say something and he just says he's sorry. Does it again." She took a long breath and disposed of it in a long sigh. "It's so bad that I start to get paranoid. The neighbor's dog dies and I wonder if he didn't have something to do with it." She laughed to shake the horror from the thought.

"The neighbor's dog?"

"You read where serial killers, when they're young, like to set fires, torture animals, that sort of thing. I mean, I know Justin didn't, really. I'm sure he didn't. There are just those moments in the middle of the night when you can't think about anything but the worst things possible. Terry tells me I'm being paranoid. He says all boys are fascinated by fire. On the other hand, I think Terry's less concerned about Justin stealing jewelry than whether he might be gay."

"Yeah."

"Of course, Terry's a whole other problem."

Unsure whether Martha wanted her to ask about Terry or not, Sally chose to say nothing.

"I'm sorry to talk so much about him . . ."

"About Terry?"

"No, Justin."

"Not at all."

"Terry just doesn't want to hear how much I've been thinking about it."

The second mention is deliberate, Barwick thought. "Men don't like to think too much about anything, in my experience."

"I even dream about Justin," Martha said. "Horrible, violent nightmares. I mean, what sort of mother am I that I can imagine my son doing such terrible things?"

"You're just concerned. The way you should be. Parents are supposed to worry. Worried parents are critical to the survival of the species."

"You're sweet, Sally." Martha paused, as if she might change the subject. Then she did. Sort of. "So what do you dream about?"

Barwick put a startled palm to her sternum, like she was trying to shut a damper in there on heartburn. She wished Martha could see the older Justin—handsome, confident, and wise—who came to her at night. "What do I dream about?" Barwick repeated. "Boys," she said.

— 28 —

Her father thought psychology was for the weak. "No one's to blame for anything. If you let them, they'll turn human nature itself into a pathology," he'd say. "People are supposed to be sad sometimes. Even depressed. Or excited. Or frightened. To the psychologist, emotions are symptoms of disease. To them, life itself is a disease." Martha's dad, an orthodontist, was frequently more dramatic than he needed to be.

The office smelled like leather and alcohol and Dominican cigars, which Martha imagined Dr. Morrow smoked in the fifteen minutes after one appointment left and before the next one arrived. She wondered about the secrets confessed here, by people other than her son. She wondered, too, what her son told Dr. Morrow, or what he divined from the things Justin didn't say—what he wrote in his notes, mumbled into his recorder, promised to keep privileged but nevertheless pondered at length, made judgments about. That scared her, and she trembled when Morrow, stout and clean-shaven, his round head topping a beige ribbed turtleneck like a chocolate ice cream cone, spoke in consultation with Justin's thin file, which was flattened across his desk.

"Justin's a mature boy," Dr. Morrow said, a professional grin taking charge of his face. "Advanced."

"Thank you," said Martha, less intimidated now that a smile was in play, but not comfortable enough to call him "Dr. Keith," which was how Justin referred to him.

"Advanced is good in many ways. In other ways it can be bad."

"Bad?" Terry said. "How?"

"Maturing is supposed to be a process," Morrow said. His voice was deep and rhythmic, like the bottom of a Parliament song. "There's a reason God starts them small. Justin is very smart. Physically, he's quite advanced, which has led to some troubles adjusting at school."

"The kids make fun of him, I know," Martha said.

"That will pass. One day, those same boys will be jealous. But he worries a lot for a seven-year-old. He wonders about things most kids his age haven't begun to think about."

"What sorts of things?"

"Who he is. Where he came from. Why he's here. For most children, those answers seem quite obvious. They are part of a family. Their purpose is to please grown-ups, et cetera. It's taken man thousands of years to identify and define the questions in Justin's head, questions he was able to pose quite plainly to me."

"All the acting out, then," she said. "That's what? Frustration?"

"Frustration, yes. Some of it might be experimentation. Justin has an extremely developed sense of self. Of *individualness*. He is able to recognize his own consciousness as a distinct person, separate from others, separate from his own body, even. Every day, he seeks to find out more about himself: who this person inside him is; *why* he is. Much of his reckless behavior would set off alarms for me in another child—fascination with fire, for instance—but with Justin I suspect he might be testing himself in ways that the world does not normally test little boys. I don't think he's after attention, or control. I don't think he has malice. I think he's an explorer. An explorer of his own mind. He's very special."

As he did once every session, Morrow turned his eyes briefly to a desktop barometer that had belonged to his father. When he died, Keith had joined his brothers and sister—an accountant, a banker, a teacher—at their dad's house in Philly, and with a magnum of wine they walked from room to room, each of them in turn claiming one possession, one story at a time, rescuing the old man's life from dismemberment at the estate sale. A worn book of poetry; a homemade tabletop baseball game; old vinyl jazz records; this barometer. Keith's father used to reset the barometer at night so he would know in the morning if pressure was rising or falling. "Looks like rain," he would say. "Ozone's dropping, I can smell it." He was uncannily accurate, the Morrow children remembered. Of course, their father watched the television news every night, got the weather that way too, and Keith had no evidence that the curious instrument on his dad's big desk was an effective barometer of anything. Still, he often thought of psychology as being like his father's attempts at meteorology: the children would come to his office and Keith would tell their parents if he could smell the ozone dropping.

"What can we do, then?" Martha asked.

"I think you need to expose him to people who have thought the same things he's thinking about. There aren't many books of philosophy written for first-graders, of course, but there are some very basic overviews of the subject, and he's extremely intelligent. I would let him start reading fables. Stories with morals. Aesop. Then you might seek out some watered-down summaries of the classic thinkers. He won't get all of it, or even most of it, but the important thing is to let him know that he's not alone in asking these questions; that as he matures, there will be places he can go to seek answers. As he gets older, he'll start to form his own opinions. The greatest danger to one who thinks too much is despair. You have to let Justin know that he won't always feel so alone with his thoughts."

"Are there any writers or books in particular we should start him on?"

"I don't think it matters much at the beginning. The important thing is that it's written in a way that he can begin to grasp it. You'll want to read with him, of course. Maybe make a game of it. At educational stores, I'm sure you can find some children's biographies of Plato or Socrates. The earlier thinkers."

"Socrates. Christ, Dr. Morrow, he's seven," Terry Finn said. "What if he's not interested?"

"He'll be interested. Trust me. You'll also want to accompany the reading with your own thoughts. Once Justin gets going, he's going to perceive everything he reads as literal truth. You'll want to counter that with your own sense of right and wrong. Justin is not looking for, nor does he need, a foundation in moral relativism. He needs to understand good and bad. I'm not sure he does yet."

"What do you mean, Dr. Morrow?" Martha asked.

"Justin sees things very abstractly. When he sets a fire, for instance, he understands that the fire destroys, but he also knows that the flames themselves take the place of the thing that burns. He does not see that as bad. He has created. The creation, not the destruction, is what interests him. Allow him to explore his creative side, but make it very clear to him where the boundaries are. He needs to understand that there are consequences."

Terry scooted forward on the leather chair. "Well, we try to explain to him . . ."

"This isn't a lecture on parenting, Mr. Finn. Justin is a special child. Once you understand the way his brain works, you'll understand that some of his needs are counterintuitive and you'll respond accordingly. You don't need to plan for every situation today."

"Doctor, could this have anything to do with the circumstances of Justin's—you know—conception?" The Finns had never discussed the particulars in this office, but they knew Justin's origins were spelled out in the initial paperwork, as required.

Dr. Morrow made a reassuring grunting sound behind closed lips. "I don't think so. I have to file a report based on my observations of Justin, and if they find any similar behaviors among other cloned children, then someone—probably someone at a university—will conduct a study. Investigate. To me, to you, to himself, Justin is a boy. A normal boy. If there's anything that makes him stand out from other kids, it's that he's above average. That carries with it some difficulties, some pain, some angst. But he doesn't have superpowers. He's not a freak. I treat other cloned children, and their troubles are as different from one another as noncloned children's. Certainly no more or less serious."

In the car on the way home, Martha's head hummed, and contempt for her husband's performance in the doctor's office felt like bees massing under the surface of her skin. He had complained about Dr. Morrow for weeks—*This is a waste of money; that boy doesn't need his head shrunk; just do what you want and leave me out of it*—and then he makes it to one meeting and pretends to be the concerned father. She didn't say anything, though. Justin was with a sitter and they'd be home soon and she'd made a determined effort not to fight in front of him anymore. Any fight she started now would carry into the house for sure.

She told Terry she would pick up some books tomorrow. There was a store just like Dr. Morrow described in the strip mall on 41, and she'd try the chain bookstores, as well as the indie one in downtown Winnetka. The counsel they'd just received was odd, she thought, but certainly the kind of thing a parent likes to hear from a psychologist—your child is smart, advanced, mature, *normal*. She thought psychologists didn't like to use that word, generally, but Dr. Keith had said it anyway.

She had a plan. She felt better. Her son was going to be okay. Kids are never as good as parents think they are, nor are they usually as bad as parents fear. And as Martha expelled months of stress with a long sigh, as the car approached the yellow fire hydrant that marked the outside range of their garage door opener, Terry finally confessed to her that he was having an affair.

— 29 —

Maybe it was only the sense of being away from himself, or at least away from the part of him so tautly tethered to the Chicago suburbs in which he had been born, schooled, and married, but there were tiny villages in New

England, incorporated into the sides of mountains or settled in the distant wake of advancing glaciers, that stirred a longing in Davis for country life. Brixton, Nebraska, on the other hand, did not. When he and Joan penetrated the town limits with a rented Taurus following a three-hour drive from the Lincoln Airport, he thought he could read hopelessness into every kitschy mailbox, countrified door decoration, and red-and-white Cornhusker garage door mural. Immediately, he felt empathy with every child whose adolescence in this town must be waited out like a juvenile sentence.

"Did you see that?" Joan asked.

"No. What?"

"That sign." Her tongue printed it from short-term memory: *"Brixton, Nebraska. Childhood home of pro football's Jimmy Spears."*

"Well, we're in the right place, then," Davis said as they passed a gas station with pumps so old they counted off gallons with rolling odometer-style meters. "Damn, look at that."

Jesus, what am I doing here? Davis asked himself. When he first received it in his e-mail inbox, he thought this lead actually held some promise, unlike the half dozen others he'd followed up on over the last two years. Its appeal was probably only relative, however; he hadn't received nearly as many tips as he'd expected. One thing Davis had learned was that most of these crime-fighting Web sites barely had an audience outside the webmaster's bedroom. The whole world might be on the Internet, but the Internet was a lousy way to reach the whole world.

What is Joan doing here? he thought. The reasons he'd asked her to come were obvious. Joan had an internal device that alerted her to poisonous character the way a Geiger counter clucked at decaying uranium, and he had been waiting for the chance to lure her deeper into his conspiracy. Selfishly, he knew the more he involved her, and the less she rebuked him, the better he'd feel. The search for AK's killer had become the most significant thing in his life, and Joan was the only person with whom he could talk about it. If he were still seeing a marriage counselor, of course, the therapist would tell Davis that every relationship he had with a woman was somehow related to his marriage. In this case, he knew it was true.

The tips didn't arrive in his e-mail very often, but Davis checked his anonymous Internet mailbox once in the morning and again every evening. The messages were typically from an untraceable account, with a lead or a suggestion, or just words of encouragement. Most of them were crackpots, fishing blindly for the twenty-five-thousand-dollar reward. He collected and cataloged them all.

The composite of AK's killer got better with every new batch of photos he received from the private investigator, or so Davis hoped. He had the help of new technology—a beta version of software used to enhance and age ultra-sounds for the purpose of identifying birth defects—and it had sharpened details in the image. In reality, he had no way of knowing whether the picture was becoming more like the face of the man he sought. It was looking more human, more realistic, however, and after he had plugged in all the variables, the FaceForger software (which he had upgraded twice now, and become more skilled in manipulating) spit out fewer and fewer possibilities.

There were dozens of Web sites devoted to true crime, and Davis found several willing to publish some version of his story. He omitted many of the giveaway details, including location, to protect his identity, but the composite picture was out there and so was the reward. To date twenty people claimed to know this man, or to have seen him, usually on the bad guy's way out of their town.

Several leads he eliminated for one reason or another, incoherence being the most common. Others he pursued from home with searches of public records. Following one tip, he drove to Milwaukee and snooped around a Toyota dealership to meet a salesman named Dave DiBartolo, who looked spookily like FaceForger's imagining of the killer. He even test-drove a Corolla and received a travel alarm, after which he put DiBartolo at the top of a sad group of potential suspects mostly labeled "too young" or "not a chance."

Then he received an e-mail from Ricky Weiss of Brixton, Nebraska.

"The fellow you're looking for is from here," Weiss wrote. "His name is Jimmy Spears. He's famous."

In an exchange of messages, Davis learned that Jimmy Spears didn't actually live in Brixton anymore, although his parents did. Spears was a third-string quarterback for the Miami Dolphins, and in telecasts could be glimpsed most often on the sidelines, wearing a headset and a baseball cap, gesturing to the huddle: a high-salaried turquoise-and-orange signal flag transmitting coded messages from the offensive coordinator to the line of scrimmage.

Photos of Spears were easy to come by and Davis collected them all, even going so far as to send away for a Dolphins media guide so he could add the most recent official mug shot. Blond, handsome. Davis agreed that he looked very much like the FaceForger composite—not so much the hair and nose, but certainly the eyes and chin and around the corners of the mouth—and if he put the composite side by side with pictures of Justin, it was easy to imagine one being a younger version of the other.

What interested Davis most, however, was a biographical detail first provided unsolicited by Ricky Weiss and later confirmed by Spears's media guide biography.

"Jimmy was a great college player," Weiss wrote. "He finished sixth in the Heisman voting the year Northwestern went to the Rose Bowl."

Davis was not a football fan, but he remembered a big to-do about Wildcat football across several seasons some years back. Joan was a college fan (though partial to her alma mater, Cal) and Gregor was a Northwestern grad, insufferable and often clad in obnoxious purple when the Cats were winning. Still, Davis shivered when he turned to Spears's bio:

> Jimmy Spears
> QB-12
> AGE: 29
> COLLEGE: Northwestern

Ten years ago, at the time of AK's murder, Jimmy Spears was attending school less than five miles from downtown Northwood. And while the campus was shuttered for Christmas break that week, Davis confirmed that the players would have been in Evanston, practicing for the Gator Bowl.

Good enough to make Jimmy his best lead. For now.

They drove in a circle following a downloaded map with a less-than-thorough accounting of Brixton's streets. Eventually, Davis backtracked to the gas station they had passed on the way in.

At the counter Davis paid in advance for fifteen dollars of unleaded, and shouted through Plexiglas so scratched and dirty the burly and bearded attendant on the other side looked like a trial witness whose identity had been obscured for television. "I'm looking for the elementary school?"

"Elementary school, high school, same difference," the attendant replied, his voice muffled and lowered an octave by the bulletproof barrier. "Both at the end of Clifton." He told Davis how to get there from here.

"What do you think the chances are that it's him?" Joan asked when Davis had finished fueling and restarted the car, initiating a conversation they'd had dozens of times in the past week. "Seriously."

"I don't know any more than you do," Davis said, not wanting to prejudice her with his doubts.

"He looks like Justin, I'll admit."

Davis recalled both a recent photograph of Spears and a printout of the composite, and his eyes drifted up and to the left while his mind compared them. "It's so hard to know."

Brixton Elementary (constructed, appropriately, of red brick) sat at the end of Clifton Street, separated from the high school by a cinder running track and a field shared by freshly painted football uprights and soccer goals with chain nets. A pair of five-tiered bleachers sat parallel to one sideline.

There was no designation for faculty or guest parking, so they left the Taurus in a space next to an aging but clean Honda Civic, and made their way to the principal's office, according to a plan they'd formulated shortly after buying plane tickets.

"Hi." Joan smiled at the receptionist, who operated an enormous old phone with square plastic buttons representing each line in and out: some labeled with the appropriate number; some lit white, some not; all depressed only with great effort from a locked finger. "My husband and I are considering a move to this area and were wondering if we couldn't take a quick look around the school." Davis noticed an involuntary shiver along his arms and back when he heard Joan refer to him as "my husband."

"Oh, wonderful," she said. "Welcome to town—that is, if you decide to move here. Where do you live now?"

"Saint Louis," Davis interrupted, unsure if he and Joan had covered that beforehand, although he was certain as soon as he said it that Joan would have been capable of a good or better lie. On second thought, it might have been better to have just said Chicago. It might have helped them keep their stories straight.

"Well, I wish you had called ahead so we could have arranged for a formal tour." As the receptionist looked about the room—for what, it was difficult to say—the door behind her opened and another woman emerged, younger and more sternly dressed, in a tan suit with a paisley scarf covering her neck and clavicle, and her hair piled and styled in a knot above her head.

"Hello," she said.

"Mary"—the receptionist stood now—"these are the Deavers. They were hoping to get a tour of the school, but they don't have an appointment."

"Lovely," Mary said. "I'm the principal, Mary Ann Mankoff."

They introduced themselves again as Greg and Susan Deaver. "We won't get in the way. We just wanted to walk around the school, if that's okay."

"I'll take you around," Principal Mankoff said. "It won't take a few minutes, as you can see."

"We hate to bother you," Davis said. Truthfully, they hoped to explore on their own.

"Not a bother," she said. "Alice, we'll be back in fifteen."

Up and down the two parallel hallways, Mary Mankoff quizzed Davis and Joan on their fictional biographies. They had a son who was seven, and they were doctors who were hoping to set up a general practice here in the country.

"Really? Well, out here in the country, you can never say no to a couple of new doctors."

Joan tried to get the principal in the rhythm of answering questions instead of asking them, and Davis thought Joan sounded appropriately curious about such things as Iowa tests and the percentage of graduates from the high school that go on to university. Principal Mankoff even took them briefly into a classroom, opening the door quietly to a few tiny turning heads. She gave an apologetic wave to the teacher, who returned it with a curious but understanding nod.

Principal Mankoff counted off statistics on her hand—rank in the state, reading scores, ACT averages from the high school—and as they approached the office again, Davis wondered if he'd have to ask specifically, when they stopped at a narrow hall he hadn't noticed.

"Let me just show you the library," Mary Ann said. "We're quite proud of it."

The room was, indeed, large for a grade school, with books arranged across shelves along every wall, and also on four freestanding stacks that filled up one half. On the other side, fifteen or so children sat on tiny rectangles of carpet as the librarian read them a story about teenaged detectives foiling a smuggling plot. Mary Ann whispered that a locally famous author had donated the library. "He built one for the high school as well," she said.

They stood for another moment as Davis and Joan pretended to marvel at the built-in shelving and brass plaques counting off the Dewey Decimals. Joan nudged Davis when her eye caught something in one of the stacks. She pointed and he saw it, too: a sign that read BRIXTON SCHOOL ARCHIVES.

Another teacher, a woman who, Davis presumed, was responsible for these children the other seven periods of the day, tugged at Mary Ann's elbow. "Can I talk to you a second, Mary? About the assembly Friday?" Mary Ann excused herself and she and the teacher left through the narrow door to the hall.

Davis and Joan walked over to the archive shelves, and Joan quickly skimmed with her eyes and fingers the years on dozens of leather scrapbooks. Davis did the math in his head—Justin's age today, Jimmy Spears's date of birth—adding and subtracting from the current year in adjacent columns.

"There. That one. First grade."

Joan spread the blue volume across the flannel-skirted lap she had forged sitting on her heels and flipped through the acid-free pages as Davis stooped behind her. Each page held, in pasted photo corners, a pair of class pictures, the students divided up by teacher. Unlike the class photos Davis remembered from his own school days, the children were not lined up on expandable bleachers, with short kids segregated on the gym floor. Instead, each class was represented by twenty individual head shots, with a similar picture of the teacher. Underneath each class was a typed listing of the students by row, cut out with scissors and taped to the page (carelessly, with yellowing Scotch tape), and Joan and Davis scanned the years and names together. She spotted it first:

Preston, P.; Spears, J.; Thoms, L.; Yaley, L. . . .

"There." She pointed.

Davis looked at the photo. He checked the name. He looked at Joan. She shrugged. Young Jimmy looked nothing like seven-year-old Justin.

"Sorry for leaving you like that." Principal Mankow stood over them. "I see you found our school history. That's Jimmy Spears. There. Second from left. The football player."

"Very interesting," Davis said.

"You must be proud of him," Joan said.

"We all are," Principal Mankow said.

A half hour later, at a restaurant called, with extreme lack of irony, the Brixton Diner, Davis and Joan took opposite sides of a window booth, sliding themselves across benches made from nearly equal amounts of old red vinyl and blue vinyl patches. Weiss was to meet them here at 1 p.m., which was now.

The door frame was crowned by a bracket with a bell, and Joan and Davis, the only customers for the time being despite the lunch hour, turned together toward its tinny chimes. The man who entered was very short, with most of that lack of height in legs rather than torso, cursing him with a bit of a waddle. He was also hairy in undesirable places—up from his collar and out from his cuffs—but less so on the top of his pink and freckled head, seen through the thin mesh of his baseball cap.

"Hello, Judge Forak?" Rick Weiss said, shaking hands.

Joan squinted curiously at Davis but didn't say anything.

"Hello," Davis said.

He took a seat next to Davis. "What did you find out? Should I notify my banker to expect a deposit?" He said it with a derisive snort that suggested to Davis that Weiss didn't have a bank, much less a banker.

"He's not our guy," Joan said.

The bottom half of the man's face went slack while the top half became scarlet and taut. "What do you mean? You sent around a bad drawing of Jimmy Spears and I showed you where to find Jimmy Spears."

"It's like she told you," Davis said. "He's not our guy."

Rick Weiss slapped his palms on the tabletop and pressed his fingers hard against the Formica until his cuticles were bleached. "You're trying to rip me off."

"It's not like that," Joan said.

"I knew it! There ain't no money."

"If we were planning to rip you off, would we even bother to meet you here?" Davis was disgusted with having to defend himself. He muttered the next at low volume, knowing it should matter, sure that it wouldn't. "This is a courtesy."

"It's him. It's Spears, I'm telling you." Ricky was fighting the temptation to yell, and so his words came out in a hoarse cry. He was blaspheming the local hero. He produced a piece of paper with a picture of Spears, clipped from the Brixton weekly paper, pasted next to one of the sketches Davis had posted on the Internet. "Jimmy's capable of just about anything. I know the man, known him since we were kids. He thinks he's special. *Entitled.* You should hear the stories some of the girls used to tell about him. What he forced them to do. How he took advantage because he was this big football star, even back then. High school football is big around here, and that fame, I think it went to his head. Made him psycho or somethin'. Like I said, you should hear the stories. I could get some girls I know to tell you firsthand . . ."

Davis didn't want to hear stories. "Jimmy just isn't the man we're looking for." He took a fifty-dollar bill he'd preplanted in his shirt pocket and slid it across the table. "For your trouble."

Weiss crumpled the fifty in his fist as if he was about to throw it back. He didn't. "Screw you, Forak." He pushed himself up from the booth and waddled toward the door. He pointed at Joan. "And screw you too, bitch!" The waitress behind the counter cringed as the door slammed and tinkled behind him. She looked at Davis and mouthed an apology. On behalf of the whole community, he assumed.

That night, back in Lincoln, at the Marriott by the airport, in the bar, under a baseball game on TV, Joan also told Davis she was sorry.

"Sorry?" Davis wondered aloud. "For what?"

"I wanted it to be him," she said. "I thought it could be him."

A gulp of the Macallan leaked down Davis's throat so quickly he didn't even taste it. He took another sip and let it sit on his tongue. "I didn't. I mean, I wanted it to be him, but didn't think there was much of a chance."

"Seriously?"

Davis shrugged. "Football star by day, rapist/killer by night. It seemed a little far-fetched. The guy who killed AK was a sick bastard. Not everyone's All-American."

"Varsity practice is where you find the sickest bastards around, in my experience," she said. "But if you thought it was a dead end, why are we here?" Davis peeked to see if she was smiling. She was.

He had hoped this lead would be the one, of course, but he realized now Jimmy Spears wasn't the only reason he had come all this way. He realized now that it was for a moment with her like this—alone, in secret, a little bit illicit—in a strange bar, miles from home, an elevator ride from a pair of rented hotel rooms—no smoking, king-sized—one in his name, one in hers.

"You never know," was all he said.

To Davis, Joan looked ready to confess, though to what, he could only guess. He had imagined the two of them intimately together—frequently, in fact—but allowed himself only glimpses before banishing the image and reproaching himself. His dreams brought to life other boys and men who must have had her: high school infatuations, college toys, med school flings. He envied them all. And he hated the monster that had taken Joan in Houston, hated it almost as much as the thing that had stolen his daughter from him.

"Speaking of sick bastards," she said, "have you looked at Justin's psych reports?"

The "bastard" crack stung. He understood Joan's sense of humor, loved it even, but since she'd first confronted him with evidence of Justin's unique sort of illegitimacy, he'd been defensive about flippant references to the secret they kept, and despite her willingness to come along on this trip, a little hurt at the degree to which Joan's efforts as accomplice continued to be reluctant, and even sarcastic. Plus he felt responsible for Justin. Paternal, in a way.

And he asked himself again, *Why is she here?* He considered the question when she agreed to come along, then again on the plane after they had wordlessly negotiated a sharing agreement for the armrest, their forearms pressed together.

"What about it?"

"You're not concerned?"

"He's a kid. Kids get in trouble."

"Some kids do, yes. That's why we call them 'troubled.' "

"What are you getting at?"

"Aren't you at all concerned that Justin has the genes of a killer and, at *seven years old,* already exhibits many of the warning signs of being a violent person himself?"

"Are you trying to say we made a monster?"

"Well, first of all, knock off the 'we' shit, Kemosabe." Joan gestured for another Cabernet. "Second of all, aren't *you* worried about it? Christ, Davis. Look at what's happening. This kid is messed up."

"Feh. Nature. Nurture. There hasn't been a single cloning study that shows a hereditary link for the kind of violence you're talking about. Genetics have nothing to do with it, Joan. If there's ever been a killer who had a killer for a son, it's because the child learned the behavior from his pop. Or because their socioeconomic circumstances were similar. Not because he scored the evil gene."

"Stealing. Fascination with fire. Cruelty toward animals. That's three of a kind, Davis. Jackpot."

"You won't convince me with mixed gambling metaphors." He pinched his eyes. "Cruelty to animals? What are you talking about?"

"The neighbor's dog died."

"And?"

"The mother thinks he might have had something to do with it."

"What about Morrow?"

"He's not so sure. Justin denies it. Morrow likes him. Thinks he's just bored."

"Well, there you go. Probably a coincidence."

"How can you be so flip about this?"

"His own psychologist isn't worried."

"And how worried do you think Morrow would be if he knew the truth about Justin?"

Davis's glass was still half full of whiskey but he had the bartender's attention so he ordered another round. The drinks were sipped more or less in silence and without regard for the man with the mustache and the expensive suit and the tiny leather notebook sitting alone at the table farthest from the door but in a chair with a good view of the bar.

They walked to Joan's room and stood outside it for a long moment, as if something might be decided there, as if either one of them could change the entire trajectory of their lives with a smile, a raised eyebrow, an embarrassed laugh.

"Who's Judge Forak?" Joan asked, and their eyes became tethered long enough for both of them to be comfortable with it.

"I have no idea," Davis said. He laughed with a nervous release.

"Hunh," Joan said, turning a few degrees toward the door, but letting her eyes float in her head, locked to his face like a compass to north.

"Good night, Joan," Davis said finally.

"Good night."

— 30 —

"He's not giving you the money?"

"No."

"Why not?"

Rick Weiss hurled himself into the back of a kitchen chair and its legs belched against the linoleum. "He's an asshole. An asshole that's trying to rip us off." He slapped the underside of the table with his knees.

"But it's him, right? Jimmy Spears? Jimmy's the guy he's looking for?"

"Of course it's Jimmy," Rick said. "A rich judge like him don't come all this way just to say no thanks. He could've done that on the computer." He pushed aside the mail in dull number 10 envelopes and opened up the September 20 *Sports Illustrated,* paging through it without glimpsing a single photo or head-line. Peg, his wife, sat down across from him, her pale face lined and worried, but not yet betraying that she had already run up a six-thousand-dollar debt with Visa that she had planned on paying with the bounty on Jimmy Spears's head.

"Then why won't he pay?" Peg squealed.

"Asshole," Rick said.

"Asshole!" Peg said.

"Fucking crooked judge!" Rick said.

Every Saturday night, Ricky and Peg watched a TV show that profiled bank robbers and murderers and molesters on the lam, and twice they phoned in tips that, privately, they knew to be thin as 20-weight oil. When Peg came across the composite Davis had created at a crime stoppers Web site, however, she was certain they were clutching a pot of gold with both hands.

"Who does this look like to you?" Peg had asked that day, handing him the printout.

"Hell," Rick said, curious, having not yet read the vague paragraph Davis had written to accompany his query. "That's Jimmy."

"That's what *I* thought."

"Sure as shit."

Jimmy Spears had been in Rick's class, two years ahead of Peg. Rick was in a different social circle than Jimmy—shop/wrestling/chewing, as opposed to AP English/football/smoking—but Rick always thought Jimmy was a good guy. Since Jimmy's appearance in the Rose Bowl, every between-classes encounter Rick had once shared with Jimmy in the Brixton High School hall-way had been embellished into a hilarious buddy story to entertain the Thursday night crew at Millie's Tap Room on Pioneer Street.

When he saw Jimmy's face on that piece of paper, however, Rick conjured a new fantasy, one that would pay him and Peg $25,000. After exchanging e-mails with tips@justiceforak.com, after the visit to Brixton had been arranged, Rick could imagine a five-figure balance on every ATM receipt.

"I fucking *gave* that judge Jimmy Spears. Whatever the fuck Jimmy did to him, I handed that boy, *my friend,* over on a golden platter, and now he's gonna screw me. You just watch. Next week, Jimmy will get arrested or he'll show up dead. Dead's my bet." He shook his finger at Peg. "Yeah. That's why Forak's so secretive. He's gonna kill the sonofabitch."

"Oh damn," Peg said. "You think?"

Rick nodded. "Remember these words: Jimmy Spears will show up deader'n a doornail. It'll be in all the papers." His voice had gone quiet. Conspiratorial.

"Jesus," Peg said. "And then we'll turn Forak in, yeah?"

"Yeah, we will," Rick nodded. "No, we'll do better than that. We'll go to the papers."

Giddiness and love pushed a flat smile across Peg's face. "Yeah."

Rick picked up the magazine and turned the cover to face her.

"*Sports Illustrated,*" Rick said. "*They'll* pay us twenty-five grand."

"You think?"

"Hell, that's a fraction of what those swimsuit models make. We'll sell more copies than them. This guy, the judge, and the lady who're looking for Jimmy. He's a smart sonofabitch. Nice clothes. And he's got connections, all respectable and shit. He's gonna kill Jimmy and he'd get away with it, too. But you and me, we're gonna crack the case. *Sports Illustrated* will get the scoop. We'll get the money. Be on *Dateline NBC.* Maybe Oprah. Jenny. Ricki. All that shit."

"Fa-a-a-amous," Peg cackled, and twisted in her chair.

"Fame and fortune, hon. Fame and fortune."

— 31 —

Jackie Moore had been a high school beauty, a college cheerleader, a public relations executive, a stay-at-home mother, an active volunteer, a lonely suburbanite, an ignored and indifferent wife, a psychiatric inpatient, and an untreated alcoholic. As she approached fifty, the only roles she still recalled with affection were the first, the last, and motherhood. Of those three, there was only one she could still claim.

Sometimes she slept during the day, more as an escape from the light than anything resembling rest. The shades in the house were almost always drawn. Davis either preferred it that way, too, or didn't notice.

She rarely used her husband's computer, but this morning she sat at his desk in the blue room with a Tanqueray and tonic, staring at the screen. Soon her fingers were snooping mindlessly across the keys. She wasn't sure what she expected to find—perhaps naked photos of Joan Burton. She snorted at the thought. Davis would never be so obvious. Or tacky. She scanned through a year's worth of e-mail. Nothing. Only a handful of messages exchanged between them. All work-related.

Snooping through the nested folders and directories, however, she found something she couldn't explain. Dozens and dozens of files—*Christ, hundreds!*—each containing an illustration of a man's face. The pictures were almost photo-realistic, but there was something not quite right about each of them. The dimensionality was wrong, the shadowing too severe, and the broad areas of uniform skin color not quite accurate. They had the look of a sophisticated police sketch in that they resembled a human being, but could never be mistaken for a real picture of one.

The file names were dated (going back five years or so) and then lettered for versions. The later ones looked better than the older ones. And in the later files, the versions were more similar, with the differences being mostly in the hairstyle or the age. In some, the man looked to be about twenty, in others, ten or fifteen years older. Clearly, they were all supposed to be the same person, though. Variations on the same traits and hair and eyes. Each head was the same shape, more or less, and although this seemed to have more to do with the software that had done the illustrating, the eyes had the same tired, indifferent, three-quarter stare. If every person drawn by a machine can be said to look "detached," this fellow seemed especially so.

She also found many digital photos of a young boy. When she clicked through the first few, a dense and knobbed mass formed in her stomach. Her suspicions of his affair with Joan forgotten, she now worried that her husband was involved in something unthinkable.

Jackie supposed one might find photos of all kinds on a middle-aged man's computer: posed porn stars in impossible positions, dressed in costumes or populating plywood fantasy environments, hands caressing their artificial secondary sex characteristics. She didn't understand the static visual mechanics that turned men on, and allowed herself to be amused when she caught Davis's eyes lingering on a sexy advertisement, or staring unsubtly at photos of swimsuit models, which appeared incongruously in sports magazines and catalogs. But these pictures, chaste and darling, of a young boy she did not know, a young boy who, along with his parents, was almost certainly unaware that his image occupied pixels and bytes on a suburban doctor's home computer, gave her chills.

As she opened more and more of the files, however, her fear became puzzlement.

Each picture showed the same blond-haired boy. Like the adult composites (and typical of Davis), each file was labeled with the name Justin, a number between three and eight (roughly corresponding to the boy's age, Jackie thought), and a letter. Not only were the pictures not salacious, most of them were adorable.

Justin was usually dressed in his best clothes and posed in some seasonal setting. There were prop pumpkins and footballs in the autumn and straw hats and wheelbarrows in the spring. There were Christmas poses and red-white-and-blue-themed photos for the Fourth of July.

If she had given more consideration to the other files she found, the illustrations of the strange man, and noted the similarity between their labels and the labels on the little boy's photos, she might not have leaped to the conclusions she did. Instead, sitting at her husband's desk in his basement room, Jackie assembled the pieces as best she could, and then she began to cry.

An hour later, when Phil Canella's cell number appeared on her caller ID, Jackie felt numbing heat up her neck and over her scalp, as she did when a doctor returned with test results. This world of mercenaries, of money traded for information, was foreign to her, but she had to admit it felt good to have secrets, and although her current state of constant anxiety was unpleasant, it was at least a respite from the everydayness of depression.

She hushed the ringing phone with a press of her glossy thumbnail. "Hello?"

"Mrs. Moore," he said. Jackie could hear activity in the background. Music, voices, glassware, doors opening and closing. A bar. Canella, who had as little self-consciousness as any man Jackie had ever met, seemed unconcerned that others would be wondering about his business. Listening in. Watching him. She found this odd for a man in the business of other people's business. She was certain paranoia would be a collateral effect.

"Well?" Jackie said, settling on just the edge of her living room couch.

"Your husband and Dr. Burton flew in to Lincoln, and drove to a tiny little town, not even a town, really, called Brixton. They took a tour of the elementary school."

"The elementary school?" Jackie was distressed by this, though she didn't know why.

She heard Canella turn a page in his pocket notebook. "After that I followed them to a diner where they met a local guy. A fellow named Richard Weiss." He checked again. "Ricky. Does that name ring a bell?"

"No," Jackie said to Canella as she heard a bartender approach.

Canella's voice became muffled but through the hand he had placed over the phone, she heard him order a beer. "Didn't think so. He's a golf course greenskeeper, apparently. Anyway, they talked long enough to order coffee, but not long enough to drink it. Then they drove back to the Marriott in Lincoln. Dinner. Drinks at the bar." He paused for false effect. "Then they turned in."

Jackie inhaled a deep breath and let it out in a wheeze. "Don't dance around it, Mr. Canella."

"Well, Mrs. Moore, it's not just dancing. I can only give you the facts I know. They had separate rooms, but adjoining ones. The maid said both beds had been slept in, and she told me there was no, uh, physical—*physical*—evidence of sexual contact."

"He could have used a condom, though," she said, sharpening the words as she said them.

"Yeah. He could have done. There were no condoms in the trash in either room, however."

"He might have taken it with him. Disposed of it elsewhere."

"Yes," Canella admitted, pausing. Jackie heard the thud of a full glass settling on a bar top. "That would be an unusual level of caution, though."

"But not unprecedented?"

"In my experience, ma'am, nothing is unprecedented."

Jackie said, "So you aren't certain if they are sleeping together?"

"I'm not trying to give you hope, Mrs. Moore, if that's what you're looking for. From where I sit this doesn't look much different than most of my stakeouts. I happen to know that Joan Burton kept this trip secret from her coworkers, her friends, her parents. The list of things people keep secret from their friends and family—and especially their wives—is short and consistent."

"She didn't tell *anyone*? And you know this how?"

"The Lincoln tickets were bought with cash. As you know, Dr. Moore purchased an additional ticket on his credit card—a ticket that went unused—to Boston, where there is a pediatrics conference this week. That's someone covering his tracks, I'd say. Deception."

He took a loud slurp of his beverage and Jackie could hear it go all the way down in an audible gulp. "Your husband and Dr. Burton were up to something, Mrs. Moore. Ninety-nine times out of a hundred, *something* means sex. I don't know about your particular circumstances, but ordinarily the people who hire me already know their spouses are cheating. They want me to get evidence for a divorce proceeding. They want leverage in a custody battle. They want revenge. If that's what you want, I'm afraid I haven't found anything that couldn't be explained away or refuted by a half-decent divorce attorney.

"If you're looking for encouraging news, I'd say that East Jesus, Nebraska, is not a popular place for romantic getaways. Dr. Moore may or may not be sleeping with Joan Burton, but regardless, there's something else going on. I'm sure there was something other than the old-fashioned mess-around that brought them to Brixton. What it is, I don't know at this point."

Jackie stood and began pacing the Persian carpet. "Maybe he's preparing to leave me. Maybe he and Joan really are planning to move to—to East Jesus—because they'll be too embarrassed to stick around here after everyone finds out what they've done to me."

"I can't say, Mrs. Moore."

"There's something else," she said. "Something new. I don't know if it's related or not." She told him about the strange sketch of a man she found on Davis's computer and about the photos of the boy. What could they mean? Is it possible Davis has another child, a boy with another woman? When their daughter was taken from them, could Davis have started an entirely new family without her? In Nebraska?

"If you want me to pursue this further, Mrs. Moore, you can e-mail that stuff to me here at the hotel. I'll try to check it out."

"And if I do want to pursue this? What will it cost to find out what Davis was doing in Brixton?"

"I'm in Lincoln now. It'll mean going back to Brixton. You have my rate. Expenses would be about the same. Figure the same as I quoted you before." Jackie felt her willingness to pay being sized up over the phone. "Maybe a little more, depending on how easily the information turns up."

For once, Jackie was grateful Davis had surrendered the household bills— and the joint checking account—to her. She could write a check from their joint account for five, ten, even fifteen thousand and he wouldn't know.

"Do it," she said. "Go do it."

That night, after Davis returned from his trip and offered some sketchy details of the conference in Boston, Jackie did her best to keep contempt on her half of the bed. It had been months—years, to be honest—since Davis had touched her sincerely. They made love on occasion, but only selfishly, when it happened that both of them so needed another's touch that the sex occurred like a spontaneous chemical reaction, perfunctorily, naturally, not always unpleasantly, but never as an expression of love, either. In the years since they'd been married, Jackie had never thought of sex as a physical need, but since AK had died, she began to see it differently, and their infrequent coupling gave the marriage a license that had allowed it to survive.

If Davis were sleeping with Joan, their fragile understanding would end.

And Jackie had already decided that it would never end with divorce.

— **32** —

Phil Canella knew that most people didn't listen much or look much, and when they did look and listen, they didn't pay attention, and even when they did pay attention, when they did see or hear something they shouldn't, they never gave it a second thought. They never attached any significance to the man in the alley, the woman at the bar, the bump in the attic, the click on the phone, the murmur in the engine, the tap at the window, the car on the street, the sourness in the scotch.

As long as other people were unparanoid, Canella's job was uncomplicated. He could tail them from a single car length, take their pictures without a telephoto lens, record conversations with conspicuous microphones, get spontaneous answers to pointed questions. On most days Canella could pick up the truth as easily as his childhood hero, Harold Baines, picked up the laces on a slow, hanging curveball.

At the Brixton Diner, Philly's waitress still maintained the ghost of a pretty smile but her hair and hips and the years since high school had beaten away the beautiful bitch she once was. "Ricky Weiss?" the waitress scoffed. "What do you want with him?"

"What do you care?" Canella asked.

The waitress, whose name was Debbie, laughed. "Whatever."

"So you know him?"

"I know Ricky," she said. "It's a small town. And as far as that jerk goes, I wish it was bigger."

"No good, huh?"

The waitress shrugged. "He's all right." Philly could tell how it would be with this one—she would offer an honest clue and then retreat. Another clue, another retreat. But he had time and money for a nice tip, and the diner was mostly empty.

"Do you know where he lives?"

"In a *trailer*," she scoffed. "Why do you want to know?"

"Maybe he's won a prize."

"A cash prize?" The waitress opened her eyes wide, scraping mascara against one lens of her glasses.

"Maybe."

"How much?"

Philly threw up his hands. The waitress gave him directions.

When lunch arrived a few minutes later, Philly engaged her again. "The other day, was Ricky in here with a couple of strangers?"

"Yeah, he was, actually." The waitress didn't ask what this had to do with Ricky's prize. "A man and a woman. The man was a judge."

"A judge?"

"Yep. Ricky kept calling him 'Judge' something."

"Do you have any idea what they talked about?"

"No, but they left fifteen dollars for three coffees."

"Hmm."

"And whatever they were talking about, it made Ricky real mad. He was yelling something about them not having some money for him that they were supposed to have. He yelled something about a rip-off or something like that." The waitress looked down at Philly as if she'd suddenly figured something out. "Ohhhh, okay," she said, and grinned.

Philly smiled and nodded, wondering what sense the waitress was making of it all in her head. Then he asked in a whisper, "Is this the best coffee in town?"

The waitress shook her head. "Mess-o Espresso," she said in a loud voice.

An hour later, Canella sat on a short wall of cut shale that bordered some young trees and other flowering greens outside the elementary school. Alice Pantini, school receptionist, sat to Philly's left, her red skirt stretched judiciously around her knees. Between them were two Mess-o Espresso coffees.

"Yeah, the Seavers or Deavers, something like that. They were both doctors. Said they were moving to town." Alice took a sip from her cup, judged it too hot with a pucker, and set it back down. "I don't know what they make these cups out of at Mess-o Espresso but it'll keep your coffee hot all day."

"They said they were doctors, is that right?"

"Yeah. But they aren't, are they? They seemed nice at the time, but I knew something was fishy."

"Really? Why's that?"

"The only doctors ever want to practice around here are the ones that grew up here. People are mostly trying to get out of Brixton, not into it."

"Huh."

"So if they're not doctors, who were those two?"

"Actually, they really are doctors."

"Oh." Alice seemed disappointed.

"Any idea what business they'd have with a guy named Rick Weiss?"

"Ricky Weiss?" Alice tucked her lower lip under the upper and leaned away. "Could be just about anything with that one. He's always got some sort of scheme going."

"No kidding?"

"He never has any money, though, which is just as well, because if he did he'd just throw it away on some crazy thing or other."

"Do you know what he's been planning lately?"

The temperature of Alice's coffee was finally to her liking. "I think I heard it was mulch."

"Mulch?"

"Yeah. He knows a guy at the lumberyard. He knows another guy with a chipper. Ricky's got an old truck. He's going to be the mulch magnate of Brixton, I guess." She laughed.

"He still works at the golf course, though, right?"

"Oh, yeah. And he does mulch on weekends. Any of that help you?"

"Maybe," Philly said. "But you're very kind. Thanks for having coffee with me."

"Oh sure," Alice said. She held up her cup and licked her lips. "Mess-o Espresso."

Canella looked at his watch. He'd never make the last flight back to Chicago. "Is there anything to do around here?"

"We're not known for much," Alice said. "Nothing besides being the birthplace of Jimmy Spears."

"Who's that?"

"Jimmy Spears? The football player? You didn't notice the big sign on the way into town?"

"No, didn't see the sign. But I remember him. Played at Northwestern." Canella remembered a game in which Spears threw for some ridiculous number of yards and knocked him out of a five-dollar gambling pool he'd entered with some friends. "Is he still in the NFL?"

Alice nodded. "Miami. We all wish he'd play more than he does. It makes the games on TV a whole lot more fun. Some people got satellite dishes just to watch him stand on the sidelines every week."

"Were you working at the school when he went here?"

"Yes, I was." Alice leaned forward again. Her smile was tobacco yellow and the joints where her teeth met were dark brown.

"Nice kid?"

"Very nice." Alice said. "All the teachers liked him. All the girls liked him. All the boys liked him. By the time he graduated he was president of student council, captain of the Class A champion football team, won a bunch of ribbons showing cattle. Everyone's still real proud of him. Of course, the good ones get up and leave town, to Omaha or Lincoln or wherever. The others, the losers like Ricky Weiss, they're the ones that stick around, which is why this little village will never be more than it is. Jimmy and Ricky were in the same class, I think."

"What about these kids?" Canella nodded at the bunches of children improvising their recess on a grass infield framed by a bus circle.

"These kids are still young," she said. "It's up at the high school they all become stinkers. All except Jimmy."

Canella drove in rectangles around the local farms, which radiated from the town like bonus squares on a Scrabble board. When he became tired, he pulled over and called Big Rob.

"What are you working on out there?" Big Rob asked, after his friend had described the remoteness of his location. "The usual. Cheating husband," he said. "Wife wants some more details, but I don't know if they're out here to be found. To tell you the truth, I dread this kind of shit."

"Cheating spouses?" Big Rob said. "That's our bread and butter, Philly."

Canella said, "I'm telling you, Biggie. Get out of the city. Come up by me. The North Shore. Do you know what the fastest-growing part of my business is? I call it 'babysitting.' No shit. Eighth-graders. Ninth-graders. Sometimes even older kids. Sometimes even *younger*. Three to four grand a pop. You follow them after school: to parties, basketball games, on Saturday nights while they cruise Main Street. The parents wanna know if they're tripping on X. Or diddling. Or hanging with the wrong crowd. They just want to be sure the kids are going where they say they're going, and it's *so* easy, Biggie. Christ. These boys and girls have no clue I'm following them, and the parents will pay more to have their kids chased than they will their spouses."

"Because they aren't trying to hide the withdrawals from one another," Biggie said with an understanding lilt.

"Yeah, they're both in on it. This predivorce legwork takes it out of me, though, I tell you."

Around six, Philly trolled by Ricky Weiss's trailer and saw a red pickup in the drive that hadn't been there two hours before. He parked his rented Focus in the street and walked up to the aluminum door without any thought to what he expected to find inside. He wanted to see his face, hear his voice, and get a look around his home just so he could tell Jackie Moore he did it. Fatten her file. Maybe he could get him talking somehow. Find out something that might connect him to Davis Moore.

He had thought of a story to tell Rick Weiss, and it was a thin one as far as Canella was concerned. He was counting on Ricky being as dense as everyone said.

Philly knocked and a man appeared on the other side of the screen. He was short and thin, and his back and legs bent in strange places, like pipe cleaners. On his head was a mesh baseball cap with the name of a manufacturing company Canella didn't know. He wore a white V-neck undershirt with so many stains and handprints Philly guessed he rarely wore anything over it. Through its cheap synthetic weave he could see matted brown chest hair that spread like kudzu up to the shaving line just above the man's collarbone. There was a tattered leather belt looped around the waist of his grass-streaked jeans. In front was a big buckle with a horse on it, which made Philly wonder when he last saw a real buckle worn unironically on a belt. The man didn't open the door.

"Yeah?"

"Hi. Are you Ricky?"

"Rick," he said.

"Rick. Right. Sorry. My name is Phil Canella and I'm a reporter for the *Miami Herald*. I'm doing a feature story about Jimmy Spears and I heard you knew him growing up."

"Yeah." Weiss put his nose against the screen and peered at him. "I know Jimmy. What do you want to know?" Philly thought he looked appropriately suspicious.

"Can I come in?"

Ricky pushed the door open and Canella stepped past him. A city boy, he had never been inside a trailer home before and this one was nicer than he expected, larger than he would have thought. The kitchen to their left had only a small number of tiny cabinets but the counters were clean and clutter-free. The living room was dusted and the end tables flanking the couch were bare except for a beer can centered on a wooden coaster. Through a cracked door Philly saw the made bed, and the decorative pillows lined up across the headboard. Ricky has a wife, he thought. Or a girlfriend.

"So what do you want to know?" Weiss said, looking him over slowly.

"Just a few quick questions," Philly said, getting Weiss's permission to take a chair at the kitchen table.

"Yeah."

"What was he like in high school?"

"What was he like?"

Philly nodded and began writing in his black, pocket-sized, vinyl-covered notebook, which he had plucked from a leather over-the-shoulder briefcase. He wrote down the brand of beer Weiss was drinking and the size of his television and doodled the shape of the scar that intersected with his right eyebrow.

"He was all right. For a jock," Weiss said. He retrieved his beer and took a chair on an adjacent side of the table. "He didn't hold it over everybody like some of them."

"How well did you know him?"

"What are you after?"

"Like I said: a story about Jimmy Spears."

"There are a hundred people in this town who knew Jimmy better than I did. Why don't you talk to them?"

Again, no good answer. "Maybe I already did."

"If you had, then you wouldn't need me, would you?"

Canella shut his notebook. "I'm sorry. Someone told me you knew him. I've made a mistake." He was trying to act nonchalant, and in doing so, left the notebook unprotected on the table. As soon as Philly said the word "mistake" he understood that he really had made one.

Weiss reached over and snatched it, turning in his chair to protect it.

"Hey!" Philly stood up and tried to reach over Ricky's shoulder, but the greenskeeper spun away. He tore quickly through the pages and Canella tried to imagine what sense he might make from his notes.

They faced each other, Philly in the kitchen and Ricky in the living room but hardly more than a body's length apart, and Canella watched helplessly as Ricky squinted his way through scrawled transcriptions of conversations at the diner and the elementary school and notes from other cases that would make no sense at all to him. The one thing Philly knew he wouldn't find was a single word about Jimmy Spears, NFL football, or the Miami Dolphins.

He stopped on one page and put his finger on the paper, either to mark his place or to make a point. "You're with the judge, aren't ya?"

Judge? Philly thought. Maybe this wouldn't be a waste of time after all. "Who's that?" he said.

"Don't fuck with me," Ricky said in a growling drawl. Canella punctuated his conversation with that word all the time, but Weiss was able to startle him with it now.

"I'm not *fucking* with you," Philly said. "Give me the notebook."

Ricky held it behind his back. "I know what the judge is up to." There was a nervous edge to his voice, but he was also laughing with the relief of an Italian grandmother leaving confession.

"Why don't you tell me?" Canella said.

"*Now* you're fucking with me." Ricky Weiss glanced at the detective and then turned back to the notebook, which he held very close to his face. "You and Forak are in this together. What are you supposed to do? Take care of me? Blackmail me? Shut me up?"

"I don't know anybody named Forak," Philly said truthfully. "I don't know any judge. But maybe we can help each other."

"Bullshit."

Canella was frustrated and embarrassed enough to think about leaving. He stood between Weiss and the door. Even at his age, it would be fairly easy to make a run for it. He hated to lose that notebook, though. "A man came to you a few days ago," he said quickly. "A man and a woman. You met at the diner."

Ricky smiled with half his face. "I thought you said you didn't know the judge."

"He's not a judge," Philly said. "He's a doctor."

"What's going on?"

Canella, who was a professional liar, hesitated before telling the truth. "That's what I came here to find out."

Weiss took two aggressive steps forward and his right arm snapped like a whip over the table, snatching Canella's bag and pulling it toward him. Philly, now resigned to honesty in dealing with the enraged greenskeeper, made no attempt to stop him, a gesture he hoped would win the man's confidence.

But he had forgotten, somehow, about his gun.

"What the *fuck?*" Ricky took the .38 out and held it in front of him, pointing the barrel toward the ceiling. Philly could tell by the assured grip of Weiss's long, thin hands that he'd handled a firearm before. "What the hell is a reporter doing with one of these?"

Philly cursed aloud. He was so stupid. When he had been a cop, he never would have made that mistake.

The door opened behind him. "Ricky!" A woman shrieked.

"Shut the door, Peg!" Weiss yelled.

She did, quickly, closing both the screen and the wooden door behind it. A plastic bag from the drugstore swung from her wrist and a can of shaving cream inside it banged against the door frame. "Ricky, what's happening?"

"Shut up, Peggy! I'm thinking!" He kept the gun pointed up and away as he brought his hands to his head.

"Who is *he*?" Peg asked. She squeezed hysterical tears from her eyes. "Where did that gun come from?"

Ricky twitched at the first question. He pulled Canella's wallet out and pried it open with the end of the .38.

"My name is Phil Canella," he told them. "I'm a private investigator from Chicago."

Weiss nodded and showed his driver's license to Peg, who was at his side now. "Okay. Why did Judge—Doctor, whatever—why did Forak hire you?"

"His name isn't Forak. His name is Dr. Davis Moore. And he didn't hire me. His wife did."

"To do what?"

"To find out if he was having an affair." Now that Mrs. Weiss was here, Philly was hopeful they could talk their way to a resolution. He wondered if he could ask for a glass of water. His throat was burning.

"An affair?" Peg muttered. "Ricky! Put that gun down!"

He ignored her. "That lady. She wasn't his wife?"

"No."

"Put the gun down, Ricky!"

"Who was she?"

"A colleague. Possibly his mistress. I don't know. That's why I'm here. I'm trying to find out."

"Do you think she's in on it?" Ricky asked. "The mistress?"

"Put the gun down, baby!"

"In on what?" Weapon pointed at his face or not, Canella was collecting information on his case.

"He's a lunatic," Ricky said. "But you know all about that, I bet." Psychologists, Philly thought, would accuse a man like Ricky Weiss, waving a gun around on a Thursday afternoon and calling another person a lunatic, of projecting.

"What are you talking about?"

"Jimmy Spears," Ricky said. "Forak's going to kill him."

"What?"

"Don't lie to me."

"Ricky! Give me the gun!"

"I'm not lying," Philly said. "What are you talking about?"

"I'm talking about your guy. Forak. He wants to kill Jimmy."

Canella almost laughed. "Kill Jimmy Spears? That's crazy."

"He told me himself." This was a lie, but a lie to which Ricky thought he was entitled, since he was holding the gun.

"Look, I've never met Davis Moore, but I'm pretty sure he doesn't want to kill some second-string football player—"

"Put down the gun, Ricky!"

"—and I don't think you mean to hurt anyone, either."

"You're a liar," Ricky said. "He sent you to do me so he could go ahead and kill Jimmy and there wouldn't be anyone left to know about it and go to the papers or the cops."

"I'm not lying to you, Ricky."

"Ricky, get rid of that thing," Peg said. "Put it down and let's talk about it."

"I don't mean to hurt anyone," Ricky said. "I don't." But he didn't put down the gun, which was now pointed uncertainly at Philly's chest.

Canella could feel the desperation and fear emitted in hot waves from the trembling Peg. He sensed the situation had turned unpredictable, and that whatever Ricky Weiss knew about Davis Moore had made him desperate. It was no longer safe to be here. He made a decision.

Run for it.

When Ricky saw Canella turn, his spinning brain increased its workload by many revolutions per minute. His internal tachometer was redlining. He needed to know more. If he escaped and told Moore that Ricky had figured out the doctor's plan to kill Jimmy Spears, Moore would just send someone else to do the job right. He had to stop Canella, but Peg had stepped away from the door, and once this man was outside, sprinting to his car, what could Ricky do except run him down and tackle him, which wouldn't be easy? Someone was likely to see them fighting from the road, especially with Peg screaming the whole while. But even if they didn't see, what would Ricky do then? Drag Canella back to the trailer? Tie him up? He wasn't a kidnapper. He couldn't take care of a dog, much less a hostage. But he had to stop him.

His brain, running too fast now, too hot, and—in Ricky's defense—without his explicit permission, knew of only one way.

Ricky squeezed the handle of the gun without really aiming it. Peg cried out in harmony with the report. Phil Canella's head jerked back toward him and blood appeared in chunky patterns across the screen door and on the back of his hand, which he had used to push it open. His body contorted in a spasm, his shoulders turned back toward the gun, and then collapsed in an inanimate free fall straight down to his knees and then forward like a tree, his head hitting the aluminum stoop, his feet still inside the trailer, his body propping the door ajar.

"No, no, no, no, no, no, no, no, no," Peg sobbed.

Ricky brought the .38 slowly to his hip and let it fall to the floor, where it made a hollow, impotent sound like a plastic tumbler dropped at a picnic. He was processing everything very quickly. He hadn't meant to shoot Canella, but he accepted the fact immediately and was already dealing with it. He would need to get rid of the body. He would need to clean up the trailer. He would need to do something about Davis Moore, the only person, as far as he knew, who could link him to this dead man when somebody noticed him missing.

First, he would need to calm Peg down. She would help him clean up the blood, and help wrap the body in cheap guest sheets, which she bought with her Wal-Mart discount, anyway. He would get rid of it alone. The less Peg knew about the details, the better. He wouldn't ask friends to help. On TV, that's how people were always getting caught. Somebody asks somebody else to help him and the second guy gets caught and cuts a deal with the cops. He wouldn't be stupid that way.

He thought he might need a good saw.

Justin at Eight

— 33 —

Because it's ridiculous, that's why. Weird."

Instead of watching television, Martha would often watch Justin read. Sitting on the couch, with Justin in the big red chair opposite, his seat and hers angled acutely toward the TV, she would drink coffee or hot chocolate, or tonight, with her mother visiting, a glass of Fumé Blanc.

"It's not weird, Mom," Martha said, whispering unnecessarily. When Justin was into one of his books, really inside the pages as he was now, the words being silently dictated to his head in a hypnotic patter, his eyes pinched together so tightly that Martha had taken him twice in the last year to see if he needed glasses, she could have fired the antique rifle Terry had left behind when he and his mistress moved to New Mexico, fired it into the ceiling, and not been able to make him flinch.

"He should be reading Harry Potter. Or the Hardy Boys. Nancy Drew, even," Martha's mother said. "That psychiatrist is filling his head with ideas. He's too young for ideas, and he comes up with too many on his own already."

"You're being silly."

"The point is, I don't think it's helping. He should be playing sports. Baseball. Football. Hockey. He has problems socializing. Relating to people. Other kids."

"The other kids don't challenge him. The other kids bore him. That's why he acts out."

"Nonsense, Martha. Do you know what your father would say about all this?"

"He'd say, *Nonsense, Martha.*"

"That's right, nonsense. He doesn't need to be challenged by the other kids. He needs to have fun. His little brain isn't ready for all this grown-up

114

thinking. The telescope and the astronomy, that's all right. But this other stuff." She shook her head. "You're going to make him into something. Turn him into something."

"Turn him into what, Ma?"

"I'm just saying."

"Then say it."

"The fires, the stealing, the acting out." Now her mother was whispering. "Those are all early signs, you know. What do they always say about the bad ones? After they've been caught by the police? They say, 'He was smart. He kept to himself.' "

"You'll fall in love with any cliché, won't you? You know, they say those things about the CEOs of software companies, too."

"Bundy, Gacy, Ng—all intelligent. They all had too many thoughts in their heads."

"Charles Ng? Ick. You should never have gotten a satellite dish, Mom," Martha said. "Justin's not crazy. He's smart. Way smart. I'm not going to ignore that. I'm going to encourage it. In an anti-smothering, noncrazy-mom, totally normal way."

Her mother shook her head. "Buy him a math book, then. I don't trust philosophy any more than psychology. Philosophy is ideology, and ideology leads to narrow minds."

"That's Dad talking, all right."

"You know what I mean. Ideas come with responsibility, and he's too young to know the meaning of that. In what cubbyhole of his mind is he supposed to stick a Greek philosopher?"

"Do you even know what Plato was all about?" Martha asked.

"No. Do you?"

"A little. What I remember from college. And from the back of Justin's book."

"You know a *little*. So he knows more than you now?"

"About Plato?" She looked into Justin's intense eyes. He was nearly halfway through the book. "I don't know. Probably."

"Here's a tip," Mom said. "Never let them know more than you. About *anything*."

"Yeah. Okay."

"Are you seeing anyone?"

"You know I'm not."

"Terry's been gone a year."

"Don't want to talk about it, Mom."

"No, I suppose not."

"Well, there you go."

From the atmosphere, Rita's could have been one of two dozen North Side Italian restaurants: thirteen tables, eclectic chairs, young staff, short menu, large portions, three-fork *Sun-Times* review in a black frame on the wall. When Big Rob and Sally walked in, the place was already nearly filled with lunching employees from neighborhood galleries and design firms.

"You're really going to buy me a meal," Sally said with mock disbelief as he held her chair. "This is a first." Big Rob didn't explain, but as he sat down across from her she thought the smile on his face seemed false. He had brought a yellow file folder with him, and he set it down next to his plate.

Big Rob waited until the server had recited the specials and returned for their order before beginning. He didn't whisper. Even though the distance between tables was less than ten inches—measured each morning by the owner with a piece of custom-cut crown molding left over from the remodeling of her den—this space somehow felt as private as an office.

"Phil Canella's dead," he told her.

"What?" Her disbelief was genuine this time.

"On a job. In Nebraska. Chasing a cheating husband."

Sally reached across the table and touched his arm. "Oh, my God, Biggie. I'm sorry. I know the two of you were close. You were on the Chicago PD together, right?" He nodded, and she understood now the formality of the setting was part of his mourning process. By giving her the news this way, in a nice restaurant instead of his hot, cramped office, he was showing respect for his friend. "When did it happen?"

"He went missing a few weeks ago. Police haven't found his body, but, you know . . ." His face went blank as he tried to choke off an unwelcome emotion. "I went down there for a few days to help out if I could. The town where Philly was last seen, Brixton—their force is a little understaffed for this kind of thing."

"Was there anything you could do?"

Biggie shrugged. "He was staying at a Marriott in Lincoln. I went through his things, looking for anything that might tip us in the right direction." He held up the yellow file folder. "I found these in his room." He handed it to Sally.

Barwick opened the folder. She covered her mouth with her right hand. "Oh. Jesus. God. No. *God, no.*"

Inside were many of the photos Sally had taken of Justin Finn over the years. The posed shots she had taken at Martha Finn's request and sold to Gold Badge Investigators.

"How? How did he get these?"

"According to his e-mail he got them from his client, Jacqueline Moore. She lives up in Northwood."

Sally continued to leaf through the photos, their familiarity shocking under the circumstances. "I didn't have any idea who the client was on the photo job. Scott Colleran never told me."

"Jackie Moore told Philly she found these on her husband's computer."

"The cheating husband?"

Big Rob nodded. "His name is Davis Moore. Does that ring a bell?"

"No."

"He was the doctor who cloned Justin Finn."

Slowly, Sally's hands abandoned the folder on her lap and began scratching the sides of her face. "Davis Moore hired Gold Badge to acquire photos of his former patient? Doesn't make any sense. What about Mrs. Moore? Does she know who the kid is?"

"No. As far as I can tell, she was afraid he was her *husband's* kid. By some other woman."

"So Moore might not have been cheating after all. Jesus, what a waste. And Philly's death? I mean *disappearance*? Related?"

"I'm going back to Brixton to find out."

Sally saw the waitress approaching with two plates of pasta and she discreetly closed the folder. She couldn't imagine eating right now. Philly was dead. It horrified her to think the photos she took—that she already felt so guilty about—might have had something to do with his murder.

"When are you going back?"

"Not for a few days. Philly and I made a deal a long time ago. I'll go through his cases and settle up with his clients. Take on the ones I'm able. God, I have to call Jackie Moore and tell her Philly was killed while working on her case."

"What are you going to tell her about the photos?"

Big Rob mumbled through a giant forkful of linguine. "I don't know. What do you think I should tell her?"

"Well, the truth, of course," Barwick said. "There's just no way to know what the truth is."

Big Rob put down his fork, which for him was a gesture of seriousness. "There's something else I wanted to prepare you for, Sals. The cops are gonna want to know what Philly was looking for down there. They're going to chase every angle. Interview witnesses. These photos"—he nodded at the folder—"are gonna come out."

It took a few seconds for the scenario to play out in Sally's head. "Omigod," she said. "Martha."

Big Rob nodded. "You might want to start thinking about how you're gonna handle that. I predict you're going to have one pissed-off mother on your hands."

That night, grown-up Justin came again to Sally's dreams wearing Eric Lundquist's face. They were sitting on top of a tall building downtown. Not the Hancock or the Sears Tower, but one of the early-twentieth-century sky-scrapers, ten or twelve stories up. Taller glass-and-steel buildings formed privacy walls in every direction. Gothic gargoyles—cats and bats and monkeys and dragons—lined the edge of the roof all around them. It was night but the air was warm and still. They were having a picnic.

"Have you heard of Plato's cave?" Justin asked.

Sally had taken two semesters of philosophy at the University of Illinois, but in the dream she said no.

Justin opened the picnic basket and transferred the contents—fruit and cheese and bread—to the blanket underneath them. "Plato believed an idea was the ideal state of being," he said. "When a carpenter conceives of a table in his mind, it is perfect. His conception of the table is the real table. When he actually planes the wood and saws the legs and assembles it, when he crafts it into something we can see and we can touch, the actual table is only a representation of the idea, an imperfect imitation."

"And the cave?" Sally asked, opening a thermos and pouring thick, sweet, green liquid into a pair of wine goblets.

"He said our experience is like that of a man in a cave, watching shadows projected on the wall from an unknown source. The shadows we see are only imperfect representations of the real human beings."

"So the real people? If you can't see them, where are they?" Barwick asked.

Justin took a goblet from her and leaned forward, their shoulders pressed together, his lips the smallest metric measurement from hers. "Here," he said. "On this roof. The two of us. At night. In your dreams. This is real."

He kissed Sally—an endless, heart-skipping, unforgettable first kiss that was still thick on her lips in the morning. It felt real. *God, it felt so real.*

— 35 —

Jackie hung up the phone with the private detective—Robert something-or-other, he'd said—and walked into the bathroom and shut the door. Tears fell from her cheeks into the bowl of the sink. Her hands trembled. Her eyes were pink with the bad news.

She had sent a man to his death.

Detective Robert had assured her there was no evidence linking Phil

Canella's disappearance to her case, but he never would have been in Nebraska if she hadn't asked him to go back. Her lungs filled with asthmatic guilt. Exhaling became impossible.

He told her they didn't have any more information about her case. She told him that was all right, she was so sorry. He didn't mention the sketch of the man or the photographs of the mysterious child or whether he knew if the boy was her husband's son. She didn't ask.

Whenever Jackie took an assessment of herself, she pictured the three Jackies: past, present, and future. Past Jackie, full of energy and potential; present Jackie, always in transition; and future Jackie, contented, relaxed, happy at last. In the mirror tonight, she could see only the first two Jackies. She couldn't even imagine herself without a husband, without a daughter, without this house. And now this shame on top of it.

Her husband was leaving her. A man was dead.

She could never know how much of it was her fault.

— 36 —

Big Rob checked in to the Brixton Budget Inn around 6 p.m., and after showering off the road grime with hard water and a tiny biscuit of motel soap, he got in his car and drove to Millie's Tap Room, which was not the only bar in Brixton but the only one in which Big Rob, after three visits to the village, could order a hamburger without trepidation. He made the first two trips in the weeks after Philly disappeared. The local police—a chief and four cops—seemed perturbed by his questions, but eventually they understood the pain and guilt Big Rob carried within his giant frame and began to value the unofficial input of a former Chicago cop to a staff that rarely handled missing persons and had never coped with a murder investigation, if that's what this turned out to be.

On his first trip he flew a low-fare carrier to Lincoln, with his girth expanding uncomfortably across two expensive seats. This time he drove, piling highway miles on his old Chevy van. "The Stakeout and Make-Out Mobile" he called it, to the appreciative snickers of his new friends on the Brixton PD.

Officer Crippen already had a table saved when Big Rob walked into Millie's. "Crowded tonight," Crippen said. "I had to fend off a few unrulies to save your seat."

"How unruly do they get around here?" Big Rob asked.

"That's what we all aim to find out, I guess." Crippen took a long pull on a bottled Genuine Draft.

Big Rob sat down with an expulsion of air and stress so loud and wheezy it seemed to Crippen less like a sigh and more like a breach of the ex-cop's hull. "So, what do you know?" he asked.

"What do we *know*?" Crippen shrugged. "Not much since the last time you were here. But there has been one development in the last twenty-four hours."

"Tell me."

"We found Philly's car."

"Really? Where?" Superstitious, Big Rob knew better than to release the hope locked within him that his friend might still be alive.

"Lawrence, Kansas. A student at KU was keeping it on campus. Got into a little fender bender. No insurance. The other guy's insurance investigator started poking around, saw the VIN plate had been replaced, found the serial number on the engine block. He's the one who eventually traced it back to Canella's rental company."

"Where did the student buy it?"

"A used-car lot in Topeka. The papers were pretty badly forged, but he says he bought it at auction, and the dealer he bought it from says he got it in a trade-in. That owner said he answered an ad and paid cash for it to a guy in North Platte. A fellow named Herman Tweedy. We haven't talked to him yet."

"Promising?"

"I'd say so. Herman Tweedy went to high school here in Brixton."

"You're kidding! Friend of Ricky's?"

Ricky Weiss had been the Brixton PD's only suspect from the day Big Rob had first called to report Philly missing. Interrogated half a dozen times by Crippen, once with Big Rob listening in, Weiss first denied knowing the man, then admitted Canella had come to see him, but claimed he left after asking a few questions. Without a body, there was nothing more they could do except put Weiss under very sporadic surveillance. Brixton cops had few resources they could devote to a case with no body and no motive.

In his days on the job, Big Rob had been conditioned not to care about motive. Human beings did horrible things for no discernible reason at all. Motives might matter to the D.A. and they might matter to juries, but good police—even ex-police—don't expect solutions to come in such square packages.

"The connection to Ricky's a little tenuous, but we can make it," Crippen said. "Tweedy's five years older. He has a short rap sheet. Stupid stuff—pot, vandalism, bush-league grifts—and a reputation a little like Ricky's. A wanna-be hustler, but too lazy to make a living at it. We're checking the phone records. Asking around."

"Anything I can do?" Big Rob asked.

"Might be. I hear Ricky's going fishing in South Dakota tomorrow. Four days in the woods. Lots of beer. No telephone. Crapper on the outside. Maybe this is a good time to approach Peg."

"The wife?"

"Yeah. I don't know what she knows, if anything, but Rick keeps her on a tight leash. This might be the best shot we get at her. Has she seen you before?"

Big Rob shook his head. "Any suggestions?"

"She's a drinker. If I were doing an unofficial interrogation, I might do it at night. With Ricky out of town, she's sure to hit the bars."

"I'll follow her," Biggie said.

"There you go," said Crippen. "Buy her a few drinks. Turn on the charm. See what spills out."

Big Rob snorted and shook his head. "You're a smart cop, Crip." The officer blushed. The waitress came and took their orders to the kitchen. "What do you want to be when you grow up?"

"Huh?"

"What are you, twenty-five? Twenty-six? You want to be chief someday?"

Crippen hitched his shoulders indifferently. "Not especially."

"What happens if you catch Philly's killer?" Biggie asked. "You'll be certified murder police, then. You still gonna be happy when they send you back out to put chalk marks on tires up and down Main Street?"

Crippen peeled a beer label, wet with condensation, away from his bottle. "I don't know."

"I'm telling you, you won't be. You catch a killer, it changes you. Makes you antsy. Makes you wanna catch 'em all." Big Rob unwrapped the paper napkin from his silverware and clutched the dull knife in a whitened grip. "Thing is, you can't catch 'em all," he said. "And the ones you do, you never catch them in time."

— 37 —

Ricky loaded the back of his truck with poles and nets and beer and secured everything with rope and canvas straps. He had three tackle boxes, with the spoons and minnows and flies segregated according to time of day and type of fish. He even had a spear, which he always brought but never used. The idea of spearing a fish thrilled him, but fishing the regular way could be frustrating enough. He imagined himself knee-deep in a stream, poking fruitlessly at the water as trout and salmon detoured around him. It made him angry just thinking about it.

Peg was in a good mood. Three days—almost four—with Ricky out of the house would give her some much-needed time away from his chattering, his dreaming, his needling, his pressuring. Since the day that private detective showed up at their trailer and Ricky did, well, did what he had to do to protect their future, he had hardly let her out of his sight. It was a trying time for their marriage, and Peg asked him many times if he trusted her. Ricky always said that he did, but he kept close to the house and needed to know every detail of her schedule and called the store where Peg worked every evening at 5:05 to make sure she'd left for home. Lately he'd relaxed some, but this trip would be as much a vacation for Peg as it would be for Ricky. She'd already made plans with the girls for Friday night, with drinks and then maybe a trip to the place off the highway where they bring in the male strippers twice a month.

For the first time in almost a year, Peg felt like everything was going to be okay.

The "thing with the guy" (that was what they called it on the rare occasions when it had to be referred to out loud) had upped the stakes on their latest scheme. Someone was dead (accidentally, of course), and if they didn't see some results from the Jimmy Spears plan, their killing him, all the risks they'd taken, would have been in vain.

Ricky never told Peg what he had done with the body (she had asked only once), but she knew Herman Tweedy had come and picked up the rental car. She assumed he was going to strip it down and sell off the parts. Through the kitchen window, she saw the two of them crawling in and out of it, with Ricky chattering on and on and the two of them laughing like they usually did when they got together. She didn't figure Ricky had told Herman the truth. It would sadden her to find out he trusted Herman as much as he trusted his own wife. Besides, if they had been talking about the thing with the guy, it wouldn't have been right for them to laugh so much.

Every morning, Ricky picked up the newspaper and turned to the sports pages. He wanted to be the first to know if anything happened to Jimmy Spears. Every day he expected to read that Jimmy had been killed in a car accident, or maimed in a botched mugging, or that he had mysteriously taken ill, possibly the result of poisoning. Every day he read through the sports news, and even scanned the listings of football injuries. For the editors of *Sports Illustrated,* he was certain that he could spin an on-the-field injury into some sort of conspiracy or revenge plot hatched by Judge Forak/Dr. Moore. Every day he was disappointed by the relative health of his famous classmate.

Peg suggested they look further into the history of this Dr. Moore, but Ricky was against it. Moore had already sent Phil Canella to silence them, he reasoned. There's no use getting closer than necessary to such a dangerous man. The detective's disappearance had sent a clear message. Ricky didn't trust the sonofabitch and he didn't want to deal with him anymore.

Ricky had instituted some home-crafted security measures around the trailer. He hung bells on all the doors and lined up flowerpots and tchotchkes along all the windowsills. He bought another gun, giving them four total, including the one he took off Canella, and placed them in evenly dispersed hiding places throughout their home.

Over Ricky's objections Peg decided to learn as much as she could about their adversary, and found some old articles on Anna Kat's murder on the computer at the Brixton Public Library. Reading them, she tried to imagine the horror of losing a daughter that way and tried to imagine Jimmy Spears in the act of such a savage crime. She couldn't. But if he did it, she supposed he deserved to be dead, and said so to Ricky.

"No man gets to be judge, jury, and executioner," Ricky said, ignoring for the moment that he was the one who put Davis Moore on the trail of Jimmy Spears in the first place. "What I did here, what we did—you know, the thing with the guy?—that there was self-defense. This Dr. Moore is hunting a man down in cold blood, and that's another thing altogether. If he succeeds, it's our duty to tell the world what we know." Peg made copies of the articles and kept them in an envelope under her socks.

A few weeks ago, Peg had revisited the idea of blackmailing Jimmy Spears. "We'll send him a letter saying we know what he did. Maybe we can get the money even if Jimmy doesn't get killed." They wrote the letter, but decided not to send it. "If they trace it back to us and then something really does happen to Jimmy, the whole deal will be blown," Ricky said. "They'll come after us and *we'll* go to prison instead of Moore." He didn't rule it out as a plan B, however.

On the morning of the fishing trip, Peg stood at the door to the trailer and watched Ricky and Tim Pokorny climb into the cab of the truck. She waved good-bye, and Ricky smiled and pointed to her through the open window. As they turned out of the trailer park, Peg studied the door frame. For weeks after the thing with the guy, she had noticed dry brown specks inside the door, which she then cleaned with a paper towel and a bottle of spray bleach. Today she looked hard and even squatted on her knees to look in the least obvious places, but couldn't find a single one.

Alone, she was almost giddy.

— 38 —

Joan's examining room was not the spare, antiseptic cell most physicians maintain in deference to their patients' germ phobias. Kids, Joan reasoned, are more afraid of doctors than they are of germs, and so her room, though no less

clean, was painted in bright colors and had laminated (that is, washable) pictures of Disney characters on the wall. The examining table was bright purple,
and the sanitary paper she pulled across it had cartoon balloons and Snoopys.
The floor was literally dotted with appliqués, the purple-polka-dot kind.

"What are you doing here?" Joan said to Davis when she walked in, a
leather portfolio held flat against her stomach. Davis was lying on the Snoopy
paper, reading a journal article, which he suspended above his face with his
left hand. He hopped to his feet and pulled a new sheet of paper off its roll,
tearing off the length he had just wrinkled and stuffing it in the garbage.

"Was wondering if I could sit in," Davis said.

"On Justin's physical?" Joan's frown declared it a bad idea. "Why?"

"Just to observe. I read the report from his shrink. I guess the divorce has
been tough on him."

"Tough on any kid," Joan said.

"Yeah, but especially tough on a kid like that."

"Like what?" Joan baited.

"You know. Smart. Genetically predisposed to . . . whatever."

"Wow," Joan said with a dry lilt. "Is Davis Moore actually expressing concern for this child, instead of pawning that responsibility off on me?"

"Come on, Joan. You know I care about Justin."

"Maybe," she said, closing a drawer she noticed was ajar. "But that's the
first time I've heard you admit that Justin might have a genetic disposition to
anything. Are you finally admitting to some second thoughts about this?"

"No," he said. "We're all predisposed to some vice, some evil. I didn't create the genetic matter that made him. Nature had already mixed it in that
combination."

"You didn't create it, Davis, you just doubled the recipe. Instead of one
monster, you have one monster on the loose and maybe another in the
making."

"We don't know that. I just think we need to watch him more closely."

"Whatever, Dave."

Davis examined an anatomical drawing on the wall. It was a poor attempt
at looking indifferent. "I called you last night to talk about this," he said.
"Where were you?"

"A date. Jazz at the Green Mill."

"Great," he said, too quickly.

"I'm not getting younger, Davis. It's tough to meet single men my age."

"Why limit it to men your age?" he said. Joan didn't have to wonder if the
question had a flirtatious subtext.

"*Single* men any age. In Northwood, anyway," she said.

Davis nodded. "So it's okay if I observe? Ask him some questions?"

"You should ask him about Kepler's laws of planetary motion. Dr. Morrow says the little braniac's interested in astronomy now. You better hope he doesn't take up genetics next. If Justin starts reading Mendel, you'll be busted for sure." She paused but Davis didn't laugh. "All right. I'll tell Mrs. Finn it's routine. She won't mind."

Davis put his hand on the door. "This room is fun. I like the colors. I might do all my reading in here."

"Get out. I'll have Ellen buzz you when I'm ready."

Davis feigned a pout and skulked out of the room with heavy slapstick feet. Back in his office, he had files to review ahead of a four o'clock appointment with a couple scheduled for a conventional in vitro procedure next month. Their history remained on his desk in an unopened folder.

He pulled a drawer past his left knee and lifted out a file, which he spread across his lap. One by one, he removed seven tattered and water-damaged pieces of paper and spread them in two rows across his desk.

He had collected them two nights before, one of the many evenings he drove home past Justin's house. This particular night, something he had never noticed seemed at first unusual, then startling. He drove to the next block, up and down and across the avenue (which was broad and grand but with little traffic), and through an adjacent neighborhood. Finally, he parked his car and retraced his route, circling Justin's house as the streets of the subdivision wound and crossed in nongeometric patterns. As he walked, Davis breathed in the lake air, sweetened by magnolia and linden trees and professionally groomed grass. He examined every streetlamp and utility pole, collecting specimens along the way until he at last came back upon his car with these seven pieces of paper in hand:

LOST DOG

MISSING KITTEN

BELOVED FAMILY PET

HELP US FIND MIKO

WE MISS OUR PUPPY

HAVE YOU SEEN COTTON?

PLEASE HELP FIND OUR BANDIT!

One was written in a child's hand; the rest seemed penned by an adult under a child's direction, or at least with the grief of a child in mind. All of them included a photo of the dog or cat and a phone number to call, should the animal appear. Davis palmed the keyboard of his computer, waking up the monitor, and typed each number into a reverse-lookup engine on the Internet. He wrote down the addresses and opened a map printed by the Northwood Chamber of Commerce for last year's Garden Walk and placed it on top of the street flyers. With a Magic Marker, he plotted the approximate location of each house, and they appeared in a symmetrical, half-moon pattern around Justin's home.

"Goddamn," he said under an exhale. The presence of the flyers themselves in such numbers was enough for him to draw a horrible conclusion. But he was struck by the discipline, by the mathematical, purposeful way in which the boy must have abducted these animals. Davis wondered why precision was so much more frightening than chaos.

"Dr. Moore?" Ellen crackled through the intercom. "Justin is in with Dr. Burton now."

Justin sat on the examining table in white briefs, his thin upper torso arched grotesquely forward so his face could stare down at his dangling bare feet. He was tall and pale, and his wavy blond hair was long for an eight-year-old, a look that, in Davis's experience, betrayed hippie parents, the premature onset of adolescent independence, or possibly in this case, a single parent with more than she could handle.

"Hello, Justin," Davis said as he and the boy shook hands. "You don't mind if I sit here while Dr. Burton gives you your checkup, do you?"

"Nuh-uh," Justin said cheerfully. He straightened when Joan approached him with a stethoscope and Davis noted he possessed the sort of awareness around doctors that older sick people have. When Joan reached for an otoscope, he turned his left ear toward her. When she wheeled herself back to grab the black cuff of the blood-pressure monitor, Justin crooked his elbow and readied his biceps. He welcomed the tongue depressor without gagging and appeared unembarrassed when Joan hooked a finger inside his waistband and made a quick survey of his privates.

"How have you been feeling?" Joan asked, settling in to a wheeled stool at a tiny white desk.

"Fine," Justin said.

"No sniffles, no headaches?"

"Nope, nope."

"Are you seeing everything okay at school? Can you read the blackboard when your teacher writes on it?"

"Yes."

Joan shook the pen she was writing with. "Dr. Moore, do you have a pen I could borrow?"

Davis's hand went instinctively to his breast. "Actually, no."

"Really?" Joan smirked. "I don't think I've ever seen you without that silver Waterman in your pocket."

"I set it down somewhere on Monday," he said. "I haven't the nerve to replace it. Thing never leaked. I'm skittish about putting some old Bic in my shirt, you know?"

Justin stretched his neck to look up at the ceiling. Davis followed his line of sight to the ugly, cheap tiles that disguised the even uglier ductwork and conduit and other guts of the clinic. Justin's mouth opened, became almost unhinged, it seemed, as he stretched farther back and back and back. To Davis, the boy looked like a duckling, newborn and featherless, his pale skin untouched by age and stress and bad diet and hormones, his bones growing even as they sat there, his mind expanding, soaking, remembering, learning without effort. A growing boy is a mutating thing, and Davis thought if he could stare at him long enough and in just the right place he could see a change occur right here in the exam room.

"I lose things, sometimes," Justin said, head back.

"Really?" Joan said. "What things?"

"Just things," he said. Davis watched as the heels of the boy's bare feet began to kick against the examining table. "Sometimes I'll have a thing in my hands and I'll—I'll just lose it. It's there and then it's lost."

"Sometimes, do you find your things later? The things that you've lost?" Joan was making conversation in an absent dialect, still scribbling across Justin's file with a new pen.

"Nope," he said. "Lost forever."

Davis felt his arms go cold and his face became hot. Joan's head was still buried in her notes. To Davis, it seemed like he was watching the conversation from behind two-way glass, picking up subtleties in tone and expression, attaching a subtext to every phrase. This boy is not AK's killer, he reminded himself, but he couldn't help imagining Justin alone somewhere, in the narrow woods that partition his neighborhood, cradling a neighbor's cat in his arms, his fingers lightly around its neck, and then an older, crueler version of him behind the counter at the Gap, straddling Davis's daughter, watching her struggle, thrilled by her fear.

— 39 —

A police station is a lousy place to primp for a night on the town, Big Rob thought. It's loud and the lighting's bad (all fluorescents) and the mirrors are cracked and warped and marred with capillaries of water damage. Big Rob was a good-looking fat man, according to just over a dozen women in the last twenty years. Looking at himself in a mirror, not this one, a good one, Rob wistfully imagined what he'd look like if he were thin. He had dense, dark hair and his chin, the top one, was strong and square. His teeth were white and original. Although he carried excess weight in his face and around his belly, he was six and a half feet tall and his frame was proportionately large. God had given him the fat, he joked, because he was strong enough to carry it.

The squad room of the Brixton police station was small and communal. The chief had a cluttered and claustrophobic office, but the half dozen other employees and officers shared desks and made do. There were big windows on three walls, and the spaces between them were painted yellow—very different from the enclosed, whitewashed workrooms Big Rob was used to from his days with the Chicago PD. The break room was clean and the refrigerator, which seemed to hold little besides condiments and freshly packed lunches for that day's shift, didn't smell.

Civilians needed little more from this place than advice or a Samaritan's hand. The Brixton cops helped people get keys out of parked cars and collared loose pets. Occasionally they took congenial statements from opposite sides of a fender bender, and Brixton had its share of drunk-and-disorderlies, as well as vandalism and domestic squabbles. Working out of the Brixton police station seemed to Big Rob like working in an ad agency or a bank.

"You all set?" Crippen's delighted grin appeared in the mirror. Biggie gave him a thumbs-up. "This is exciting shit," Crippen said. "Be careful, and don't push it too far. Just try to get her loosened up with the margaritas and then let her talk."

Big Rob nodded. "You know how you get to be a success with the ladies, even with a body like mine?" He tugged on an earlobe. "Be a good listener."

At a bar called Hounds, Biggie easily found Peg at a square table with four friends. Peg had secured a fifth chair from another part of the bar and made camp on a corner that, due to a pair of lost screws underneath, tilted awkwardly toward her. In the center of the table, downed drinks left their fingerprints in thin pink films on the insides of the glasses, which were grouped together like the small woods that separated property lines in suburban subdivisions. It had been so long since a waitress had cleared the table that the ladies had only its perilous, slanting fringe on which to place their current beverages, although in the waitress's defense, the women were emptying the glasses so quickly their drinking could have been mistaken for sleight of hand.

The bar was decorated with a half-assed British theme. Store-bought posters of green countryside, ruined castles, and ocean cliffs hung on the walls at angles in cheap black frames. A few kitschy Sherlock Holmes items—ceramics, toys, books—were scattered about on shelves. A reproduction movie poster was tacked next to the door. Displayed randomly were some Irish and Scottish items, as well. They poured Guinness at the tap, which made Big Rob hopeful for a pint of Tennent's, but he should have known better. He backed away from the bar with his Harp and casually maneuvered through the crowd until his giant torso was only a few feet from their table, like a cruise ship anchored off a port of call. All five women turned.

"Good evening, ladies," Big Rob said. "Do you mind if I buy the next round?"

— 40 —

When Sam Coyne was fifteen, a hornet stung him during cross-country practice.

An abandoned Milwaukee Northern line ran behind Northwood East High School, and Coach Carne had the team train over the split and rotting sleepers, on their toes, up to three miles out and three miles back for the varsity. The exercise steeled Sam's will and fattened his calves, and by midseason he held the number-three spot on the roster, after Bruce Miller and Lanny Park, and even finished second at the Oak Park Invitational, which had a famously flat second half.

Lanny and Bruce and another teammate, named Bryan, had turned back at two miles, this being a Friday, with a meet the next day and a party rumored for that night. Sam promised he'd meet them later at Jan Tenowski's, whose parents were in Lake Geneva. If she wasn't already planning on taking advantage with a beer-baited get-together, they were sure they could talk her into it.

As the balls of his feet sprung again and again off the timbers, Sam's legs felt good, which meant he could hardly feel them at all. There was a certain point in the middle of a quality run when they seemed to propel themselves. There was no pain, no effort, the oxygen arrived in sufficient quantities, and the rhythm of the footfalls both propelled and recharged him. At this pace, on this cool evening, he was certain he could run forever, and in the seconds right before the hornet struck, he was convinced that Lanny's number-two spot could be stolen from him on a regular basis, starting tomorrow.

He had joined the cross-country team in the seventh grade, mostly because of girls. That's not to say Northwood runners had significant numbers of groupies, although the cheerleading squad scheduled an appearance at one meet every fall in a display of pep they probably counted as charity. For an awkward and easily embarrassed thirteen-year-old, however, a spot on an athletic roster seemed like a minimum standard to meet socially, and Sam had always been blessed with good stamina, if not world-beating speed. Running allowed him to work alone, which he liked, but it didn't single him out, either. The team shared the credit for success, but the blame for failure was distributed just as equally, and that was all fine with Sam. Most important, he was an athlete, which, in the eyes of girls, was the high school equivalent of having a good job.

There were other benefits, as well, his parents noted. Sam's grades improved, and he gained confidence. He thought the teachers gave him more respect and, when he needed it, the benefit of the doubt.

The yellow jacket landed on his shin about six inches below the right knee. Sam looked down at it, but didn't stop or break stride, as doing so suddenly on such a treacherous path would cause him to stumble. He stared down at the hornet, which clung to his skin even as his feet found tie after tie, sending vibrations up and down his legs. He leaned forward and tried to swat it away.

It stung.

Sam pulled up like a wounded horse and he slapped at it, meeting some resistance, as the insect hadn't yet let go of the stinger. He fell and his left ankle turned painfully against the half-buried right rail.

"Dammit!"

In just a few seconds, the sting had become swollen and purple and painful. Sam stood panting beside the tracks and watched the wound mutate. It was the first time he'd been stung by an insect, and in the minute or so it took for him to catch his breath, he realized he was allergic.

The next time he was stung—by a bee, while playing in a three-on-three basketball tournament in Chicago—he was much older. That particular night, he called his parents.

"Did you go to the emergency room?" his mother asked.

"No, Mom," Sam said. "I took a couple of Benadryl."

"I remember the day you got stung during running practice."

"Cross-country practice," he corrected.

"Cross-country *running practice*," she snapped back, but then she chuckled. "Your ankle was as big as a softball when you got back."

"It wasn't my ankle, it was my shin. And that was a lot worse than the one today. I had to walk two miles on it."

"Well, it was huge."

They talked about his sister's family in Milwaukee until they'd exhausted the topic, and both he and his parents—Mom and Dad on separate cordless extensions—sat quietly with the headsets at their ears. It wasn't uncomfortable silence—each party knew the call hadn't yet reached maturity—but no one said a word for almost half a minute as they waited for the conversation to start itself again.

"Sam, there's a little boy here in Northwood who looks exactly like you," Mrs. Coyne said finally.

"Really?" Sam was paging through *The New York Times Magazine* with the phone wedged between his shoulder and head. There was an article on a jazz guitarist he liked and he didn't feel like waiting for his parents to hang up before he started reading it.

"Yeah, it's really something," his father said. "Are you sure you didn't get any of those girls pregnant in high school?"

Between another father and son, the remark would have been laughed away as familiar joshing. Between Sam and his father there was subtext.

The period of Sam's worst battles with his father ran roughly the same duration as World War II: from September of his thirteenth year until the August after his graduation from Northwood East. Sam drank a lot of beer and smoked a lot of pot on weekends. He brought girls to the house, girls he knew his mother and father wouldn't like, and when he slept with one of them he did nothing to conceal the fact from his parents. Freethinkers, Mr. and Mrs. Coyne didn't mind the sex so much—not after he turned seventeen, anyway—but they were appalled by his lack of discretion. Smart girls, dumb girls, skinny girls, fat girls, rich girls, poor girls: teenaged Sam screwed in the same bored fashion that he flipped channels on the television, with each program being no more or less interesting than the next.

His promiscuity had much to do with the deep supply of willing partners, of course. Sam attributed this to a story that circulated the school concerning his private girth. As it spread, the tale had become exaggerated, of course, but not by much. By the time Sam reached his junior year, he found there was always a curious girl willing to bring him home or follow him home or go for a drive or take in an unpopular movie from the back row. It wasn't always intercourse—some only wanted a preview—but the attention was all the same to him, frankly.

"So, who is he?" Sam asked.

"The boy? Oh, we don't know his name," Mrs. Coyne said. "Dad saw him at the fruit store, and then pointed him out at the butcher."

"It was uncanny, really. We came home and pulled out the old photo albums. You could be twins—if you were still in second grade," Mr. Coyne said.

"Did you see the mother?"

"About your age. A few years older maybe. Pretty. Thin," his mom said.

"You remembering something, son? Did you ever have a rubber go on 'spring break'?"

"James." Mrs. Coyne's frown translated into a sour murmur over the phone.

"There's nothing to remember, Dad," Sam said.

"Are you sure? Are you sure you didn't slip one past that chubby field-hockey goalie? What was her name? Rebecca?"

"He's kidding, dear."

"Yeah, Mom. Anyway, that's funny. This kid. He looked just like me, huh?"

"They say everyone has a twin," Mrs. Coyne said. "Yours just showed up twenty years late."

"Weird."

"So how's work?"

"Busy."

"Any good cases?" his father asked. "Have you taken any dirty drug money this week?"

This joke, on the other hand, was not as caustic as it sounded. James Coyne was proud of his son's work as an attorney, and he boasted to his friends about Sam's big-moneyed clients. Mr. Coyne often used the phrase "dirty drug money" as an ironic and not-too-subtle reference to his own activist college days. He wasn't ashamed of them, exactly. He wasn't embarrassed about his objection to the war, or the editorial pipe bombs he tossed on the back pages of campus newspapers in the direction of the White House. In middle age, however, he had become a pious capitalist, starting his own business, building it large enough and quickly enough to sell it by the time he was fifty, and in retirement he considered the demonstrations of his early adulthood as another stage of growing up. He saw his son's teenage promiscuity the same way in retrospect, but he couldn't resist the sharp needling over it, then or now.

Regardless, Sam was happy to talk about something other than his tiny, chocolate-smudged look-alike. He was certain he didn't have a son wandering around Northwood, but he did have secrets, and this conversation had his parents poking around in the dirt under which they were buried.

That night, however, after he'd hung up the phone, the name of Anna Kat Moore haunted him for only a minute or two. He exorcised it from his mind with a cold shiver, played for an hour on the computer—a new multiplayer game called Shadow World that one of his clients insisted would be the next big thing (the client was so sure, in fact, he'd bought five thousand shares of stock in the company that created it)—then fell asleep watching a basketball game from the West Coast.

— 41 —

Lying in Ricky Weiss's bed, an arm under Ricky Weiss's sleeping wife, Big Rob didn't struggle too much with whether or not it had been ethical. He wondered if it had been ironic—that this began with an investigation of an alleged cheating husband, and ended with him between a married woman's sheets—but then decided he was confusing "irony" with another word, one that wouldn't come to him just now. It didn't matter what you called it. It was what it was: inevitable. Hell, that wasn't the right word, either.

It made him ill to be in such an intimate array with a woman he now knew to be complicit in Philly's death. Complicit? Was that right? Did he even know what really happened to Phil Canella? The drink and the dark and the postejaculatory haze dulled his ability to sum up.

The girls had consumed three rounds of juice and alcohol in various combinations before the six of them moved to a just-liberated and more comfortable round table. Big Rob delivered the promised charm in the form of compliments and jokes and reciprocal laughter. He told adventure stories from years back starring his formerly svelte self on high school lacrosse fields and in the navy and on the police force.

Late in the night, Big Rob was telling how he'd almost invested in the stock of some biotech company—human cloning, gene treatment for cancer, that sort of thing. He spent his money on a boat instead, and all of his friends got rich. "And I don't even have the boat anymore," Big Rob said to hearty, high-pitched laughter.

"Ricky and I are gonna be rich," Peg blurted out, bringing a cranberry-colored drink to her lips almost as if she hoped the glass would act as a muzzle to keep her from blabbing.

"Tell us," the blonde one named Linda said, demonstrating her faithfulness by a lack of skepticism.

"I can't tell you all the details," Peg giggled. "It's a secret." She made a not-so-discreet nod toward Big Rob, but when her eyes caught his, they stuck there, and she parted her thin lips in a way that Big Rob found incidentally sexy.

"I'm just passing through town," he said. "Your secrets can stay here, as far as I'm concerned. What happens in Brixton, stays in Brixton, if you know what I mean." He winked at no one in particular.

Peg brought them all together in a woozy huddle around the table. "Ricky and I have the goods on this rich doctor from Chicago. And when the time is right, he and me are gonna cash in." She burped. "That's all I'm saying."

Big Rob waved at the waitress for another round and she warned him with a painted nail pointed toward the clock that this was last call. "So, this doctor, what? Has he done something bad?"

Peg's burp had apparently been a hiccup, and it repeated. "Not yet. He hasn't done it yet, and that's all I'm saying." Big Rob patted her gently on the back, as if that were a folksy cure.

"Well, if he's going to do something bad, shouldn't you go to the police before it happens?" asked Jo.

"Shhhh!" Peg said. She reconvened the huddle. "We don't know for sure he's going to do *anything*." She paused to take control of her rib cage as Big Rob continued to rub her back with his left hand. "But if he does, we're not gonna let him get away with it."

"What's this doctor going to do?" Big Rob asked when he was afraid no one else would.

Peg grabbed a random glass from the waitress's tray. "I can't tell you *that*." She fought her hiccups with big gulps. " 'S all I'm saying."

When the bar closed, Big Rob was the first to offer her a ride home, and when she accepted, the other girls retreated into the darkness of the parking lot behind the echoes of coy good-byes. Big Rob helped Peg into the front passenger seat of his van, and by the time he walked around to the driver's side, she was already in a light sleep. He stroked her hair and she stirred.

"Are you going to invite me back to your motel room?" Peg asked, her eyelids heavy from drinking and napping.

Big Rob had known from the purposeful way her hand had repeatedly touched his knee in the bar that he would have no problem getting her alone. The trick would be keeping her awake, and he knew one method of doing that was a way frequently practiced between strangers in motels. But he was convinced something had happened at Ricky Weiss's house, and his offer to drive her home was, first and foremost, an attempt to see the crime scene without a warrant.

"I sort of have a roommate," he said. "Budget cuts at the home office and all." She frowned. "Can we go to your place?"

Peg endured a sudden spasm down her spine and knocked her head against the window. "Ow," she said. "I'm married, you know."

Big Rob turned away. It seemed chivalrous to him. "Is your husband home?"

"No."

"Will he be home tonight?"

"No."

"Well, then."

"Well, then."

Big Rob had driven past Ricky's trailer a dozen times, and he steered the van toward it in silence. Careless. He was only a mile away when Peg said something.

"How do you know where I live?" she asked.

"I don't," Biggie said. "It's a small town. I figured you'd say something if I was going the wrong way." In her condition, this seemed reasonable. "Is this right?"

"Left up here," she said, tucking a finger under his shirt sleeve and rubbing the cotton between her fingers. "So what did you say your name was again?"

"Biggie." He grinned and Peg covered her mouth at the delightful naughtiness of it and them.

They parked in the street and tiptoed in exaggerated silence to her aluminum door. Big Rob expected the place to be messy, but when they pushed themselves inside he found it to be just the opposite, and it struck him that a clean trailer almost seemed kind of upscale—like someplace a movie star passes her time between takes.

They stood there in the space between the spotless kitchen and tidy living room like, well, actors who'd forgotten their lines. The air was a stale combination of chlorine and air freshener. "Do you have anything to drink?" Big Rob asked. As full of liquids as they were, Peg laughed, chose two cans of beer from the refrigerator, and pointed him toward the couch.

He sunk into the sofa as delicately as he could. She put a bony knee against a cushion and, still holding both cans, pressed her open mouth against his. She folded herself into his lap and abandoned the beers to the black-painted coffee table.

He endured their fumbling embrace for ten minutes or more, even enjoyed it in spite of himself. Peg was not the prettiest woman to have sat on Big Rob's lap over the last twenty years, nor was she the homeliest. He put her in the middle somewhere. Around fifth. But Peg had information about Philly, she may even know something about Philly's death, and the crazed probing of his teeth and gums by her tongue seemed more than inappropriate. It seemed like betrayal.

But then, James Bond had sexed bad women, hadn't he? Women who were spies, who were plotting to kill him, who had killed his friends. Hadn't he? Big Rob was almost sure, although he couldn't name the films in which it had happened. The early Connerys and the later Moores all ran together in his head even at the most ordinary and sober times. But he was certain James Bond had sexed evil women and allowed himself to enjoy it. Toward a greater end.

His hand reached for the front button of her jeans. At some point in the next hour, they moved to her bed.

Finally, between oddly configured and suffocating clenches during which there was circumstantial evidence of her climaxing, but before he had done the same, Big Rob said to her, "Hon, I can't lie to you."

She gave him a puzzled and tired look. "Baby, lie to me," she said. "Please lie to me."

"No," Big Rob said. "This isn't a game."

She grunted. Peg wanted to reciprocate, quickly, and go to sleep. But Big Rob knew there would never be a better time to interrogate this witness than right now.

"Something you said. About a Chicago doctor."

Peg's eyes snapped open. Her teeth set but didn't quite meet, the result of an uncorrected, genetic asymmetry.

"I'm looking for a doctor and it sounds like he could be the same man," Big Rob said.

She squinted into the darkness and imagined a path from the bed to the door.

"It's okay. Maybe we can help each other."

She relaxed some and sat up against the headboard. "What do you mean?"

Big Rob backed off the bed and found his pants. He pulled out the illustration that Jackie Moore had sent Philly. "Do you know who this man is?"

She took it and turned on the light. "Oh, fuck," she said.

"What is it?"

Her mind sorted the possibilities like an old mail machine. "You know Davis Moore?"

"I do," Big Rob said. "I mean, I know who he is."

"Fuck," she said again. Big Rob didn't know if she was going to say anything else.

"Look, I don't want your money. Your big payday. You and Ricky. I just want to know who the guy in the picture is and what he has to do with the doctor. Like I said. Maybe we can help each other."

"So you're saying, I help you, and you'll let Ricky and me sell our story to the magazines?"

"Magazines?" Big Rob said. *That was their big plan?* "Sure. I'll drive you right to *Vanity Fair*'s front door, if that's what it takes. Look, you said yourself you were waiting for something to happen so you could cash in on your story. Maybe I can help move things along a little bit."

Peg was very tired and still a little drunk. Given the events of the last hour, the heavy, shirtless man in her bedroom had gained her trust. "That's Jimmy Spears."

"The football player?" Big Rob looked at the drawing again. He knew of Spears—he played for the Dolphins. Or maybe the Falcons. He'd heard the name a hundred times since he started coming to Brixton, but like most football fans, he wouldn't know what the guy looked like without a number and name on his back.

"Jimmy Spears grew up here in Brixton. Davis Moore thinks Jimmy

Spears killed his daughter. Ricky thinks Moore is gonna, I don't know, get revenge or something."

"No shit?" Big Rob wished Philly were here, then looked down at his mostly naked body and at Peg half covered by a sheet and he almost laughed. "No shit."

Peg continued. Big Rob recognized the tired, relieved—almost tearful—tone of a confession. "After Moore used Ricky to track down Spears, he sent some guy here—a private eye with a gun, to kill Ricky, and Ricky . . . well, Ricky wrestled the gun away from him. Here at the trailer. Then the detective started running. He ran to his car." She sighed and closed her eyes. "I saw it. He came here to kill Ricky." Then, in a confused and tired lapse that shattered Big Rob's most fragile hope, "It was self-defense. I saw it."

"Self-defense. I believe you. Anybody would," Big Rob said. His heart was beating at a speed that would terrify his doctor. "What did Ricky do with the gun?"

Peg climbed out of bed and opened the sliding closet door. On tiptoe, she reached up to a high shelf and pushed aside a number of boxes and single shoes. In the moonlight, the skin on her back was shiny like wet sand. She turned around and presented the gun to him carefully, at arm's length.

"It's okay." Big Rob hooked his pinky through the trigger guard and checked to see if the safety was on, and he set it on top of his folded pants. He took her in his arms and she squeezed him. Her hands were sweaty against his back. Later, remembering this, he would cry.

"So you're gonna help us?" she asked, sniffling into his ear. "You're gonna help me and Ricky get our money?"

What could Big Rob say except yes?

That's when her hand went under the waistband of his boxers.

Big Rob closed his eyes and coaxed himself to the finish. Toward a greater end.

— 42 —

Barwick kept her apartment dark and cool. A friend in Arizona often asked why she lived in Chicago, why she put up with those Northern winters, but Sally never understood the question. With layers, it was easy to escape the cold, and snow was only a temporary nuisance, like boxes piled in a hall-way. Northern winters were preferable to Southern summers—which were unrelenting and bright and hot. You could hide your worst flaws in the short, cold days of winter, but the Southern heat and sun only exposed your worst features to the world. Even now, as spring intruded, Sally, with drawn shades, made her home a bunker from the early mornings and lengthening afternoons.

She turned on her computer and with a keystroke rejected an offer to enter Shadow World, which she had just started playing in the past week. She had heard about the game from a friend and although it wasn't exactly a mainstream phenomenon, the alternative press had been raving about its potential. She understood the appeal. Being inside the game was like being in one of her dreams.

Sally opened her word processor and began a letter to Martha Finn.

She told Martha who she really was. What her job was. What she had done. She said she was sorry. That she had accepted the assignment without realizing they would become friends. That once she started the lies—the most necessary tools of her business—it became impossible for her to stop them.

A man is dead now, and I don't yet know if I have any culpability for his murder, Sally wrote. *I once asked that same man about conflicts of interest in our profession. Philly told me, "Lawyers have conflicts of interest, Barwick. Not us. We're more like priests. The husbands confess to us. The wives confess to us. We hear their worst secrets. Act on their worst impulses."*

You deserved less cynical consideration from me, Martha. You are a good person, far better than me. You have a wonderful son, destined for wonderful things. Even now it is easy for me to imagine him as an older boy, as a man. A man of duty and great responsibility. I have not only betrayed you, my friend, I have betrayed Justin. I will live with that pain all my life.

When my boss returns from his business trip I am quitting. Leaving this job for good. All I have to show for my falsehoods are dead colleagues and lost friends. There must be a better living in honesty, a better way to pursue the truth than through lies.

She printed the letter and signed it, then stuffed it in an envelope, which she addressed and stamped and left on a tiny sideboard that flanked her door. She deleted the original from her hard drive so it could never be edited, never be changed.

— 43 —

Davis left work at about ten o'clock. He liked coming home after Jackie had gone to bed but before she had gone to sleep. In the darkness of their bedroom, lying in their king-sized bed like parallel lines, never touching, they could talk. They could discuss the highlights of their days and the miscellaneous nuisances of their lives—bills, home repair, social obligations, and so forth. All of that was harder in the light of downstairs. Except for the bedroom and sometimes the dining room, the rest of the big house had become like a time-share in which they both lived, but never together.

He ate an unbruised portion of banana from a bowl and then walked upstairs. The stereo was tuned at high volume to a classical station. Haydn's Twenty-second Symphony, he realized, and was amazed he recognized it. Davis preferred jazz, but he and Jackie had season tickets to the Chicago Symphony Orchestra, and went often, even over the last few years. Davis didn't hate his wife. Their marriage had just lost its tolerance for long silences. At Symphony Center, silence was never an issue.

The door to the bathroom was open three inches and the light was on. Davis sat on the bed, dropped his head between his hunched shoulders, and put his palms flat atop the comforter.

The boy. Christ. The boy.

Davis had decided his path in the first year of medical school, but he told his mother and father that he planned to be a surgeon. His father was never churched, but he was a devout believer. An engineer, he taught his children that the purpose of life was to discover God from the inside out. The old man loved science, especially physics. The language of God was not Aramaic, or Latin, or Hebrew, or Arabic, he used to say, usually with a dismissive wave at a church or a Bible. The language of God, he'd say, is mathematics. When we reconcile the randomness of the universe with the precision of its rules, when we can see no contradictions in the chaos of nature and the equations of natural law, then we will understand his hows and whys.

Niles Moore believed God wanted us to deconstruct the world, to lay it in pieces across the kitchen table and, in doing so, understand him.

Davis believed that, too, which is what drew him to genetic research and, when Congress and a friendly administration assented, to fertility. For him, cloning was never about playing God. It was about replicating God's work, following the blueprints of God's greatest achievement and creating life.

The old man wouldn't see it that way. The old man, back when cloning was only a possibility that made half the electorate excited for mankind and the other half afraid for their souls, thought that scientists who pursued human cloning were not observing nature but foiling it.

And so the deception throughout medical school—an easy enough thing considering the years of study and residency, unobserved outside the hospital. When he went into practice, it was more difficult.

By that time, Davis, privately (never to his patients), had become an agnostic. He had lost his faith like so many, gradually, slowly coming to the conclusion that his father's God had not lived up to expectations. Davis didn't blame his lack of faith on a godless universe—he still believed in some sort of power—but on the ridiculous demands religion placed on God. Omniscience? Omnipotence? Omnipresence? How could anyone who believed in a God like that not be disappointed with the world?

Jackie was still in the bathroom.

He had a sudden, horrible feeling.

Many times Davis had found his wife passed out in the bathroom—on the toilet, in the tub, under the sink—and had to undress her and put her to bed. He never resented her more than when pulling a nightgown over her limp, sour-smelling body, and he never felt less culpable for her unhappiness.

He walked to the bathroom door and kicked it open, gently, with the toe of his right shoe.

"Jackie?" he called to her, hoping she would answer, hoping she would give him some indication, even a sentient grunt, that she could walk on her own, any gesture at all to demonstrate that she was capable of reclaiming some dignity tonight.

The bathroom was barely lit by thick purple candles that smelled like berries—cherries, it seemed to him, although he guessed it was blueberry or boysenberry the makers intended. The faucet dripped like an abandoned metronome keeping time atop a silent piano. On the tile next to the tub was a mostly full glass of white wine and an empty brown prescription bottle with JACKIE MOORE written at the top of the label and DAVIS MOORE typed at the bottom. The tub was half filled with lukewarm water and displaced almost to the point of overflowing by 115 pounds of naked lifelessness.

For the second time in his life, but not the last, Davis stood over the hollow body of a person he had once loved.

Justin at Nine

— 44 —

Folks had called Sam Coyne many cruel names as a child, but none had stung him more than "mama's boy." Perhaps it was the insinuation that he was weak, or maybe he simply didn't want to be identified so closely with his gregarious and eccentric parents, but all these years later he was still reluctant to ride with his mother to the store when she asked. Running errands with his mom around town, around Northwood, where he grew up, made him self-conscious.

"Heck, Ma," he said, trying not to whine. "Why don't you make me a list? I'll go get it myself. Save you the trip."

"Jesus, Sam," she said. "You're thirty years old. The other boys won't make fun of you when they see you with your mom."

"It's not that," he muttered. But of course it was, and when he thought about it again, he realized how ridiculous he was being. Maybe it was his thirtieth birthday (for which his buddies from the law firm had surprised him with an expensive hooker at the Drake) or maybe it was just being home for the weekend, but Sam was having a tough time accepting himself as an adult. He looked at people in their early twenties and was convinced they were older than he. He always assumed certain kinds of celebrities—athletes, for instance—were older, and he suffered tiny spasms of panic when he read that this shortstop or that seven-foot center had a birth date ten years later than his.

"Anyone new in your life?" Mrs. Coyne asked from the passenger's seat as he backed out of the driveway, where, in an earlier family car, Sam had accepted a blow job from a cheerleader named Alex who also had a twin brother named Alex, a fact that Sam couldn't put out of his mind through the duration of the act.

"No," Sam said. In truth there were many new anyones—Samantha, Joanne, Tammy, the hooker at the Drake—and he knew them all about equally well. When he called a girl for a date it had more to do with matching her preferences to his mood—this one's a baseball fan, that one likes to be bent over a leather chair—than it did with any desire to advance a relationship. Unless a woman was especially good at scratching that month's sexual itch, he usually let pass just enough time between dates so that she and he were starting over each time. It kept complications at bay.

Sal Faludi had been butcher to Northwood for all of Sam's life and longer. He was in the shop every day, commanding about fifteen employees in a downtown space that over the years had expanded across four storefronts. Rare were the times when you didn't have to wait your turn at Faludi's. On summer Saturday mornings like this one, you took a number. Sam's was seventy-four.

When Sam was in high school, he and the others would sometimes leave campus for lunch and they would usually end up here. When the weather was nice, Sal set up tables made from black steel mesh on the sidewalk, and the kids would each grab a sandwich from the deli and race for one of the al fresco seats.

"Sixty!" Sal called out.

A pretty young woman, about Sam's age or a little older, pushed open the glass door with her rear end and her shoulders. Sam noticed the appealing shape of her right away, even before she turned around to reveal her white teeth and giant eyes. She had a brown grocery bag in her left arm and was holding the hand of a boy—seven, eight, nine, ten years old, somewhere in there, Sam thought—with her right. The woman smiled curiously at Sam, who was staring, and said hello to Sam's mother before looking away and taking a number from the big snail-shaped dispenser.

"Oh, good!" Sam's mother said, pinching his arm. "Sam, look!" She took two long steps and a graceful skip to the woman's side and she pulled the woman and the boy back in Sam's direction. "Martha!" Mrs. Coyne said. "This is my son, Sam. The one I've been telling you about all these months."

"You know, I was wondering." Martha laughed. "I see what you mean. Hello, Sam." She let go of the boy's hand long enough to shake Sam's. The boy looked into each of their faces and sighed politely. This turn of events wouldn't get him out of the store any sooner.

Sam was gracious and puzzled, quietly assuming his mother was match-making again. If that were the case she had done better than usual, except for the presence of a child, which triggered an automatic preemptory challenge for him as far as dating was concerned. This Martha was extremely pretty. She had short, reddish blond hair with fashionable bangs that transcended the common suburban bob. Her lips were full and her neck was long. Her eyes were so large and green they reminded Sam of sexy girls in comic books. She wore a green sleeveless top with narrow openings for her thin and angular gym-toned arms. Under a long abstract leaf-patterned skirt he could make out shapely athletic legs. He liked the way her head tilted when she said hello. The shy but confident way she shook hands. The silent manner in which she respected (and received respect from) her little boy. She must have been young when she had him, he thought.

"Sam, I've mentioned Martha to you a hundred times," his mother said. "We're always running into each other downtown. Little Justin here looks exactly like you did when you were his age."

Right, Sam thought. The little boy. The bastard child his father was always kidding him about. Nope, it wasn't his. Sam couldn't remember every woman he'd slept with, but he would have remembered Martha. Now imagining her, flesh against flesh, he chuckled and looked at the boy's face for the first time. Yeah, he supposed he had once looked like that. A little. Not so much that his mother should have been going on and on about it for the last year. But then, one never sees himself, or remembers himself, exactly the way others do. Self-recognition is a sign of intelligence, his freshman psychology professor had claimed. Only advanced mammals are capable of looking in a mirror and acknowledging the image there is their own. But the mirror also distorts. How many times have you heard people say, *That's a terrible picture of me,* when the photo, in fact, is quite accurate? We disavow the correct images of ourselves because they don't match against the idealized snapshots we all carry in our heads.

"Well, I'll be," Sam said.

Mrs. Coyne opened her purse. "A month ago I started carrying this old picture around so I could show it to you when we ran into each other, and then I haven't seen you since. Isn't that always the way?" She made paddling motions inside the huge bag, pushing aside innumerable contingency items like lip balm and pens and tissues and the keys to her sister's house in Rockford.

"Here," Mrs. Coyne said, her fingers on something. "Oh, yes. This."

Sam and Martha huddled close for a better look while Justin stared out onto the sidewalk. The photo of Sam was taken when he was about eight years old. It was winter and Sam was dressed in snow pants and a parka and he was holding a sled. He wasn't wearing a cap, but Sam wondered why his mother chose this photo to demonstrate his youthful resemblance to Martha's son when she could have picked from dozens of others, in which he was not so obscured by nylon and fleece. He guessed it was because the house in the background showed off the Christmas lights his parents were so famous for in their neighborhood. Looking at it, however, he had to admit the resemblance to Justin was startling. They had the same blond hair (although young Sam's had been shorter), similar cheekbones, the same chin.

"Wow!" Martha grinned, pulling away from the photo and then bending back down for a better assessment. "Justin, take a look," she said. "Look at Mr. Coyne when he was your age. He looks just like you."

"Wow," Justin said flatly, blinking at the photograph. There was a moment of curiosity, when his eyebrows curled, indicating to Sam that the boy saw the resemblance, but it also was apparent that Justin wanted no part of a conversation that would keep him out shopping with his mother longer than necessary. Sam sympathized.

Martha handed the photograph back to Mrs. Coyne and looked Sam in the eyes. "Well, he has a lot to look forward to if he grows up as handsome as you."

Flirtatious, Sam thought.

"Seventy-four!" Sal cried out.

Sam held out his ticket. "Here," he said to Martha. "I'll trade you. It looks like Justin would like to get this over with."

Martha raised her eyebrows. "That's kind, but you don't have to."

Mrs. Coyne stopped Martha's hand as she tried to give the ticket back. "Take it. Really. We're in no hurry."

"Gosh," Martha said. "Thank you so much."

"Divorced," Sam's mother whispered to him, in answer to an unasked question, after Martha had waved good-bye and disappeared toward the checkout.

Sam returned to the city following an early supper on Sunday, and on the way home he called innocent-looking-but-uninhibited Tina, whom he had met and balled at a client's holiday party last December. Tonight, their second night together, he lay on his back and Tina straddled him, facing away. The television news was on, with the sound turned down.

"Oh, Looord," Tina purred. "This guy on the TV looks a little bit like you."

Sam had forgotten how chatty Tina was. Even when they were coupled in her boss's office the night of the party she was telling him stories about the weird guy in accounts payable who came by her desk every morning when she was in the ladies' room and tongued the lipstick off her coffee mug.

"I've been getting that a lot lately," Sam said, hands firmly on her hips, keeping her in proper time. "Who is he?"

"A football player. Jimmy Spears, it says." She giggled and dug into his thigh with her red nails. "He's *hot*."

"He sucks," Sam said. "What's he doing on TV in the middle of July?"

"Don't know," Tina said. "Don't care." She arched backward and Sam snarled one hand in her auburn hair and slipped the other around her neck, just under her jawline, and when a finger got close to her mouth, she bit it hard enough to draw blood.

Later, as his hands caressed the faint but exquisite bruises, both his and hers, left by the scratching and teething and openhanded slapping, he tried to imagine Martha's contours in place of Tina's, tried to conceive of the sort of clandestine, muffled, normal sex they would have with the little boy who looked just like him asleep in the next room.

To his surprise, he almost could.

— 45 —

WEISS TRIAL DATE SET FOR FALL

Vic Fabian, Brixton Courier

It has been 32 years since John Francis McCullough was found guilty in the stabbing death of Calhoun resident Molly Bowman, but Brixton officials insist they will be ready on November 14 when Richard Cantrell Weiss becomes the first individual in three decades to be tried for murder in the Main Street courthouse.

The facts of the case might not be fully apparent until the end of testimony in what is expected to be a four-week trial, but a glimpse of the case was revealed recently in the prosecutor's indictment.

Weiss, a graduate of Brixton High School and a former greenskeeper at Brixton Country Club, has been charged with the murder of Phillip Canella, a private investigator who had been making inquiries around the village last October. Canella was looking into the alleged infidelity of a Chicago-area doctor at the behest of the physician's wife. Neither police nor the district attorney would comment on the connection between Weiss and the doctor (whose name was redacted from the indictment), although sources say he could be called as a witness.

The prosecutor's office refused to comment on persistent rumors that Miami Dolphins quarterback Jimmy Spears, a Brixton native and high school classmate of Weiss, might be called to testify, as well. Originally alleged on the sports network ESPN, the story has been repeated in the *New York Post* and *The Miami Herald,* with reporters in each case citing "anonymous sources." Spears has admitted that Brixton officials have been in contact with him concerning the case, but declined further comment.

Police were alerted to Weiss's possible involvement in Canella's murder after one of Canella's associates supplied them with evidence allegedly obtained from Weiss's wife, Margaret. A subsequent interrogation of former Brixton resident Herman Tweedy led police to a wooded area near Beck City, where Canella's decomposed body was discovered. Margaret Weiss is said to be cooperating with police and charges against her are still pending. Herman Tweedy recently pled guilty to obstruction of justice and being an accomplice after the fact.

Although he was a longtime resident who was well known around town, Weiss's close friends have been reluctant to comment. In Millie's Tap Room, a favorite haunt of the accused, a recent patron (who requested his name be withheld) said, "Am I surprised that Ricky's on trial for murder? Sure I am. Am I shocked about it? No, not really."

Chicago newspapers covered the arrest of Richard Weiss, but Philly had no family in the area to add local interest, so ongoing coverage consisted mostly of Metro section wire stories and an occasional update on the sports page. Citing "anonymous sources close to the investigation," a suburban paper, the *Daily Herald,* named Davis as the Chicago doctor purged from the indictment. The other papers followed, with the *Sun-Times* also naming Joan Burton as "Dr. Moore's associate," hinting that she was the alleged mistress Phil Canella had been trying to expose. Davis's attorney, Graham Mendelsohn, noting his client had lost his own daughter to murder, his wife to depression and suicide, and had himself been the victim of an assassin's bullet, refused comment. The local press didn't pursue the Moore angle aggressively, but that could change, Graham told Davis, if he were called to testify.

"It could change dramatically, depending on what you have to tell them," Graham said.

"I understand," Davis said.

"Is there anything you want to tell *me,* at this point?"

Davis said there was not.

On the day the assistant district attorney from Carlton County, Nebraska, traveled to Northwood to take statements from Drs. Moore and Burton, around the time she and two other attorneys from her staff were landing at O'Hare, Davis and Joan met in his office to chatter nervously about the appointment.

"What have we decided?" Joan asked, lying on a stiff brown couch that was hardly ever used. "We're going to have to tell them, aren't we?"

"Are we?"

"Goddamnit, Davis, they'll be here in an hour."

Davis rubbed his knuckles into his eyes and sighed. "What are they really going to ask us? They're going to want to know how we came in contact with Ricky Weiss. I'll tell them I've been trying for years to find the man who murdered my daughter. Weiss e-mailed me because he thought he had identified the sketch I'd posted on the Internet. You and I went to Brixton to check it out and we told him he was wrong. My wife hired that detective to follow us down there. I wasn't even aware of it until the police told me, weeks after Jackie had died. That's the extent of our connection to the case."

"They'll want to know where you got the sketch."

"I drew it on a computer."

Joan adopted an interrogator's tone. "Really, Dr. Moore? Based on what?"

Davis had practiced this lie. "Based on the profile created by police during their investigation into AK's death."

As herself now: "They'll want to know if we were having an affair."

The truth again. "We weren't."

"And the photos you had taken of Justin?"

Davis nodded. "I handed over everything I had to police. I told them I was collecting data for a longitudinal study of a young patient."

"Oh, Davis. Really. A secret study?"

"I didn't want the parents to bias the results," Davis said. "You didn't know about it, either. I asked you to help me find AK's killer and that was the end of your involvement. They'll probably assume we were sleeping together. They won't suspect our trip to Brixton had anything to do with Justin."

"You'll take a hit for this secret study crap. The Board of Oversight—"

"Yeah, and I'll take the hit alone."

"I don't want to lie."

"I'd never ask you to."

He wanted to go to the couch. To hold her. He didn't. Several times since his wife's death, Davis had considered advancing his relationship with Joan to something beyond colleague and coconspirator, but each time he decided he couldn't. It wasn't that it was too soon—although he mourned Jackie, he hadn't felt like a husband to her in years. It just never felt right. It hadn't been right that night in Lincoln, and it hadn't been right a dozen times since. Today, with a prosecutor headed to his office to ask them point-blank why they were making clandestine trips to Brixton, Nebraska, it still wasn't right.

His love for her, all by itself, wasn't enough to make it right.

— 46 —

Twenty years ago, when Sam Coyne was ten, downtown Northwood was a poorly zoned collection of vacuum-repair stores, coin shops, a discount furrier, a used book store, and a handful of eateries (including a few second-tier chains) all claiming to grill "the North Shore's Best Hamburger." Northwood's homes were as old and stately as the neighboring suburbs, but its zip code was less prestigious and its public services reliant on property, rather than sales, tax. If any of its residents needed a birthday gift or a nice meal, they got it in the city or at the malls in Skokie and Gurnee.

Then came revitalization. Almost in unison, Chicago suburbs began reimagining themselves as self-contained communities. Tax breaks were offered; boutiques and clothing stores and fine restaurants gobbled them up. Within five years Northwood had a face-lift and the kind of prestige that its residents—many of them had bought homes here as a compromise when they realized they couldn't afford the neighboring towns—always coveted.

Tony Dee, a Chicago chef who had bounced for ten years between Taylor Street's three-star Italian restaurants, opened Mozzarell here with the following simple calculus: low taxes plus low rent plus high incomes. On a Saturday night these days, there were as many Mercedes leaving the city to dine in Northwood as there were BMWs headed in the opposite direction, and Mozzarell was one of the toughest reservations. Despite Sam's usual desire to impress dates with one of his downtown culinary discoveries, he had asked Martha to meet him here because he guessed (rightly) she'd find it pleasantly upscale and also because he knew she'd save money on a babysitter if he brought her home before eleven, a consideration he made sure to mention when she had called him. That's right, he reminded himself. She called *him*.

The salads arrived and Martha had just finished describing all the places she had lived. "Then Terry and I moved to Northwood shortly after all this stuff went in, I guess. I never saw it the way it used to be."

"What a shit hole," Sam said, and then sputtered a quick apology that he didn't wait for her to accept. "It's nice now, but I hated this town when I was a kid."

"I guess we all resent the place where we grew up," she said. "Because it reminds us of all the stupid stuff we wish we could do over again."

"You sell real estate now, though?"

Martha tipped her head to the left and back, a sideways nod that was something of a tic and often imitated in fun by people who knew her well. "Yeah. I made out pretty well with the alimony, but it's still not enough with a boy in the house. Not if you don't want to deprive him, anyway, and he shouldn't have to suffer because his dad is a, well, you know. It's a good time to be selling homes in Northwood, though. The market is tight here. Let me know if you ever decide you want to move back home."

Sam made a sarcastic face. A scenario such as you describe, the face said, is highly unlikely. "How about you?" he asked. "Where do you come from?"

That's sort of a funny way to put it, Martha thought. *Where do you come from?* It reminded her of the questions—the nonstop, vaguely existential questions—that Justin was always putting to her. "South suburbs," she said.

"Huh," Sam said. He'd hardly ever been south of Thirty-fifth Street, where the Sox play, but he'd seen a concert or two at the outdoor theater in Tinley Park. "So ... Terry ... what did he do?"

"Futures trader. The whole LaSalle Street thing, you know. Make a ton of money one year and try not to spend it all before the market turns against you the next. He did okay."

"Where is he now?"

"New Mexico. He's remarried."

"Hunh. You'd think he'd want to stay closer to Justin and all."

"Yeah, you'd think." She smiled and then looked down at her salad, a sign she didn't want to talk about her ex-husband anymore.

Obliging, Sam offered, "You said you wanted to ask me about something."

"Yeah," she said. "And please tell me if I'm out of line."

"Not at all. Please," he said.

"You know the murder trial in Nebraska? The one where the victim was a private detective from here?"

"Sure."

"Well, I'm sort of ... involved," Martha mumbled.

"Why? What do you mean?"

Her reply wasn't really an answer. "I'm on both the prosecution and defense lists of potential witnesses."

"You're kidding. Why?"

Martha told the story of Sally Barwick's friendship and betrayal. How the photos of her boy ended up in the dead private eye's possession via the wife of her former physician, Dr. Davis Moore. "Terry and I had some trouble getting pregnant," she explained. "We went to New Tech and Dr. Moore helped us conceive Justin."

Sam paused and drew a breath through his nose until he was certain he'd locked in a vaguely concerned but otherwise unreadable expression. "What's Moore's connection to all this?"

"I haven't gotten much from the defense attorney—he said he might not even call me—but the district attorney's office has been a little more helpful. From what they can piece together about his defense, this guy, the defendant, Ricky Weiss, he claims Dr. Moore sent Phil Canella to kill him."

Sam paused, pretending to chew his veal. He wanted to be careful not to let on how much he knew about Moore. She was apt to start asking a lot of questions and he was in no mood to keep track of his lies tonight. "The news accounts haven't been real clear, but you can sort of piece it together. Some crazy story about a football player murdering the doctor's daughter, right?"

"Right. Moore says that's not true, but the D.A. tells me Moore had hired a detective agency in Gurnee, and *they* had hired Sally to take pictures of my son for him. Lots of them over five years. I *only* knew Sally as a photographer and I had her take photos of Justin a couple times a year. You know, for family."

Dr. Davis Moore, pedophile? Sam thought. If this gossip were true it would be more delicious than the meal. "*Jesus.* Are you kidding? What did the doctor want the pictures for?"

"I don't know. Moore apparently says it was for some sort of study he was doing, a fertility study, but the D.A. isn't really buying it."

"That's creepy. Are they looking into it anymore?"

"They say it's not part of their theory of the case."

"And what *is* their theory?"

"Well, Sally was some sort of freelancer. It's not clear she even knew the pictures of Justin were going to Dr. Moore. But Phil Canella was working a case for Dr. Moore's *wife*. She thought he was cheating on her, apparently, and I guess Dr. Moore and Dr. Burton had gone to Brixton to meet with Ricky Weiss, and Canella followed him there to spy on them for Mrs. Moore."

"And he runs into Ricky Weiss and he's a paranoid freak and he blows the dude away," Sam said. "I got that much from the *Tribune.*"

"Anyway, the D.A. thinks maybe the defense is going to bring in these pictures of Justin as evidence. They're going to throw all of these bizarre connections at the jury and hope that they buy the conspiracy theory Weiss is floating."

"It sounds like there *are* a lot of coincidences," Sam said.

"It gets worse," Martha whispered, leaning forward and hunching down below an invisible blind that might shield them from the eyes of other diners. "Terry and I hired a detective agency six years ago. Not North Shore. One based downtown. One of Terry's buddies from the pit had used them."

"What did you need a private eye for?"

She dismissed the relevance of the question with a wave of her hand. "It was a—a genealogy project. Just going through birth records back east, looking for one of Terry's lost ancestors. But guess who they sent for the job?"

"Sally? Now you're just making the shit up."

She nodded. "It's all true. But I didn't know. I never met her back then."

"Unbelievable. Have you been deposed yet?"

"No, and the D.A. says I probably won't be unless they decide to call me, and even then it might be at the last minute. If that happens, I was hoping you'd help prepare me for it. Not as a favor. I mean I'd pay you."

Sam frowned and wiped his mouth with his napkin. "Don't worry about it. Is there some reason you think you might need a lawyer?"

She closed her eyes, her lashes long enough, it seemed to Sam, to graze her cheeks. "I'm just confused. Feeling a little betrayed. A little embarrassed that I ended up as a tangential player in a weird Nebraska murder. I'm just feeling really cautious right now."

"I can recommend a criminal lawyer if you'd be more comfortable..."

"No, I don't think it'll get that serious," she said. "I'm just nervous. This isn't the easiest thing to talk about."

"It's so fucked up," Sam said, wondering if he should have cursed like that, but then again, he decided it was a ridiculous thing to be sensitive about, considering what he had planned for Martha later. He became conscious of the silence in the impolite wake of his comment and filled it with a casual remark. He thought it best to tell a little bit of the truth. "I think I went to high school with Davis Moore's daughter."

Unsurprised, Martha said, "The D.A. from Nebraska said he wasn't certain Dr. Moore had done anything illegal with regard to the photos. He didn't have jurisdiction, in any case."

This was getting interesting, Sam thought. He remembered how much Anna Kat had craved her father's approval. How difficult she said it was for her to get his attention. "Illegal? Maybe. Maybe not. It sounds a lot like stalking to me. Invasion of privacy. Exploitation of a minor. You might think about pressing charges. That could help pave the way for a civil suit."

"Really?"

"Sure. Whatever he was up to, it was sleazy. He was your doctor. A doctor who betrayed you. Nine juries out of ten would fall all over themselves just to stick it to him."

She blushed. "I can't tell you how upset I've been over it. I can't imagine what he would want pictures of Justin for unless it was something—" She shivered.

"Pederast," Sam spit. "He's a pervert, I bet."

"I really liked him," Martha said. "And Dr. Burton, too. I can't believe she would have anything to do with something like that. It makes me think there's a lot more to the story. But then I never dreamed that Sally was spying on us all those years, either. It's so strange."

"Well, that kind of case—I guess it would be medical malpractice—isn't really my bag, but if you decide to pursue it, I'll give you the name of someone at my firm."

She smiled. "Gosh, I'd appreciate that."

Gosh, Sam thought. Just great.

Sam paid for dinner with his Platinum Card and for the waitress he added a generous tip, in case Martha was looking over his shoulder.

At her home, the same one Martha had moved to with Terry eleven years ago ("He still pays the mortgage," she said with an embarrassed turn of her mouth), Sam insisted on paying the babysitter from the cash-station twenties folded into his money clip and tiptoed upstairs with her to peek in on sleeping Justin, whose body was contorted, facedown on top of the sheets as if he had been dropped there from a great height. His snoring had a delicate, white-noise quality that Sam, a snorer himself, found something close to soothing.

The room was filled with books—more books than toys, even—and in the darkness, although he could not make out any titles or authors, Sam noted from their thickness and from their serious-looking spines that they seemed to be books for older kids, or even adults. Martha had said he was smart, but he figured moms say that about the dumb kids, too.

They closed the door and Sam followed Martha downstairs. If Sam's intuition was right, Justin's wouldn't be the last bedroom in the Finn house he would see from the inside tonight. Who would have imagined, at age thirty, that Sam Coyne would be trying to bed an older woman? Certainly not Sam, although he figured the differences in their ages couldn't be more than four or five years.

Martha opened a bottle of red wine and Sam, with his twin prejudices about the suburbs and single moms, correctly guessed it would be Merlot. Martha sat on the couch and Sam settled in daringly close to her. He stared at her for a minute, letting a smile develop slowly, and not taking his eyes off her when he leaned the bowl of his glass on his bottom lip for a long drink. Martha became nervous in the silence, and when she couldn't think of anything to say, broke the stare and looked away, shyly.

"It's been a while since . . . since I've been on a date," she said.

"I can't believe that," Sam said, reaching his right hand for the ends of her hair.

When Martha had called him for dinner, he had agreed without hesitation and immediately began planning their first intercourse. Sam made notes in a pocket-sized leather-bound notebook he carried (coded notes, in case they were ever lost or discovered), with everything he knew about Martha (which was little) and everything he assumed based on women like her he had known. The letters and symbols added up to a formula (of sorts) equal to some combination of techniques, positions, and bawdy requests from his sexual repertoire.

So determined was he to get it exactly right, he arranged for a run-through the week before, hiring a pricey hooker, whom he arranged to meet at the Swissôtel (he never gave hookers his real name, and never brought hookers to his apartment—if they knew who he was, he couldn't be *unrestrained*, and it protected him if things got out of hand, which, regrettably, had happened twice). He was specific with the escort service, describing Martha's height and weight and hair color, the relative size of her hips and waist and shoulders, and even her voice, which was in a lower register and rounded on the edges without the nasal Midwestern vowels. Martha sounded as if she came from either money or Ontario, and that was how he put it to the service's automated receptionist.

They did well with the match. She called herself Fonia ("as in Sinfonia," she said at the bar, as if that was supposed to have relevance for him), and while her features didn't especially resemble Martha's, they certainly could have shared wardrobes, so close were their shapes. She was much younger than Martha (she might have been as old as twenty), but up in the room, once he had started the script, he could easily imagine Fonia's thighs and ribs and nibbles and moans were Martha's. He never gave her specific words to say, but several times asked her to tone down the enthusiasm when he thought she was overplaying her part. "You're making it hard, baby," Fonia said over her shoulder, and Sam smiled and said nothing more about it.

Once, he slapped her across the jaw a little harder than he intended. Not hard enough to leave a mark, but harder than he thought Martha would accept from him. Fear crossed Fonia's eyes for just an instant, but Sam apologized and sounded sincere and Fonia seemed fine with it after. Just a little startled, she said. This was exactly why he wanted to practice.

On Martha's couch, Sam grabbed tangles of her hair and put down his wine and leaned forward, head tilted so his open mouth could make a landing on her neck. Startled, she set her glass on the coffee table in a panicked rush and it tipped on the edge of a thick magazine, spilling onto the beige carpet.

"Oh *shit*," she said.

"Leave it," Sam whispered sternly, hoping to set the tone for the kind of sex he had in mind: unhurried, choreographed, a little bit painful in the moments just before release, but not so harsh as to leave a lasting mark. Something she'd never experienced before. She hesitated, the arm that wasn't pinned between them suspended in the air over the glass, then kissed him uncertainly—with curiosity and hunger and ambivalence. She *hadn't* been on a date in a long time, Sam thought. She *had* been lonely. She *had* felt unwanted. He was counting on all three.

With a wrestler's control, he grabbed her wrist and spun her away from him, facedown on the couch, pressing his hips against her spine and twisting her head back so her mouth could join his. She protested unconvincingly, struggling in small fits but still reciprocating with her lips and tongue. He lifted her dress and pushed down on her shoulder, waiting for her to submit completely before he entered her. Sam wriggled free of his shirt and belt and threw them past her head onto the floor. She cried out for him to stop: once, twice, and again, the third time desperately as he pressed harder against her.

She lifted herself onto the armrest like a frightened swimmer to a pier, and told him again, no. He laughed and pushed and waited. She would give in soon. If he was right about her, she would give in.

Instead she reached for a ballpoint pen on the end table and, clicking it once, drove it backward into the soft part of his thigh.

Sam yelped and reared back on his knees. The point hadn't entered him with great force, but it surprised him. He looked down to see if the mark there was blood or ink as Martha wriggled free and slid to the floor, gasping. Sam composed himself and silently customized his conciliation speech, the one he pulled out on nights of miscalculation like this one. *I'm sorry, baby. I thought that was what you wanted. I was getting a thing from you, a vibe. Wow, you haven't been out on the scene in a while, have you? A lot's changed in ten years. Men and women are less inhibited. More in tune with their animal urges. Hell, they write about S & M and rough sex in the weekend section of the* Tribune *now. But we can do it your way. Any way you want.*

He never got a chance to deliver it.

When he lifted his head he saw Martha on the floor beside the sofa, her hair dissembled, her eyes angry and wet, her lips shaking with bewildered rage, her neck red where he had gripped her, her body bent roughly like an Adirondack chair, propped up on her arms, her legs tensed, ready to bolt if he moved toward her. She was waiting for him to say something, trying to think of something to say, in that segment of a second before she saw in Sam's face that he'd seen something shocking, and she figured out that the boy was standing behind her.

She flipped and crawled to Justin in a scramble, standing and wrapping her arms around him, forcing his face to her shoulder so he couldn't see her or the half-dressed man in their living room. "I'm sorry, baby," she whispered. "I'm sorry, Justin."

Sam stepped off the couch, glad that he hadn't undone his pants completely. He stepped the long way around the coffee table to avoid mother and child and wondered if she was going to send the kid out of the room so they could resolve this. If he could rattle off an insincere apology and get an indication from Martha that she wasn't going to call the cops, he'd feel better about leaving.

"Get out," Martha said. Her words were less hysterical than they might have been if she didn't have the boy pulled against her, shielding him from Sam, from even the sight of him. She was exposing a degree of shame with which Sam was unfamiliar, and it made him pity her a little.

"Okay, yeah, okay," he said softly. "Jesus, *sorry.*" He picked up his shirt and flipped his arms through the sleeves. He didn't bother to button it. He folded the belt in his hands, the way he had intended to do later when he thought she might let him raise a wonderful red-and-blue mark across her buttocks. Now he slid past Martha and Justin, turning away from them as he walked toward the front door, thinking how fucked-up this all was and, from the way she was holding her kid, that she was raising a little wuss. A *mama's boy*. As much as the thought of doing a hot suburban mom had excited him this past week, he should have known better.

As his midsection twisted in the narrow space between Martha and Justin and a glass cabinet against the wall, Sam's shirttail flew up and away from his body, revealing his bare back and a few inches of blue boxer shorts where his unsuspended pants had slid down his hips. As it happened, Justin opened his eyes and peered past his mother's shoulder, bare now where the strap of her dress had fallen, and he wiped his damp nose against her skin, which smelled faintly like the deodorant he was only now beginning to use every day; and he watched the man leave and realized even in that instant that he could never tell his mother that he remembered the man from the store or how much of what happened tonight he had seen and understood.

On the porch, Sam yanked the door shut behind him just to hear the sound of heavy things thudding together, and he walked stiffly to his black BMW, casually glimpsing about to see if a neighbor had heard or seen anything of concern. When he turned the corner, he barked at the microphone in the steering column, and the in-dash phone dialed information. He asked the automated operator for a number downtown, and the call was forwarded.

"Lily Escorts." It was yet another automated female, produced with more sophisticated voice-recognition software than even the phone company had access to.

"I was wondering if Fonia was available tonight," Sam said.

"Have you been on a date with Fonia before?" The voice was pleasant and real-sounding, but tinny and shallow, like what you might expect from an undersized woman.

"Yes, I have."

"What night was that, sir?"

"Three nights ago. Wednesday. We met at the Swissôtel."

"And your name, sir?"

"Paul." That was the name he used for prostitutes and phone-sex lines and Internet chat rooms. He couldn't even remember when he'd started using it.

There was a short pause. "Yes, Mr. Paul. Fonia is on call tonight."

"What does that mean?"

"It means she can see you for her usual rate plus half."

"Fine."

"Where would you like her to meet you tonight, Mr. Paul?"

"Mother's. On Rush Street. At the bar."

"She can be there in an hour."

"Perfect."

Sam turned down the ramp onto the Edens Expressway and leaned on the accelerator. It was a clear night and the concentration of fluorescent city lights made an artificial glowing dome in the distance. His skin was hot and his heart was throbbing and he could feel the pulse in the muscles of his neck without even putting a finger to it. The ache that sometimes came to his head spread in a high arc over his right ear. He opened the glove compartment at sixty-five miles per hour and fished out a bottle of pills, forcing two down his dry throat, but they wouldn't make the ache go away or stop the artery to his brain from flexing. The only thing that could help would be the sight of a woman's face contorted in pain beneath him and then, just before she cried out, the sight of that pain transformed into pleasure, lips twisted in fear becoming round, a wince turning into a wicked grin, narrow eyes becoming wide with understanding. *Yes, my God, yes!*

He was about to drop a thousand dollars on a hooker and he wouldn't even enjoy it. Not really. But he needed the release. The violent release.

Later that night, around the time Sam could feel the ache in his head subsiding, when Justin could no longer hear his mother sobbing in her bedroom down the hall, Justin slipped from the sheets again and opened his closet door. There was a cheap mirror mounted on the inside, and when his mother dressed him in nice clothes, she liked to stand behind him and look at him in it, as if she could see more of him in the reflection than she could by inspecting him directly. Justin turned to his left and in the glow of the reading lamp from his nightstand, tried to make out the birthmark on his hip, the one he rarely gave a thought to, and he wondered if there were many other boys or men who had it also, or if somehow he and the man from downstairs, the man who had tried to hurt his mother, were just special.

— 47 —

Fifteen years of this shit. Like an aging rocker, Mickey had been on the road for fifteen years, and he was tired. His hair was mostly gone and what remained made a wispy horseshoe around the back of his head. His face and hands were weathered like a hobo's, and he had ailments in his back and feet and at least three expanding blemishes on his skin that should probably be checked by a doctor but wouldn't be. He'd die when God called him in from the field. If Mickey the Gerund needed a doctor to save his life, the irony and humiliation would be worse than death, and the Hands of God didn't provide insurance, besides.

It hadn't been a life without satisfaction. He had many successes. As measured on Harold Devereaux's Web site, there were some fifty-seven cloning professionals killed and another sixty or so retired, and better than eighty-five percent of them belonged in Mickey's column. There was no serious legal threat to cloning these days (if anything, Mickey's work had earned sympathy for the other side in a *we can't let the terrorists win* sort of way) but the *business* of cloning was under siege. Fewer students were taking up the specialty in medical school. Despite advances in technology, requests for cloned children were down fifteen percent from a decade ago. The Hands of God were slowly winning a war of attrition.

After three kills in six weeks (bullet in Detroit, bombing in Minneapolis, auto "accident" in Des Moines), Mickey agreed with Phillip and the others that he should cool it for a couple of months. The FBI hadn't stopped looking for Byron Bonavita, although some in the bureau suggested it would be less embarrassing to speculate publicly about the legendary fugitive's death than it would be to admit they might never catch him. The feds now claimed several different groups were active in committing anti-cloning terror. This was a generally positive development for the cause, as it made violent opposition seem widespread and it still meant they weren't looking specifically for Mickey. It did mean he had to be more careful, however. The Hands of God were under close scrutiny back in Ohio, and they didn't want to do anything that might disabuse the feds of their bad assumptions.

That didn't mean Mickey had to stop operations altogether. He was free to conduct nonlethal maneuvers, although if Phil and the others suspected the risks Mickey assumed in the process, surely they'd have told him to knock it off.

Mickey slept three nights in the rusting Cutlass in a rest stop on I-35 outside Austin. During the day he'd go into town and scope out the streets around Neil Armstrong High School. It was busy, with lots of old trees and routes of escape. He followed the kids at lunchtime, with his eyes after one in particular. On the second day he came across an electric bike outside a comic book store and in a matter of seconds had it hotwired. That night he slept across the front seat with a charger running from his car battery to the bike, which he'd jammed across the back bench.

By day four he'd discovered his subject's routine. Around three o'clock Mickey checked into a motel that offered "nap rates" and took a shower. He changed into clean clothes, sat at the tiny particleboard desk, and pulled a blank sheet of graph paper from his bag. He unfolded a second piece of paper, this one old and brittle. It was the illustration he'd drawn the first time he'd tried this particular tactic. That operation had gone awry and he wasn't able to give the drawing to his target, but he liked the idea of it so much that he'd kept it all these years and copied it whenever he needed a fresh one. The graph paper allowed him to divide the paper into quadrants to get the drawing just right. He also thought drawing on graph paper added a touch of meticulous insanity that ratcheted up the fear factor a couple of notches. He dug out a black pen and a red pen and started to work.

He sketched a heart (a medically correct heart) with a snake coiled around it and a pair of hands, one pointing skyward. He drew a sword surrounded by flames. He made an elaborate calligraphic monogram—HoG—and colored it red and black. He listed the names of six recently dead doctors (updated many times over since the original drawing) and crossed their names out with a red pen. Beneath them he wrote the name Oliver Bel Geddes but didn't cross it out. In careful letters, he printed a verse from Genesis, one of many parts of the Bible he had memorized:

"SEE! THE MAN HAS BECOME LIKE ONE OF US, KNOWING WHAT IS GOOD AND WHAT IS BAD! THEREFORE, HE MUST NOT BE ALLOWED TO PUT OUT HIS HAND TO TAKE FRUIT FROM THE TREE OF LIFE, AND THUS EAT OF IT AND LIVE FOREVER."

All the words were written in black ink except for HE MUST NOT BE ALLOWED TO . . . LIVE, which he wrote in red. When he was done and the ink was dry, he folded the paper into quarters, slipped it into his back pocket opposite his wallet, and returned the original to his bag.

Mickey checked out of the Pegasus Motor Lodge around five-thirty and drove to a residential street he had scouted earlier. The houses were large and irregularly kept. Many of the lawns were overgrown and the trash cans filled with beer empties. Mickey assumed the renters here were mostly students from UT. He parked the car and unloaded the stolen bike from the backseat. As he rode he started to feel the rush, the anticipation of close contact.

Mickey took his time, careful to obey traffic laws, making a full stop at intersections. He hated people on bikes, especially kids, who thought they could drive on the wrong side of the road or blow through stop signs, expecting licensed drivers in cars and trucks to look out for *them*. It was still summer and still muggy, but a light breeze cooled his aging skin a bit, especially when he was in motion at twenty-five miles per hour, and when he arrived at the grocery store he dismounted and turned the bike around. He didn't know the area well and wanted to make sure he didn't become so lost in the getaway that he'd have to backtrack past the grocery after the cops arrived. If there were any cops at all, of course. One could never tell just how a target might react.

He entered the grocery, which belonged to a chain, although not one of the Texas-sized conglomerates with the travel agency and the copy center and the bank. At the registers, he turned into a small deli with four booths and a tiny pizza oven and a machine that made milk shakes. Four people stood in line ahead of him, and he stared indifferently at the menu board while he waited. When it was his turn he made sure not to put his hand flat against the stainless steel counter (not that they had his fingerprints in their database, or that fingerprints were even used much to ID people anymore, what with DNA being so much more reliable, but it didn't serve any purpose to be leaving the ghost of his palm behind everywhere he went) and he ordered a turkey club sandwich, no cheese, and stood in another line by the register while they built layers of mayonnaise and sliced meat and lettuce and bacon on a slice of white bread.

His sandwich arrived at the cashier at the same time he did. A boy around seventeen asked him what he'd ordered and Mickey described the sandwich to him and produced a ten-dollar bill. The boy counted out his change, and when he handed it over, Mickey cupped the kid's fingers in his hand, making sure that he felt the scales of Mickey's raw, chapped skin.

"Are you Christopher Bel Geddes?" Mickey asked the boy casually. He knew the answer. He only wanted to get the kid's attention. Most of the time when you talk to them, teenagers aren't listening to you.

"Yeah?" The kid looked up.

Mickey leaned in and spoke in a low voice. The kid leaned forward as well until his lobe was near enough to Mickey's mouth that Mickey could have bitten it with an attacking lunge. "Tell your father that he might be innocent in the eyes of the law," Mickey said, his breath hot in the boy's ear as he shoved the folded drawing roughly into his apron pocket, "but he still has to answer to the Hands of God." He said this last bit in something like a Southern accent—*Haints of Gwad*—partially as a nod to Byron Bonavita and partially because, when he practiced it, he liked the menacing way it sounded to his own ear. He called that voice "the Sinister Minister." It reminded him of De Niro in the remake of *Cape Fear*.

Christopher Bel Geddes was still bent over the counter when Mickey grabbed his sandwich and spun toward the door. He walked with his head down out into the grocery store, behind the row of fifteen registers, which counted off in backlit numbers above the cashiers' heads. He walked in the direction of the double sets of automatic doors, which did their best to lock the cool air inside.

"Sir?" a voice asked. Mickey didn't look up.

"Sir?" the voice said again. It was following behind him. "Can I see your receipt, sir?"

Mickey stopped. He didn't even know if he had a receipt. Christ, they weren't going to pinch him for shoplifting. Talk about an undignified end. He wished he had left the sandwich on the counter. Taking it was just cocky. He turned around. The security guard was small and his tie was too short and his uniform pinched the fat around his middle. "Um, I paid for it," Mickey stammered. "They put it in this paper bag."

"They should have given you a receipt." The guard turned as if he wanted to lead Mickey back to the deli. Christopher Bel Geddes appeared from behind a stack of Coca-Cola, his leather-soled shoes sliding on the worn linoleum floor. From a hundred feet or so, his eyes brought Mickey and the guard into focus.

"Hey!" the kid yelled.

Mickey ran, his right shoulder checking the second set of sliding doors when they wouldn't open fast enough. The security guard yelled after him. He saw his bike. No, screw the bike. He'd never get it started in time. He ran as fast he could across the parking lot and back down the road by which he'd come. Already he was winded. He had no chance of outrunning a seventeen-year-old kid. A cloud of shouting gained on him from behind.

He turned a corner and leapt awkwardly over a low chain-link fence, sprinting through someone's yard. He climbed the fence on the other side and found a gulley that separated backyards between rows of homes along parallel streets and ran down the middle of it, his feet heavy against the mud and the weeds. This was too dangerous. They might see him from the side street.

Mickey jumped another fence, this one in the middle of a block, and ducked behind a yellow plastic playhouse to rest. He didn't have a gun or even a knife with him. He had change in his pocket and, what else, the damn sandwich. He still had the damn paper bag in his hand.

"Hi," a little girl's voice yelled in his right ear. Mickey jumped, but he was too tired to run. There was a kid in the playhouse, maybe six years old. Her black hair was thick, and her new, grown-up teeth were too big for her pea-shaped head. She was leaning out the window and her head was beside his and she was giggling. "I'm Talia. I'm an eye doctor," she told him, and with a pudgy finger she pushed the lower lid down and away from his right eye and leaned in until her irises were this close to his. Mickey didn't swat the girl's hand away, didn't do anything to make her shout or cry or yell.

"Are your parents home?" Mickey asked. Then he added, "Dr. Talia."

The girl nodded, still pinching the bag of skin under his eye. Of course her parents are home, Mickey thought. Parents don't just leave the house when there's a six-year-old in the yard. Good parents, anyway. "What about them?"

Mickey asked. He pointed to a big white house with aluminum siding next door.

Dr. Talia shook her head. "They don't have babies. Mommy says babies would crank their lightstyle."

"Great. Thanks." He waved good-bye and duckwalked into the neighbor's yard as Talia called good-bye after him. She ran into her own house, no doubt to tell her mother about her new grown-up friend. Mickey made his way around the side of the garage and pushed a window screen in. They had a second car, thank God, an old Audi. He lifted himself up and squeezed through, landing on an empty rubber trash can. Using his own keys to expose the wires, he had the Audi started in less than two minutes. The remote for the garage door was on the passenger-side eyeshade. He backed out slowly.

Down the street and getting closer, he could see a handful of men darting in and out between homes. There were no cops yet, just an assortment of teens and old baldies in deli aprons. He caught a glimpse of the fat security guard catching up to the pack at last, still thinking they were chasing a shoplifter, no doubt. He was talking into a radio. Mickey reached for the clicker and closed the garage behind him as he pulled into the street, just like any home owner taking the Audi to meet his wife for dinner. Young Chris Bel Geddes and the rest of the deli crew hardly gave him a thought as he drove away.

That was a rush, Mickey thought to himself. When they go bad like that, it's always a rush.

— 48 —

Graham Mendelsohn didn't usually make house calls to his clients, but he and Davis had a scheduled round at the Northwood Country Club at one, and Graham phoned him at New Tech to say he'd be coming in a little early to talk business. Davis didn't like the sound of that.

Tall and thin and about Davis's age, Graham wore pressed khakis and a pink Polo, which put Davis at ease when he saw the attorney turn the corner into his office. A man bearing grim news wouldn't deliver it in a ridiculous shirt like that. Davis tried to put him off message before Graham could turn the mood sour.

"Did you hear they almost nabbed him?" Davis asked.

Graham stopped rehearsing the announcement he was about to make and froze, resting his briefcase on an extra chair by the door. "No. Who?"

"Byron Bonavita," Davis said. "He threatened Oliver Bel Geddes's boy down in Austin and the kid chased him for a few blocks. Bastard got away, though."

Graham frowned. "Balls. They get a description? DNA? Anything?"

Davis said, "No. A little girl got a good look at him up close, so I'm sure they'll be out searching for Tigger tomorrow. Anyway, I hope you brought something to cheer me up."

"Well, the good news is you won't have to testify," Graham said. "Ricky Weiss is taking a plea."

Davis grinned. "No shit?" He made a move for his clubs. This would be the first truly relaxing round he had played in a year.

"I told you he'd fold eventually. Between his own wife and that Tweedy fellow, he was totally screwed."

"Graham, after that I don't *care* what the bad news could be." Davis started to shut down his computer. They could celebrate with cigars on the first tee. "There *is* bad news, right?"

Graham nodded. "Martha Finn is pressing charges against you with the Lake County D.A. for stalking her son. I negotiated a voluntary surrender at noon tomorrow. They won't announce it ahead of time. There won't be a perp walk. That should keep it off the television news, anyway. The daily papers will probably bury it in the eighth 'graph of the Weiss story."

The room around Davis tilted and shook like a cheap carnival ride. "Jesus Christ!"

Graham opened his briefcase and pulled out a stack of papers prepared just that morning by a paralegal. "Relax. Relax. We can look over the sentencing guidelines, the precedents. You'll make bail at the arraignment, we'll plead it to a misdemeanor, there'll be a small fine, community service. I don't expect the legal ramifications to be that bad."

"Not bad?" Davis shrieked. He stood and hustled across the room to shut the door. "What about my practice? My medical license?"

"I scheduled a conference call at one-thirty with a firm in D.C. that's more in tune with the medical ethics side. You'll have to cancel our tee time, I'm afraid."

"God. What a mess," Davis said, falling back into his chair.

"Don't worry. We'll clean it up. But I think you should start today by finally telling me the real reason you bought all those pictures of Justin Finn."

Davis shook his head. "Like I've told you many times, the last being at dinner Thursday, I can't tell you. It was an experiment. Beyond that . . ."

The attorney leaned back in the leather chair and under his shifting weight it made a sound like an old record scratching. "Is the boy yours?"

"Justin?" Davis nearly snickered. "No. He's not mine." He tried to determine how little he'd have to confess. "In fact, he's a clone."

A thin brow tented over Graham's left eye. "If that's out there, the daily papers just became more interested in this story, especially the tabs. What's special about him?"

"Nothing. He's a healthy nine-year-old boy, conceived like dozens of others in this clinic."

"But you don't take the same interest in all your cloned children."

"None of the other children I've cloned live a mile and a half from my door. Graham, you were sitting in the room when I answered all of this in my deposition for the Weiss trial."

"She didn't ask that many questions, frankly, and we were able to dodge most of the tough ones due to confidentiality laws. It's a good thing you were never cross-examined. When you plea this out, and that's my recommendation since you've already expressed a reluctance to testify about this matter publicly, you'll have to stand before the judge and elocute. Say exactly what you did. I'd rather not hear the whole story for the first time at your sentencing."

"All right," Davis said. He had, after all, considered that it might come to this someday. "I had a theory I was trying to prove through Justin. Or I have one."

"What theory is that?"

"That cloned children are even more like contemporaneous twins than we've imagined. That they share personality traits, interests, abilities, even when raised in a radically different environment. I was hoping to put together a longitudinal study following Justin's development through childhood and compare it to the development of his cell donor."

"Aren't there other doctors, psychologists, doing the same thing?"

"Lots."

"All with the parents' permission, though."

"That's why they're flawed. If Martha Finn knew what I was doing, she'd start to get curious about Justin's donor. She'd ask a lot of questions. More importantly, it might affect the way she raised Justin."

Footsteps thumped in the hall outside and Graham worried for a moment that they were talking too loudly. "Well, I have three things to say about that. First, you've made her very angry. Second, I don't think you can hide behind scientific method with a story about half-assed secret research, and third, did you know that when the boy was three years old, Martha Finn and her now ex-husband hired a private investigator to track down Justin's cell donor?"

Davis brought a hand to his face. He hadn't shaved today and he'd noticed earlier, in the washroom, that more of his whiskers were coming in gray. He kneaded the woolly hairs with his fingers. "I didn't," he said, now fearing his attorney knew more than he had allowed. "What did they find out?"

Graham opened his briefcase again and removed a folder with a summary of discovery from the Weiss case. He flipped through it to a highlighted section. "Eric Lundquist. Syracuse, New York."

"There you go," Davis said. "Eric Lundquist. I wish I had known they knew about him. I'd have canceled the study. It would have saved me a lot of sneaking around."

"If it had kept you from sneaking around the Finn boy, it would have saved you more than that," Graham said.

"I suppose that's true."

"I just want you to know that I can't help you suborn perjury," Graham said.

"Then I won't ask you to," Davis said. "But you think I should plea it out?"

"If this is as good as your story gets? Yes."

"Dammit," Davis said. "Okay. But I want to make it a condition of the agreement that they won't pursue Joan or anyone else here at the clinic. Joan was helping me with the other thing, in Brixton, helping me look for AK's killer, but she had nothing to do with Justin. This is all on me."

"We'll ask," Graham said. "If they believe you're being honest with them, it shouldn't be a problem."

"Do you believe I'm being honest with *you*?" Davis asked.

"I'm your lawyer," Graham said. "Believing you is the best I can do."

— 49 —

Unprotected from the assault of cold rain that seemed to materialize from nothing in the yellow domes of streetlights above his head, Detective Teddy Ambrose walked around the blue apartment dumpster and felt his insides twist: everything above the equator of his navel clockwise, everything below it in the opposite direction.

He tried to remember what his life had been like yesterday, just hours ago, before this shift began. His wife was pregnant with their second, but they hadn't told anyone; the two of them glowed from their shared happy secret. If he could finagle a way around the department's residency requirements, they were thinking about renting out the two-flat he'd inherited from his parents and moving to a bungalow in the suburbs. In the meantime, he and another cop, a guy he'd been through academy with, were ready with the down payment on a boat in Belmont Harbor.

Yesterday, as he'd driven up Grand Avenue toward Area Five headquarters, through the wet curtains of an all-day storm, he'd thought of the dozen closed murders he had credited to his name. He had so few open cases he had been likely to draw the next call. That was fine with him. *Bring it on.* His luck had been amazing of late: the pregnant teen who turned in her ex for clubbing his brother with an anchor and dumping his body in the lake; the hit-and-run who'd left just about the most costly paint flecks in the history of painted Porsches on the victim's artificial leg; the carpenter who abandoned a screwdriver engraved with his own initials in the eye socket of his wife's lover. The night before at Dante's Tavern, Ambrose had boasted to his fellow cops that there was a point at which luck had to be considered destiny, and the number of cases Ambrose and his partner, Ian Cook, had sent to the D.A. in the last six months was surely on the verge of qualifying.

"You'll jinx us." Ian laughed.

The phone rang at 1:47 this morning with word of a female body discovered under a dumpster in a North Avenue alley. And when the evidence technician met their car with an umbrella and recounted the meager evidence at the scene, his partner spat angrily into a garbage can.

"You jinxed us, Brosie. I told ya you'd jinx us."

Ambrose knelt beside the dumpster and turned his head. The victim's hand was brown and stiff and cupped as if it were a wax demonstration for the proper fingering of a two-seam fastball. The hand was at the end of a brown arm and the arm disappeared behind the wheeled coaster of the dumpster. Still in a crouch, Ambrose took two sliding steps away and flattened his body, stomach down, against the wet concrete, letting the beam of his flashlight follow his panning eyes. The brown arm was connected to a shoulder, and the shoulder was connected to a torso, and at the top of it all was a head. A blue-and-tan dress had been torn almost from her body. There was something unnatural about the pose.

The concrete was raised in the middle of the alley, and the whole area sloped slightly to the east. A river of rainwater washed around the body, carrying away blood and hair and transferred skin cells and depositing them in a drain twenty yards on, along with Ambrose's near-perfect clearance record.

"A fucking whodunit." Ian scowled as his partner pushed himself to his feet and brushed pebbles from his dark blue slicker. "An honest-to-Jesus whodunit."

"We don't know that, man," Ambrose said in his least assuring tone. They would find out who this girl was and if she had a husband or a boyfriend. If she was messed up with drugs. They would talk to her friends. Find out where she'd last been seen. But even if those queries presented them with a good suspect, say an asshole boyfriend with a weak alibi and a history of threatening behavior, the assistant state's attorney wouldn't be happy about the lack of physical evidence. Crime scene technicians had become expert at collecting even the smallest traces of DNA, and juries had become accustomed to seeing a genetic comparison between the perpetrator and the accused. Defense attorneys routinely cited a lack of DNA evidence as constituting reasonable doubt all by itself. Frequently juries agreed. The increasingly sophisticated science of DNA made the dumb criminals easier to catch and the smart ones (or the lucky ones) that much harder.

Reading his own twisted guts, Ambrose worried this case might be on his desk for a long, long time.

— 50 —

Martha never pressed charges against Sam Coyne for attacking her. The only person with whom she discussed the incident in detail was a therapist she began seeing a month or so after. The therapist helped her some, and she always had felt that the therapy mandated by cloning regulations had helped Justin, and so, as she entered her mid-thirties, she began to think even her father could have benefited from a few sessions with an understanding professional. She directed her anger at Davis Moore instead, and tried to forget that the idea of suing him had originated with Coyne. She found a different lawyer to help her through it, of course.

By now, Justin was devouring the works of great philosophers in the least turgid English translations. His impatience in class had brought Martha to the school for a dozen or more teacher conferences, and his irritability (coupled with his obvious intelligence) eventually pushed his third-grade teacher into a conspiracy with the school's fourth-grade teachers, and the result was a joint recommendation that Justin skip ahead.

He didn't attract more friends in the fifth grade, of course. The older kids thought him an even bigger geek than the third-graders had, but none of this seemed to bother Justin. He received excellent grades in every class and even excelled in gym when the physical skills being rehearsed weren't the team kind. He proved outstanding in gymnastics and he was faster than all but three or four of the older boys, which earned him a certain amount of respect. He was a bit smaller than most of his new classmates, but he was growing at an advanced rate and didn't appear so out of place in the class pictures. Throughout the first semester of the fifth-grade experiment, Martha was certain she'd made the right decision.

Justin stepped off the bus every afternoon dragging a bag heavy with books, but his broadening back was able to manage the burden. When Martha unzipped it one evening looking for evidence to lodge a complaint over the mountain of homework being assigned, she discovered only a few slim textbooks. The rest were books Justin was reading on his own: not philosophy, to her surprise, but true crime.

In his room, under his bed, she found more books on Bundy and Berkowitz, Starkweather and Speck. Even Charles Ng, whose name, unappealingly, caused Martha to think of her mother. Shaken, she gathered them in her arms, a dozen or so volumes, and brought them to the kitchen table.

"Where did you get these?" she asked.

Justin seemed surprised at the accusing tone. "A boy in my class. James. I'm only borrowing them." He said this as if he feared theft were her only concern. "His parents read them."

"Justin," Martha said, choosing words with care, not wanting to sound worried or judgmental, "why do you want to read these horrible books?"

Justin blinked a few times and touched her on the arm with a grown-up's confidence. "The Wicker Man," he said. "I want to keep us safe from the Wicker Man."

Of course, Martha thought, expelling a relieved laugh. She leaned forward and hugged him. The Wicker Man was all over the news, and much of downtown was living in fear of him—dating in groups, loading up on pepper spray, even staying home at night. He had killed six people so far in the Wicker Park neighborhood on Chicago's Near West Side, five women and one man. The police assumed there were more victims as well, better hidden, perhaps elsewhere in the city. The women had been sexually assaulted and stabbed. The man's throat had been cut. They found fiber evidence, bloody shoeprints, but they had no good witnesses, no DNA, no links between victims, no evidence that could lead to a suspect. It horrified Martha to think her son had been getting such gory details from the news, but it was almost unavoidable. If the Wicker Man was the biggest local news story of the fall, then the second-biggest story was the degree to which talk of the Wicker Man had saturated the Chicago media.

"Justin, sweetie, the Wicker Man isn't going to hurt us. He lives far away from here."

Justin didn't speak but implied with a disappointed expression, a flat smile, and puffy eyes that he didn't believe her. That broke Martha's heart.

"Can I go up to my room and play Shadow World?" Justin asked. Shadow World was a computer game her sister had bought Justin for Christmas. It was generally thought to be for grown-ups, but lots of kids played it too, and Martha had activated all of the strict parental controls.

"Sure, honey," she said. As he padded toward the stairs, she tried to read his state of mind. The worst thing about Justin was that he soaked everything in, but the best thing about him was the way he bounced back. It wasn't that Justin couldn't handle the truth as much as that Martha couldn't handle him knowing. She would talk with him about the Wicker Man, or Ted Bundy, or even goddamn Charles Ng, but she knew she would never be able to talk with Justin about what happened that night between her and Sam Coyne.

— 51 —

There are thousands of views of Lake Michigan from the city, but none quite like that from Abbott's, the pricey glass-enclosed two-story restaurant a hundred yards out on Navy Pier. From the right table at Abbott's you felt surrounded by water, protected by it. Davis had hoped for, asked for, and received such a table, and was so comforted by the environs he had to be cajoled by the waiter into finally opening his menu.

The dress Joan wore was black—her little black one, he presumed—and she was as stunning in it as it was stunning on her. It was difficult to tell, in fact, whether she or the dress benefited more from the pairing. Davis had seen her in dresses before, at holiday parties and professional functions, and once by coincidence at the symphony, a night Jackie had been unnecessarily rude to Joan and her date, leaving Davis alone with them at intermission, stammering to cover his jealousy and embarrassment. For all he knew this might have been the same dress she wore that evening, but tonight she wore it specifically for him, specifically to please him, and he was suddenly ashamed of his brown suit, not because it wasn't flattering, but because he had given so little thought to putting it on.

"Frankly, I'm surprised you wanted to be with me tonight," she said after the waiter had refilled their glasses with pricey sparkling water and then drifted out of earshot.

"Who else?" he asked, almost suavely.

"On the night before your sentencing? I don't know," she said. "I'm just surprised." Her smile was self-conscious.

"I don't have many friends anymore, to be honest." Davis realized almost immediately how unseductive that sounded, and also how true it was. "I've seen enough of Graham the last few months. My next-closest friend is Walter Hirschberg, I suppose, and I'm not sure this would be the most comfortable evening to spend with an ethicist."

"Well, even if I was at the top of a short list, thank you."

"Not at all."

"And not just for dinner."

Davis was foolishly optimistic about her intentions.

"Thank you for keeping me out of it," she said, reaching over and brushing his hand. "They might have been easier on you if you offered them something. Given me up. Many people would have, to save themselves."

"I'm hardly worth saving," Davis said. "Besides, you had nothing to do with it. If anything, I used you. They should tack time *onto* my sentence for that, not shave it off."

Joan retracted her hand and placed it over the pearls at her neck. "I thought you said you wouldn't have to go to prison."

"Graham doesn't think so, but there's always a chance. It's actually mandatory in the guidelines, but he thinks they'll suspend it."

"And then?"

He let a sip of Shiraz trickle down the back of his throat. "Put it behind me."

"Really?" she asked. "Put it all behind you?" She had her hair up for the night, but it refused to be contained. Long, wavy tendrils hung down past the corners of her brown eyes to her cheeks.

"It's been ten years since I did it. A fifth of my life. The *worst* fifth of my life. I made a lot of other people miserable or worse. Including you. For all I know, the guy who killed Anna Kat is dead or rotting in jail by now, anyway. Odds are, he is. It's time for me to stop caring and see that the next fifth of my life is better. I don't have many fifths left."

"Don't be ashamed of what you tried to do," Joan said. "It was stupid." She looked at him honestly. "But you did what you did because you loved Anna Kat. And what happened to Jackie wasn't your fault."

"Yes. It was."

"No. God, Davis. I don't want to speak ill of her, but she was deeply troubled." A pair of waiters arrived with their plates and Davis and Joan gazed at each other in silence until they were alone again and she was able to finish the thought. "Did you know Jackie slashed the tires on my car?"

"No! When?"

"Maybe four months before she passed away. It was parked in the driveway of my condo. On a Tuesday night. I found it the next morning."

"How do you know it was her?"

"She didn't try to hide it. She came to my house the next day and warned me to stay away from you. I told her there was nothing going on, which was a lie, I guess, but nothing *sexual* was going on."

"Why didn't you call the police?"

"Oh, *really*, Davis. Call the cops on your wife?"

"You should have told me . . ."

She puffed her lips. "That would have been worse."

"I don't believe it."

Joan allowed herself a breather for a few bites of pumpkin ravioli. "So, was there something going on?"

Davis squinted. "What? With you and me?"

"With you and anyone. I mean, the woman was suspicious about *something.* She might have been unbalanced, but I don't think it came from nowhere."

The restaurant was full now, and the late setting sun reflected against the glass of downtown in an orange glow. "Yeah, well, *nowhere* was kind of a theme with Jackie."

Joan whispered, "Even I wondered about you once. That day at the Finns' house." She took a sip of Chardonnay and said, almost inaudibly, "Maybe I was just jealous, too."

"I remember," Davis said. "But no. I never cheated on Jackie."

"See? You always had that perspective. Take care of the people closest to you. At all costs."

"I wanted to once," he told her.

"Cheat? Really?" she said, mouth full, somehow unsuspecting. "When?"

"Brixton," he said.

She nodded, slowly, sincerely. He didn't feel bad for having said it.

After dinner, they walked to the end of the pier to enjoy the blackness over the lake. To their left was Festival Hall, part of the original pier built in 1916. He and Jackie had been married there, in the Grand Ballroom, and it suddenly struck Davis as inappropriate that he should be here with Joan. Some subconscious gremlin had caused him to make reservations at Abbott's, where he and Jackie had celebrated a handful of their early anniversaries (although the restaurant had another name then). It was impossible that this wouldn't have occurred to him before now, impossible that he couldn't have seen how callous it was to be here with Joan on what amounted to, if he was being honest with himself, their first date—his first date with the woman Jackie had accused of threatening their marriage. And although Jackie might have been half crazy, about that she was at least half right.

For that reason, demonstrating what he recognized as too-little-too-late respect for the memory of his wife, Davis didn't take Joan's hand as they walked, and if she had expected him to, she didn't show it. Joan, her fingers holding a light black sweater over her bare shoulders, seemed content, commenting on the wonderful smells of the shore and the pleasant breeze and the number of children about at so late an hour.

At the tip of the pier stood a crowd of maybe thirty people, staring off into the darkness. In the back a young man in shorts hopped on his toes for a better view, but all Davis could see from his six feet three inches was a couple of midsized boats—not pleasure craft, but not the massive party-and-tour yachts that docked here in the summer, either—about seventy-five yards out. They were working boats, with electronic gear and a radio dish and men in uniform scurrying on deck and men in diving gear going over the side.

"What happened?" Davis posed the question to the back of the crowd, offering it to anyone who thought they knew the answer.

"They found another girl," somebody said without turning around. "Another dead girl."

Part Two

Justin at Fourteen

— 52 —

Davis pushed the remains of an overcooked chicken back and forth across the heavy white Prince Hotel Palm Springs catering plate. He knew he was being watched, and the scrutiny had poisoned his appetite. Every one of the three hundred or so doctors and researchers and ethicists in this room probably brought with them to this conference an opinion, rumor, or assumption about Davis Moore. He still wasn't comfortable with the kind of celebrity he had become.

His difficulties with the Lake County state's attorney had resolved themselves much as Graham had promised. Davis pled to a misdemeanor and paid an affordable fine, was sentenced to seven days in jail, suspended, and worked at a free clinic on Chicago's West Side every Tuesday for six months. Martha Finn followed up with a civil suit, which Graham settled out of court for less than $75,000. Following his community service, the Congressional Board of Oversight and the AMA suspended his license for another four months, a slap on the wrist considering the full menu of their options.

When the suspension was up, however, he didn't return to the clinic. The Chicago dailies lost interest in him after Ricky Weiss was sentenced, but the stalking charges against him became front-page news in the suburban papers. That brought him notoriety, and not just the shaming kind he expected. People sympathized with him. He had lost his daughter and his wife, and for the love of God he'd been shot himself by a religious zealot, and maybe he *had* crossed some ethical lines with his mysterious "study" of Justin, but no one suggested he'd been a danger to the boy, no one except for Martha Finn in her restraining order (which remained in place until Justin was eighteen).

In place of his practice, Davis accepted generous fees to speak at seminars and dinners and fund-raisers. He became a regular pundit on the Sunday television roundtables as the violence at fertility clinics became more intense and the ethics of cloning were debated with increased frequency on the front pages of newsweeklies. At the age of fifty-six and with no patients of his own, Dr. Davis Moore had become cloning's most distinguished spokesperson.

Of course, he could never admit publicly the real reasons he quit his practice. For one, he was exhausted, weary of the violence that had now taken four of his close friends in the profession, and too tired to cope with new clinic security—the armed guards, the gated parking garage, the metal detectors, the name badges, the bomb-sniffing dogs, the drills, the threats, the bimonthly evacuations and the subsequent "all clear's." Even here at the conference uniformed guards stood by the exits, making and remaking every attendee, memorizing faces, and quantifying risk.

Davis also felt guilty. Guilt over the bodies of Anna Kat and Jackie and even Phil Canella, whom he never even met. Guilt over the trauma he'd caused the Finn family. Guilt over Justin, a boy who never should have been, and guilt over Eric Lundquist's discarded DNA, the blueprint of a boy who should have been but never was.

The conference was sponsored by the California Association of Libertarian Scientists. Traditionally, they lobbied Congress on any issue related to "researcher rights," but over the past year, as the anti-cloners in Washington gained support (up to forty-three percent in some polls), CALS had become almost exclusively a cloning advocacy group.

"Our guest tonight has made many sacrifices in the name of science," began the introduction from a Berkeley-educated medical doctor named Poonwalla. "He has been persecuted, prosecuted, and has even taken a bullet for the causes all of us in this room hold dear. But you can't keep a good man down, especially a good man who has right-thinking, free people like you on his side. Ladies and gentleman, from Chicago, Dr. Davis Moore."

Davis stood up and smiled and shook hands with Dr. Poonwalla. As he took a breath and began, Davis thought of three true statements: This speech wasn't especially good. He was a hypocrite for giving it. This audience would love it.

"There is a computer game, maybe some of your kids play it. Actually, about forty percent of the adults in this room play it every week, if the adults in this room are typical and the statistics I read in the paper are worth a damn. Worldwide, they say five thousand new players sign up every day. The game is called Shadow World."

A murmur of recognition pulsed from table to table. Everyone had heard of Shadow World. It was the most popular multiplayer game in America. At several tables, husbands elbowed wives and wives elbowed husbands as if to say, *He's talking about you, hon.* Couples who played the game together, and there were many, squeezed hands.

"I've never played Shadow World myself, and I don't have any children"—Davis hadn't meant this as an oblique reference to Anna Kat, but guests who were familiar with every part of his biography became suddenly silent, as if any noise they made would be interpreted by the speaker as pity—"but in its ads the makers ridicule other online games, in which the players take on fictional personas and go on magical adventures in make-believe lands. The Shadow World is the exact world we live in, every building, park, bus stop, and store in the thirty-five hundred cities around the world—and counting—that the TyroSoft programmers have drawn in the game to date. Within any city, you can walk or drive down most any street or alley, enter any building if the door's open or you have a key. You can even travel from city to city through working airports and train stations and a skeletal interstate system. Every player begins the game with a character representing himself. You start with your real-world job, your real-world family, your real-world education. But in Shadow World, the player can do all the things they are afraid to do in real life. You can choose new destinies or take outrageous chances. You can ask models out on dates or tell off your boss. The price of failure is nothing worse than the forced start of a new game, beginning again as the real you, with another shot at deciding what choices will make you happy.

"I'm told different players use the game in different ways. Many people try to live their dreams in the game, hoping to become actors or musicians or famous writers. Some use it to practice—a dry run at real life, if you will—working out scenarios to determine what might happen if they asked for a raise or cheated on a spouse. Many people, oddly, mirror their real life in the virtual world down to every detail, going to work in the morning, ordering lunch from the same places, coaching their kids in Little League. In the gaming vocabulary, these individuals are called 'True-to-Lifers,' and they apparently enjoy watching their lives play out realistically on-screen as if it were an animated documentary elevating their mundane lives to something like art.

"Now, when Shadow World was introduced, many people thought it could provide a road map to Utopia here on earth. Through virtual experimentation, we would discover that life truly does offer limitless choices. With Shadow World as a guide, mankind would discover its real potential. We would invent synthetic fuels, find cures for terminal diseases, happen upon new and better systems of governance and diplomacy.

"As you know, that hasn't happened. Or it hasn't yet. Six years after its creation, life in Shadow World has become almost an exact copy of life in the real world. The crime rate is about the same. Disease spreads with the same efficiency. Wars between nations occur with the same frequency. Government corruption and corporate malfeasance turn out to be as seductive in Shadow World as they are in this one.

"Why do you think that is? Sociologists who study this sort of thing, which is nice work if you can get it"—laughter—"suggest several possibilities. First of all, the so-called True-to-Lifers make up more than a quarter of the gaming public. In fact, sociologists say these people, replicating their actual lives on the Internet, are critical to the stability of the game. Their presence ensures that Shadow World isn't populated entirely by aspiring movie stars and rock singers." Laughter. "In the game, True-to-Lifers aren't always taking outrageous risks, failing, and starting over. Their lives go on and on, running the insurance businesses and the bakeries and the movie theaters. They are the invisible matter that makes Shadow World so real. So livable. So popular. And that's the irony. The fantasy world is seductive because it is so very much like our own.

"I have a good friend named Walter Hirschberg, who's a respected professor at the University of Chicago, and he has another theory: perhaps Utopias can't exist because in a reasonably free society, happiness is a constant." Davis paused here at the introduction of an abstract concept. "Of course, it goes without saying that misery would be a constant, too, and some people will be happier than others. But when you add up our talents, our aspirations, our capabilities, our treachery, our selfishness, our generosity, our technology, our addictions, our hope, our anxiety, our love, our anger, you find that collectively we tend toward a certain level of happiness. That level can change slightly, in the short term, but it always works its way back to equilibrium.

"Now, what does any of this have to do with science or liberty? Walter suggests that when we are at our natural level of happiness, restrictions on liberty can only result in a net loss of that happiness." Applause. "Now, of course we need certain laws to preserve order"—ironic boos—"yes, yes, I know who the anarchists are among us"—laughter—"but laws that seek to restrict liberty because of fear, because of ignorance, because a wrong-headed idealist is trying to construct his own version of Utopia: these laws cause a ripple effect through society, one that affects us all for the worse. The Buckley–Rice Anti-Cloning Act is exactly that kind of unnecessary legislation." Enthusiastic applause. "And we might even have proof.

"One year ago, inside the game of Shadow World, the United States legislature *passed* the Buckley–Rice Anti-Cloning Act. The result, in the universe of the game, has been an *increase* in infant mortality, an *increase* in reports of clinical depression, an *increase* in violence committed by mothers suffering from postpartum depression, and an across-the-board increase in the suicide rate. Not much of one, just a few percent, but it didn't correspond, as such things usually do, to an increase in the real-world suicide rate. Can I tell you for certain this overall *decrease* in happiness is a direct result of Buckley–Rice? No, I'm not that smart. But I can tell you what Walter Hirschberg would say. I can tell you because I called Walter up and I asked him.

"First I must tell you that Walter, despite his friendship with me, is not a supporter of cloning. He and I have had that ethical debate many times over the years. But even Walter agrees that Buckley–Rice would be a horrible mistake. Laws are not equivalent to ethics. They do not effectively answer questions of whether we should or shouldn't do things. Laws address whether we *can* do things, and with respect to cloning, clearly the answer is yes. The mapping of the human genome and the successful, even routine, cloning of man is one of the great accomplishments of our lifetimes, and if the United States Congress tells us, all evidence to the contrary, that we *cannot* clone stem cells in order to prolong life, *cannot* use cloning to treat infertility and stop the spread of hereditary disease, *cannot* seek out every resource and tool at our disposal to reduce the suffering of our patients, they are not creating a better America, they are *increasing* American *misery.*"

The applause was kick-started by a chorus of supporting cheers. One of the middle tables stood first, the diners kicking chairs back from the table and straightening their legs in the space between. In a moment, most of the gathered were standing and the applause grew in celebration of the consensus. Davis smiled and let the cheers subside until he could finally hear chair legs rubbing against the thin carpet as the guests returned to their seats.

Davis continued: "This is not meant to end the discussion about cloning. Walter and I debate this issue every time we get together. He suggests that just because we *can* clone human beings doesn't mean we *should*. I tell him he's answered the wrong question. If we *can* do something—to increase health, to increase happiness—doesn't that mean we *must*?" Applause. "A couple comes into your office. They can't have children, or they're afraid to. They ask for your help and you have the ability to help them. How could it possibly be ethical to do otherwise?" Louder applause. "Walter says that what cloning professionals do is remarkable—and I agree, but not for the same reasons. He is amazed that we can take a cell, a fraction of a fingernail, and from that make a human being. I tell him nature has been doing that for years. *Conception* is still the bigger miracle to me. From two, one. It's the lower organisms that usually reproduce asexually, after all.

"We do not 'make people' as Walter suggests. What we do is give them moms and dads. That truly *is* a remarkable thing." Sustained and satisfied clapping.

"I agree with Walter on another matter, however. Our profession *must* have an ongoing and rigorous discussion concerning the ethics of *all* our practices.

One of the reasons I support the efforts of this organization"—Davis gestured to the CALS banner behind him—"is that a free society must make difficult ethical decisions, must weigh the consequences of its actions, must debate and justify the validity of its works. To live under an oppressive government is to live without ethical dilemmas. In Castro's Cuba, in Saddam's Iraq, in the North Korea of Kim Jong Il, ordinary people did not debate whether they should do this or should not do that, only whether they *could* do this or *could* do that.

"Utilitarians ask us to consider the *greatest good.* That's a valid philosophical approach, I suppose. The attorney general, along with the sponsors of Buckley–Rice, uses that rhetoric all the time. He claims the greatest good will be served by government regulation of scientific research, by the banning of all cloning procedures, by letting Congress set the agenda for scientific research in this country. But what about the *greatest evil?* The only thing the Luddites have against technology is their own fear of it. But if we stop, or even slow the pace of genetic research, thousands will die, tens of thousands will suffer, and billions—all the world's free people, in fact—will find themselves worse off for it."

Davis used eight true examples of current research to demonstrate his points, and he projected slides and videos on a giant screen behind him for illumination. He made sure to mention the work of a half-dozen people in attendance—Dr. Seebohm, Dr. Harmon, both Dr. Carters, Dr. Manet, Dr. Huang. CALS members grinned through it all, laughed three or four more times, and cheered him vigorously when he was through.

"Terrific!" Dr. Poonwalla said over his shoulder as guests lined up at the conclusion of the event to introduce themselves to Davis and express concurring opinions. "Just the thing to rally the troops!"

When the last well-wisher had made off for the coat check, Davis rode the elevator alongside a balding drunk wearing a name tag (not from the CALS conference, Davis ascertained). He leaned against the back wall of the cab and couldn't even spit out the number of the floor he wanted. Annoyed, Davis got off on fourteen and when the drunk tried to follow, he pushed him back on and lit buttons for random floors with a slap of his hand.

Davis turned several corners, following arrows on painted wall plaques until he found his room number, then dropped his key card through the vertical slot and leaned on the door. The room was silent and he guessed without looking that she would be wound into the armchair by the floor lamp, reading one of the three paperbacks she had packed for the thirty-six-hour trip. It was dark except for a dim light in the foyer, however, and when he stepped gently into the room he saw she was asleep. He detoured into the oversized bathroom, where he peeled away his charcoal suit and brushed his teeth and ran a comb of wet fingers through his silver hair.

"How was it?" Joan asked, making a mockery of his exaggerated attempts at stealth. He continued them anyway, easing weightlessly into the bed next to her, pulling the sheet to his neck without billowing the cool air underneath.

"Just another day preaching to the converted," he whispered.

"Mmm. That's good. The converted don't shoot at you, generally." Joan made a reference to his old wound at least once a day, but she never mentioned Jackie's death, according to the never-discussed rules of their partnership. They used to talk about Anna Kat all the time, but now her name was spoken less and less. Davis no longer felt he had to prove to Joan that he remembered his daughter.

Joan had left New Tech shortly after Davis, setting up her own practice at a clinic affiliated with Northwestern Hospital. As his legal troubles were confronted and dispatched, their relationship advanced as an inevitability, with each step toward intimacy seeming as preordained as a precocious child's graduation from one grade to the next. When they were finally married, late last year, Joan worried her husband's notoriety would scare away patients (or the parents of her patients, anyway) but she discovered, as he did, that people had long ago ceased to find the difference between fame and infamy interesting. There were a few extreme anti-cloners who no doubt imagined eternity in hell for any parent who put their child's well-being in the hands of Davis Moore's wife, but if anything, appointments increased when she changed her listing from Dr. Joan Burton to Dr. Joan Burton-Moore.

She reached across him with her right arm and placed her palm against the top of his stomach. With the nails of her left hand, she scratched him on the right temple. He smiled and rolled to his side, where she met his mouth with hers. She was naked, to his surprise—she always slept in a long T-shirt—and he kissed her with enthusiasm. His eyes adjusting to the light by the minute, he paused above her long enough to make her smile, and he delighted in his proximity to her, that she allowed him to touch her, to kiss her, to enter her. The marriage itself having been decided on as casually as a weekend at the lake house in Michigan, he still marveled that she returned his passion at night, she who was beautiful and smart and generous and ten years younger, when he was flawed and shamed and selfish and older and had failed badly at marriage once before.

She watched his eyes. There was a time, before they were together even, that she was certain she'd lost him. His preoccupation with AK's killer had left him like a warehouse filled with empty boxes, with nothing inside yet no room for anything more. She had played along with his insanity in order to protect

Justin, certainly, but also to protect Davis from his own madness, and also because she could think of no better way to be near him than to share the only thing that seemed to matter to him. Her love for him in those days was compartmentalized. She held little hope for it, and tried several times at relationships with more available men, but she always returned to the improbable dream that a life could be had with Davis Moore.

She was still young enough to have children—Davis himself had coaxed babies from countless women older than she—but Joan understood how unfair that would be. He was only now accepting that his daughter was gone. If she could have Davis—all of him—to herself, it would be enough, Joan thought.

Later, together, tangled, asleep, they each had horrible, sheet-twisting dreams in which the other was absent.

— 53 —

When Davis Moore shoved Mickey the Gerund back into the hotel elevator cab, it took just about all the willpower Mickey had not to laugh, or to grab Moore's arm, or even to shout some epithet after him while remaining in drunken character. Instead, he stumbled silently back and watched the doors close and felt the elevator lurch upward. Mickey thought Moore was an affront to God, an obstacle to God's will, and he had shot him once because of it. It was a source of some irritation to Mickey, all these years later, that he hadn't killed Davis Moore. That he hadn't felled him with a head shot the way he intended. Mickey hadn't missed many times in his career. Occasionally he killed a person he didn't intend to—collateral damage—but he rarely missed a doctor he wanted dead.

Sometimes he fantasized about a second chance at the man. Maybe someday, after he had finished the mission, he could go back and correct his mistakes. Others in the movement never gave it a second thought, probably, but to Mickey, his errant shot at Davis Moore was an irritating black mark on his own fearsome reputation.

Still, Moore wasn't the reason he was here. Moore had left his practice, at least, and although the man's public advocacy would still make him a legitimate target, the ex-doctor had become a sympathetic public character over the years. Taking another shot at him now would do more harm than good. Mickey was trying to make dead doctors, not unnecessary martyrs.

Because Moore had palmed the control panel, the doors opened and closed four times before Mickey arrived at the twenty-second floor. He stumbled out, still pretending to be drunk although he was alone in the halls (except for security cameras, he reminded himself) and made his way, head down, to room 2240. In his pocket was a gift from Harold Devereaux.

Phillip had advised him not to go to the CALS conference. There were too many people who might remember him from the scene of a previous operation. Given Mickey's busy schedule over the last four years, there were probably two dozen doctors and lab rats in the ballroom downstairs who had seen him before. Whether they could connect him to a shooting or bombing or specific act of intimidation was another matter. Mickey didn't much care, anyway. He hadn't planned on showing himself at any of the seminars. The Hands of God didn't make his agenda anymore. He'd earned the right to designate an appropriate target, to determine what was an acceptable risk. And although he had already ninety percent decided to come to Palm Springs, the envelope from Harold Devereaux had sealed the deal.

Who knows where Harold got it. He had friends and supporters everywhere. Many of them were so timid they wouldn't even enter into an argument about religion or science with their families and coworkers, but privately they did what was right. What had Reverend Falwell called them years and years ago? The silent majority? One member of the silent majority must have mailed this to Harold, and Harold knew just what to do with it. He sent it to the Hands of God with a note to forward it on to the Gerund. The envelope had a message in Harold's handwriting and all it said was, "Good at any Prince Resort Hotel worldwide." Mickey hadn't even told Harold of his plans to be here, but Harold knew a device like this would come in handy sometime.

A master key card.

Mickey slid it through the vertical slot of the lock at room 2240. The security light blinked once yellow, then Mickey heard a click and the light blinked green and he opened the door and slipped inside. The room was dark and empty and cold. He sidestepped into the bathroom to see if the shower had a curtain or a door. It had a frosted-glass door, translucent enough to make for a poor hiding space. He walked back into the room and slid open the mirrored closet. The hangers were bare. The couple must have been vacationing out of their suitcases, or possibly they had hung up their formal wear, the clothes they were wearing tonight, and left bathing suits and blue jeans and golf shirts folded in their bags. They were scheduled to be here for only three days.

Inside the closet, Mickey slid the door shut and scooted to the opposite end, the side least likely to be opened. He grabbed a pillow from a high shelf, placed it between his aching back and a miniature ironing board, and cracked the door a few centimeters in case he had to stay in here for several hours.

Dr. Poonwalla and his wife arrived forty minutes later, announcing themselves with exhausted sighs and loud whispers.

"That Davis Moore is a charmer, isn't he?" said Mrs. Poonwalla.

Dr. Poonwalla said, "Yes, such a tragedy what has happened to him, although I'd like to know the real story behind that unpleasantness in Chicago. His story about *secret experiments* was a bit hard to swallow, I'll admit."

"Still, a good man."

"Yes. Yes, he is."

After washing up, the Poonwallas draped their clothes someplace other than the closet and went to bed with a kiss reaffirming their vows. Mickey waited until he heard snoring, then stepped out of the closet and through the fat extra pillow fired two shots from a pistol at close range, one into each of their foreheads.

— 54 —

When she took time to consider it, Ms. Eberlein thought it an odd and even disturbing subject for a social studies report, but she had to admit it qualified as current events. Off and on for three and a half years, the Wicker Man had been reliable front-page news in the city, a recurring nightmare for six million people. He didn't strike in a regular pattern—at one time there was a nine-month gap between homicides with the killer's signature—but every time the city relaxed, every time the nightclubs on the West Side filled up with carefree twentysomethings, every time folks felt safe alone on the El, every time people stopped calling friends and family to let them know they arrived home safely, another body would appear, a lifeless message breaking across the morning news programs.

News of a fresh killing was particularly stressful for young single females like Ms. Eberlein. All but two of the Wicker Man's eleven victims had been women, and police suspected the men were not intended targets. In both cases they believed the men had responded to cries for help, or had been killed because they witnessed the crime. Like thousands of other young Chicagoans, Ms. Eberlein had taken a self-defense class at her neighborhood gym and armed herself with pepper spray. After four years of living by herself downtown, Ms. Eberlein sold her condo (paid for by her parents when she received her master's degree) and moved into an apartment with space enough for a roommate and a rottweiler.

So it wasn't entirely surprising that one of her juniors wanted to do a report on the Wicker Man murders. What concerned her was the student's age. Justin Finn had skipped three grades before landing in her class, and he was so bright it was unnerving to think he was only fourteen. When he first came into her classroom last semester, she wondered casually if he had a single hair on his body beyond the long, curly blond mess that sprawled across his head, then she banished the thought with a self-reproaching scowl. It was bad enough when she noticed the emerging sexuality of the older boys in the school. She couldn't deny that Justin would be a good-looking young man someday, however, probably around the time he got his law degree at nineteen.

"What's amazing about the Wicker Man is that he hasn't left any physical evidence," Justin explained to the class. "Nearly all violent criminals leave something behind—blood, hair, semen"—a boy in the back of the room guffawed, and a girl sitting in front of him rolled her eyes and grinned—"but not the Wicker Man. This has given him an almost supernatural aura in the mind of the public. I'd compare him in some ways to the Zodiac Killer in San Francisco, whose cryptic notes and spooky costume compounded the terror of his killings. The Wicker Man is a real-life bogeyman."

"How do you think he's been able to avoid leaving evidence?" Ms. Eberlein asked. Students were encouraged to interrupt the speaker at any time with a relevant question. It made the exercise less boring for her, kept the class engaged, and made it difficult for the presenter to learn only fifteen minutes of facts. Usually she had to ask the first question herself, however.

Justin nodded and held up his bound report as if to say the answer was within. "Clearly he spends a lot of time with the bodies after they're dead. We know this because of the peculiar pose he leaves them in—the details of which police have managed to keep secret. Obviously this also gives him time to clean up. Some police believe he uses a condom"—another muffled snicker—"and that's certainly possible, but just about every one of the attacks have taken place on nights when it's raining. I think that's deliberate. He lets nature wash away any trace of him. Also, people with their heads hunched under an umbrella or a hood are less likely to be aware of other pedestrians or suspicious activity. His victims can't see him coming, and potential witnesses are less likely to notice."

Impressive. Ms. Eberlein hadn't heard that theory before. She mentally added it to the list of street-smart facts that might someday save her life.

A girl named Lydia raised her hand and Justin nodded at her.

"I remember, like, three months ago, the police said they had a suspect and this guy with a bad mustache was all over the TV, but they never arrested him and then I never heard anything more about it. What happened to him?"

Justin grimaced. "That's been a major embarrassment for the police. The suspect's name was Armand Gutierrez, and he was connected to two of the female victims. One had been in a ballroom-dancing class with him at the Discovery Center and another was a regular customer at the grocery store where he worked. Investigators thought it was just too big a coincidence, and so everything about him seemed suspicious after that. He had some kind of weird porn collection—nothing illegal, but it piqued the interest of the cops who searched his apartment. He was also a butcher in an Italian deli, and one of the male victims had been carved up brutally with a big knife. The police have been under intense pressure from City Hall to solve the case, and they leaked his name to the press last October in order to get some good news out there before the mayoral election. But Gutierrez had alibis for almost every night a body was found, and they just couldn't make the case. Some cops still think he's the killer, but the state's attorney and the FBI have pretty much written Gutierrez off. He's suing the city, by the way, and will probably make out with a bundle."

"You mentioned the FBI." A popular boy the kids all called Foo didn't wait for Justin to call on him. "Do they have a, you know, what do you call that, where they look at the crime scenes and they write up what they think the killer is like—"

"A *profile,*" Justin said. "Yeah, they believe he's a white male, between the ages of twenty-five and forty-five, highly intelligent, if not educated, probably lives in Wicker Park or Ukrainian Village, or at least on the North or Near West Side. He's shown incredible restraint—being able to go months, it appears, without killing anyone. The FBI believes this means that he is either in a highly supervised situation—that is, he's institutionalized in some way, perhaps in a treatment facility or a halfway house, and his opportunities are somehow limited—or that he leaves the city for long stretches of time, or that he's killed many more people than we know and has just done a better job of hiding their bodies."

Ms. Eberlein, who was sitting in Justin's usual chair, raised her hand. "You've obviously spent some time with this subject. Which of those scenarios do you think is most likely?"

Justin was standing behind a portable lectern that had been set up on Ms. Eberlein's metal desk and he ducked his head modestly, as if he were looking for something among the notes in front of him. "None of them, actually." He smiled. "I think he leads a pretty normal life—he might even be very successful, given that everyone agrees he is intelligent—and that he has another way of blowing off steam. Whatever it is that compels him to kill, he has another way of sublimating"—scoffing from somewhere, as if to say no fourteen-year-old would use that word if they weren't just showing off—"his desire. Maybe he has an aggressive hobby, like boxing. Or maybe he's into sadomasochism"—outright laughter—"and he's able to get his kicks in non-lethal ways. But every once in a while, something just builds up inside him and he can't help himself. He has to kill."

Ms. Eberlein raised her eyebrows and whistled. "I think you'd make a pretty good FBI profiler yourself, Justin. It sounds like you've really gotten inside this guy's head." For better or worse, she thought to herself.

The bell rang and the students offered up lazy applause, and Justin smiled at Ms. Eberlein and switched places with her long enough to retrieve his books from under his chair. As the students bottlenecked at the door, she shouted the names of tomorrow's presenters after their backs and opened her black vinyl grade book, where she wrote next to Justin's name, "Creepy. A+."

— 55 —

The panoramic cityscape through the window of Sam Coyne's apartment was like a Realist painting on the days and nights when fog or rain or snow didn't entirely obscure the view. However, on blustery days, which were common, even the pleated flannel curtains had more depth than the flat gray haze of the Chicago sky.

This night the air had clarity worthy of the pricey window-washing service Sam hired as a redundancy to his own fastidiousness. The empty sky-scrapers glowed at twenty percent of their maximum wattage, lighting floor upon floor of unoccupied space. From thirty-nine stories up, the Lake Michigan shoreline was discernible only as an imaginary line separating the fluorescent city grid from the black void of the water. Sam loved how empty Lake Michigan was at night, loved the depth of its nothingness, and earlier this night, when he'd turned a twenty-six-year-old Leo Burnett art director onto her hands and knees, he made sure with the push of his hips and the pull of his hands that she could see the same blackness in the lake that he saw, and he could tell from her response—her narrow pelvis tight against his thighs, and the base of her skull pressing against the heel of his palm—that she was like him, that she recognized the blackness inside her was the blackness of nature, the blackness inside every one of us.

Sam slid out of bed and the sleeping girl spread her arm dreamily across the sheet to fill the divot in the mattress he'd left behind. He slipped down the hall to a guest room he'd converted into an office and opened his laptop. The screen brightened at his touch, as if it were glad to see him.

He clicked an icon for Shadow World and the game loaded, unspooling copyright notices and legalese and an animated intro, which he skipped after only a few frames. Recognizing him, and noting the time, the screen revealed an aerial shot of Chicago at night, the point of view soaring in off the lake and between buildings heading north. The game was plugged in to the National Weather Service so the Chicago on-screen was enjoying the same cloudless weather as the real city outside. In a matter of seconds Sam could see the steel-and-glass exterior of his own building, and then up, up, up thirty-nine stories to Sam's home-office window. The on-screen point of view then entered the apartment as if the glass in the window had dissolved like sugar candy.

Sam donned a headset and manipulated the POV until it was identical to the one from his desk. He walked his avatar down the hall and looked in on the sleeping woman in his bed, his gaming persona, naturally, being as promiscuous as he was in real life. He had Shadow Sam go to the walk-in closet and put on a pair of khaki cargo pants and a black turtleneck. Shadow Sam walked quietly from the bedroom to the kitchen. He opened a drawer and removed a long knife, which he wrapped in a dish towel and placed in one of his roomy side pockets. He left the apartment and took the elevator to the garage and found his BMW in its assigned spot (his Shadow car had been stolen once, but it had been insured). He drove north along Shadow Lake Shore Drive. There was little traffic and he rolled the top back. The speedometer on his dash was frozen at sixty miles per hour, about fifteen over the speed limit. In his earpiece, the car hummed through the whistling night air. An old pink eyesore of a building appeared on the horizon and as he passed it he remembered reading that its real owners had managed to have its landmark status revoked and planned its demolition for later in the week. Sam wondered how up to speed the Shadow World coders could be and made a note to have Shadow Sam drive this way on Friday to see if the pink building were still part of the game.

He exited LSD at Fullerton and drove west, away from the lake. The white moon disappeared into the canopy of tall buildings and trees in Lincoln Park. He turned northwest on Lincoln and passed a bar called the York, which had a 4 a.m. license. He circled, found a parking spot, and walked back to the bar. The inventory panel on his screen reminded him of the contents of his pocket: one wallet, $300, one knife, one dish towel.

The York was crowded but a couple abandoned their seats at the bar, and Shadow Sam took one. He ordered a beer, left a fifty on the counter, and turned around to scope the room. Youngsters, hipsters, a desegregated mix of straight and gay. A pair of girls danced together to the jukebox Rolling Stones. They were both blonde and shapely and pretty in a cartoon way, as most everyone was in the game, save the True-to-Lifers. Sam took pride in the fact that his icon looked a lot like him. In fact, last year, when he was stuck in a gymless Saint Louis hotel and gained five pounds in a week, he updated his avatar with the extra weight. That kind of honesty was unusual among gamers.

He watched the girls dance for a while, their hips swaying and arms lifting in a repeatable programmed loop based loosely on the hustle, and then he asked if he could buy them drinks. He stood up and offered them his chair as well as the stool next to it. The bartender made more change from what remained of the fifty.

Their names were Donna and Lindsay. No one handed out his or her last name in Shadow World, except the hard-core True-to-Lifers or people looking to start a relationship. He said he was Sam.

"Lindsay, that's a nice dress," he said into the headset microphone. According to conversation protocol, gamers used the name of the person being addressed when there was more than one person within listening distance, or in the "halo of conversation."

"Sam, thanks. I bought it at Saks." That is, she bought it with Shadow dollars at the Shadow Saks Fifth Avenue. Lindsay put her hand on Sam's leg just above the pocket where he'd put the knife.

"Lindsay, you have pretty hair. Is it real?" Sam was asking if the actual Lindsay looked anything like this or if she had created a sexy avatar through which she could live the virtual life of a prettier woman. He didn't care one way or the other, but these were the flirty and inane conversations one had in Shadow World just to advance the time, to get to the next, better thing.

"Sam, it's real," she said. "Dyed, but real." In his earpiece, he heard her giggle.

"Lindsay, Sam, bye," Donna said. She already saw where this was going and moved down the bar to play with someone else.

"Lindsay, do you want to go for a walk?" Sam's avatar asked.

"Sure!" Lindsay replied.

They walked outside and turned right on the sidewalk and had more ridiculous conversation of the real world rather than Shadow World kind. Sam turned down an alley and Lindsay followed. There was a car parked under a broken light, thirty or so feet from the street. Sam pressed Lindsay against it and started kissing her.

In Shadow World, players were constantly pairing off with strangers and having sex in public places. Countless magazine articles on the subject quoted psychologists who explained this was a common fantasy for both men and women, and it made sense that people would use the game to act it out in a world with no lasting consequences (venereal disease should have been more widespread in the game, but Shadow World public officials had taken the threat seriously and infection rates were only slightly higher than in the real world). If Shadow Sam spotted a woman alone in a bar, he could usually get her to an alley in even shorter time than this.

Shadow sex wasn't the most visually stimulating thing. Programmers hadn't yet mastered the code to make on-screen characters seem realistic or sexy. The naked icons appeared as textureless flesh-colored versions of their clothed selves, and the same visuals (her with mouth open, him with eyes closed, hips thrusting together in mechanical rhythm) looped and repeated again and again. Online sex was a big draw of the game, however, so the makers were working on a more explicit, adults-only plug-in for version 5.0.

Shadow World sex was similar to a dirty two-person (or sometimes three- or four- or seven-person) chat. As player icons mashed together on-screen, the players would shout and moan and call each other filthy names and describe how close they were to climaxing and what unexpected things they were going to do next to please their partners. Voyeurs, mostly kids whose parents had never bothered to activate parental controls, scanned the back streets at night looking to spy on illicit couplings like this one and record them to their hard drives. There were several Web sites devoted to the playback of amateur Shadow World pornos.

Unsuspecting Lindsay whispered many of the usual erotic clichés. When Sam reached into the puddle of pants around his ankles, she must have thought he was looking for a condom because she said, "Sam, do you want me to help you put it on?" As she spoke, the mouth of her avatar opened into a small black oval and collapsed into a flat red line like the mouth flap on an old Saturday morning cartoon. The subtleties of lip movement were still beyond Shadow World's capabilities.

Sam's avatar shook the towel from the blade and said, "Lindsay, no thanks," and plunged the knife into her left side.

"Goddammit! Sonofabitch!" Lindsay yelped. They weren't cries of fear or pain, but frustration and anger. Whatever riches or fame or happiness her character had amassed in Shadow World would be wiped out as the life bled from her avatar. She would have to start the game over as her own boring self again.

Shadow Lindsay collapsed backward onto the hood of the car. Sam picked up the towel and wrapped the knife in it and returned them to his pocket. He surveyed the alley to make sure he hadn't left any clues and to make sure there wasn't a punk voyeur hiding in the shadows. He walked back to Lincoln Avenue and found his car, and he drove east to Lake Shore Drive, past the pink building on his way home. He closed the door to his apartment quietly, washed the knife in the kitchen sink, and tiptoed into the bedroom. The woman was still asleep in his Shadow World bed just as the young art director was still in the actual one. The real Sam Coyne had never left his apartment.

— 56 —

The red message light on his screen had been flashing for an hour before it finally woke Justin from a vivid dream in which he was being chased by a cougar through the halls of his school. He rolled to the floor and thought for a moment that he would pull the blankets down on top of him and finish the night's rest on the soft blue carpet, but when curiosity caught up with his consciousness, he knew he couldn't go back to bed. He strained to see the clock on the desk. Four-thirty.

He trotted across the room on his hands and knees and lifted himself into his chair. The screen awoke and blinked into focus in a matter of seconds. As he suspected, he'd been sent a Shadow World news alert.

When news broke in Shadow World, it was reported in the Shadow media. For most people, this consisted of e-mailed news alerts, updating the player on matters of specific interest to his character. An alert might tell you that your favorite Shadow World singing group had scheduled a concert in your town, or that a work by your favorite Impressionist painter was going up for auction. Justin had subscribed to receive only a very specific type of news. If his e-mail light was flashing at four-thirty in the morning, someone in Shadow Chicago had been murdered.

In another Shadow World parallel, researchers observed that murders took place in the game at almost the same rate at which they occurred in the corresponding real cities. For Chicago, that meant over one per day. It was known that Shadow World thrill killing was a popular pastime for gamers, but no one seemed to understand why Shadow World murders, which were assumed to be perpetrated by different people and for different motives than their real counterparts, leveled out at the same rate.

Justin had asked to be notified only if the murderer hadn't been apprehended at the scene and if the killing didn't appear to be connected to a domestic dispute. That eliminated more than three quarters of them. At least once a week, however, Justin received a gruesome summary in his mailbox.

He scanned it quickly and it appeared to be a good candidate. He put on his headset and logged in to the game, and when his avatar materialized in his Shadow World bedroom, he started work. Shadow Justin dressed himself, snuck out the window, and jumped to the ground. He grabbed his electric bike from the garage and rode it to Shadow Northwood's Metra stop. His inventory panel showed he had $40 in his pocket, a notebook, pen, camera, and Metra card, and he boarded the first train headed for downtown.

There weren't many other players on the train at this hour. A tired-looking woman in a nursing uniform sat with her head resting against a window. A man in a suit, possibly a True-to-Lifer on an early commute, read the *Sun-Times*. A more casually dressed man sat in the first seat by the doors; Justin settled himself across the aisle and three seats up from him.

The train rumbled past dark houses and dark streets, the red lights of the crossings indicating when the train intersected a major road, and by counting them, Justin could determine the train's location even without listening for the garbled announcements over the public-address system. After three stops the casual man approached and sat across the aisle from him. Justin turned and said hello. The man wore a yellow sweater with a collared shirt and glasses. He leaned forward and tried to speak, but the words in Justin's headset were obscured by long beeps, and a text window above the man's head printed the words <AGE INAPPROPRIATE>. Whatever he was saying, the parental controls disapproved. The man stood up and walked quickly out of the car, in case Justin planned to turn him in to the conductor.

After arriving at Northwestern station, Shadow Justin walked to the El and rode up to Lakeview. The news alert said the murder had taken place in the 2400 block of North Lincoln, and he ran to the address, triggering a mild on-screen energy warning to remind him that his avatar hadn't eaten breakfast.

Three policemen stood on the sidewalk sharing a box of Krispy Kremes. Shadow World cops were almost all wannabes in real life and they spoke and acted in keeping with the worst television clichés. They ate a lot of doughnuts and talked about "running down perps." Justin found them annoying.

"Kid, nothing to see here," one of the cops said as Justin tried to duck under the yellow police tape. "Move along."

"Officer, come on," Justin said, trying to peek down an alley blocked by the blue-and-white police car. Justin took some photos, which were saved to his hard drive. An evidence technician, possibly computer-generated, was measuring distances from the body to various parts of the alley and making notes on a clipboard. A reporter scribbled in her notebook.

The cops had turned their backs to him, getting on with their non-cop-related conversation. Justin slipped a doughnut from the box, slid across the hood of the car, and ducked under the yellow police tape.

"Kid! Hey!" one of the cops yelled after him, but didn't give chase. The reporter looked up from her work and took a few steps in their direction until Justin was behind her.

"Officers, it's okay," the Shadow reporter said. "He's with me." The cops waved. She and Justin walked on to the body.

The parental controls were efficient at blocking out swearwords and improper propositions and obscuring nudity and sexual activity on-screen, but they did nothing to protect child players from violence. If youthful gamers were immune to violence, the makers reasoned, they could never be killed or even injured, and that would compromise the integrity of the game. In their minds, it was necessary for Shadow World children to fall down wells and get caught beneath tractors and be chased by cougars if cougars escaped from the zoo. Few parents knew about this loophole. Martha Finn certainly didn't.

The body had fallen facedown by the front left tire of an old sedan. There was a lot of blood in an oval pool underneath her that dispersed in red canals under the car. Her clothes were soaked in it.

Justin turned to the reporter. "Sally," he said, "what do we know?"

Twelve months ago, three years after their last photo session, Sally Barwick, Justin Finn's first crush, made contact with his avatar outside his Shadow World school. She couldn't contact him in real life, she said, because his mother still had a restraining order forbidding it. Sally was even afraid to come to Justin's Shadow World home, in case Martha played the game. Sally told him she was sorry about the photos. Sorry she had been disloyal. She always thought he was a special kid. She thought about him often.

Justin was too embarrassed to have his avatar say it, but he still thought about her, as well.

She explained that her character had worked her way up to crime reporter for the Shadow *Chicago Tribune*. They traded theories about the real-life Wicker Man. Sally invited him to his first virtual midnight crime scene. Since then, they had met (behind Martha's back) about twice a month over the corpse of a dead avatar in a Shadow Chicago alley.

"Justin, hi," Shadow Barwick said. "Her name is Lindsay. Stabbed in the gut. Found by a couple of voyeurs about two hours ago. No witnesses. No murder weapon."

Justin looked under the car. "Does this remind you of anything?" There was no one else within earshot so he dispensed with the formality of addressing her by name.

"What?"

"Three weeks ago. Shadow State Street. Blonde. Stabbed."

"Yeah, her and about a hundred others," Sally said. "This is just another thrill kill. Probably a teenager showing off for his buds."

"You know what else I can't help thinking about?" Justin said. "Something else this reminds me of?"

"What?"

"Not in here. Out there."

"Don't say it."

"Okay, I won't."

"You got Wicker Man on the brain, little man."

"You don't think it's weird? There are a lot of similarities."

Barwick waved her pen in the air. "Okay, so it's a copycat. You get a lot of those. A year before you joined the game they found a crazy guy in the Shadow suburbs with a couple dozen avatars buried in his crawl space. Some high school kid thought it'd be a laugh to be John Wayne Gacy for a few weeks. What an <AGE INAPPROPRIATE>."

"I have a theory," Justin said. "Wanna hear it?"

"Sure. Why not?" Sally said.

"I think the Wicker Man has some outlet for his anger. That's how he can go so long without killing sometimes."

Leaning against the car, Shadow Barwick said, "Oh, <small>AGE INAPPROPRIATE</small>! That's crazy. You think the guy who did this is a True-to-Lifer?" Sally pointed at the lifeless avatar. "A serial killer in real life who's also a serial killer in the game?"

"I've been charting the dates of the Wicker Man murders against the dates of similar murders here in the game," Justin said.

"And?"

"Well, I haven't figured out an exact pattern yet, but there are some interesting coincidences . . ."

"That's all they are, Justin. Coincidences." The police tech shooed Barwick's hand from the car. She yawned and offered Justin a stick of gum from her bag. Sally unsheathed a second one for herself. "This here is just teenage boys messing around. Playing a sick game their conscience won't let them play in reality."

"Yeah?" Justin asked. "If you're so sure there's nothing to these killings, how come I see you taking detailed notes at every one?"

Shadow Sally stepped outside the police tape and threw the gum wrapper foil into a dumpster. "Heck," she said. "I'm just doing my job."

— 57 —

The whispered joke around the station was they made Ted Ambrose a sergeant, and then a lieutenant, because they felt sorry for him. Any one of two dozen detectives could have taken the first Wicker Man call, could have been stuck with all these unsolved murders. It was just too bad they had to get stuck on a good cop like Teddy.

He now supervised the Wicker Man task force, which handled the day-to-day investigation, and Ambrose still marked off milestones in his life according to their proximity to the Wicker victims. His mother passed away the day before the body of victim number three, Carol Jaffe, was found on the 1400 block of West Wabansia. His wife left the day before number seven, Pamela Ip, turned up in the parking lot of the 60622 post office. The last one, LeeAnn McTeer, was discovered over on State Street, more than ten blocks east of the Wicker Man's comfort zone. Ambrose was certain McTeer was number twelve, however, because the killer had left the body in the same condition as all the others—stabbed and sexually posed—and also because Ambrose received word the day before that his daughter needed expensive braces for her teeth.

He sat in his office and stared at a painted cinder-block wall on which he had pasted connections between the Wicker Man victims and the suspects Ambrose still liked for the murders. Any individual who had ever been under suspicion in this investigation had been assigned a letter, but most of them had been cleared one way or another. Three names remained taped to his wall.

Suspect A was the deli worker, Armand Gutierrez. "The Butcher," Ambrose nicknamed him for grins. Many of his colleagues had moved on from Gutierrez. The local media had all but acquitted him, and the FBI said he didn't fit the profile. Ambrose wasn't so sure.

Suspect F was Bryan Baker. "The Baker" was Ambrose's departmental code name for the man. Baker was a cab driver who came to police attention because of some odd statements he had made to patrons in a tavern over the course of several weeks last summer. Baker was obsessed with the Wicker Man case, and he told anyone who would listen that he was acquainted with some of the girls. In fact, police were able to place three of the women in Baker's cab in the year prior to each of their deaths (two had charged the fare on a credit card; a third had called the cab company to report a lost wallet). Unfortunately, that strange coincidence was all the evidence they had, and Ambrose frankly doubted the Baker was smart enough to be his man. Still, the cabbie remained on the board.

Then there was the most recent addition: Suspect M. Privately, Ambrose called him "the Candlestick Maker."

He came to their attention through one of hundreds of anonymous tips phoned in to the Wicker Man hotline. The day of the call, Ambrose had sold his two-flat for twenty grand over asking price. A sign, he thought. This guy, the Candlestick Maker, set Ambrose's famously instinctive guts churning. He was educated. Successful. Handsome. Smart. A real Ted Bundy type. The caller, an insomniac, said she had noticed him coming and going from his downtown condo at weird times, within hours of each of the last two killings. Not much to go on, but he fit the profile almost perfectly. Ambrose put his name on the wall and ordered his building on intermittent overnight surveillance.

Pressure to solve the case came in waves. Sometimes quiet months would slip past and the papers would speculate that the Wicker Man had moved away, or been picked up on some unrelated charge and was trapped in a jail cell downstate. Then another body would turn up and the heat would come down on Ambrose's neck like desert sun. It never seemed to bother him. Even though the murders remained unsolved, most on the force agreed Teddy was the guy for the job, if only because he was so good at handling the mayor and the police superintendent.

At one of the Wicker Man press conferences, an ornery and sarcastic Ambrose gave a reply to a reporter's question that since had been e-mailed to nearly every police district in the country. Some cops were said to have printed it out and framed it in their squad rooms. It was known as "the Ambrose Doctrine."

"There are *never* any clues," Ambrose said. "Murderers, rapists, and thieves *never* leave evidence. Why would they? Christ, if they left evidence, *real evidence,* we'd catch them in a day. Just pull up outside their house or apartment with a tactical team and a warrant and kick in the door and arrest them.

"In reality, the job of a detective is to empathize with the victim. You do that enough times, and listen to your gut, you'll catch your share of bad guys."

Justin at Fifteen

— 58 —

She decided to tell him on his birthday, more as an instrument of procrastination than ceremony. Maturity wasn't an issue—Justin no doubt had been capable of digesting the news five years ago, when he built his own telescope and taught himself conversational Spanish. Martha half expected him to tell her he'd already figured it out. That would be a relief. It would be far better than the response she feared, which was disappointment and possibly anger. Stoic Justin had amazing self-control and she hadn't seen him truly angry since he was a small child, but this might be the kind of news that could set him off. If not the news itself, the fact that she had been keeping secrets from him. If she waited any longer it might just make the inevitable tantrum even harder to control.

Not that she could take him in a confrontation even now. Justin had grown taller than she and no longer looked like the runt of his class. He had more friends now, oddball types, admittedly, but they weren't all the same kind of oddballs. They were nerds and jocks and stoners and band kids who, for some reason, were all drawn to her son. He was more popular with girls than he had been, especially smart girls, but the fact that he was three years younger than everyone else in the senior class made him pretty much off limits as far as dating went. He had the kind of quiet charisma that would make him a star as an adult, she was convinced, but it was lost on all but a few of his high school peers.

He'll show them, she thought. One day he'll show them all what he's made of.

He had opened his presents—mostly books Martha couldn't read for three pages without falling asleep. Michel Foucault was his latest obsession, and she had found some fine used hardcovers. Justin didn't enjoy paperbacks to nearly

197

the same degree. He liked to grip a book with both hands, as if the knowledge were entering through his fingers instead of his eyes.

"There's something you should know," she said, and motioned for him to come off the floor and sit next to her on the couch, where she could grab his arms if they started to flail, or wrap her elbows around an ankle if he started to flee. Then she told him, without much preface but with a brief rationalization having to do with heredity (which she knew he understood) and with Huntington's disease (which had taken his grandmother and which would probably take her someday), and in the end she said she hoped the news didn't make him unhappy because a natural-born son wouldn't have been him and it was him whom she loved, him she couldn't imagine life without.

Justin wanted to know about the procedure: where had it been done, how had it been done, who else knew? *Does Dr. Keith know?* He asked about the donor and Martha explained that he was dead, but that he had been a good boy who lived out east and he had died in an accident when he was very young, but in death he had given three very important gifts—*his eyes to a blind person, his liver to a sick person, and a single blood cell to your father and me so that we could have you.*

Justin could tell she was nervous, and he calmed her. He wasn't upset. He was glad that she had told him. Did his father know she was going to tell him today? *He did? Well, it's no surprise he didn't want to be here for this, either.* They laughed. She cried a little. Never worry about telling me the truth, he told her, and she promised she wouldn't. Never again.

It wasn't the whole truth, and at the time Justin assumed his mother knew, as he did, that the story was a lie. Soon, he would find out differently and he would hate himself for mistaking her for a coconspirator. Even now, wondering if she was holding something back, he loved her for telling him. For giving him on his birthday the thing he had been searching for in all of those gift-wrapped books.

— 59 —

In New York, being a liberal didn't mean putting a target on your back.

When he took the job as managing editor of the *Chicago Tribune,* Stephen Malik knew the publisher was using him. The *Tribune* had long been a Republican paper in a Democratic town, and he understood the editorial page would always try to preach to its conservative suburban base. Malik was brought in to answer charges from city readers (and supporters of the current governor) that the news division had a right-wing bias as well. Malik's liberal credentials gave the *Trib* some cover. And of course, Malik knew, his presence provided them with a convenient fall guy if things ever went wrong.

Beginning in June, boy had they.

The frayed end that unraveled it all was a story on an anti-cloning protest in front of the Dirksen Federal Building. The protesters—or more accurately, advocates—were expressing their support for the Buckley–Rice Anti-Cloning Act. Written by a young and promising reporter named Scott Harmon, the article estimated the size of the crowd at around 150, and described in detail the signs and the banners they carried: STOP THE BOYS FROM BRAZIL. MAN CAN CLONE A BODY BUT ONLY GOD CAN CLONE A SOUL. CLONING = SIN. Harmon also quoted a small group of counterprotesters. "These people are just afraid of progress," said one, identified as Cameron Straub. "They're ignorant." Another young man, a Naperville resident named Denny Dreyfus, claimed to be a clone himself, as well as a Catholic: "I feel like [the protesters] are denying me my humanity," he said. "It's like they're telling me I'm not human. That I'm an affront to God."

A freelance writer living in Wrigleyville took an interest in the second quote. His name was also Denny Dreyfus, and he began working on a feature story about this clone who shared his name. He thought he could sell it to *Chicago* magazine, for which he'd written several articles in the past.

There was a problem, however. He couldn't locate the other Denny Dreyfus. Not in Naperville or anywhere else in Illinois. He tried looking for Cameron Straub, thinking the two might be friends. He couldn't find anyone by that name at all.

When an e-mail query from Dreyfus the writer arrived at Stephen Malik's desk, he felt ice against his spine. He remembered that story. He remembered looking at an early draft of it and wondering how it got past the Metro editor in the shape it was in. It hadn't a single quote from pro-cloning counterprotestors. There must have been at least some of them making noise at a protest that size. Word came back that Harmon had interviewed several but didn't think the quotes were that strong. "I don't care," Malik said. "Get the other point of view in there somehow." The next version had the quotes from Denny Dreyfus and Cameron Straub.

Dreyfus wanted to see Harmon's notes on that story. With twenty years in the business, Malik was certain he knew what would happen next.

Dreyfus's story ran in the *Chicago Reader* and included a dozen or more cheap shots at Malik's expense from anonymous discontents in the *Tribune* newsroom, each accusing him of trying to undermine the objectivity of his reporters by injecting news stories with his own political and personal agendas. By that time, Scott Harmon had been fired for fabricating quotes, but that had only made him disgruntled, and he spoke on the record with Dreyfus. "I felt pressured to get certain points of view, certain liberal points of view, in my stories," Harmon said. "Malik never complained if the conservative side wasn't represented."

Others suggested to the *Reader* (anonymously, of course) that Malik's aggressive attempts to create "diversity" by hiring reporters without a solid background in journalism had forced unqualified people into prominent assignments at the paper. The implication (the way Malik read it) was that the Harmon incident was an example of this, even though Scott Harmon was a white kid with a degree in film, the son of a wealthy advertiser, in fact, whose hiring had been imposed upon Malik from higher up. In fact, Malik was proud of many new writers he'd managed to lure into the ranks.

Sally Barwick was an example. Bright. Hardworking. African-American. Her prose was efficient and almost entirely free of cliché. If there was anything he would change about her, it would be her insistence on working the police beat. As a matter of philosophy Malik didn't think any reporter, especially one with such promise, should stay in the same department for more than twelve months at a time. Sally, however, a former private eye, had convinced him of her passion for cops and crime scenes and courtrooms. Also, as a matter of smart management, Malik believed in keeping his best writers happy.

He had heard about her hobby. There had been snickers about it in editorial meetings practically since the day she was hired, and Dreyfus even made a snide allusion to it in his *Reader* story, although he didn't mention her name. Malik thought it was ridiculous. Tens of millions of people played Shadow World, and yet there was still this crazy stigma attached to it. The *Tribune* had done countless stories about the phenomenon, and he remembered one citing studies in which one in five people who said they weren't gamers actually were, and more than half of those who admitted to playing lied about how much time they spent inside the game. If it didn't affect her work (and as far as he could tell, it never had), then why the hell should he care what she did in her spare time? They had a sportswriter who was a snake handler; that was a lot weirder than playing some video game.

"You wanted to see me, Stephen?" Barwick asked.

Malik waved her into his office and motioned for her to shut the door.

"What's going on?"

"I just wanted to give you a heads-up. I don't know how long I'm going to be at this paper."

"You're quitting?"

Malik knew her shock was feigned—Barwick was aware of newsroom politics. She heard the talk in the hallways and across the street at the Billy Goat and from gossipy colleagues at other papers. He appreciated the gesture, though. "Not exactly."

"They're forcing you out? Over this Dreyfus bullshit?"

His head drifted unconvincingly to the left and right. "Not yet. I might even survive this one, but I've learned something from it. Next year it will be something else. And the year after that, there'll be another 'Dreyfus affair.' One of them will have my number on it. They won't back me up indefinitely."

Sally sat in a green chair with upholstery that felt more like scratchy carpet. "You don't have to worry about me," she said. "I'll back you all the way."

"I know," he said, not smiling where another man might. "That's why I wanted to talk to you. One day, they might ask you to choose sides. When they do that, I want you to look after yourself."

"Not a chance," Barwick said. "I owe my career to you. If you hadn't put me on the murder beat, I'd still be transcribing obits over the phone."

"Just trust me on this. Save your job. This is a good paper. I'll land on my feet somewhere. And wherever that is, if you're interested, you'll have a job. No matter what. Maybe you'll get lucky. Maybe it'll be a city with even more sicko murders than this one."

"One can hope," she said darkly.

"But the rest of this crap doesn't have anything to do with you. And I don't want it to. That's an order, or whatever."

"An order, huh?"

"Uh-huh."

"Well, maybe it won't come to that."

"Maybe not," he allowed. "Things change. Before it all comes down, maybe you'll break open the Wicker Man case and win a Pulitzer. Make me look good." He didn't smile this time, either.

She left without making any promises. Malik tapped his computer keyboard to retrieve a dozen e-mails, all received while Barwick was sitting in his office. She could be a lot of things in this business, he thought to himself, a columnist or an editor. When she first came to the *Tribune* she said she wanted to be a journalist because she liked having an audience but hated crowds. That made Malik laugh. She could be anything she wanted to be.

He wondered what kind of person she was in the game.

— 60 —

Davis sat in a big leather chair by the front window in the big house on Stone Avenue, reading a paperback called *Time of Death*. It was about a convicted murderer named Hughes whose appeals have been exhausted. His execution date is set. At midnight. He knows the precise second at which he is going to die and he finds the burden of that knowledge unbearable. Through another prisoner, Hughes hires a third con, one whose identity is unknown to him, to kill Hughes at some random date before his execution. This uncertainty makes Hughes happy—so happy he can no longer accept dying. So he tries to foil his own exercise-yard assassination.

It was a silly book and Davis was hypnotized by it, reading the first two hundred pages in just a few hours. Improbable novels like this—sci-fi, thrillers, mysteries—had been his weakness as a teenager, when he read two or three of them a week. He always kept a book with him back then and never let a minute of idle time pass without bending back the shiny cover and holding it with one hand in front of his face. He read at breakfast, on the bus, between periods, at lunch, during his breaks at the hardware store, and even while riding his bike.

He read less and less for pleasure as he got older and various obsessions held his dwindling free time hostage. In med school it was fly-fishing, although he did more practice casting in a park near his apartment than he did wading in Wisconsin streams. In his early thirties he took up track driving—with an inheritance check he paid off his student loans and purchased a BMW coupe—and he rented time on the raceway in Joliet. As AK grew older and Jackie grew sicker, he sold the Beamer and immersed himself in genealogy, trying to define himself with the sum of his ancestors, tunneling for hours through birth and death records in the windowless blue room. Genealogy was shunted in the search for AK's killer, and the search for AK's killer was abandoned for fear of going to prison.

The obsessions, one after another, had been a symptom of depression. He understood that now. A happy person looks forward to a few moments of boredom now and then, but for an unhappy person, idle time is intolerable. The unhappy mind is congested with regrets and guilt and situations out of its control and the unstoppable unfolding of worst-case scenarios. Fly rods and race cars and note cards covered with family history became occupying forces in his head, dispersing unpleasant thoughts, outlawing unwanted concerns.

Since he and Joan married, the old stresses had largely disappeared. Potential disasters and subconscious dreads were still players in the politics of his imagination, but only as disorganized, discredited third parties. The files in the blue room, both older ones relating to his family and the more recent boxes filled with leads in AK's murder, hadn't been opened in more than four years, and Joan talked about converting the space into a studio so they could take up painting together when she retired. With more free time to enjoy than at any other time in his life, idleness had now become its own reward. He treasured hours that passed with no deadlines or duties or responsibilities. Time to sit by the big window on Stone and read all the terrible and exciting books he'd missed in the last forty years. AK's memory was with him at all times, but it no longer haunted him, and he felt so removed from his own shooting that some days he wondered if it hadn't happened in a TV movie.

The doorbell rang and Davis thought about not answering it. It was likely a package delivery that could just as well be left on the porch, or a neighborhood petition he didn't want to sign. It could be kids from the middle school selling candy or candles in support of some band trip. He wasn't against band trips, but he wasn't exactly in favor of answering the door right now either, of interrupting his idle time. He was sitting by an open window, however, and his head must have been visible from the walk. After living at the same address for nearly three decades, he didn't want to be known as the crazy old man who never answers his door. He stood up, flattening the paperback on an end table.

The boy had grown in six years and was so unlike a boy now. He was less than a hand shorter than Davis, and his long, blond curls danced above his head like spiraling Chinese kites in the light breeze. Muscles had started to assert themselves on his arms under a layer of fine hair. There were a few pink scars on his hands. He wore a silver chain around his neck. Something that one day would have to be shaved loitered under his nostrils and lips. His face was breaking out around his eyes and hairline, and he had a prominent red-and-white pimple at the end of his nose. He wore a two-toned button-down short-sleeve shirt, loose khakis, and sandals, the uniform of teen indifference.

"Dr. Moore," was all he said.

Davis fought the dryness in his mouth by working the glands under his tongue, and he wondered what sort of trick this could be. He wondered who could be trying to fool him like this and what they expected him to do. He needed to know so he could do the opposite. Davis looked past the boy for some sign of his mother, scanning up and down the street for the red car she used to drive.

"What do you want, Justin? You shouldn't be here." He said it loudly in case someone was nearby, or in case Justin's broad pockets had been fitted with a microphone.

"I wanted to ask you some questions," he said, then sensing Davis's reluctance, added, "I'd be in big trouble too if my mom knew I was here. I ditched a couple periods from school. But this is important."

Davis was certain he was making a mistake, but waved the boy inside for the same reason all people do the wrong thing: the wrong thing is irresistible.

Justin paused in the foyer, polite and uncomfortable, weight on his right foot while his left sneaker dragged invisible half circles against the hardwood. Davis gestured toward the living room and followed him inside. The boy sat on the edge of the couch, knees pinned at angles to the coffee table as if black ink might ooze from the backs of his thighs if his legs came in contact with the cushions. Davis drew the front shade.

"Just a minute," he told Justin. Davis picked up the cordless phone in the next room and dialed Joan. Her last appointment was at two-thirty and she had said something about stopping for groceries on the way home. She would flip if she knew Justin had been in the house.

"Hon," he said, "could you pick me up some potting soil, and also some of that shampoo you bought last month? Yeah, that's the one. Sorry, I should have put it on your list. Thanks. Love you." That would add two stops to her route. He figured they had about forty-five minutes.

"It *must* be important for you to risk coming here," Davis said, ignoring the minutes-long gap since Justin last spoke at the door. "What can I do for you?"

"Mom told me," Justin said. He looked eager, and although he had trouble sitting still, Davis identified his jitters as a symptom of his age: a lack of comfort with his mutating body, fatigue from the pains that came to his growing legs and arms and spine at night. It wasn't nervousness. Coming here was an act of confidence, in fact. Defiance. Justin's eyes challenged Davis to be as daring. Though uninvited, Justin had risked something by showing himself here, and he expected Davis to risk something in return.

Not yet decided on what he could afford to wager, Davis decided to play it dumb. "What did she tell you?"

"She told me where I came from."

"Uh-huh."

"She told me I'm a clone."

"Yes?"

"She told me I'm the clone of a kid from New York named Eric Lundquist."

"Okay."

"Is it true?"

Davis smiled. "I'm not allowed to say."

"You're not a practicing physician anymore," Justin said, stumbling over the word "physician." Davis winced, thinking suddenly of the fires and the lost pets and the fog of concerns and guilt Joan had raised eight years ago, which had long burned off in the sunny joy of the present. He was surprised to find himself frightened, not of what might happen if he was caught violating the restraining order, but frightened of Justin himself. He couldn't pin down exactly why. "What can they do to you?" Justin asked.

"Lots," Davis said without elaborating. "When did your mom tell you?"

"About six months ago."

Davis subtracted in his head. "Let me guess. Your birthday?" Justin nodded. "They always do it on a birthday. That must be in one of the books or something. Okay, your mother explained things to you, but you still want to hear them from me. Why? Do you think she would lie to you?"

"No."

"Well, then."

"I don't think she's lying. I think she's wrong. There's a difference."

Again, Davis considered that Martha Finn was putting him up to this. Or the cops. Maybe someone suspected. Maybe someone wanted him to do prison this time. "Why do you think she's wrong?"

"Because I *saw* him," Justin said. The boy leaned back now in a low slouch, his head on top of the cushions, staring at the light fixture in the ceiling, his arms crossed in front of him and his hands clasped the wrong way around, pinkies out, resting between his legs.

Arteries up and down Davis's body pumped two parts adrenaline to one part plasma, the way they had when he'd received the last promising lead in Anna Kat's murder via e-mail from Ricky Weiss. That had ended in the worst way he could have imagined. Davis tried to slow it all down, saying nothing for a long time. The boy seemed fine with that, even closing his eyes as though a nap were coming before a thought fired across a synapse in his brain and he blinked awake, eyes on the ceiling, waiting.

"Where?" Davis said finally. "Where did you see him?"

"Nuh-uh," Justin said. He sat up straight, as if his waist were a hinge, and leaned until his head was closer to Davis's chair than Davis's own knees. "I tell you stuff. You tell me stuff."

Christ, what did this kid know? How could he have seen AK's killer? Forget that, how could he have *identified* him? Understood what he was looking at? Was it someone from Northwood? Had the monster been so close all along? He couldn't let Justin out the door now, not without reaching some sort of understanding. Whatever the kid knows, it might be enough to put Davis in prison for ten years. Still, he had to know. After everything Davis had gambled, how could he not play this hand out? And if he had to trust anyone, why not Justin, who was as much his child as he was Martha and Terry Finn's? If not for Davis, this particular arrangement of carbon and neurons and blond hair and curiosity would never have existed.

"Tell me what you want to know," Davis said.

Justin stood up and walked around the coffee table, sprawling across the carpet at Davis's feet. He twisted his torso, and his spine cracked like a roll of caps. He rested his head on an elbow. "You're not supposed to make clones from living people."

"That's right."

"But you did."

"I did."

"You could go to jail for that."

"You're right."

"It must have been important."

"It was."

"So tell me."

"I will," Davis said. "But I just confessed a secret to you. Something serious. I'd like something in return now."

"That's fair."

"Where did you see him?"

Justin paused, but didn't seem reluctant. It was as if he had to play back a recording in his mind before he knew he could get it right. "He attacked my mother."

"Shit!" Davis cursed with a reflexive gasp. "Is she all right?"

Justin nodded with a sneer that seemed inspired by equal amounts anger and guilt. "Yeah. She's okay."

"When did this happen?"

"Six years ago," Justin said. "Right before she filed the lawsuit against you." Davis considered that. "Just a coincidence, though. Now, who is he?"

"You don't know?" The questioned betrayed disappointment, and that seemed to confuse the boy.

"I want to know what you know first."

Davis nodded, asking himself if he needed more than an hour from Joan, if he should call with another errand before she returned from the office to find her husband and the Finn boy trading information like distrustful double agents. "He attacked my daughter."

"Is she okay?" Justin asked.

"No," Davis said. "She's not."

The story came out in a long exhale, and Justin seemed shocked by none of it. He listened and nodded and looked concerned. At other times he appeared relieved and even excited. He never interrupted. He allowed Davis to describe, to explain, to rationalize, to apologize. He seemed so sympathetic, so non-judgmental, Davis thought he could have cried in front of the boy, and almost did, twice.

"I feel bad," Justin said when Davis was through and they had both thought silently on it for a few minutes. "I feel bad I don't have more answers for you." He sighed. "I can't remember his name. It was like money or something. Mr. Cash, maybe? I think he lived in the city. I think he used to live in Northwood. Or his parents did."

"His parents live here now?"

"They did six years ago. His mom introduced him to my mom. They talked but I wasn't really paying attention. I remember everybody was saying he looked like me. When he was a kid, anyways."

"What else?"

"He and my mom went to dinner one night. I thought I heard something after they came home and I went downstairs. I just saw the end of it. I think he tried to rape her, although she never said, exactly. My mom was crying. She kicked him out and he walked past me and I really looked at him this time, looked him in the face, in a way that I hadn't done when we met in the store. It was like, you know how you look at an old picture of yourself and you don't look like that anymore, and you don't spend that much time looking at yourself in the first place, but still you just know the face in the picture is you? Right away. That's what it felt like. Looking at him."

"Do you think he saw the same thing you did? Do you think he saw himself in you?"

Justin picked at the carpet with his fingers. "I don't know. I doubt it. He just wanted to get the hell out of there."

"Does your mother have any idea?"

"Nuh-uh. Like I said, she thinks my donor was Eric Lundquist."

Davis wanted to believe it. "Are you positive it was him? The guy who hurt your mom? He is your donor?"

Justin's head bobbed with a barely perceptible motion, more like a vibration than a nod. "Oh, yeah, shit!" he said. "There's another thing." He pushed himself to his feet and lifted his shirt up over his head, turning his back to Davis. Davis stood up too and Justin turned his head, looking down over his shoulder, his shirt twisted around his forearms. "That."

"What?" Davis leaned back and scouted the white planc of the boy's backside. "What? The birthmark?" Davis put his hand very near it but never touched the boy's skin. It was shaped like the top of a teakettle and disappeared under Justin's belt. "He had this?"

"Exactly like it," Justin said. "Right in that spot."

"Jesus Christ," Davis whispered.

Three rooms away, the back door opened and Joan shouted, "Hi, Dave!"

"Jesus Christ!" he said again. "You need to go now. But we need to keep talking. Saturday?"

"Yeah, I can do Saturday. Where?"

"I don't know." He heard Joan's footsteps leaving the kitchen and pushed Justin toward the front door as the boy struggled to get his shirt back on. Davis took a card out of his wallet. "This is my cell phone. Call it tomorrow. I'll figure it out." Justin snatched the card and ducked out the door without saying good-bye.

"Who was that?" Joan had entered the foyer. He couldn't tell what she'd seen.

"Hmm? A kid selling candles. For a band trip."

"You ordered one?" Joan asked.

Davis realized he had his wallet in his hand. "Two," he said. "They're going to Saint Louis." Christ, he hadn't warned Justin, hadn't told him not to tell anyone, hadn't told him he might be in danger if this Cash fellow put together the same pieces Justin had. Now that he had run out the door, there was no way of telling him. Not without violating the restraining order or involving a third person.

Joan waved a bottle of shampoo and walked into the living room. She leaned over to shut out the draft coming through the window and picked up the open copy of *Time of Death*. "I've read that," she said, handing it to Davis without a review. He took another card from his wallet and used it to mark his place before setting it down again.

— 61 —

Just as she was leaving private investigation and starting a new life, Sally, like millions of others, became immersed in Shadow World. The depth of the digital creation was fascinating to her. Every time she discovered a new spot in the game—a restaurant, a thrift store, a car wash—she sought it out on the real streets of Chicago and was always amazed when she found its twin. If she faced disappointment in the real world, she could usually find same-day redemption on her computer. The new duality of her life was both exciting and comforting, and her days were now divided almost equally—nine hours in the world, nine hours in the game, six hours sleeping.

Although they remained physically apart for more than three years, grown-up Justin never stopped visiting Sally in her dreams. The mornings after such meetings she felt invigorated but a little woozy, often unsure of what had been said, what intimacies had been exchanged. That sensation was almost always followed by sadness. Martha had been Sally's friend, but she found it was Justin she missed most. Not the real, flesh-and-blood boy almost twenty years her junior, but, as Justin/Eric himself once put it, the *idea* of him. No real man would ever measure up. Now that they were friends again in Shadow World, she could actually get to know Justin, the ideal Justin, separated from his teenaged body.

It was getting so Sally was almost looking forward to a fresh Shadow World murder.

— 62 —

Female secretaries, paralegals, and summer interns at Ginsburg and Addams shared a regular appointment. Law firm politics stratified employees into sections and subsections—those with a law degree and those without, those with testes and those without—and so the workers who fell into both of the without groups, thrown together by sexism and caste, met informally once a week for happy hour at a bar called Martin's (frequently called Martini's, in an ongoing, unfunny joke). Once together and half full of gin and vermouth, they explored other things they had in common—the weather, fear of the Wicker Man, vacations, men, and horror stories about a senior associate named Sam Coyne.

Coyne had parallel reputations in a number of categories, all of them bad. He was a cruel boss, an overly competitive softball player, an arrogant negotiator, and a strange, selfish, and violent lover. Stories regarding the last of these were usually told in the gossipy fashion of urban legends, and these stories were repeated often as the staff turned over, month by month. In fact, if the gathering at Martin's included, on average, a dozen young women, three of them had probably slept with Sam Coyne (or performed an act other than intercourse most people would count as sex, or had started such an act and not completed it because of something he said or did, or had tried to stop but felt compelled to see it through because of alleged physical or psychological coercion on Coyne's part). In most cases, these women never told their coworkers of their own involvement, but instead passed along embellished accounts of the events with the names of long-gone Ginsburg and Addams employees substituted for their own. Occasionally, one of the women would get drunk enough and fess up to a tryst with Coyne. Such a person would earn head-of-the-table honors at Martin's and would be pressed for explicit details. At the very least, she'd be expected to comment on the most notorious Sam Coyne rumor of all, that the handsome young attorney who specialized in mergers and acquisitions had a cock like the grip on a tennis racket, and a woman in the know would always confirm this by contorting her mouth into a wide oval and holding her hands apart at an exaggerated length, and a soprano-pitched roar would go up from that corner of the bar and martinis would be ordered by the tray.

Some Sam Coyne stories had sober endings (and even more dubious attribution) and they drew a different reaction. There was Nancy, who had to cover her bruised arms and legs for an entire month; Jenny, who discovered the handcuffs and the crazy leather masks in his closet and also discovered that she was kind of into it; Carrie, who felt degraded kneeling in front of

Coyne in a downtown parking garage while he pulled her hair and growled commands down at her like she was in some sort of perverse puppy school; and there were multiple stories of former Ginsburg and Addams employees, usually girls right out of schools in Missouri or Indiana, who'd been briefly imprisoned by Coyne in his car or his apartment and forced to perform on him while being verbally and physically abused. The women with tenure traded legends of raped paralegals paid to shut up and sexually harassed secretaries bullied into silence—"sexual harassment harassment," they called it. Sam Coyne was handsome like a movie star, smart like a politician, mean like a jungle cat, and hung like a bell tower, and men with that combination, the Friday night cynics at Martin's agreed, can get away with just about anything.

Sam knew the women talked about him. He heard them whispering sometimes in the break room, or caught the new ones searching his slacks surreptitiously for some topographical evidence of his infamous attribute. It didn't bother him. He even worked it into his come-on when he found himself drawn to a new girl, when he saw some darkness in her eyes, some clue in the way she dressed, some unexpected piercing, or the faint arc of a buried tattoo. "What do they say about me?" he'd ask in the late hours of overtime when one of the newbies volunteered to stay late and help him with copying or filing or whatever she could do. "Nothing," the new girl would say, looking at him with her big eyelids at their apex and her mouth turned down in a determined attempt to appear naïve. He'd say, "Half of it isn't true, you know," which would make her blush, betraying the fact that, yes, they did talk about him, and much of it was juicy and even shocking, and then he'd say, "Does that disappoint you?" and the girl would say, if she were mature beyond her years, "It depends on *which half*," and that's when he knew he'd have her in his bed or on his desk or in the copy room or in his car (or on his car), depending on the mood and circumstances and whether or not this one would lose her nerve at the last minute, like too many of them did.

— 63 —

Davis met Justin in the forest preserve, on a narrow road between the dog park and the picnic area. No one drove this bit much except to fish a tiny stream about a quarter mile ahead, and in the middle of the day it seemed as safe a place as any for a secret and illegal midday conference between a man and a teenaged boy.

Through the open window of his SUV, Davis heard the spritzing of a bicycle tire on wet pavement, and catching Justin's attention in the rearview mirror, he waved him around to the passenger side. Justin ditched his bike in the tall grass by the door, and when he climbed in, throwing his backpack on the floor mat, Davis offered him a Pepsi. Davis felt a little bit dirty: the two of them in the front seat, the bike on its side by the road, the kid's pant cuffs wet from the ride, the Pepsi, which felt like some sort of lure. He considered how happy he'd been just a week ago and how bad he felt at this moment—how his stomach seemed like it would be knotted now for the foreseeable future—and told himself this was surely a mistake. But an overlapping thought assured him there was no choice here, really. He couldn't conceive of a future in which he didn't follow up on all the boy knew. He couldn't tell Justin to forget it. He couldn't ignore him. This wasn't about options anymore, or right or wrong, or vengeance or justice or the word that used to get thrown around after AK's death: closure. Davis knew that he and the boy had only one path beneath their feet and they would follow it until it stopped, and Davis would spend the remainder of his life in whatever place they ended up.

"I forgot to tell you," Davis said. "You can't tell anyone else about this. If this guy 'Mr. Cash' found out who you were, I think you might be in danger."

"I thought of that," Justin said, pausing to expunge a carbonated belch. "Don't worry about it."

"Can you remember anything else about this guy?"

Justin's lips were severely chapped, and the skin around his mouth was red and irritated in a wide circle. It looked like he'd applied lipstick on a roller coaster. "Lived in the city. Looked like he worked out. Good-looking, of course." Justin patted himself ironically on the chest, then stopped, recalling something new. "He drove a nice car. European, like a Porsche, or maybe a Beamer or Mercedes. It might have been a convertible."

"He could be driving anything now," Davis said. "Still, expensive car. He's probably a professional. That's something of a surprise."

"What, you had this guy figured for a maniac? A psycho?"

"After what he did to my little girl? Yeah." He realized too late the question was a trap.

"So how'd you expect I would turn out?" Justin said. "Did you figure I'd come up the same way?"

Davis sighed. "There are a lot of things that make a man's character, Justin. Very little is predetermined."

"Is that why you kept such close tabs on me? Why you were *stalking* me?" He seemed to be using the language of the lawsuit deliberately, to put Davis on edge. " 'Cause you were worried?"

"A little bit."

Davis hadn't turned the radio off, only dialed the volume down to practically nothing. Justin turned it back up until a melody was recognizable—

Brahms, Violin Concerto in D Major, Davis noted to himself. Justin made a face and turned it to a top-forty station.

"So I was what?" Justin asked. "Some tool in your investigation? Like an artist's sketch. Something like that?"

"I guess you could see it that way."

"But if you had given my mother that Eric kid's DNA like you were supposed to, she'd have had a different boy. Not just me in a different body but a different consciousness altogether. Another self. I wouldn't exist at all."

"I guess not. I really don't know how it works, Justin." Davis was staring down the road through the spotted windshield. A dog, its face low to the ground, following a scent, emerged from the woods and made a circle in the road. A woman in her twenties followed with an unattached leash folded in her hand and fired off a series of rhetorical doggie questions—*What is it? What you got? Where you going?*—before the pair headed down toward the stream.

"At night it gets quiet and I try to think, and then I also try to keep track of my thoughts," Justin said. "It's like if I can figure out what I was thinking just before the thought I'm having now, and how it's connected to the thought before that and the thought before that and the thought before that, at the end of it I'll be able to find the real me." Davis noticed how different Justin appeared even just a few days removed from the meeting at his house. The breezy morning had swept his mess of hair into an unruly pile. He had as many pimples as before, but they seemed rearranged, melting away in some places and reappearing in others. He continued, "We're not made up of our thoughts, you know, even though that's the only way most of us can approach the question of identity. I am the one who makes the thoughts, and that's who I'm looking for at night: the thinker, separated from his thoughts."

The dog and the woman were just visible now. She made a throwing motion, a fake apparently, and the dog didn't fall for it. When the woman threw a ball for real, the dog bounded away and the woman disappeared after him, around a bend in the road.

Justin looked out his window, squeaking a finger against it as if trying to remove something on the other side of the glass. "What if everything about Mr. Cash and me is exactly the same except for our thoughts?" Justin asked. "I mean, our DNA is the same, our appearance is the same. What if we also have the same thinker? What if at the very core of it, our thinker, our self, is exactly the same? What if we are the same person, thinking different thoughts?"

"Honestly, Justin, I don't know. Would you say the same thing about twins? Or identical triplets? Do you think they might be one person split into three different bodies?"

Justin smiled and sought out Davis's eyes in the rearview mirror. "That would really be something, wouldn't it? I mean, why can't a person exist more than once? Physicists theorize that time travel must be possible. That you and I could go back to the meeting we had at your house and watch ourselves talking. That would require two versions of each of us coexisting but acting independently. Millions of people believe in reincarnation. Is it such a stretch to believe that a person could live more than one life at the same time, with the individual selves not even aware of each other?"

Davis twisted his hands on the leather bands wrapped around the wheel until he felt worms of grit forming in the friction against his skin. "I don't want to change the subject, but maybe this is related, somehow." He reached for an envelope in the backseat and pulled out the old computer sketch of AK's killer. The one Ricky Weiss had identified as Jimmy Spears. "What do you think about this? Does this look anything like Mr. Cash?"

Justin stared at the paper for a long time. He whistled through clenched teeth and paused and whistled again. "Little bit, yeah," he said finally. "A lot, actually. Where did you get this?"

"I got it from you. Years ago."

Justin let Davis know with uncurious silence that he understood. "That business with the football player? And the dead guy in Nebraska?" Davis nodded. The boy unzipped his backpack and took out a pen. "Can I?"

"Yeah. Sure."

Justin made a desk on his lap with a textbook and a magazine and began to draw careful lines on the sketch. The hairstyle changed, cut shorter now. He added sideburns and widened the eyebrows. He gave depth to the eyes with a few shadowing strokes, and performed similar surgery on the chin, narrowing it, making Mr. Cash thinner. Davis marveled how a few lines of ink drawn by a living hand (and not a computer) made the sketch seem more realistic. More alive. More like the boy sitting next to him.

"There," Justin said. "I can see me in there now. That's Cash."

Davis took the paper and angled it away from him into light refracted through the windshield. He had spent untold hours with this face, but was only now seeing it as an actual person as opposed to an abstract idea—a person to be found, to be confronted, to be feared. It gave him a chill and he wondered what it would be like to be this close to the real thing.

"So how do we find him?" Justin said.

"There's no chance you could get any more info out of your mom?"

Justin made a noise with his lips like air leaking from a basketball. "No way. She's never mentioned it since that night. I think she's hoping I repressed it or something. If I bring it up now she'll get my shrink involved, and her shrink, too. She'll freak."

"No good," Davis agreed. "We can't let her suspect."

"Yeah. She finds out about this she'll have my butt grounded and your butt thrown in jail."

"Probably. I'm going to work on this a little. I used a detective agency a few years ago . . ." He stopped.

Justin giggled. "Gold Badge? The one that hired Sally Barwick to take the pictures of me? My mom's got a restraining order against them, too." He reached into his backpack and pulled out a notebook. He paged through it, looking for something among the class notes and elaborate ink doodles. "This is the guy Sally used to work for. His office is downtown. Mr. Cash lived in the city, remember?" He wrote something and tore off a page corner.

Davis stuffed the paper in his pocket. "You still talk to Sally Barwick? What is she doing these days?"

Justin shrugged. "Dunno."

Davis didn't press him on it. He really didn't care. "Do you ride your bike to school every day?"

"Until it gets too cold."

"When I find something out, I'll put a white piece of paper in an upstairs window of my house. The one on the far right as you're looking at it. Ride by in the morning from now on and if you see it, call me on my cell. And don't use your own phone. If your mother sees my number on your bill it's all over."

"Right," Justin said. He checked his bag to make sure it was zipped tight and opened the passenger door.

"Justin," Davis said. The boy stuck both feet on the ground where the pavement surrendered to the wild grass and leaned back into the cab. "That stuff you said, about the self, about the thinker separate from his thoughts. One self occupying two bodies . . ."

The boy blushed. "That's just stuff I kick around. I'm embarrassed to talk about it with people I know, so when I get a few minutes with a stranger . . ."

"Well, you're a smart young man," Davis said. For some reason the words had a difficult time coming out of his mouth. His eyes rinsed themselves and his nose went numb. He started to say he was proud of him but realized how stupid and wrong that would sound.

Justin shrugged and squinted in a manner that fell just short of being modest. "Yeah, smart," he said. "That's gonna make me a real bastard to catch."

— 64 —

Big Rob's tiny Ogden Avenue office hadn't been altered in even small ways since he quit the force and started taking on clients. The walls had the same rose tint. The furniture, two decades out of date when he opened up shop, was now approaching the forty-year mark and was nearly but not quite retro chic. The carpet was industrial-grade, the kind they used in department stores, and along well-traveled routes he had treated the periodic coffee stains with dish soap and a damp cloth. Surrounded by dust, an old CPD bowling trophy stood on a filing cabinet like a statue anchored in concrete.

"Dr. Moore," Big Rob said. "I'm surprised to see you here."

"Really?"

Biggie nodded. "I hardly know you and yet I feel like we've been through some traumatic events together."

"Phil Canella was your friend, I understand," Davis Moore said.

"He was. And I'm very sorry about your late wife."

Davis nodded, thankful that such business could be dispensed of quickly. "I'm looking for a man. I don't know much about him. But I need you to get me his name and to tell me where he lives."

Biggie held up a hand and stood from behind his desk. Although there wasn't room for a man his size to walk freely in this office, when he was with a client he liked to be on his feet. It felt like exercise. "Who are we looking for?"

Davis took a small notebook from his pocket. He had written down pages of thoughts and notions since meeting Justin in the forest preserve three days ago, and he had done his best to filter the speculation from the facts. "His last name could be Cash, or something similar. He grew up around Northwood— was probably living there eighteen years ago, and one or both of his parents might still live on the North Shore. He likely has some history of violence against women, although I can't say if he has a record or not. He has money— he's possibly a doctor or a lawyer or a banker or an entrepreneur—and he probably drives an expensive European car. As of six years ago, he was living in the city of Chicago." He paused while he decided if the next piece of information would be helpful. "Around the same time, he went on a single date with Martha Finn."

Biggie groaned and pointed at Davis. "Gold Badge hired my assistant, on your behalf, to take pictures of her son. Mrs. Finn has a restraining order against Sally now. She has a restraining order against you, too. I read that in the paper."

"That's fine. I don't want anyone to bother her."

Big Rob looked out the window, deciding how he was going to live with the regrets that were already taking shape in his head. *Christ.* "What else do you know?"

Davis turned to a pair of notes he'd made after contemplating the things Justin said in the car. "As a child he might have been fascinated with fire, or connected to the disappearance of animals or pets. He'll be extremely intelligent. Probably much smarter than you or me."

"Great," Biggie said. "A psycho, in other words. And a genius. What is he, like a mad scientist or something?" He chuckled.

Davis opened his briefcase and pulled out the sketch. "Finally, he looks like this. Or he did until recently."

Big Rob pulled the paper across his desk, touching it only at the edges. "I know this picture. Philly had it when he died." He looked into Davis Moore's eyes for signs of truthfulness.

"My wife found it on my computer and sent it to him, thinking it might be related to"—he wasn't sure how to put this—"her case. It's been refined a little since then."

Big Rob held it up in front of his face, blocking the sight line to his client. "Philly died over this face." He forced an impassive expression onto his eyes and lips and set the sketch down, fixing his gaze again on Davis.

Biggie told Davis his fee. "And you'll pay my expenses in the meantime?"

"I will." Davis unfolded cash from his pocket. Biggie sighed and accepted the money without counting it.

— 65 —

The sheets on Justin's bed hadn't been changed in a week and a half, and Martha felt terrible about that. She had been showing four houses a day, many of them for the same client, a young woman (just married to an older doctor) who had convinced her husband they needed a suburban house with a yard and a playroom and a big kitchen more than they needed a downtown apartment with a view of the lake. "If he thinks I'm going to raise kids in the city just so he can be close to his Gold Coast mistresses, he's nuts," she told Martha. The woman confessed she knew about her husband's Gold Coast mistresses because until recently she had been one of them.

For a boy's room, Justin's was unusually tidy. He spent a few minutes at the end of every day organizing, arranging his books at alphabetical attention, blowing the dust from his computer keyboard, coordinating his clothes for the following morning. Although he never showed signs of fatigue, she couldn't imagine how he had time for sleep, between school, his own independent study, his fastidiousness, and the hours he spent playing that blasted computer game. She had read an article about how thousands of kids (and adults, too) spent so much time playing Shadow World they had become indifferent to, if not outright neglectful of, their own, real lives. Extracurricular and athletic team enrollment were both down dramatically in high schools across the country, and many educators claimed, credibly, that Shadow World was to blame. It made sense: just in Northwood, Martha personally knew of three— *three!*—marriages that had broken up because one spouse had left the other for someone they'd met in Shadow World. At least Terry left Martha for his personal assistant. There was something almost old-fashioned about that.

Not everyone agreed the game was entirely bad for kids, though. Some psychologists claimed teens who experimented with adult scenarios in Shadow World were better prepared for college and the pressures of leaving home. They were said to be confident, less risk averse, and more likely to be content once they entered the working world. Never having played the game herself, Martha was skeptical about such claims, but it was easier to believe them than to try taking the game away from her son (or her son away from the game), so she chose to have faith.

Martha pulled the dirty sheets from the mattress and aired out the clean ones, measuring the sides of the fitted sheet and folding the corners of the top sheet. Then she reassembled blanket and comforter and pillowcases, trying to be as neat about it as her son would be. He never complained but Martha had caught him more than once remaking the bed after she had done it, to his mind, in a substandard way.

She had sorted the laundry and carried her own clothes into the master bedroom (compared to where she slept, Justin spent his nights in a biological clean room). Two weeks' worth of his shirts, jeans, and underwear, washed and dried in a morning-long marathon, filled three round laundry baskets, and she set about putting them away in their proper places. Blue jeans needed to be folded and stacked on the second shelf from the bottom in his closet. Shirts hung on plastic hangers, never metal. Blue socks had a different drawer than black socks. Underwear should be rolled instead of folded. Again, he never complained to her or threw a tantrum over it, but she knew he'd redo it if she didn't get it exactly right.

At the bottom of the laundry basket she found three bleached-and-dried one-dollar bills. She must not have checked all the pockets before she threw his pants in the washer. Worried she might have ruined something important—a homework assignment or a pretty girl's phone number—and not above using that concern as an excuse to snoop, Martha began feeling inside Justin's pockets. She found two more ones and a five in the first four pairs and set the money on his dresser. In the fifth, her hand felt something curious: paper, wrinkled and warped in the agitated soapy water and spin cycle, the size of a business card. She pulled it out. The name printed on it didn't even register with her at first without the "M.D." behind it.

Anger wasn't the word for what pulsed through her. Outrage was closer. Or just rage. She wondered where Moore had approached him. For how long had they been meeting? *What does that sonofabitch want with my son, and why won't he leave us alone?* She wanted to call her lawyer, but knew he'd start the clock at $350 an hour. She wanted to call the police, but knew the first thing they'd ask was whether she had ascertained all the facts. *Have you talked to your son, ma'am? It's not a violation of the restraining order for your son to be carrying around a piece of paper with Davis Moore's name and number.* The truth was she couldn't ask Justin. She was too scared. He hadn't said a cross word to her in over four years, but he still frightened her. A mother knows her son, even if he received none of her DNA. A mother knows what her son is capable of. Every time he quietly redid the bedding or refolded his jeans, Martha imagined the pressure building inside his head and inside his heart, pressing against his skull and his ribs, whistling in his ears. Sooner or later it would need to be released.

But as long as she could keep Justin close, as long as her boy studied and played under her roof and under her eyes, as long as she remained interested and up to date with his friends and his hobbies, she could guide and control and protect him.

And hope for the best.

Martha grabbed a piece of paper from Justin's printer and wrote down Davis Moore's private phone number and e-mail address, and she returned the card to Justin's pocket.

— 66 —

In the middle of downtown Northwood was a roundabout where six streets intersected, and in the middle of the roundabout was a small park with a half dozen benches, each perpendicular to one of the streets, and in the middle of the park was a statue of a soldier, erected after World War I but understood to commemorate Northwood veterans from all the military conflicts since, including the most recent mini and proxy wars in Asia and Africa. Parades on Memorial Day and Veterans Day and the Fourth of July always ended here, which made good sense for both symbolism and downtown business.

Big Rob and Davis had made an appointment to meet in the middle of the roundabout, it being a sunny weekday and close to the bank where Davis needed to withdraw the detective's fee.

Big Rob had spent three weeks tracking down the mysterious Mr. Cash— starting with Chicago and Northwood phone books, then widening his search to online databases he subscribed to for just this purpose. He worked the professional organizations—the bar association, the futures exchange—and found a few Cashes, but none that matched the few facts he had about the man. Big Rob called a friend on the force and got access to recent domestic complaints and sexual assaults, and he checked area luxury-car dealers. If the guy's name was Cash, the pool of suspects was too small, and if it was just something similar, the pool of suspects might as well be infinite.

The break came when Big Rob wasn't even looking for it.

"Fum ducking luck," Big Rob said to himself.

He had collected several months of back issues of *Northwood Life*, which seemed to exist only to print the names of as many residents as possible in every edition. He was scanning them inattentively on a Friday afternoon (but mostly using them to catch Ho Hos crumbs before they reached the floor) when he found a paragraph announcing that Sam Coyne, a graduate of Northwood East and the son of Northwood residents James and Alicia Coyne, had been named a partner at the downtown law firm of Ginsburg and Addams. The name didn't trip any neurons in Big Rob's head, but when he saw the photo of Sam Coyne, he bit his tongue. The picture in the paper was a professional business portrait. Sam was handsome, in his thirties, and blond. His suit fit precisely and he looked healthy underneath it. And the face was nearly the same face Big Rob had taped to the top of his desk twenty days ago. "Cash. Cash. Coyne," Biggie mumbled to himself. "Christ, it's gotta be."

Big Rob stood nervously behind his desk. Sometimes the cases just solve themselves, he thought. But he was also a man who believed in earning his fee.

At five o'clock he was loitering outside the glass doors engraved with the names Ginsburg and Addams and hopped on a descending elevator with a gaggle of G&A secretaries. They ranged in age from about twenty to about fifty-five, none of them wore a wedding ring, and they seemed a little happy and loud to be headed for a train home. "I just made fifteen thousand dollars without doing a damn thing," Biggie announced to the cab as it descended past the twelfth floor. "And I'd like to spend a good chunk of it tonight getting beautiful ladies drunk." The secretaries whooped and hollered.

The next day he called Philly's old buddy Tony Dee at Mozzarell. "Tony, how'd you like to do me favor? For old times' sake. For Phil Canella's sake."

Tony Dee laughed. "What you want?"

"How far back do your reservation books go?"

"I got 'em all the way back to the day I opened," Tony said.

"And credit card records?"

"The same. My accountant says I should get rid of 'em. What do you think?"

"I think you should toss 'em," Biggie said. "But only after I get a good look."

On the bench in the middle of the roundabout Big Rob kissed the sides of a strawberry ice cream cone and pinned an envelope under his left thigh to protect it from the cool autumn breeze. He waited about five minutes before Davis Moore appeared. He also had an ice cream cone. Vanilla.

"Hey, we had the same idea," Biggie said, waving his napkin around as a stand-in for his devoured cone. Davis sat down and they didn't look at each other or say anything right away, as if they had no business, as if this meeting were only chance, just a couple of men deciding to get in one last ice cream before the weather turned cold. Big Rob's clients always acted like this. Secretive. Paranoid. He guessed they saw characters in their position act this way on television, and most people had no other frame of reference for the detective business. Biggie always indulged them.

"His name is Sam Coyne," Big Rob said. Davis looked puzzled. "Coyne. Cash. You said it was something *like* Cash, so I connected the dots."

"How do you know it's him?"

Big Rob pulled the summary page of the Moore file out of the envelope and read from it. "Samuel Coyne. Grew up in Northwood. Parents still live here. He was recently named partner at the law firm Ginsburg and Addams. Leases a tricked-out BMW, always black. Has a reputation among his adversaries and peers for being a ruthless sonofabitch, and among his female coworkers for being both a slut and into the rough stuff. No criminal record. Six years ago—that's in the time frame you specified—he dined here at Northwood's finest restaurant, Mozzarell. Ordered the expensive wine."

"Was he with Martha Finn?"

"Reservation was for two."

"That doesn't prove anything. His parents live here."

"You're right," Big Rob said.

"Do you have a photo?"

"I do." Big Rob reached again into the envelope and retrieved an original of the photograph that had appeared in *Northwood Life*. He'd paid a twenty-three-year-old copy editor fifty bucks for it so Moore wouldn't think he was charging him 15K for clipping articles out of the local paper.

Davis stared at it and nodded, and the empty, narrow bottom of his cone scratched the sides of his throat as he swallowed it nearly whole. "You're right. It's him." There followed an uncertain pause. Biggie knew it as the transition when the detective's responsibility became the client's. Except for an inheritance case here and there and the really messed-up revenge divorces, no one who hired him really wanted to hear the information he provided. Biggie was the finder of bad news, and now that it was his, Davis Moore was going to have to figure out what to do with it.

"Dr. Moore," Big Rob said, "if you don't mind me asking, and please don't tell me if it's something I don't wanna know, but what are you gonna do to this guy?"

Davis took the envelope and began examining the rest of the contents for himself. "Nothing. Probably."

"I only ask because of Ricky Weiss. When he thought your man here was Jimmy Spears, he said you were gonna kill the guy. That's why he said he killed Philly. He was scared of you."

"Ricky's the killer," Davis said. "Not me."

"Yeah, that's what I figure, too. But if I find myself on a witness stand at somebody's future murder trial, I want to be able to say that I asked. That my conscience is clean. Within reason, I mean."

"You did, and it is," Davis said. "Shall we get your money?"

The two of them walked to Lake Shore Bank, where Davis had opened up an account fifteen years ago to finance his investigation into Anna Kat's death. He had kept a slush fund here to hide traveling expenses, as well as a reserve of reward money, from Jackie. He never closed the account and meant to tell Joan about it several times, but he never did. For a while he thought he might use it to surprise her with a trip or a car or a spectacular piece of jewelry. The current balance was $56,533.21.

It took about half an hour for the manager to fill out the paperwork and get all the necessary approvals for a cashier's check of that size. Big Rob and Davis waited wordlessly in a small cubed office belonging to an account manager, who brought them coffee and an assortment of cookies on a small plate. Despite the odd half walls surrounding them, on which the gray carpet from the floor seemed to be crawling toward the ceiling like ivy, voices in this place, with its high ceilings and broad tiles and marble counters and hushed tones, would carry.

When it arrived, Biggie folded one of the easiest checks of his career under his green windbreaker and into the pocket of his short-sleeved dress shirt, and they walked out the west-facing front door into the early evening, where the sun shot rays parallel to the ground and directly into their eyes. Big Rob put on his sunglasses and held out his hand to indicate the close of the deal.

"There's one more thing in there I didn't tell you about," Biggie said as his fingers wrapped around the doctor's palm. "You'll read it yourself when you go through that file, but I wanted to say it." He set his left hand on Davis's shoulder and put his mouth close to the man's ear, but he didn't whisper. This wasn't so much a secret as a confidence: "Coyne and your daughter were in the same class at Northwood East."

Davis watched the detective walk away. He didn't know how he should feel, nor could he diagnose the pain in his stomach. He had an envelope with a name and a photograph, and he'd thought it would make him happy to know the truth at last, but it made him anxious, not glad. Anna Kat had been murdered by someone she knew. Perhaps even a friend. The last thing she would have felt was not just horror and pain, but betrayal as well.

— 67 —

It had been thirteen weeks since Justin received his last Shadow World news alert. Eight killings in four months, and then nothing. No stabbed or strangled avatars discarded in the alleys or in the back rooms of bars or in dirty Lincoln Avenue motel rooms. Justin hadn't played the game at all in two months except to check in on his avatar and to celebrate his Shadow mother's birthday.

Tuesday morning, dressed for school in jeans and a black T-shirt, he poured dry cereal in a bowl and pawed through the mess of bills and home magazines and catalogs on the kitchen counter.

"What are you looking for, hon?" Martha asked.

"The paper," Justin mumbled.

"The Tempo section is on the table there," she said.

Justin kept shoving aside piles of old paper. "Nuh-uh. The front page."

Martha sighed. "You shouldn't read this stuff. You get so worked up." She opened a baseboard cabinet where she kept the big pots and removed the folded *Tribune* section. "But I guess I can't keep it from you. The radio, the television, the Internet. God knows what you talk about in school."

Justin sat down and flattened the paper on the table. The headline read:

DAMEN AVENUE DEATH

Cops say woman, 23, could be first Wicker Man victim in six months

Justin read the story quickly. She was found behind a French restaurant. Strangled and stabbed. Raped. Body left in the rain. No prints, no DNA. Police guessed time of death was between 2 and 4 a.m. Justin agreed: it was the Wicker Man, all right.

The story continued with as many details about the victim as they could gather. She was from downstate. A student at DePaul. She had eaten at the restaurant with friends earlier in the evening. None of them were considered suspects. Not much more than that. This edition had been distributed electronically (and printed directly in the homes of subscribers on large-format paper), but the reporter still would have had only an hour or so to file the story.

At the end of the article was an editorial note in italics: *"Sally Barwick helped with the reporting on this story."*

Hunh.

He put on his coat and kissed his mother good-bye. "Finish your cereal, you have time," she said.

"Gotta be in early today," he told her as the kitchen door shut behind him. "There's a science lab I need to finish before class."

Martha sighed. She felt certain that was a lie.

When he'd gone three blocks on his bike, Justin turned right where he should have turned left and circled back to Stone Avenue. The last few mornings he worried he had been looking at the wrong window. What if Dr. Moore had left him the signal days or weeks ago and he'd missed it somehow? He paused his bike a few houses down and scanned every upstairs window, eight of them across the face of the large Prairie home. In the upper-right quadrant, underneath a flat, protruding eave, there was a window separated into eight panes. A piece of white paper had been taped inside the bottom left pane and the curtains behind it had been pulled shut.

Justin picked his feet off the ground and propelled himself forward. Finally. The waiting had been horrible. With no word from Dr. Moore and nothing going on in Shadow World, his life for the last few weeks had been practically suspended.

He endured his morning classes—English, calculus, history—and rushed across the main building to get to fourth-period computer science early. He was only the sixth person to arrive. Now he just had to remember which boxes were still live with the game.

Shadow World had become so popular that Northwood East (and hundreds of other schools across the country) had to ban students from playing it during school hours. It was too big a distraction. Teachers tried to be diligent about deleting the software from hard drives and networks on campus, but the kids wanted to play more than the teachers wanted to stop them, and Justin could almost always find a machine with an undetected installation. He sat in the back left seat and searched the computer there. Nothing. He slid over to the next chair and tried again. This time he found it in a hidden folder, nested deep in the directory and renamed "HISTOR~." An indifferent teacher conducting a half-assed search would never have found it.

The students were mostly in their seats now. They were supposed to be working on independent programming projects, so their teacher, Mrs. Biden (too old to know how to do anything useful on a computer, the students all agreed), made a few brief announcements and then urged them to work quietly, as she always did. Justin had already finished his assignment, or nearly anyway, and he called it up on the screen so he could switch to it in a keystroke if someone walked behind him. Then he logged on.

The game downloaded the time from a government lab, consulted his schedule, and figured out he should be in this classroom. Fourth period was an hour long, followed by lunch, which was also an hour. He had a forty-minute study hall for sixth period and had already put in a request to spend his free period here in the computer room. That meant he had two and a half hours. He hoped it would be enough.

Typing every word he wanted his avatar to speak (at school he couldn't use the headset or the teachers would bust him in a second), Shadow Justin told his Shadow teacher he wasn't feeling well, and she excused him to the nurse's office. His avatar ducked out the doors by the gym and took a shortcut through the woods toward downtown Northwood, jogging along a path of mud and dead grass. An early snow had covered the ground a week before but it had melted from even moderately traveled places and the game reflected the messy result even along this out-of-the-way trail. He couldn't risk getting his bike from the rack. Someone in the game would see him. Looking around the room he guessed there were three others playing at the same time, and their online alter egos were no doubt skipping out on school as well.

In fifteen minutes he was on a train headed into the city. Other suburbs rolled past as the light midday ridership boarded and disembarked. At Northwestern station he got off the train and passed an arcade on Washington. He wondered what it would be like to go inside and play a coin-operated video game through his computer. Some other day.

Speed was the thing, so Justin hailed a cab and took it to Tribune Tower, just north of the Chicago River. The sidewalk in front of the Gothic stone building on the east side of Michigan Avenue was active with reporters and other workers from the paper returning from the field or heading out to lunch. Twin revolving doors, framed in glass and wood and set inside the elaborately carved stone edifice, sucked men and women into the building at the same rate they pushed them out.

The lobby was several stories high and the walls lined with a variety of reflective stones. A security guard sat at a marble half-moon desk, checking people as they came in. Two banks of elevators were behind them, and over the elevators was an engraved quote from Colonel Robert R. McCormick, the first publisher of the *Tribune*.

"Guard, I'm here to see Sally Barwick," Justin typed when he came to the front of the short line. "She's expecting me." That was a lie.

"Your name?" the guard asked.

"Justin Finn."

The guard touched a directory screen in front of him. "Sally Barwick.

She's on the fourth floor. Let me call up and see if she can come get you."
He appeared to be listening to the phone ring over the handset, and he
waved Justin aside so he could help the next person. If Sally wasn't playing
the game at the moment, he would no doubt tell Justin to come back later.
No good.

The elevator dinged and a half dozen people stepped off while a crowd of
avatars pushed forward, preparing to squeeze in. Shadow Justin quietly joined
them and the back of the guard's head was pinched away by the closing elevator doors.

It took only a few minutes of navigating the paths between cubicles up and
down the fourth-floor newsroom to find Sally's desk. Her avatar was typing
diligently at her keyboard, working on a story.

"Sally?" Justin said.

Shadow Sally looked up. She didn't appear to recognize him. "I'm sorry.
I'm very busy. Perhaps you can come back later and we can talk." A programmed response. Weird.

If she was signed out of the game, her avatar should have been gray and
lethargic. When a person was logged off, the player's avatar went on auto-
pilot, performing typical functions in a robotic torpor. If, in Shadow World,
the person had a job in a cotton-ball factory, the avatar would continue
to make cotton balls in the player's absence. A player could leave simple
instructions—take the five-fifteen train, make a TV dinner, go to bed at
eleven—and until the player returned to the game, the avatar would have
minimal contact with other players. It would even turn a washed-out blue
color so others would know that interaction was discouraged. Sally's avatar
had a normal complexion, but clearly real Sally wasn't in control.

Justin typed, "Sally, will you be coming online for lunch?"

"That's impossible to say," Shadow Barwick said. "If you would like to
leave me a note, I will see it when I am less busy."

"Sally, fine," Justin typed. He found a piece of paper and a pencil on her
desk and wrote:

SALLY,
I'M AT THE BILLY GOAT.
PLEASE MEET ME.
I'LL BE THERE UNTIL 1 P.M.
JUSTIN

Sally acknowledged the note when he set it in front of her, but the avatar
did not read it. Instead she went back to typing an imaginary article about an
imaginary subject no one would ever read.

Justin rode the elevator back down to the street and walked past the security guard, who seemed unconcerned that he'd lost track of Justin only a few minutes before. He must be a program-operated character, Justin thought. The program lets you get away with much. Real players do not.

He crossed the street, descended a concrete staircase to Lower Michigan Avenue, and walked into the Billy Goat Tavern. He ordered a hamburger, chips, and a cola and found a wobbly table with a view of the door.

The real Billy Goat wasn't much to look at, and the Shadow Billy Goat reflected that. A long L-shaped bar had been built along two walls, and several televisions hung above it, showing highlights from last night's Bulls game. The chairs were the institutional kind, with hollow aluminum frames and vinyl seats and backs with a faux wood finish. The linoleum floor was old and dirty. Frames on the walls held photographs, some autographed, of the Shadow Billy Goat's celebrity patrons. These celebrities fell into three categories—people who were famous in the real world but mostly unknown inside Shadow World; people who led anonymous lives in the real world but who had become famous inside Shadow World; and people who were famous in the real world as well as in Shadow World. Most of those in this last group were True-to-Lifers, extreme celebrity egotists who were unsatisfied with the adoration they received from actual people. They needed the love and attention of a whole other universe. Some of them were intriguing, however, like the current and popular Chicago news anchorwoman whose Shadow World character had left journalism to become a world-famous concert cellist. Now *that* was cool, Justin thought.

Back in his seat at school, the bell rang and the other students hurried out the door toward the cafeteria. Justin stretched, but hardly anyone noticed that he lingered behind. It wasn't unusual for students to work in the computer lab through the lunch period, and few of his classmates were close enough to young Justin to care what he had planned for the noon meal. Alone, he turned his attention back to the game.

He was through with his burger and about to open his bag of chips when Shadow Sally walked through the door. She stood at the top of the steps and looked around. When she located Justin she nodded, but she didn't look happy to see him.

"Justin, a little young to be in a bar by yourself in the middle of the afternoon, aren't you?" she said.

"Sally, in the real world maybe," Shadow Justin said. "They're pretty lax about that here in the game."

She sat down and nudged two fingers inside Justin's bag of chips. "What's going on?" There was no one else within listening distance, so they could stop identifying each other by name. "You're typing. Are you at school?" If she had a headset on, his voice would have sounded artificial, her computer reproducing his typed words in a flat, mechanical tone. Her spoken words, on the other hand, were spelled out across Justin's monitor in subtitles.

"Yeah, it sucks," Justin said. He attempted an awkward segue: "But you know, after all this time, I never had you pegged for a TTL."

Sally didn't reply for a moment and Justin wondered if he'd offended her. "No shame in being a True-to-Lifer, is there?"

"None whatsoever," Justin agreed. "I was surprised, is all. I figured you were just a crime buff like me who got herself a job at a Shadow World newspaper."

"I am, I guess," Barwick said. "Except I got myself a job at a real-life newspaper first. How'd you find me out?"

"I saw your byline in the paper this morning."

"And how'd you know I'd be logging on before one o'clock?"

"I figured a TTL wouldn't let a lunch break go by without getting in the game."

"Yeah," Sally said. "I'm always terrified the program will let my avatar walk into traffic, or slip in front of the El or something. I need to be controlling her as much as possible."

"When I saw you at your desk, your avatar looked live, but you weren't there. How is that possible?"

Shadow Sally smiled. "Ancient Shadow World secret. An old TTL trick."

"I don't really understand True-to-Life play," Justin confessed. "You're just putting her through the motions of your own existence."

"More or less," she said. "But that's the closest thing I can get to understanding the way others see me. That's the goal of the game, as far as I'm concerned. A lot of people play it in order to create an idealized version of themselves, but I want Shadow Sally to be as much like the real me as possible. Through her, I can get a better handle on who I really am."

"I've never heard a TTL put it that way, exactly," Justin typed. "That's kind of cool. I think about that stuff a lot—who I am versus who I think I am versus who other people think I am."

Sally said, "Interested in the existential mysteries of life? I guess that's normal for a fifteen-year-old. I forget what it was like to be that age sometimes. Still trying to figure it all out. Wondering what grown-ups know that you don't."

"Save me the trouble," Shadow Justin said. "What do grown-ups know?"

"Not a damn thing. But you have a jones for philosophy? That's good."

"Yeah, my mom got me started on that stuff when I was a kid," Justin wrote.

"Your mother? Why?"

"I don't know." Justin typed quickly, not wanting to bring up his shrink and generally trying to steer the subject away from his own life. "I think it's kind of funny that you're a True-to-Lifer, though, given some of the conversations we've had."

"What do you mean?"

"I mean the Wicker Man. I've been suggesting since we hooked up in Shadow World that he might be a TTL, a guy who mirrors his real-life killing online."

"Yeah, so? You think I'm him?" She was kidding, Justin was pretty sure.

"No, I don't think you're him. But why do you find my theory so implausible, considering you're a True-to-Lifer yourself?"

"Because there are so many other explanations that make more sense, Justin. The correct explanation is almost always the simplest one."

"Occam's Razor, I know," Justin typed.

"Huh?"

"William of Occam. Fourteenth-century Franciscan monk. *The correct explanation is almost always the simplest one.* He said that." Justin wondered if he was coming across like a know-it-all. He frequently did in real life.

"You're full of surprises," Sally said. "It's hot in here." Temperature in the game was metered on-screen, and characters were expected to act accordingly—remove clothes, drink liquids—or they would start to get tired. Eventually avatars could become dehydrated and need to go to a Shadow emergency room.

Justin didn't want to talk about the broken thermostat. "But why is it more likely that the Shadow World murders, or the ones most similar to the Wicker Man killings at least, are being done by a copycat, when we know that a quarter of the folks in Shadow World are True-to-Lifers like you? Why not explore the possibility that the Wicker Man is a gamer and he's killing in both worlds?"

"Because we have no evidence of that beyond your crazy imagination. And even if it were true, Justin, how would we prove it? The Wicker Man hasn't left any physical evidence in the real world. On a computer network he'd be a total phantom. No fingerprints, no DNA, no blood evidence." She paused, as if she were hesitant to say the next thing. "Plus there's another reason."

"What?"

"The Wicker Man's victims are posed, postmortem. The bodies in Shadow World aren't."

"Some of them looked kind of posed," Justin said.

"No, the real Wicker Man victims have their legs spread wide apart, and the left hand is covering their left breast. Every one of them," Sally said. "The cops have asked to keep that out of the papers so they don't run up against copycats."

Justin was undeterred. "Maybe he's doing it slightly different in the game.

I just think it's worth looking into. If we find out who's killing these girls in Shadow World, it might lead us to the real-life killer."

Sally's avatar covered her mouth but no titles showed up on Justin's screen to indicate she was laughing. Maybe she was yawning. "Yes, I suppose that's true." She said. "Is this what you came all the way down here for? To argue this all over again now that you've found out I'm a TTL?"

"I'm in school," Justin typed. "I'm bored."

"Smart guy like you, I'm not surprised."

"I have to go to my next class soon. I should head for the train."

"Yeah, and my lunch break's about over."

"Sally, tell me something before I split," Justin wrote. "If I had gone downtown in real life and left you a message that I was waiting for you across the street, would you have shown up?" As he typed he realized it sounded flirtatious and, given his age, presumptuous. He didn't care.

Shadow Sally reached across the table and touched him on the shoulder. "<AGE INAPPROPRIATE> right, I would," she wrote, turning his empty bag of chips inside out. "A girl's gotta eat."

— 68 —

They would have been meaningless, forgettable syllables six weeks ago, but the name took on an instant taint of evil when he heard Dr. Moore say it. He fingered through the envelope of evidence, which featured it in bold type on every page.

Sam Coyne.

In Justin's mind it was a name already as menacing, and as fascinating, as Bundy and Gacy and Speck.

Samuel Nathan Coyne. It needed the middle name to be official. For the highest dishonor.

"So what do we do?"

"I'm not sure," Davis said.

"Let's go to the cops," Justin said. "We can explain what happened. Get a judge to order a sample of his DNA. If it matches mine they can charge him with Anna Kat's murder."

"I don't think it's that simple."

"Why not? Wasn't that always your plan?"

"First of all, I doubt we have enough evidence here for a warrant. As soon as the sample of Coyne's DNA left the police station, the chain of evidence was broken. The fact that his DNA matches yours, or even that it matches the original sample, if I still had it, would probably be inadmissible. Plus there's the fact that when I created you—and you're the only evidence that fingers him—I broke the law. Any good attorney, and Coyne would have a dozen of those, would have a field day. Coyne would go free, I'd probably go to prison for ten years, and *your* life would become a media freak show. You'd be the world-famous Killer Clone Boy of Chicago."

Justin didn't look up from the thin stack of paper and photographs. "I could handle that. Could you? Would you go to prison in order to catch him?" Davis shuddered at the matter-of-fact way the boy said it. Like it was a challenge. As if he were calling Davis out. *Now you're not going to be a problem, are you? You're not going to go yellow on me?* There in the car Davis realized he was afraid of Justin Finn, the boy made from an animal. But he was also in awe of him. He had poise. Intelligence. Charisma. Talking with him, it was nearly impossible to keep in mind that he was only a fifteen-year-old kid.

"At one point, yes, I would have been willing to do that, years ago," said Davis, although he couldn't remember if that was really true. "Now I don't know. Could I do that to my wife? If it meant Coyne would go to prison, or worse, maybe. I'm not sure. But it doesn't matter. It wouldn't do any good."

Justin felt himself getting warm inside his coat and he cracked the window. The old trees of the park covered the car in a dappled shade. It had been pleasant all day, if a little cold, and the path was more crowded than it had been the last time they met. This discussion was more important than caution, however.

"I've been looking for that name for eighteen years," Davis said. "Sam Coyne. I've done unimaginable things. Phil Canella and my first wife are both dead because of it. And now that I know, I've never felt more helpless. When I didn't know who killed AK, I could imagine he was a miserable psychotic. I could imagine him suffering in some prison, or hospital. I could imagine him rotting in the ground. Burning in hell. Forced to confront the evil he committed. To pay for it. I could imagine the karmic scales had been balanced without my help. Honestly, it tortures me to know he's been made partner in a thriving law practice. That he lives in an expensive condominium on the Gold Coast. That beautiful young women are probably lined up at his door." Davis felt like he might cry, but he also felt detached and cold, like he did the night of Anna Kat's murder. He didn't cry over her body, and he didn't cry now.

Justin said, "Dr. Moore, I've read a lot of books written by philosophers. Some of them, like Kierkegaard, are trying to figure out who we are, what makes one guy different from the next guy. Some want to know if there's a God. Like Anselm or Augustine. Others—Hobbes, Hume—are trying to sort out right from wrong: what's okay to do, what isn't okay, and why. Every single one of them, in his own way, is trying to find out, *Why am I here?*" He clutched the envelope in the space between them. "Do you know how many get to hold the answer in their hands?"

Davis coughed, the spasm in his throat disguising his amazement. Justin was so much like an adult. Davis had expected something like empathy from him and instead got a lecture on metaphysics. "Come on, Justin. You're more than that. More than some investigative tool. I was callous about bringing you into this world. I should have considered the consequences, the burden I'd be putting on you if you or anyone else ever found out, but I take responsibility for that. There's nothing unique or odd about you, physically or metaphysically. You're just a teenager—an extremely intelligent teenager, obviously—but a teenager like any other." As was so often the case these days, Davis wasn't sure he believed what he was saying.

Justin waved the envelope. "I am a teenager capable of horrible things, apparently."

"We're *all* capable of horrible things. Every one of us. If there's anything you've proved in the first fifteen years of your life it's that a man is more than just the sum of his chromosomes."

Justin held Big Rob's report out the window and turned it into and against the wind with the rolling motion of a conductor's hand. "I can't just let it go. I think we have a responsibility. A duty or something."

Davis almost wished Justin would open his fingers and let the wind take the evidence somewhere into the park. Wished someone else would discover this $15,000 dossier on Sam Coyne and wonder who he is. What he had done. Wished it could be someone else's duty. "I'm open to suggestions," he said.

Justin said, "Dr. Moore, I believe that choices, all choices, are made for us. The weather, the time of day or night, our sexual needs, our survival needs, latitude and longitude, the collective will of the other six billion people on earth—these are the things that determine our fate. Maybe God works through them and maybe not. But when we pretend to exercise free will, when we make what we think are choices, we're really just signing off on that which has been preordained by the universe. A hurricane has more choices than man."

Justin leaned across the armrest that separated them. "When the right idea is *suggested,* by you or by me, it will already be inevitable."

— 69 —

Another night at home and another night Davis was spending downstairs in the blue room. Alone. Joan noticed he'd started messing around down there right after she suggested they clean it out. It was predictable behavior in some ways. Getting older and averse to change, Davis felt the room was threatened and reasserted control over it. She'd had enough psych classes preparing for pediatrics to recognize that. Still, it was frustrating. *He* was frustrating.

Joan tried not to give much credence to the horrible thoughts that sometimes crept into her head. She doubted he was having an affair. He seemed distracted, though. Inattentive. They had once spent all the time together they could, but tonight she sat in the living room with a book that held only half her interest while he sat a floor away doing what? Working on his family tree? Playing solitaire? Playing Shadow World? She laughed at the thought of Davis Moore, computer gamer. Nevertheless, one of the women's magazines that came to her office rated Shadow World as the third-biggest threat to marriage, behind money problems and poor sex. Money wasn't an issue with them—her practice was thriving and Davis had been well off even before his public speaking fees started rolling in. As far as sex was concerned, Davis's drive was healthy for his age and Joan was fulfilled. It certainly wasn't anything they argued about.

Up from her chair and into the kitchen, Joan made herself a decaffeinated tea and pushed the house intercom to see if Davis was interested in a cup. He said no, pleasantly, with a thank you, but he didn't say when he was coming up, either.

"Whatcha doin' down there?" she asked.

"Fooling around," he replied. "I'll be up in a minute."

Fooling around. She knew it was silly, but those words weren't the ones Joan wanted to hear.

— 70 —

Another animated alley on Shadow World Chicago's North Side. This one was especially detailed, Barwick thought. She walked her avatar up to one of the walls until her nose was right against it. Every brick was different, flawed in its own way. She could see mortar breaking apart, and the faded color of old graffiti tags. Above her, the fire escape creaked from old age and dropped water on her shoulder. She wondered if programmers had done this in every alley, on every street, in every Shadow World town in the world. Or was it just this one? Was this alley special? Some sort of software beta test?

The dead avatar on the pavement belonged to Victoria Persino, stabbed and dumped. She had $300 in cash and a diamond engagement ring in her inventory. Another gamer thrill kill. Or, if you believed Justin—Sally looked up. Speak of the devil.

"So whaddya say, Jimmy Olson?" Sally said into her headset. "Is the Wicker Man online tonight?"

Shadow Justin looked down at the body but didn't study it the way he usually did. He didn't even photograph it. "Sally, yeah. Looks that way." He walked the perimeter of the crime scene, but she could tell from his silence he had something on his mind, and she waited patiently for him to come out with it. "I have something I want to talk with you about." He looked behind him and then got closer, as if he didn't want the cops to hear him.

"What is it?"

"Sally, I was hoping you could do me a favor," he said. "I want you to look into somebody for me."

"What do you mean, *look into?*"

"I mean look into. Check him out. See what you can find."

"Who is he?"

"His name's Sam Coyne. Rich guy. Lives downtown. He's a lawyer for a firm called Ginsburg and Addams."

"What's this about?"

"I just need to know as much about him as I can."

Justin must be tired of getting shit from me for his crazy Wicker Man conspiracies, Sally thought. *He's trying to pretend this is about something else.* "What happened? Did you find out you were adopted and this guy's your real dad or something?"

"Something like that. Yeah," Justin said.

Liar, she thought.

"Can you do it?"

"You're my buddy. My protégé. I am sworn to look out for you, so I'll see what there is to see."

"Thanks," Justin said.

Barwick's avatar pointed to the body on the ground. The detail on this girl was much more sophisticated than the detail on Sally or Justin or anyone else Sally had ever met inside the game. Her skin looked organic. Sally could practically count her pores. "I bet Victoria here just signed up. Got the latest version of the avatar creator," Barwick said. She had read in a gamer magazine they needed to upgrade the animation in order to keep the sex freaks happy. "What's your best guess about what happened to her?"

Shadow Justin looked at the body and head-checked the length of the alley. "Maybe a thrill kill. Maybe not."

"Come on, Justin," Sally said. "What do you know?"

Justin wouldn't let her in on it. "Sam Coyne, Sally," he said. "Just please check him out."

— 71 —

Mickey the Gerund pulled the last job of his career in Seattle, blowing up a doctor, her husband, and their two college-age sons as they drove to dinner. Although he used them sparingly early in his missionary career, there was something about bomb-making he'd grown to love. He taught himself about explosives and timers and triggers, and so there was some DIY satisfaction in that. There was also the permanence of a bomb. A bomb is instantaneous and forever. Guns and knives create wounds that can be undone. A doctor can look at the knife and see where it entered the flesh, and he can sew it together again. But a bomb takes things apart—both lives and property—in a magical, secret way, and every char and shrapnel it creates is unique. If you knew how to ask it, the bomb might be able to tell you how to put it all back together, but—and here's the elegance of it—the bomb destroys itself first.

Mickey knew the Seattle job might kill a few innocents, if you could call people who ate expensive meals and enjoyed Ivy League educations paid for by the business of cloning "innocent." That had stopped being a dilemma for him long ago. This was a righteous cause, and for the cause they were fighting and winning, in no small part due to his willingness to kill "noncombatants."

Some polls showed more than fifty-five percent of Americans considered themselves "anti-cloning." There was more ambivalence over the use of cloning techniques for medical research and so forth, but on the subject of human reproductive cloning, the public was sending Congress a clear message, and although the wheels turned slowly in Washington, there was a fair chance they would pass the Buckley–Rice Anti-Cloning Act in the next few years.

Mickey sat on the end of a queen bed in an Idaho motel room and cleaned his gun. There was plenty more he could accomplish with this rifle and this box of wires and the leftover C-2 explosive, but it was time for him to retire. His back hurt from all the miles upright on the road. His head hurt from the meticulous planning. All his life he'd remained three steps ahead of everyone, but he didn't want to think ahead anymore. He wanted to meditate on the present for a change. To enjoy a sunny day without having to worry about the consequences of nightfall. To drive his car without running away. To plant and care for a real garden, with lilies and tulips and vegetables. To give birth to a yard of grasses and flowers and fruits, and let it feed on the sun. Watch it mature. That would be a fitting retirement for him. A celebration of God-granted creation.

He cleaned his gun out of habit, but this time it was more like a wipe-down. Before the sun came up he would throw the barrel overhand into the Arrowrock Reservoir, and later that day he'd toss the stock in a bend in the Snake River, and that would be the end. Back to Ohio for a life of prayer and contemplation in his house turned church turned monastery. If the Hands of God wanted to send someone else to the front lines until the war was over for certain, then so be it. He had fought bravely and fought well, and like a good covert soldier, he could never have a single body traced back to him.

That night, Mickey prayed for the souls he had saved with his bullets and bombs. Those souls were his responsibility and he remembered the names of every one he had set free from an infected body. With Mickey as their shepherd, they had stepped out of one car, in which they had sinned, and into another car, in which they could be saved.

— 72 —

Opening the door to the Shadow Billy Goat, Justin saw Sally's avatar sitting at the same table where they'd last met. The plain wrappers of two hamburgers were spent on the table and she was halfway through a third. Like she said, a girl's gotta eat. Even in Shadow World.

Justin directed his on-screen likeness down the stairs and sat across from her, while keeping a real eye out for a teacher who might catch him in the computer lab during lunch hour playing an outlawed game.

"Got your e-mail," he typed.

"Obvious," she said.

"Did you find anything on Coyne? If you did, I figured you'd just put it in the e-mail."

"What fun would that be?" Barwick said. "E-mail is boring, real-world communication. I'm a TTL, remember? This is how I play the game. This is *why* I play the game. This world is as real to me as the other. If we have business in Shadow, we meet in Shadow. We talk in Shadow."

"Fine."

"Anyway, this is big. You might be right about this Coyne guy."

"Right about him how?" Justin wrote. He didn't remember telling Sally the reasons he was interested in Coyne.

"I checked out his Shadow World stats. He's a serious gamer."

"Shadow World?" Trying not to let his real teacher read his surprise, Justin tapped anxiously on his keyboard. "I wanted you to check him out in real life!"

"You did?" Sally asked. "I thought you'd pegged him for the Shadow World thrill killer. The last time we talked—or the time before, anyway—you were going on about an investigation here in the game."

"This thing with Coyne is unrelated."

"Apparently not."

"What do you mean?"

"His stats. I got them from TyroSoft, the company that makes Shadow World."

"How did you do that?"

"They provide demographic information to potential advertisers. I called them up and told them I worked for the *Tribune*. The guy on the phone assumed I was in marketing."

"You didn't mention Coyne by name, did you?"

"Give me a *little* credit for sneakiness," she said. "I asked them for player stats on American Express Platinum Card users who live in the downtown zips. They sent me a file."

"What was in it?"

"Amazing <AGE INAPPROPRIATE>. Every player in the demo broken down by name, address, and estimated income. How much they play, and when they're online. They let you target individuals or groups of individuals with direct marketing *inside the game*. Scary stuff. Almost makes me want to stop playing."

"So tell me."

"Right. So Coyne plays mostly at night or in the early morning. I cross-referenced his usage with the nights girls showed up dead inside the game. Guess what? He was online for seventeen of the last twenty-three. And at crazy times, too. Three a.m. Four a.m. Always between sundown and sunup."

Justin didn't say anything for several minutes, and his avatar started making preprogrammed head motions, loops written into the software so characters looked alive even when the players weren't touching the keyboard. Eventually Sally asked, "Justin, well?"

"I'm thinking," Justin wrote. "None of that info you got from TyroSoft said what he was doing or where he went inside the game?"

"Nah. That's private. If another player doesn't see you inside the game, you aren't seen. TyroSoft doesn't track your movements."

"So nobody knows we're meeting right now. Or what we're saying. The game isn't keeping track of that?"

"Not unless somebody in this bar sees or hears us. If they're close enough they could record us, of course . . ."

"All right. Look, Sally. I think we're on to something really big here. And not about what you think."

"About what?"

"I think Sam Coyne might be the Wicker Man. In real life."

Shocker, Sally said sarcastically to herself. "I thought you said this didn't have anything to do with the Wicker Man." Her avatar grinned.

"It didn't. Honestly, until this moment I never thought Coyne was the Wicker Man. And it didn't even occur to me he was the thrill killer—I had no idea he was a gamer at all. But it makes so much sense now. I only wanted you to look into the real Sam Coyne because I happen to know he did a really bad thing a long time ago. If my other theory is right, though, and the Wicker Man is a True-to-Lifer, then this all fits together. I think Coyne has never stopped killing and he's killing in real life just as he kills in the game."

"Impossible," Barwick said. "Coyne can't be a True-to-Lifer. He doesn't play enough. He goes weeks without logging on sometimes."

"But there are different kinds of TTLs. Different degrees," Justin said. "Just because *you* have a compulsion to play every day doesn't mean they all do. The program is equipped to keep your character going through reasonable periods of inactivity, right? The software doesn't care if you're a True-to-Lifer or a fantasy player. I think maybe he uses the game to blow off steam. To channel his psychotic urges into something besides flesh-and-blood women. I made a chart once trying to show how the Shadow World killings increase in frequency when the Wicker Man goes a long time between murders."

"But you never made a correlation—"

"It wasn't exact—"

"Then how can you say it's true?"

"—but if we now have data that shows which Shadow World murders Coyne could be responsible for—the ones that happened while he was online—then I might be able to use it to make the chart more accurate. If we can do that, it might be something like evidence. Or at least a starting point for a story by you in the paper. The *real Trib,* I mean."

"<AGE INAPPROPRIATE>, Justin. I don't know. It's one thing to investigate a character for fictional crimes he commits in a computer game—and we don't even know he's doing that—but it's a huge leap from there to accusing a real guy, a successful lawyer, for cripes sake, of being a serial killer."

"Fine. One thing at a time. Forget about the real Sam Coyne for now. Let's investigate Shadow Sam Coyne. Like we talked about. An investigation inside the game."

"How?"

"I dunno. Stake out his apartment, I guess. Do we know where he lives?"

"I know where he lives for real."

"If he's a TTL it will definitely be the same place in the game."

"And if he's a fantasy player?"

"It still could be the same apartment. I live at home in the game."

"You're fifteen."

"Sixteen almost. Coyne might still have the same apartment—real and Shadow—if he's a fantasy player. And if he has *different* homes, then we'll know my theory is shot from the start. Do you have a car?"

"No."

"I mean in the game."

"If I don't have it in life, I don't have it in the game, Justin," she said.

"Too bad," Justin typed. "We'll need wheels."

— 73 —

"You should come with us," Justin said after explaining the plan.

"No," Davis said. "First of all, I've never played Shadow World. Second of all, we shouldn't be seen together. Even inside a video game, and certainly not by a newspaper reporter."

"Now you're being paranoid," Justin said. "Hell, the reporter is violating the restraining order, too. You should come."

Davis thought the suggestion was silly, even as he noticed a white car stopped about fifty yards behind them in the spot where two park district paths intersected. It idled there for a few seconds and drove on.

"Maybe I *am* paranoid. But the restraining order includes all kinds of communication. I can't come near you in a game any more than I'm supposed to approach you in real life or call you on the phone." Justin measured the distance between their car seats with his eyes. Davis said, "You know what I mean. Computers leave a trail. A record. Besides, you haven't convinced me Sam Coyne is the Wicker Man. I don't see any reason to take the risk."

"Which is why I'm going to follow him. For proof," Justin said. "The Wicker Man killings stop, more or less, whenever Sam Coyne is spending a lot of time inside the game. And almost every night he plays, someone in the game dies. Coyne is blowing off steam in Shadow World. He's able to control his urges in the real world by killing in the pretend one."

"A stretch. You said yourself the correlation between the real murders and Shadow World murders was shaky."

"There's nothing exact about psychology. And we know he's capable of it, Dr. Moore. He's a brutal killer. We know that for a fact. How big a stretch is it to suggest AK isn't the only girl he's killed?"

That much is true, Davis admitted to himself. "Justin, you're perfectly free to play your computer game however you want. I just don't see the point of chasing Sam Coyne around some virtual version of Chicago. From the way you describe it to me, even if he is killing other characters in Shadow World, he's not doing anything illegal. There's nothing there we could go to the police with."

"You've already said Coyne couldn't be convicted for Anna Kat's murder, even though we both know he did it," Justin said. "Our only chance of nailing him is to catch him at some other crime. Sally Barwick is a real reporter. For the *real Chicago Tribune.* If I can convince *her* that Coyne is a killer, maybe she can get an actual investigation started."

He continued, "The game is the safest place to poke around this guy's life. If we're caught following him or if we mess up or if we're just plain wrong about him, it won't matter. It's only pretend. But there's also a chance we'll find out something we don't know. Something we can use." Justin could tell he wasn't convincing him. "Look, Dr. Moore. Sally's like you. She thinks I'm really pushing it, accusing Coyne of being the Wicker Man. But she's also really into the game. She's a True-to-Lifer. She lives as much in that world as she does in this one, and what happens in Shadow World is as important to her as what happens out here. She wants to catch the Shadow World thrill killer as much as she wants to stop the Wicker Man. If I can use that to get her curious about Sam Coyne, then what's the harm?"

Davis said, "Just remember that coincidence is not evidence. I'm worried you're just looking at two things you're obsessed with and trying to make connections between them. The Wicker Man killings appear to be random. Coyne, on the other hand, knew Anna Kat. Or they were in the same class at school, anyway. She was strangled, and many of the Wicker Man victims were stabbed. I've seen practically every piece of evidence in the investigation of AK's murder, and there's not as much similarity as you might think." He tapped his finger on the steering wheel. The boy was going through with this no matter what he said. "Look, your idea is a good one. Even if he isn't the Wicker Man, Coyne must have done *something* else in the last fifteen years. Hurt another girl. An animal capable of that kind of violence doesn't get a taste of it and just quit. So see if you can get Sally Barwick interested. Maybe something will turn up. But be *careful.*"

"I will." Justin cleared his throat with an uncomfortable growl. "To tell you the truth, I like it that you're worried about me." It was one of many unsubtle cues Justin had given Davis since they'd become reacquainted, and he let a number of seconds pass before acknowledging it.

"Have you heard from your father lately?"

The passenger side lock thumped up and down a few times. "Nah. Three months probably. He's got his own kids by Denise now and they're more important to him. I'm a thousand miles away and he doesn't think of me as his real kid anyhow."

"I'm sure that's not true."

"He's practically said it to my face. I know he's said it behind my back. To Mom, not that she'd bad-mouth him to me. It's okay. Dad's right. He had nothing to do with bringing me into the world. I don't even think he wanted a kid in the first place. Don't take this the wrong way, but you're closer to being my father than he is. You're the one who made me."

Davis inhaled a whistling breath between clenched teeth. "No, Justin. I mean, I'm not comfortable with that—"

With a brooding kick, Justin tried to untangle the straps of the backpack between his feet. "Okay. But it's true whether you're comfortable with it or not. What do you think, I'm angry about it? Hell, no. Without you I wouldn't be here. That's cool. I mean, who else do I have for a father figure? Sam Coyne?" He chuckled sadly, the way people at a wake laugh at dark jokes. "That's a fucked-up couple of parents: a revenge-mad doctor and a cold-blooded killer."

Davis wanted to deny it even as he was tempted to scold Justin for swearing.

"I'll see you here next week," Justin said. "Hopefully, Sally and I will find out something by then." He opened the door and tumbled out.

In the rearview mirror, Davis watched Justin disappear into the forest preserve, the hum of his electric bike diminishing between snowdrifts until it sounded like an electric razor on a shallow beard. With his window down, through the birdless silence, Davis heard a coed football game crunching in the snow, and smelled a dirty winter grill with fresh brats and burgers and vegetables on a kabob. He wasn't the boy's father. That was practically paragraph one in the cloning professional's oath, or it would be if they had such a thing. Every seminar he ever attended had a lecture on that very topic. *This job will make you feel a little bit like God,* he heard a speaker say once. *Don't believe it for a second. We coax life into the world so that people can lead fuller, happier lives, but we don't make life. It is the nature of life to propagate, and cloning is another evolutionary step in the history of human reproduction. We are only tools.*

Davis had proved that was a lie. The physical process that brought Justin into the world was identical to that of every other clone. But the act of creation had taken place the moment he held Sam Coyne's DNA in his hand and decided he would make the switch. Justin was not conceived in a lab or in the womb but in Davis's mind. He existed because Davis had wanted him to, and what kind of being does that describe if not a god?

He didn't feel like a god, though if he did, what obligation does God have to his creations? *Any at all? God doesn't always act like it.* One way or the other he had a special obligation to Justin, and it was something like being a father to him, although not exactly.

He had an obligation to Anna Kat for certain, and on that score he was failing her. Again. Most nights he sat down in the blue room, among his old family files and eighteen years of cold evidence, sat there in the silence doing nothing. Pretending. As if just sitting in the chair where he once obsessed over her murder was the same as tracking down her killer. It reminded him of the way Jackie used to pray, in an indifferent and rehearsed whisper, as if the words meant something even if she didn't believe them. Even if Justin were only chasing his own demons, the kid was doing more to find Anna Kat's killer than he was. Davis thought, *My God, what's a fifteen-year-old doing with demons?* and then he felt guilt in his stomach incubating like a virus. He pushed back against the headrest, listened as carefree voices converged from around the forest preserve, and he thought about suicide, about men who had parked along lonely roads like this one with a rubber tube attached to the exhaust pipe and looped in through the cracked window, the rest of the opening caulked shut with a towel. He tried to block out other thoughts for a minute, his eyes closed, imagining what it must be like for the terminally desperate in the final moments when their survival instinct surrenders to the lure of permanent sedation. It was a meditation he did, not often but sometimes, in places where he was truly alone. In the car it was always a rubber tube. In the bathroom it was razor blades. In the blue room it was a gun. The instruments were location specific but his imagined last words were always the same.

"I'm sorry, Jackie," he whispered. "I'm so goddamn sorry."

— 74 —

The back door opened and closed, and Martha heard a pair of boots clunking to the kitchen floor, and she felt a teenaged body displacing air as it moved through the house, and when it climbed the stairs to its bedroom every sock-footed step seemed to be lying to her.

She learned this during her divorce: when a person you love is lying to you, everything they do or say is a lie until they confess it. Even a nominally true statement—"I want raisin bran for breakfast"—is still a lie because it takes the place of the truth. Small truths, told between lies, are just part of the cover-up.

These many years later, Martha remembered how normal her life with Terry had been during the months in which he'd carried on with his seventy-five-thousand-dollar-a-year glorified secretary. She suspected he was cheating, knew it in her gut, and yet those were happy days for her somehow. Sally Barwick had been lying to her then, too. So much of her life at the time had been a fiction, and yet she remembered it fondly, like a favorite novel. She could almost understand the appeal of a game like Shadow World.

Sadly, that brand of happiness eluded her now. She was wiser and more mature, and it was her son who was lying. Those were the differences, she supposed. Plus, she distrusted Davis Moore. Hated him even. That made the current situation unbearable. When her husband started having an affair with Denise Keene, Martha didn't even know the little slut existed. Dr. Moore, on the other hand, was taunting her through notes in her son's blue jeans.

When a two-thirty appointment canceled on her that afternoon, Martha thought she would call and see if Sara could sneak her in a few days early. She hated the way her hair was growing out, and had done as many blunt scissor repairs on her bangs as she was able. Midway through dialing, however, she changed her mind and decided to follow her son home from school.

A long bike path led from the umbrella-shaped bike-battery dock, past the athletic fields, and through a narrow gate in the chain-link surrounding the school grounds. Martha idled her cream Sable about fifty feet away and watched a hundred or more kids walk and ride out onto the sidewalk on Copes Street. The radio played an old rock song, from before her time even, and she hummed nervously along with it, even though the singer's angst over love lost reminded her of the last days of her marriage.

Her son appeared at last, bundled in his jacket, his backpack as big as a Sherpa's. A few weeks ago, when there was real snow on the ground, he'd have been walking or taking the bus. She resisted the temptation to shift out of park and followed him instead with her eyes. If he was going home he would take a left onto Delaware, she thought. When he didn't, she wondered if he was headed for a friend's house and why they weren't walking with him.

The slow-speed chase that followed was ridiculous, she knew. Several times she pulled over to the curb and pretended to be lost or looking for something under the seat so an irate driver could pass. Three cars behind him in the turn lane at a light, she was afraid he had spotted her. He made a left, accelerating through a narrow opening between oncoming cars, and by the time she passed through the intersection, he was gone.

Driving through an area with no houses and thick old-growth trees close to the shoulder on either side, Martha wondered where he could have gone. There was little out this way but commercial real estate—office parks and fast-food joints. She was more and more certain Justin was on his way to a meeting with Davis Moore, but unless she happened to see his bike parked somewhere, she was sunk.

A quarter mile past the red-and-white sign marking the entrance, she figured it out: *the forest preserve.* He'd turned into the forest preserve.

Usually a strict disciple of driving etiquette, Martha made a blind three-point turn on the narrow road and reversed direction toward the blacktopped drive that wound through the preserve. There was hardly anyone here on a

Thursday in winter, but high school students made use of the grounds all year round, for smoking or drinking or necking or, she hoped not to discover, holding secret meetings with a creepy doctor who'd been charged with stalking them when they were small children.

Martha stopped the car. What if Justin wasn't here to meet Davis Moore? What if Justin really had come to the woods for smoking or drinking or necking? How embarrassed she'd be if he discovered her spying on his ordinary teen mischief. She sickened at the thought of Davis Moore and his *experiments* (or *studies* or whatever he had called them in his deposition) and lurched the car forward again. No one said being a parent wouldn't be embarrassing.

The black SUV was parked halfway down a dead end. Martha might not have seen it except that the evenings were short and cold and Moore had no doubt left the engine running for the heat. Against the dimming horizon, she could see the curls of exhaust and the red glow of his taillights, and next to it, in the cold, matted grass, Justin's silver bike. She could see broad streaks of white on the back of the older man's head in the driver's seat. Justin was turned toward him, his profile recognizable in silhouette.

With her car angled across the only exit, they were trapped up the road, but what would be the point of approaching? She still couldn't confront them without unpredictable repercussions from Justin, and despite the satisfaction of seeing the ever more prominent Davis Moore, the darling of libertarians and television magazine programs, explaining himself in front of a judge and hiding his lying face from the news cameras, she knew she couldn't just march up to the car and start screaming at them both. When her husband abandoned her, she had at least been a party to the action. She'd had a lawyer. Some input into the dissolution. She realized that unlike a spouse, a parent was helpless in this situation. A teenager can walk out on his mother without ever leaving the house.

She let up on the brake, coasted down the road, and drove home to wait for her son.

<h2 style="text-align:center">— 75 —</h2>

Locking and chaining his bedroom door and staring gravely into its white-painted paneling, Justin let a discontented noise expire softly in his throat. Adults. They worry so much. They have much to worry about, of course, but he worried enough for all of them. Didn't they understand that's why he was sent here? Why he was brought here? Sent here or brought here, he wasn't sure which, but it didn't much matter one way or the other. His responsibility was the same: to wonder, to worry, to *act*.

Dr. Moore was a mess. Poor guy almost had his life back together before Justin knocked on his door, but what did he expect? These things were decided long ago. Very long ago. Nothing is decided when it happens.

He felt bad for his mother. It would be hard on her when it all came out. She had done nothing to deserve the pain. She only wanted a son, presumably one without a destiny, but she had no choice in the one she got.

On his bed, his hand feeling around inside his backpack, Justin gripped a leathery pouch with a zipper. Retail stores used them to make cash bank deposits, and hip teens now used them for tools and school supplies and allergy medicines and computer discs and PDAs.

And stuff.

His mother had been at the park today. He'd seen her car in the rearview mirror. So now she knows he's been seeing Moore. That was a problem. Not a fatal one, but it was another challenge. Whether the challenges were sent here or brought here, that again didn't matter much.

Justin unzipped the pouch and dumped its contents on the bed. Cloudy crystals tumbled from a plastic Baggie. A lighter, a spoon.

He turned on the radio and after he had prepared the syringe he injected its contents into a kitchen sponge and placed the sponge in a plastic bag for anonymous disposal later. From a week of this ritual, the Baggie, the syringe, the spoon all looked well used, coated in black and white residue. He capped the needle, returned everything but the sponge to the leather pouch, and hid the pouch behind a row of books on his nightstand shelf.

— 76 —

Another late night alone in the blue room. Joan was upstairs reading a book. She mentioned to him that even with her busy schedule at the clinic, she was averaging almost three thick novels a week these days. She had to go to the library almost as often as the supermarket. He understood what she was getting at but pretended it went over his head.

Davis knew there were files in here he had never examined thoroughly. Hell, there were thousands of them. Even with the dedication to the task he once possessed, he had performed a kind of triage, deciding which folders held the most promising information and attending to them first and most often. He remembered a box he'd picked up from the police station just months after AK was killed. Jackie was in their bedroom with a highball glass and a Dick Francis hardcover. He carted the box downstairs and set it on the card table in the blue room, removing the reports one at a time from within. These were witness statements from Anna Kat's friends, and after scanning just a few of the thirty or more reports, he knew they'd be too painful to read. As the detectives had warned him, none of the girls seemed to know anything about the night of the murder. Instead they filled investigators' notebooks with tearful eulogies and stories illustrating their love for AK. What a good friend she had been. How much promise her life held. How sad and different their lives would be without her. Now, though, if he could go through them once more, he wondered if he'd find that any of them had mentioned Sam Coyne, if any could help him connect the dots between the killer and his daughter.

He picked a report at random. Janis Metz. The name was unfamiliar. To investigators, Janis claimed to have been a friend of Anna Kat's since the eighth grade, but by the time they were seniors in high school, they weren't as close as they had once been. "We were still friendly," Janis said. "We just kind of drifted into different crowds." Janis had lots of stories about AK, and flipping through the transcript it was obvious that her eagerness to tell them was not matched by the patience of the detective conducting the interview. Several times he hinted that she should wrap things up, only to have her respond with another tale of Anna Kat's beneficence.

"There was this boy, Mark," began one such anecdote, "and he really liked AK. He followed her around like a little puppy dog. Mark was one of the supersmart kids, kind of shy, he's going to Stanford in the fall. These interviews aren't going to be in the newspaper or anything, are they?" The detective assured her they would not be. "Anyway, in ninth grade Mark finally got up the nerve to ask AK to go roller-skating, and she told him she didn't think of him in that way, and the poor guy was just crushed. But she stood in the hall and talked to him for, like, twenty minutes after she rejected him, and asked him about his family and his classes and stuff. He was on the debate team and a few months later she went to one of his matches or games or debate things, whatever you call them, and in the spring she nominated him to be class president. I mean, they were little things, but she let him know that he didn't have to be embarrassed. That they could still be friends, you know? Even though they'd never be *close* friends. That was really cool. I would have been, like, afraid that the guy would start stalking me or something. Not AK. She didn't care what clique you were in or how cool you were. She liked everybody."

Davis felt a pinching sensation in his nose, the prelude to a tear. He felt pride and love—and loss, too, but in manageable amounts. He skimmed the rest of the interview quickly for Coyne's name and, not finding it, reached into the stack and grabbed another one.

Bill Hilkevitch. Davis remembered him. He was one of AK's "guy friends," to be differentiated from her boyfriends. He liked Bill. Smart. Genuine. Polite.

Bill had spoken at Anna Kat's funeral, eloquently, until he had to stop and cry, which was a kind of eloquence in itself.

"Anna Kat used to get a little grief from a few of the other kids about her dad," Bill told the police sergeant. "I'm not saying that any of these kids, you know, *killed* her or anything, it was nothing like that, and it actually died down a lot after her father was shot, but it was still there. I remember—it was like tenth grade, I think—and we were reading *Frankenstein* in English class and somebody grabbed her book and wrote something on the title page. The full title of the book is something like *Frankenstein, Prometheus Unbound.* This guy had crossed out 'Prometheus Unbound' and written 'Davis Moore, M.D.' underneath it."

At this point the detective asked who or what Prometheus was. "Prometheus," Bill explained. "In Greek mythology. He was the guy who took all mankind's troubles—you know, diseases and whatnot—and put them in a box. Eventually Pandora opens it and life sucks forever after. He also stole fire from the gods and gave it to the mortals. The thing this guy wrote, Dr. Moore's name, it doesn't even make sense. The guy who wrote it was just copying what he'd heard his parents say or something. You know, that clones are like Frankenstein monsters. That's what the anti-cloners are always saying. It's stupid, but a lot of people think that way.

"At school right now there are only two kids who are out as clones. They say that at a school our size, it's probably more like thirty, but most families keep it a secret. It's not a surprise because the two kids, the clones, they get a lot of shit. Even though one of them's, like, this superathlete. He's a freshman and already on the varsity soccer team. The rumor is his cell donor was a big-time college football player or something, although that could be a load of crap. Anyway, he's going to be a huge star at the school and it doesn't matter. A lot of kids treat him like he's got a disease or something. He used to be really depressed all the time. But AK always finds those guys—or she did, anyway—found them in the hallway or after school, asking them to volunteer for this or that or to come to her volleyball games. That was the funny thing. She was the kind of girl who could ask you to do her a favor, like work the charity car wash on a Saturday morning, and you felt so good because she asked you. It was like she was doing something for *you.* And it wasn't just guys that felt that way, you know. It wasn't just because she was cute. Girls liked her, too."

The detective asked about the person who wrote in her Frankenstein book. "Oh, yeah. Steven Church. One day, months later, we're playing this coed softball game in gym. Steven's playing first base and AK hits a grounder to short. She's thrown out by two steps, but as she crosses first base she takes off her helmet and swings it around—whap!—knocks him right in the back of the head. He went face-first into the dirt and AK acted like it was an accident—

I'm sorry, I'm so sorry—but a few of us knew. And she never said anything about it and Steven never gave her any trouble after that. She was always real protective of her pop."

Davis smiled for the millionth time at the thought that AK was the one looking after him instead of the other way around. Given how helpless he had been searching for her killer, that was no doubt true.

Where had he heard that name before, Steven Church? There had been a Natalie Church, a nasty woman, who used to show her face at the occasional protest in front of the clinic, shouting hackneyed slogans at his patients *(Hey hey! Ho ho! Genetic research has got to go!)*. He assumed Steven was her kid. If Davis hadn't stopped reading these files fifteen years ago, and had come across this story, he would have checked Church out as a potential suspect. The police apparently had the same idea because on the last page of the statement someone had written in pen (before it was photocopied), *Church's alibi checks. He and his parents were in Saint Pete.*

The cops were doing something, at least, Davis thought. He tossed Bill's statement back and fished for another one.

Libby Carlisle. Libby he knew well. She and Anna Kat played together on the volleyball team. Libby had slept over here at the house on Stone dozens of times. He would hear them giggling late into the night, sometimes whispering into the phone with a network of conspirators who were spending the night in the homes of other girls.

The nocturnal back-and-forth between AK and Libby could get loud (the intensity of teenagers' conversations, like the intensity of an old Borg–McEnroe tennis match, increased with every volley), but Jackie usually slept through it with some soundproof combination of antidepressants and liquor. Lying in the dark, Davis wondered if a responsible father should knock on his daughter's door and break it up. Order them to bed. He never did. Instead he would eavesdrop, and although the girls were too many rooms away for him to make out the content of any conversation, the happy notes of his daughter's voice were informative enough.

Libby's statement was long, and Davis flipped the pages with his thumb, starting with the last one. Because he knew Libby, and because she no doubt held many of Anna Kat's confidences, he felt as if reading it too closely might constitute a betrayal of sorts. But it was also Libby's tightness with AK that gave the statement promise. If AK knew Sam Coyne, so did Libby.

The first time through, he just missed it. Maybe he was looking specifically for the word "Coyne," the big capital *C* and the single descender from the *y*, like a lowercase letter stretching its arms and legs. He turned the pages more deliberately the second time.

Libby said, "AK and I went to the mall on Monday. She had a night home with her mom on Tuesday. Wednesday night we took the train downtown with Dennis and Sam and this friend of Dennis's who goes to Madison."

That was it. The only mention in over a hundred pages of transcript. Could this Sam be Sam Coyne? It had to be. Were many parents naming their kids Samuel thirty-five years ago? He couldn't remember. It had been his business, bringing little boys into the world, and yet he couldn't remember how many of them had been named Sam. The detective interviewing Libby hadn't even asked for their last names. Sam *who?* Jesus Christ, Libby had given them the name of the killer and the cop didn't even have the sense to ask what his last name was. What kind of an investigation was this? A botched one, but he already knew that.

Davis threw the rest of the bound statements back into the filing cabinet and went upstairs to AK's old room. For years it had remained almost as Anna Kat left it, not for sentimental reasons but because Davis had no stomach for the day's work it would take to pull everything out. Jackie would sit in here sometimes and mourn in her own way. When he married Joan, she turned it into a guest room. They never discussed it. She just did it herself and he didn't object.

Some of AK's things were still here, though. On a bookshelf were four years of yearbooks, including the one that had been delivered to the house after she died. Every margin on every page was covered with anguished eulogies and melodramatic farewells from teenagers dealing with the death of one of their own for the first time. There were song lyrics, lots of song lyrics, and drawings of flowers, and even sketches of Anna Kat, some of them skillfully done.

Laying it flat on the bed and kneeling beside it, Davis examined the senior class row by row. He found Sam Coyne easily: handsome, smug, wearing a novelty tie with a cartoon cat. He looked so much like Justin. Exactly like Justin, but with a crew cut. A shiver went through him, top to bottom. This was the last face to see his baby alive, and it was Justin's face.

Coyne was the only senior named Sam. There were three boys named Dennis in her class. Among the underclassmen he discovered four more Dennises and one other Sam. But he hadn't thought about girls. Turning to the index now, he came across six Samanthas, three of them in the senior class. Libby could have been talking about a Samantha, and when he looked for their pictures, a couple of the girls looked familiar.

Absently he started reading through the messages inscribed to her. They ranged from sentimental ("Parting is all we know of heaven / And all we need of hell") to cruel ("Have a nice summer!"). How odd friendship is between teens, Davis thought. So intense. Every acquaintance is as close as a lover. Every minor slight an act of betrayal. The loss of a peer unthinkable.

The last two pages, left blank by the printer, were black-and-blue with ballpoint ink, irregular blocks of words covering the spread like a quilt. Davis rotated the binding, reading messages from less concise members of the Northwood East senior class. One of them, a poem—or more likely, song lyrics—froze the book in his hands:

> They can't hurt you now
> It doesn't matter what they say
> You can still feel anger across the grave
> But it was fun anyway
> Sam

He read it again. And a third time.

A confession. Maybe.

The handwriting was precise, but it was definitely a boy's—no teenaged Samantha would print with such bold, angular confidence. The words were not written hastily, but deliberately copied. The margins were careful and even. The strokes almost carved into the page.

You can still feel anger across the grave / But it was fun anyway. The words drilled into his heart and uncorked a gusher of rage. He was still trying to hurt her, still taking pleasure in her pain. Laughing. Taunting. Missing her only because he wasn't done torturing her.

I'll bury you, Coyne, he thought, his fingers on the front cover's raised letters—ANNA KAT MOORE. *I was so long without a child, I forgot I was a father. I got comfortable. I lost sight of you. I forgot what you did to her. Forgot that I wasn't supposed to let you have the last word.*

Davis thought, *I'll show you her anger.*

— 77 —

"Do you even have your learner's permit?" Shadow Barwick asked.

"No."

"God."

"Relax," Justin said into his headset. "It's like playing a video game. In fact, we *are* playing a video game. Remember."

"*You* might be playing," Sally said. "This is real to me. I'm risking my life here."

"We're not going to *die.*"

"We're chasing a serial killer!"

"So you're convinced he's the killer now?"

"I didn't say that. You know what I mean."

The blue Camry belonged to Justin's Shadow mother. Unlike his real-life mother, Shadow mom hadn't upgraded to a Sable, and the digitized import showed its age in the frayed floor mats and worn steering wheel. Tonight, for the fourth time in a week, Justin snuck out with the car, picked up Sally, and parked across the street from the garage underneath Sam Coyne's apartment building. In reality, of course, they were both sitting in their pajamas at home.

"I've topped two hundred and fifty thousand points on Ultrathon Grand Prix," he reassured her. "I'm a good driver."

"Maybe you'd be better off playing your little driving game tonight," Sally said. "I don't think he's coming out."

"He has to sooner or later."

The last Wicker Man killing had been ten weeks ago. According to Justin's theory (illustrated on his revised chart), there would be a killing either in the game or on the real streets of Chicago very soon as Coyne felt the need to release his aggression. For many reasons, they were both hoping it would be in the game. Sally in particular was hoping it would be tonight. She was tired.

That's not to say she didn't enjoy her time with Justin. He was the only man in her life. He had read more books than many adults, and understood them better than she did. He could argue a point without being personal. He wasn't an intellectual and could talk about movies and music and television, and also at length about Sally's primary interest—life in Shadow World. If he weren't so young, she'd no doubt be dating him by now. Given all the time they spent together, between the game and her dreams, some version of Sally practically was.

"Unless he doesn't," Barwick said. "Have to, I mean. At some point we need to give up on your theory, Justin. I don't want to, but with all these late nights I'm having trouble staying awake at work. Both of me are." The dashboard and computer clocks both said 12:30 a.m.

"Well, *I* have to go to *school*," Justin said, as if this stakeout had been her idea. Sally was reminded that when she was fifteen, she had been certain high school was so much harder and more boring than work would ever be.

"Wait." She nudged him. "There!"

The garage was technically underground, a dead end in the maze of arteries carved underneath downtown known collectively as "Lower Chicago." At night, however, visibility was just as good as it was on the upper streets bearing the same names. A black BMW glistened in the fluorescent light as it nosed under the corrugated door and turned onto the street. Shadow Justin checked the license plate.

"That's him!" he said, and in a small window showing third-person point of view, Barwick watched her on-screen avatar lurch forward as Justin took the car out of park. From a dozen car lengths, they followed Coyne's taillights up Shadow Wacker Drive to the surface, then West on Madison to the old meat-packing district. There weren't slaughterhouses here anymore—only galleries and nightclubs and condos, with the odd restaurant-supply store on Lake Street, the neighborhood's only secondhand memory of its past life. Barwick's townhome was a few blocks north and west, in fact.

"I think I know where he's going," Sally said. "Stay on him just in case."

Coyne parked the Beamer on Aberdeen, and Justin stopped short and backed up to a space more than a block behind. Coyne stepped out of his car and the lights flashed when he locked it with the remote. "Crap!" Justin said.

"What?"

"I don't know how to parallel park."

In her bedroom, behind her computer, real Sally chuckled. "Take your time," she said.

"No! We'll lose him!" Justin said. "You wait here and I'll chase after him."

Shadow Sally reached out and held his arm before he could unbuckle his seat belt. "You'll never get in."

"What do you mean? Where is he headed?"

"The Jungle," Barwick said.

When it opened six months ago, the Jungle was celebrated with local headlines that were half mocking and half adoring: *New Meat Market Opens in Old Packing District* was typical of the press. In fact, Sally, making a rare contribution to the features department, had written that article for both the real and Shadow *Tribune*s. The nightclub took its name from Upton Sinclair's book that exposed the once-unspeakable practices of Chicago slaughterhouses. The modern-day incarnation of the Jungle, however, was nothing but high-tech glamour. With three stories, six dance floors, more than a hundred yards of bar if you put all nine of them together and laid them end to end, the Jungle was the hottest dance spot, pickup joint, and celebrity hangout in Chicago, real or otherwise.

"I can pass for twenty-one," Justin protested. "In the game, anyway."

"That's not the problem," Sally said.

"What?"

"You look like you're dressed for softball," she said, fingering his avatar's T-shirt and baggy shorts. "We discussed how Coyne must be picking up women in bars at night, and these clubs have strict dress codes. Why do you think I've been breaking out the tight dresses for our stakeouts this week?" It was an opening for a come-on line, and when Justin didn't take it, Sally was reminded once again he was just a kid. "You stay here. I'll check it out." She stepped carefully onto the sidewalk, balancing herself on a pair of high black heels. "Keep the engine running and keep your eye out for me."

"Wait," Justin said. "I should go, or give it a try anyway. Like you said, it could be dangerous."

"Not because I'm a girl, I hope."

"Of course not. Because you're a TTL. If something happens to me, I shrug it off and start the game over. I have nothing to lose."

Sally smiled. "Nothing's going to happen to me. I'm just walking into a bar. I do it all the time. Did you happen to see what his avatar was wearing?"

"It looked like a black overcoat," Justin said. "But under that was a dark shirt with a vertical yellow stripe down the left side."

"Good," Sally said.

The entrance to the Jungle was up a short flight of concrete stairs. At the top of them a bouncer with a black ponytail and a square goatee protected a glass door with a purple curtain behind it. Having been judged lacking in some way, a small group of avatars stood on the sidewalk. They were mostly men, and had likely been rejected for wearing tennis shoes or committing some other fashion offense. In most cases, Sally guessed, they hadn't left for another bar because the bouncer had nodded their girlfriends inside and the girls had gone dancing, abandoning the men in the virtual cold.

Shadow Barwick paused to glance at herself in the window of a gallery that earned its reputation setting outrageous prices for artists no one had ever heard of, hoping to make them stars right out of the box. This tactic had worked once or twice, but now it looked to Sally like the gallery was going under. It shouldn't matter to the landlord. This neighborhood—although still a bit gritty and industrial—was red-hot. Another gallery would take its place before anyone noticed. In the window's reflection, Sally looked good, in a tight black dress with a red scarf and a small red purse. Although now in her mid-thirties—and even with Shadow World sucking up so many hours—she still made the gym three days a week and made certain her avatar was as fit as she was in real life, right down to her current weight in ounces. Earlier in the week, Sally had downloaded the latest update of the avatar builder and the difference in appearance was stunning. The skin tones and facial expressions were lifelike. The stitching in her clothes was twice as detailed. The animation in her straightened hair was so good she could differentiate between strands. Although it was a violation of the unwritten TTL code, she took advantage of the new installation and made some minor adjustments to her face—lengthening her nose, widening her eyes, slightly adjusting the shade of her brown skin—nothing too drastic, but she was both delighted with the way the new look made her feel and ashamed of having done it. Such tinkering was counter to the True-to-Life ethic, but the new technology made it irresistible. The first night of the stakeout, Justin had commented, shyly, that she looked great, but she couldn't tell if he was referring to the higher resolution of her avatar or to the minor surgery she'd done on her face. She promised herself she'd change it back, but was unconvinced she actually would.

Threading herself between the castaways on the sidewalk, Sally climbed the concrete steps and the bouncer opened the door with a big grin. "You look fine, honey." She wondered if this was the same doorman she had interviewed in real life at the opening, and if he recognized her. Either possibility was a stretch.

Inside, patrons were packed into the most inconvenient places. The coat check was as difficult to get to as any of the bars. Fortunately, Sally's avatar wasn't thirsty and she'd left her coat in Justin's car.

Not thirty seconds inside, a tall Asian man asked her to dance. She couldn't even see the dance floor and the music was so loud she could barely understand the request in her headset. She turned him down and continued to push her way deeper into the Jungle.

The center of the club boasted a fifty-foot ceiling and an enormous skylight that would have revealed a brilliant display of stars if the sky were clear and the city not so lousy with light pollution, a detail Shadow World's programmers had written into the Chicago code. When there were no clouds, you could make out a handful of the brightest planets and stars, but mostly you'd see the blinking lights of airplanes in holding patterns over O'Hare and Midway. Last month, during a meteor shower, the club—the real Jungle—had a party to celebrate. There had been little to see through the skylight but patrons partied on, soon forgetting the promotion that had brought them there in the first place.

Two more offers to dance followed in quick succession, along with a third suggestion that prompted Barwick to push away the propositioner with the heel of her palm. Disgusting. When yet another avatar asked if she wanted to join him for the next song—*what were they, taking numbers?*—she finally said yes. From the dance floor she could move around better and also get a decent look at all sides of the club.

Out in the middle of the room, under the big skylight, Sally loosened up. She felt self-conscious when she danced in real life, but in Shadow World she could relax. Let the music lead her. The motion of her fingers across the keyboard was a dance of its own, and the easy manner with which her avatar responded was much more satisfying than any real-life two-step. This was why she felt more alive in the game than she did in real life. This feeling of confidence and control was something she had tried to describe to her family but never could. They would just shrug and laugh and say they'd never understand this True-to-Life obsession of hers.

Tonight, though, even more than other nights she'd spent clubbing in Shadow World, Sally really had it going on. The motions of her new avatar were so fluid. So natural. Changing to third-person in the point-of-view window she could watch herself as others saw her, and what others were seeing was a sexy, sexy display. The way her hips rolled, the way her hair fell in front of her eyes, the fluid way her arms turned above her head as if she were undersea.

In the main panel of the screen, she saw her dance partner—dressed up, trying too hard, a good but not great dancer, handsome face, shaved head, broad shoulders under a ribbed turtleneck. He had a grin on his face and an empty, fixed stare that Sally recognized from thousands of hours in the game as lust.

Of course.

That was why she was getting all the attention. Most of these guys were in here for online sex, and she represented the newest technology. They were after some high-resolution in-and-out with her. She was both flattered and nauseated by the thought. Scanning the area around her, she found a lot of eyes on her body, men and women, some horny and some just curious. She counted a few others who had obviously upgraded, maybe one in twenty players at this point. TyroSoft predicted that in one month the penetration would be close to ninety percent.

It had been stupid to upgrade so early. She was here on surveillance, for crying out loud, trying to be stealthy, not sexy, and she stuck out like one incredibly desirable sore thumb.

On the other hand, maybe that wasn't such a bad thing.

Winking at her dance partner, she spun away from him and began walking the perimeter of the club. She found an opening at the bar and ordered a vodka and tonic and then resumed her patrol, although she had to stop every ten feet or so to deny a request for dancing or sex or both. Sally was becoming irritated, waving away suitors like gnats.

There: dark blue shirt with a yellow stripe. He was standing three bodies out from the bar, talking with a couple of blondes. Coyne had made the upgrade as well, she noticed, and she wondered if he also had cheated on his looks a bit, chiseling those cheekbones and squaring that jaw when he redid his avatar. Her investigation hadn't turned up a photo. The real Sam Coyne was probably a stereotypical fantasy player: short, fat, and bald.

She watched him from this safe distance, simply ignoring the propositions when they came now and taking small sips from her glass to make the drink last. She'd feel conspicuous standing here alone and without a drink, and she was afraid of losing sight of him if she had to go back to the bar.

He became focused on one of the girls now, his eyes boring into her. One blonde tried to inch her way into his line of sight, but he seemed more and more interested in her friend. They were too far away for Barwick to hear what they were saying (sound in the game carried about the same distance as it did in real life), but it seemed to her to be all smiling and flirting. Sam Coyne was a charming man, it seemed.

He looked up from between the two blonde heads and made eye contact with Sally. Not a casual glance, but a long, unbroken connection. Barwick was slow to look away, and then it was too late to do anything but return his gaze and look indifferent. She didn't, apparently, seem indifferent enough.

In a matter of seconds he had excused himself from the blondes and they turned and pouted as Coyne made his way over to Sally. This wasn't what she wanted, but she couldn't run. And what did she expect would happen when she walked into this bar, anyway? Sally realized too late that she had no plan.

"Hello, I'm Sam," he said. Sally noticed another benefit of the upgrade. The lip sync was almost perfect. Forget about flesh, she thought. Even dirty talk would be sexier in the new Shadow World.

"Sam, hi," she said. "I'm Sally."

If he was a TTL, and he looked anything like this in real life, Sam Coyne, attorney-at-law, was quite a catch. Wavy blond hair. A big white smile. Athletic waist and thighs. Coyne might be the Shadow World thrill killer, but she was finding it harder and harder to buy into Justin's thinking. She'd met a lot of serious gamers and this guy was too good to be true.

"Sally, do you want to dance?" he asked.

Did she? Heck, it's a crowded club. "Sam, sure," she said.

Coyne was better than a decent dancer, although she acknowledged that dancing in the game was all fingers and wrists—a different skill set than dancing in a real club. It still took rhythm, though, and he had it. As he moved on her screen, she couldn't help seeing in him something like what men had been seeing in her all night. Casual sex wasn't Barwick's thing, in Shadow World or in life, but she was attracted to him. Or to his avatar, anyway. Of course, the avatar *was* a real man as far as Shadow Sally was concerned, and whether or not danger had anything to do with it, Shadow Sally was turned on. And he was picking up on it.

After just one song, he leaned in next to her ear and said, "Sally, do you feel like going for a walk?" She had been playing the game long enough to know what that meant. She was scared. Excited and scared. She needed that plan now.

Barwick had entered the Jungle to spy on Coyne, not to bait him. Or become another of his victims. She had a life here in Shadow World, a life she loved as much as its mirror in the alternate universe of the real world. She simply couldn't risk it all chasing the crackpot whim of a high school kid she barely knew. She had to give Sam Coyne the same answer she'd give in real life if he asked her to go somewhere for quick and meaningless sex.

"Sam, no," she said. "Thanks, but no."

He stared at her for a minute as if others in this situation had changed their minds in the line of his hypnotic pupils. She didn't doubt they had.

"All right, Sally," Coyne said. "Some other time." She watched him turn and walk back to the bar where one of the two blondes was still waiting. At just a word, she hopped off her stool and followed him toward the coat check. Sally waited until they were lost between bodies in the crowd, then set off after them.

Her escape from the dance floor was as littered with oversexed obstacles as her entrance, however. "No. No. No thank you. *God, no!*" she insisted to one poorly rendered avatar after another until she finally reached the cold air outside. Snow had begun to fall. At her computer, Barwick looked out the window. The flakes were just beginning to stick to the boxwood outside. She marveled again how the Shadow World programmers were able to make the world on her screen so responsive and complex.

It was nearing last call and the bouncer had left, locking the entrance door behind him. The sad crowd of boys on the sidewalk were gone. The street was visible for several blocks in either direction, but she couldn't see Coyne or the blonde. Sally began walking to the Camry, her head twisting in all directions, but a hand on her arm stopped her. Justin was out of the car.

"Sally, they walked into that building!" he said. "Across the tracks!" Barwick looked in the direction he was pointing and saw a large tin garage used by a private disposal company to warehouse garbage trucks.

"Eww," she said. "Are you kidding me?"

"Maybe he's testing out a new technique," Justin said, looking over his shoulder as Sally tried to keep up with him in her heels. "Or maybe he's done this very thing dozens of times as the Wicker Man, in the real world. Maybe he dumps the bodies with the garbage, and they're never found. Who knows what his body count might be?"

Barwick didn't buy it. "Sex next to a garbage truck has got to be an in-game-only fetish," she said. "Stink doesn't go through the computer. Besides, I'm not so sure this guy's a TTL."

"Why?" Justin asked.

"He's too good looking."

In his bedroom, Justin smiled.

A door to the giant tin barn was left open and Justin and Sally slipped inside. Dozens of blue trucks were lined up in rows, ready to make their rounds in just a few hours. A few fluorescent lights were on, high in the rafters, and they could hear loud echoes—a man and woman breathing and giggling—from somewhere inside the barn. Barwick put a finger to her lips and Justin understood. *If we can hear them, they can hear us.*

They walked with gentle footfalls up and down the rows, and the sounds from Coyne and the blonde became louder and more passionate, but they couldn't tell if they were just inches away or dozens of yards. The crazy acoustics of the metal roof and walls, and the directional limitations of their headsets, limited their ability to home in.

Until they heard the blonde screaming.

"That way!" Justin whispered, running off before Sally could get her bearings. She slipped her heels off and followed the screams, which became more and more angry.

You sonofabitch! You sonofabitch! You goddamn crazy sonofabitch!

At least she wasn't a True-to-Lifer, Barwick thought. If she were a TTL, the screams would be more terrified. More real. This chick's just pissed.

Ten seconds later Sally ran right into Justin's back. He was frozen between the front and rear bumpers of two garbage trucks. Because he was six inches taller than she was, Sally couldn't get a look at anything on the other side of him.

"I can't see!" Justin whispered desperately. "I'm blind here. I can't see!"

It took Sally a moment to figure out what he meant. This was a fine time for his computer to freeze, or for a glitch in the software to show itself. He turned to face her. "I can see you," he said. "But I can't see out there." Then she understood. Around the corner, there must be a scene so deranged or sexually explicit (or both) that it set off the parental filters on Justin's computer. His screen had gone black.

"Look away," Sally said. "Turn around and get behind me." She pushed him aside and nudged in front of him, almost wishing she had the parental filters activated herself. Even if the blonde wasn't a TTL, Barwick wasn't sure she wanted to see what Coyne had done to her.

And when she stepped out to look, she wasn't able to see it. Not right away.

The instant she maneuvered in front of Justin, Sally was hit in the face with something hard and metal. The pain meter at the bottom of her screen redlined. "Ow!" she said instinctively. She rolled over onto her back and looked up. Sam Coyne, pants buttoned but belt unbuckled, stood above her holding a shovel caked in dirt and filth. He sneered at her.

"What are you doing?" he asked. His voice was calm and measured—and calm and measured, under the circumstances, was cold and creepy. "If you wanted to come along so badly, *Sally*, you should have just said yes when I asked."

Barwick tried to push herself backward, but the blow had injured her avatar, making it unresponsive to commands. "Sam, stay away from me," she said. Through Coyne's legs, she could see the blonde's naked, lifeless avatar lying in an expanding pool of red. Somewhere in Chicago, the woman who had been playing the game with that character had no doubt stomped into the next room and was already watching television in a foul mood.

From one of his deep pockets, Coyne pulled a bloody towel. The towel dropped to the ground, unveiling a long knife with a black handle. "Sally, I usually like to get to know a girl first," he said, crudely grabbing his crotch with his other hand. "Too bad."

Barwick tried to stand, and managed to lift herself up on a straightened arm before falling back to the ground. Coyne lunged at her, then stopped himself, taking a slow step, then another lunge, a slow step, a lunge. Toying with her. When he was so close his right shoe gently kicked her bare left foot, Sally managed a scream.

And not some prissy, fantasy-playing, nothing-at-stake blonde-girl scream, either. It was fat and loud and high-pitched and it echoed through the old tin barn like a soprano aria. Coyne was startled then, not just by Sally's yelling, but also by footsteps.

Seconds later, Coyne was on his side against the concrete, the knife skidding away with a sound like a shuffleboard disc. Justin was on top of him, flailing at the man's face, but most of his blows missed or were blocked, and a few even struck concrete, punishing his own knuckles and forearms. Sally tried to right herself and looked around for the knife. By the time she saw it, deep under a truck at least a hundred feet and three rows away, Coyne had reversed positions with Justin. Now he was attacking with jabs, like a boxer, and Justin could do nothing but cover his face.

"Justin!" Sally yelled.

"I can't see!" he managed to spit out between desperate breaths.

Shit! Barwick thought. Coyne likely thought Justin was babbling or referring to some temporary condition caused by the blood in his eyes. Sally knew better. As long as the blonde's naked body was in his line of vision, the parental controls on Justin's computer forced his screen to go black. Because Coyne was standing between Justin and the naked avatar, when Justin faced Coyne he couldn't see anything in the game at all, much less defend himself against the man's blows.

Sensing an opportunity, Coyne backed off a few steps and reached for the shovel, which had fallen behind the tire of one of the trucks. Barwick's avatar had regained enough strength to wobble to her feet, and she circled around Justin in the opposite direction, testing Coyne. He didn't make a move for her. Justin was his concern. The boy was twenty years younger and could no doubt take him in a fair fight. Coyne needed a weapon. Justin bobbed his head toward the sound of the older man's breathing, trying not to reveal his handicap.

Sally walked backward, toward the dead blonde. Coyne knelt slowly by the giant tire, feeling for the shovel. Justin began throwing uncertain taunts in Coyne's direction, trying to appear cocky.

"Sally, a little help!" Justin shouted.

When Coyne had walked from the car to the door of the Jungle, Justin said he was wearing a long black overcoat. *It must be around here somewhere,* Barwick thought. She saw no clothes around the body, however. Coyne must have thrown anything that had become bloody during the attack into the back of one of these trucks. She kept searching. She heard the first blow strike Justin in the side. Another crunched bone and she hoped it was an arm. She saw his avatar slump. On the back of one truck, camouflaged by the vehicle's blue paint, sat a tarp of the same color. It was covering an open bed full of waste that hadn't yet made it to the landfill. She jumped up and grabbed the edge, but the tarp slipped out of her hand. She tried again and this time got a better handle, but it was stuck.

"Help!" Justin called as Coyne swung the shovel again with a thud.

She leaped a third time, looping a thin finger inside a metal grommet, and pulled down with all her weight. The tarp came loose and brought several pounds of rotting meat and fruit down with it. Wet, Shadow Sally dragged the tarp over to the lifeless blonde avatar and tossed it on top of her, covering her naked body.

"Justin! Look!"

His screen blinked to life just as Coyne was bringing the shovel down on the crown of his head. Responding to Justin's expert keystrokes, his avatar ducked and rolled, and the blade clanged against the concrete. Standing, he got a glimpse of Sally pointing to his left, in the direction away from Coyne, who was recovering from the stinger shuddering through the wooden handle.

What the hell is she pointing at?

He waited to be sure Coyne was after him, not Sally, and he dashed off in the direction of her gesturing. Coyne followed between the rows of vehicles.

"Under the truck!" Barwick yelled. *What was she talking about?* Justin thought. *Why wouldn't she just come out and say it?* The trucks were parked nearly bumper to bumper and in the narrow space between them, Justin couldn't put any distance between him and Coyne. He heard the man gaining behind him. He heard Coyne breathing. Close. Coyne lifted the shovel over his head, and it made a whooshing sound past Justin's ear.

Under the truck! Duh!

Justin dove forward on his belly and slid on some sort of greasy sludge, which propelled him beneath the carriage of the truck in front of him. The shovel came down, just missing his foot.

"Bastard!" Coyne shouted.

All right, Justin thought. *Now it really is personal. Mother. Fucker.*

On his belly he slithered away from Coyne, using the trucks as cover. Coyne hadn't followed him. Justin could see his feet circling around the perimeter of the trucks, trying to cut him off. Justin backed up and changed direction. Sensing his motion, Coyne retraced his steps. *Dammit.* He had to find a way back to Sally.

"Little <AGE INAPPROPRIATE>, where are you?" Coyne shouted. He was practically jovial about it. Laughing between taunts. Sally and Justin hadn't foiled his plans, they'd just made the game more challenging for him. More fun. Justin wondered if the extra energy Coyne spent killing him and Sally might actually save a real girl's life. He hoped he wasn't doing this for nothing.

Then he understood what Sally had been warning him about. *Under the trucks.*

Three vehicles to his right he saw the blade of the knife wink at him in the reflected light. Beautiful. That was his way out of here.

"Why don't you come under here and get me?" Justin answered as he made his way toward the weapon.

Coyne snickered. "Maybe. Or maybe I'll just back you up into the lot until there's no place for you to go, and then double back to your girlfriend there."

Justin took the knife in his right hand and crawled until he was inches away from the aisle where Coyne was standing. Justin waited a second, then bent his right knee, kicking a gas tank with his boot. To Coyne, the noise was loud and close. He ran toward it.

"Gotcha!" He bent down and swung the shovel under the truck. Justin stopped it with his left hand, the blade making a gash in his palm, and pulled the shovel toward him. Coyne refused to let go, fighting with Justin for control of the tool. In an effort to break it free, Coyne pushed the shovel further under the truck, exposing his hands at the end of the handle. Justin saw and struck.

"<AGE INAPPROPRIATE>!" Coyne yelled. When Justin slashed unexpectedly into Coyne's arm, the game created an involuntary response to the pain, causing Coyne to drop the shovel and recoil. Justin pushed himself out from under the truck and went after Coyne again. Sitting on the ground, the older man could do little but try to defend himself. He rolled onto his back and started kicking at Justin's hands. Justin swatted the man's shoes away and made a few crazed stabs at his legs.

Barwick called out, "Justin, what's happening?" Her voice stopped Justin in the middle of his assault. The most important thing was to protect her. She was the one putting her online life at risk. Cocky again, Justin grabbed the shovel and retreated between the trucks, back toward her voice. "Fuck you, Coyne!" Justin called out over his shoulder, for no reason but to make the lunatic aware they knew his name. "Go to hell!"

On the blue tarp, blood beginning to ooze from underneath it, Barwick looked up with a start when she heard Justin approach. He knelt beside her and took her hands in his, and she turned his left one over and started at the open wound.

"We need to get to a hospital," she said.

Justin shook his wrist. "Naw, I'm fine. It's just a game."

"I mean for me," she said. She pointed to the shovel in his hands. "While you were blinded, he smacked me with that thing." Sally lifted her hair and on her finely rendered temple Justin could see a large bruise growing toward her eye.

"All right," he said. "We should get out of here *now*. I lost sight of him, but he could try to cut us off." He held out the knife. "Can you hold this? Or wave it around, anyway? Look menacing?" She wanted to stab Justin with it, to tell the truth. Justin had saved her with that blind tackle, but it was his insane scheming that had put her in danger in the first place. What the hell had she been thinking? And they weren't out of it yet. She tapped her bruise with the handle of the knife and the pain meter shot to life. She might have a concussion.

Practically hanging from his shoulder with one hand and making a conspicuous presentation with the blade in the other, Sally and Justin walked out of the garage the way they'd come in. Neither mentioned to the other how relieved and disturbed they were that Coyne didn't show himself again.

— 78 —

Joan felt Davis come to bed late, after midnight, and he settled inertly and heavily into the left side, his side, as if eased there by a dockside crane. She recognized the sigh, the murmur, the groan, and knew he wasn't coming to sleep, but only to seek refuge from being tired, from the thing that was causing him stress and unhappiness. Oddly, even though the place he chose to hide was only inches away—was, in fact, the very spot on which they had made love countless times before and since their wedding day—she was convinced the thing he no longer wanted to face was their marriage.

She stretched an arm across his thickening belly nevertheless. "What is it?" she said.

"I've been keeping something from you."

Oh God.

"I didn't tell you because I didn't know what you'd say. How you'd react. I know you thought I was past it."

Wherever he was heading, this sounded bad. Bad for her. Bad for *them*.

"I know who did it," he said. "I know who killed her."

Awake now. Wide awake. "What are you talking about?"

"Sam Coyne. That's his name. He killed AK. He was a boy in her class."

In the dark, with the dense red curtains blocking the streetlamps and the moonlight, she could barely see his face, but his white hair reflected what little fluorescence there was in the room. He was staring at the ceiling and she wondered if he planned this, planned to tell her all along, if he knew she'd be awake tonight and planned to tell her, or if he was just tired, tired of not sleeping, tired of not telling. It didn't matter much either way, now that she knew what had been bothering him.

"Do you know where he is now?"

"Chicago. He's an attorney. Ginsburg and Addams."

"No," she said. "Shit."

"No shit."

"Honey, are you sure? How do you know?"

He inhaled a long breath, as if he had to tell the entire story before it expired. "Justin came to me." He held up a preemptive hand. "I never called him. Hadn't even laid eyes on him in years, but he came to me a few months ago. In the fall." It came out then, not in one breath but in pieces and tangents and in forgotten bits where the tale had to be stopped and backstory recounted.

When it was done, he said, "I don't know what to do, Joan."

She pulled herself closer to him. "Can you call the police?"

"If the point is to land *me* in jail for fraud and genetic tampering, sure."

"Well," Joan said with a hopeful sigh. "This isn't going to sound like much of an idea, but you could do nothing. You could let it go. A lot of lives have been disrupted or even ended because you started on this path. And I take responsibility for that, too. But if you really can't get this guy without hurting anyone else—and by anyone else I mean you and me, of course, but also Justin and Martha Finn—then maybe it's just time to walk away."

Davis said, "That's probably an excellent idea, Dr. Burton. But it might be out of my hands."

"What do you mean?"

"I mean the boy. He's fixated on Coyne. I think he plans to do something. Something irrational."

Joan was up on an elbow. "Do you think he'd kill him?"

"I don't know. He's convinced Coyne is the Wicker Man, and he's trying to prove it."

"God. I mean, do you think it's possible? That Coyne is a serial killer?"

Davis frowned. "No. I mean, is he capable? Sure. He's proven that. But Justin was obsessed with the Wicker Man before he even found out he was a clone. Before he found out he was cloned from Sam Coyne. In his head, he's obviously put these things together on the flimsiest of evidence. You know, he plays that video game—"

"Shadow World."

"Right. And like a lot of other gamers, he talks about the things that happen in Shadow World as if they actually happened, but then he'll disclaim it and say something like, *You know, it's only a game . . .*"

"But you think he has a hard time distinguishing the game from reality?"

"No, I think he has a hard time distinguishing reality from the game. I think he looks at *real life* as if it's some sort of contest. As if life is a puzzle to be figured out. That there's an objective. Winners and losers. A purpose. And now he's convinced his purpose for being here is to bring down Sam Coyne for murdering AK."

Joan whispered, "How do you know he's wrong?"

"What do you mean?"

"Maybe there *is* something each of us is here for, and maybe our lives *are* supposed to be spent figuring out what that is. I mean really, Davis, Justin actually *was* created for a purpose. *A very specific purpose.* And you know what? That purpose was exactly what he thinks it is."

Davis propped himself up on one arm. "Justin wasn't created so that *he* could find AK's killer. I wasn't thinking clearly, and I shouldn't have done it. The question is, what do I do now? What do I do with the knowledge that the monster that took my daughter from me is living it up as a partner at a prestigious law firm? How can I let that be? And what do I do about Justin? He's my responsibility."

Her hands wet with her husband's sweat, Joan went to the closet for a towel, and she brought him a clean T-shirt, peeling the dirty one from his shoulders and drying him off the way a nurse would.

"We'll figure it out," she said. "Just promise me when this is over, whatever happens, we'll stop keeping secrets and I'll have you all to myself."

Cooled as she lifted the dampness from his chest and arms, Davis smiled in the dark. "You'd be the first," he said. "But I promise."

— 79 —

When a fantasy gamer gets sick or injured, she usually lets the avatar die. A Shadow World hospital is about as much fun as a real one, and nobody wants to sit through stitches and a physical when she can start the game over instead. There are only two kinds of people with enough at stake to bring their characters to Shadow hospitals: players who've achieved great success, fame, or wealth inside the game, and True-to-Lifers. Fortunately, that means the emergency room wait is only half as long.

In front of the computer in his room, Justin worried his mother would hear him talking into his headset. It was getting closer to dawn and his mother—his real mother—would be sleeping less soundly. She had patience with his gaming, but she'd flip if she knew he'd been staying up all night, driving around town with a thirty-five-year-old woman, and getting in knife fights with serial killers. He started typing words for his avatar instead of speaking them.

Shadow Sally sat on an exam table, needlessly dressed down to green scrubs. A doctor, Hannah Wright, conducted a series of unconvincing tests (Justin guessed she was a fantasy player pretending to be a doctor) before telling her she was going to be okay.

"Sally, you have a concussion," Dr. Wright said. "I've ruled out a serious head injury and your spinal cord seems fine. Take acetaminophen when the pain gets to you. Stay away from aspirin or ibuprofen, all right?"

"Dr. Wright, sure."

The avatar named Dr. Wright took a seat in an orange plastic chair; her eye line was at least eighteen inches below Barwick's, and she looked up at her with her head tilted to the right. "Sally, do you have someone to stay up with you tonight? Just in case you start showing disorientation? How about your friend here?"

Shadow Justin took a step away from the wall. "Well, yeah. Sure. I mean, I have to go to school in a couple hours," he said. "But my avatar could stay with her. And I could check in on her every few hours."

God, he still doesn't get it, Sally thought. *What it means to be a TTL.*

"Good," Dr. Wright said. "I'm sure she'll be fine. I'd like the two of you to sit here for another half hour, just to make sure there isn't any unexpected swelling or disorientation."

"Thanks, Doctor," Sally said. Dr. Wright left the exam room to see other patients.

At home, Justin—real Justin—was tired. The fight with Coyne had been intense and he wanted to shut down his computer and get an hour of sleep before school. But he knew if he left his avatar alone with Sally's, it wouldn't be able to monitor her "orientation."

"You don't have to stay," Barwick said.

"No, I want to," he typed. "How are you feeling?"

"Better," she said. "Avatars heal quickly."

"Yeah, but did they factor in all the symptoms right? On a percentage basis? You could just drop dead from an aneurysm or whatever."

"Thanks."

The energy meter on Justin's screen dipped to a critically low level, and he grabbed the orange chair. Even if he wasn't going to sleep tonight, his avatar could use a little rest.

Shadow Sally sat on the exam table, her fingers tucked under her thighs. Her bruise was already healing, an indication from the game, Justin suspected, that her injuries weren't going to be so bad.

"Can I ask you a question?" he said.

"Of course."

"Why is this life so important to you? I mean, I play the game. It's fun. Why did you need to come here to the hospital? If your online life is exactly the same as your real one, why can't you just start over if something happens to you? It seems like you wouldn't even lose a day."

Sally said, "The best way I can explain it—it's sort of a Zen thing. The goal of being a True-to-Lifer is to make the two existences, online and off-line, equally important. Equally real. Some TTLs treat their avatar like a yin to their yang, trying to channel their less attractive impulses into a fictional character so they can be a better person in real life. Others, like me, are trying to lead two nearly identical lives. If I were to die in Shadow World, I would feel the pain as if a real person had been lost. And if I were to die in real life, my avatar would hopefully go on without me."

"Go on without you? What are you talking about?"

"If you don't log in to the game for sixty days, Shadow World shuts down your account. Your character disappears, and if you perform a necessary function, you're replaced by another player or game-controlled character. But a good True-to-Lifer can fool the program. His avatar is so realistic even when a real person isn't controlling him, he can continue on in the game for months or even years after the player who created him passes away. If you pay attention, you can see them, walking around Shadow World. They have a sad look. Mournful."

"So you're something like twins," Justin said. "Twins with the same mind."

Sally nodded. "I like that."

Justin stood up and walked to the door. Nurses were leading worried avatars between exam rooms, medicating them. Healing them. Sitting at computers, their players no doubt were praying the ailments and injuries weren't serious. "The yin and yang thing. What if Coyne is one of those kind of TTLs? What if he's not just trying to blow off steam? What if he's trying to . . . to banish the Wicker Man from the real world into the game? What if he wants to rid his real self of these horrible impulses and put them all into his character online, where he can't hurt flesh-and-blood people?"

"*Oh God.* I don't think so," Barwick said.

"Why not?" Shadow Justin was annoyed. "You dismiss everything as soon as I say it, but you have to admit, some of my nutty theories have proven right.

Isn't it possible that the real Sam Coyne is trying to stop himself from killing, and he's trying to use the game as a way to rid himself of the illness that compels him to attack women?"

"I doubt it," Sally said, "because right now I think the real Sam Coyne is standing outside my window."

— 80 —

Through a window in the spare bedroom, cracked even in winter because of an irritating anomaly in the ductwork that always baked this corner of the town house while other rooms froze, Barwick heard him when he jumped the iron fence into her tiny, neglected back garden. In a sweatshirt and black jeans, he looked like a panther against the new covering of snow, but less graceful, putting his face clumsily to the downstairs windows, peering inside. If he was a predator, he didn't seem to be stalking prey so much as peeping it.

That was Sam Coyne for sure. She recognized the blond mess of hair and, when he looked up into a streetlight, those cheekbones. *Maybe he is a TTL after all,* she thought. *The avatar didn't lie.*

Still online with Justin, she dialed 911. She also tried to come up with a way to defend herself. As she gave her address to the emergency operator, the closest thing to a plan she could manage was to grab a softball bat from under the bed.

"How did he find out where you live?" Justin asked. "Or even who you are?" Sally could hear Justin's own voice again. He must have picked up the headset.

"I don't know," Barwick said, standing at her computer now, whispering, trying to figure out where Coyne had gone. "Maybe someone at the club recognized me from the story I did on their opening."

"You think?"

Without her even commanding it, Sally's avatar looked around the hospital room and then down at her own hands. Watching it on-screen, the action jolted real Sally. "Oh *shit!*" she said into her headset. "My purse! I left my purse in the garage! My Shadow ID is the same as my real one. Shit!"

"Do you have a weapon or something?" Justin asked. "Like a gun or a bat?"

"You know, for a deep thinker, you're about two minutes behind the curve," she said. "Do you think I should hide? In the closet?"

"No!" Justin yelped. "How will I know you're okay if you're away from the computer?"

"Not a priority for me right now, Justin."

She removed her headset and bounced from window to window, following the man as he made the perimeter of the house. If he *was* the Wicker Man, so notorious for leaving no evidence at the scenes of his crimes, Coyne was having an off day. The bottoms of his boots had made dozens of impressions around the foundation. She took that as a hopeful sign he wasn't here to kill her.

"What's going on?" Justin asked at intervals.

Hearing his muffled voice from across the room, Barwick grabbed the headset and held it to her face. "He's just walking around the house."

"Like he's looking for a way in?"

"I don't know. Why doesn't he just bash in a window?"

"Noise, maybe?" Justin said.

"This is insane!" The ends of her sentences were starting to betray fear.

Justin was still trying to grasp the strangeness of it—the way they were having a real-world conversation and navigating this tense situation through avatars sitting quietly in a hospital waiting room. His real life suddenly seemed like the surreal one. "Don't freak out," Justin said.

"Easy for you."

"Just stay away from him. You've already beaten him once tonight. This time you've got an advantage. It's your house. He's got more to lose. The cops are on the way . . ."

Knock. Knock. Knock.

"Are you kidding me?" Barwick said.

"What?"

"He's knocking on the front door."

"Maybe it's the police."

"Have you ever called the police?"

"No."

"They're not that fast." She dropped the headset and lifted the bat to her shoulder. *The simplest explanation, remember? The simplest explanation for that knocking sound is that the deranged madman I saw lurking outside my house wants to let him in so he can kill me.*

She was exhausted. The last four hours had been long and intense. She was more *tired* of being frightened than she was frightened. Frankly, she had been more scared when Coyne had been chasing her in Shadow World. Her whole life seemed inverted.

She decided she was going downstairs. She let Justin get her into this for the sake of a story, and now the story was knocking on her door. It was probable the story wanted to kill her, of course, but she was going to ask Sam Coyne a few questions, nevertheless.

Knock. Knock. Knock.

"I've called the police!" Sally shouted from the stairs.

A pause. "I just want to talk!" Coyne said through the door.

"I know who you are!"

Another pause. "I know. That's why we need to talk. Call the police back."

"And tell them what?"

"That you made a mistake."

"You can't cancel a nine-one-one call," she said. "I already gave them your name." That was a lie but she wondered why she hadn't.

"You're a reporter. For the *Tribune*."

"You're a murderer. Nice to meet you, asshole."

A long silence. She thought he might have left. Or gone around back. "How did the boy know my name?" he said finally.

Sally said, "That's right. He *does* know who you are. And he knows you're here. We're sitting together at Shadow Stroger Hospital right now. I've been telling him everything that's happening."

The doorknob shook. "Please, if we could just talk for a few minutes."

"Not a chance. I saw what you did to that girl in the garage."

"But . . ." he said. "That was just a *game*. Sally. Miss Barwick. I was *playing*. We all were."

She took another step toward the door. It was thick and heavy. Mahogany or something. It was the first thing she'd loved about this house and she was never more thankful for it than now. She wondered if he had the balls or the sense of drama to crash through a window. They were five feet above the ground outside and he'd have a tough time climbing through. She'd get a few swings at his hands with the bat before he hoisted himself up, anyway. "That's sick," she said. "And I don't believe you."

"Don't believe me?" Coyne seemed puzzled. "Hell, you saw . . ." He was recalling something. "You're a TTL, aren't you? I checked it out. You write for both *Tribune*s. Shadow and real."

Checked it out? How did he do that so fast? In the middle of the night?

"I know it must have been scary for you. In the garage. I didn't know. If I'd known you were a True-to-Lifer I wouldn't have come on so strong."

Come on so strong? Jesus.

"Why did you do it?"

"Kill the blonde?"

Incredible. "Yes, kill the blonde."

Pause. "I don't know . . . It's a *game*. Look, I want to talk to you because, well, maybe we can work something out. I'm an attorney."

"So?"

"So, you're writing an article, aren't you? For the Shadow *Tribune* or the real one, or both? Whatever it is you're going to write about me, there would be certain things that would be, obviously, embarrassing if they were to get out."

No kidding. "How many other girls have you killed?"

He sighed. It was an odd and frightening sound, Sally thought. The discontented sigh of a serial killer. "This isn't an interview, Miss Barwick. Not unless you can guarantee my name will stay out of the paper with regard to tonight's incident."

Barwick placed her hands and her right ear against the door. *Where were the cops?* "I can't guarantee anything, Mr. Coyne."

"You have to let me give my side of the story, then, at least," Coyne said. He was just beyond the door, his head only inches away from hers.

Sally thought about his offer. An interview. An interview with the Wicker Man. To expose him. Capture him. When the police arrive, the opportunity will have vanished. She checked the chain to make sure it was secure. She put her hand on the knob. This is what it means to take risks for your career, she thought. She turned and pulled the door open until the six-inch chain stopped it. Coyne leaned from the other side, expecting to be let in the house. He wrapped his fingers around the door and pulled his face into the opening between the door and the molding. "Miss Barwick?" he said.

Face-to-face at last, she looked him in the eyes.

And as the short, loud *braaaap* and blue-and-red lights of a police car pulled to the curb, she got the answer she'd been pursuing for nearly thirteen years.

— 81 —

With no word from Sally after five minutes, Justin called the police from his cell phone. The emergency dispatcher told him a car was on its way to her address. Justin ran a search on his computer for Sally's number and dialed. No answer. He left a breathless message.

After half an hour with no sign that Sally had returned to the game, Justin discharged her from Shadow Stroger Hospital and drove her back to her Shadow condo. Periodically he tried to start a discussion just to see if he could see some sign of the real Sally. Although her avatar hadn't gone entirely lethargic from her absence, she showed no signs of warmth toward him, either. Shadow Sally thanked Justin politely and perfunctorily and let herself in with her key.

Speeding through wide gaps between early-morning reverse commuters, Justin got his avatar home before dawn. He gave his Shadow mother a ridiculous story about going for an early-morning jog, then shut down the game and hopped into his real bed. It was almost time to get dressed for school. He removed his sweatshirt and his pants and pushed them down to the foot of the bed with his feet.

He heard the phone peal down the hall. His mother hushed it on the fourth ring and a moment later rapped on his door.

"Justin?" Martha Finn called.

"Yuh?" he said with manufactured grogginess.

"It's for you. It's a girl."

Justin wondered if Sally had the guts to call here. If her name would show up on caller ID. If his mother would recognize her voice all these years later. He rolled out of bed and unlocked the door and opened it just enough to slip his hand through the crack. He gripped the phone and pulled it back inside, shutting the door behind him.

"*Sally,*" he whispered, even though his mother might have the extension to her ear.

Silence.

"Are you okay? What happened? Where's Coyne?"

Nothing.

It occurred to Justin that it might not be Sally on the other end. It might be Coyne. But how would he know who Justin was? Or where to find his number? Sally and Justin had never spoken outside Shadow World, not since he was a kid anyway.

"Sally, are you all right?" he asked again.

"I'm fine," Sally said finally. "The police came. He's gone."

"Thank God."

Neither one of them said anything more for at least a minute. Justin couldn't explain the awkwardness. Despite their close friendship in Shadow World, it was almost as if they were strangers in real life.

"Anyway," Sally said.

"Anyway," Justin said. "I'll meet you in the game later. After school. We'll talk then. You'll tell me everything."

"All right. Good," Sally said, and then, before she hung up, "Wait a minute, Justin . . ."

"What?"

Another long silence. A sigh over the phone. "Nothing. No. I mean . . ." It sounded to Justin like she was crying. She said, "Happy Birthday."

Justin at Sixteen

— 82 —

These stones had been brought to America on ships from Egypt, and the tomb reconstructed here inside the Field Museum years and years ago, Davis noticed, when you could still pull a stunt like that. The exhibit twisted along narrow hallways and opened into small chambers where ancient artifacts were displayed alongside reproductions and bits of history unfolded on metal plaques. Twenty-three actual mummies were the main attraction, though, a graphic demonstration that no resting place is ever final.

Sally Barwick had asked to meet him here, in a small, dark room with two old urns and some re-created hieroglyphs. She was comfortable here. It was a place in the real world she could go when she couldn't escape to the game. And it was important this conversation be private.

Unpressed, yesterday's dress hung from her body in unsightly relief, creases and wrinkles charting imaginary glacial topography across the fabric. Barwick said, "Justin knows, doesn't he? He knows he was cloned from Sam Coyne, not Eric Lundquist."

"Yes," Davis said. "How did you figure it out?"

She could have told him it was the eyes. That Sam Coyne's eyes were the same eyes she had photographed when Justin was a child. They were the eyes that romanced her in her dreams. "What did Coyne do?" she asked instead. "Justin said he did something terrible. A long time ago."

Davis sat on a small bench and she took a seat beside him. "He killed my daughter."

An icy fright radiated from Barwick's stomach to her scalp and to her hands and feet. She felt like an investigator again, felt the rush of the end of a case. This one had been open for thirteen years, since she'd turned the stiff pages of the photo album in Mrs. Lundquist's living room. "You cloned him

271

from the evidence." She realized she felt burdened with the answer. She didn't know what she was supposed to do with it. "Why didn't you go to the police with that? Or the newspapers?"

"Let's see," Davis said, sadly. "Because what I did was illegal? Because I'd go to prison? Because the evidence is totally inadmissible. Because Coyne would go free." He was embarrassed. About to be exposed. A headache was forming above his ears. Sally Barwick was being pleasant enough—calm even, considering what she'd just discovered. Still, this felt like an interrogation.

"Why does Justin think Coyne's the Wicker Man?"

"Honestly, I don't know. I haven't shared his . . . his *enthusiasm* for that theory. I think Justin's desperately looking for connections between things. He has trouble accepting the existence of coincidences. In his mind, our world is frustratingly disconnected."

"I thought Justin was crazy, too," Sally said. "Not after last night, though."

"What happened?"

"I saw Coyne kill a girl. Slice her up. Let her bleed out."

"What? Where?" Then he understood. "In Shadow World. That's not the same, is it?"

Barwick didn't feel like explaining the True-to-Life aesthetic. "He also came after *me*. In real life. He came to my house to kill me."

"*Jesus!* What happened?"

"I called the police."

Davis became excited. His face turned hopeful. "So they have him? He's been arrested?"

Barwick shook her head. "He told the cops it was a misunderstanding. That he was just playing a game and that he came to my house to try to explain what I had witnessed on-screen. They couldn't hold him."

"Goddamn," Davis whispered. "He'll just come again, won't he? Are you safe?"

"I filed a restraining order against him," she said.

"Means little," Davis said.

She knew that. The fact that they'd both been meeting with Justin (although Sally only met him in Shadow World) was an illustration of that. "I want to tell the cops," Sally said. "I think Justin's right. I think Coyne might be the Wicker Man."

"They'll laugh at you."

A couple walking through the exhibit paused in the chamber where Sally and Davis were talking. Uncomfortable in the sudden silence, they pointed quickly at the urns and moved on.

"What about this?" Barwick said. "Let me tell *your* story. Write a feature for the Sunday *Trib* magazine. We'll expose him. There'll be a cry for an investigation. Coyne will never survive the scrutiny."

Davis snorted. "Neither will I. I'll be locked up for the rest of my life."

"I'll make the story as sympathetic as possible."

Once more, Davis asked himself how much he would sacrifice in pursuit of AK's killer. "It's not only me. There's another life that would be ruined."

"Justin," Sally said.

He nodded. "It's bad enough for people, especially kids, when they're just outed as clones," Davis said. "If it became public that Justin was cloned from a killer, his life would become a freak show. He'd never get it back."

Sally was thinking. *Coyne knows where I work. Where I live.* She was thinking that as long as he was out there, it would be virtually impossible to sleep in her apartment. She was thinking the offices of Ginsburg and Addams were only three blocks from Tribune Tower. She was thinking her life would be lived from now on in almost constant fear. "No matter how I feel about Justin, given what I know, I can't do nothing. Coyne needs to be exposed. The Wicker Man has to be caught. He's killed dozens of people. He'll kill dozens more."

"I can't tell you what to do," Davis said. "Coyne is still a killer, whether you believe he's the Wicker Man or not."

Barwick looked up at the hieroglyphs etched into stone above the doorway. She couldn't know how they translated. She thought of the nearly forgotten son of a pharaoh who'd been buried in this tomb, uprooted, transported, put on display in a New World city, a world that wasn't discovered for more than a thousand years after his death. What kind of a person was he? What kind of a friend? A son? A father? Did anyone care? Those tourists passing through—did they consider at all what kind of a man he was? If they didn't, what was the point of this monument? What was the point of remembering a life that was no longer of any consequence?

— 83 —

By the skin of my teeth.

That was the phrase Stephen Malik had been using in reply when sympathetic friends and colleagues asked him how he was holding up, or whether he was hanging on, or if, as of that day, he still had a job at the *Tribune*. He'd been saying it for so long, in fact, that it had ceased to be an honest answer. If it was true one was holding up or hanging on or keeping one's job by the skin of one's teeth, it's assumed one could not do so indefinitely. In Malik's case, however, everyone agreed that his era at the *Tribune* was in its final hours. A Web site dedicated to journalism gossip had a regular feature called "Malik Watch." Several times a week, it published an anonymous quote from inside the newsroom detailing a grievance against the managing editor, or a rumor about his replacement. Unidentified sources spied the *Tribune* publisher courting candidates for the job at pricey restaurants in New York, Los Angeles, San Francisco, and Miami.

But still he remained. He remained although he'd run out of excuses he could sell even to himself. *Maybe I really am the wrong man for this job,* he thought. He was ready to leave. He had rehearsed his farewell newsroom speech, decided on a graceful, gracious exit with nothing but kind words for the filthy saboteurs upstairs who had recruited him and then plotted against him. He and his wife had discussed retirement in the north, Wisconsin or maybe the Upper Peninsula, to a small town with a weekly paper, because seeing a daily on his doorstep every morning would be painful for a time. He had once loved this business so much.

It was amid such an atmosphere, on a sunny spring day, that he found Sally Barwick lurking outside his office. He invited her in and shut the door.

"Stephen, I've been keeping something from you. From everyone here."

He expected she was going to tell him about her gaming. It was something, at this point in his free fall, that he couldn't care less about. "What's that?"

"I've been working on a story for a couple months. I haven't told you or anyone else about it. Now it's almost got me killed."

Not what he thought. "Are you talking about this business with the lawyer? The creep who was stalking you?"

She considered the accuracy of that statement. "Actually, I was sort of stalking *him*. At first, anyway."

"What? This Coyne guy? The one you took out the restraining order against?"

"Yeah."

"What are you talking about?"

Fidgeting, Sally realized she was sitting in the chair she hated, the most uncomfortable chair on the 400 block of North Michigan Avenue, and she wondered why she hadn't chosen another of the three in this office. "Sam Coyne attacked me because I've been trying to prove he's the Wicker Man."

"Jesus, Barwick." He snickered because it had to be a joke.

"I'm serious."

For a moment, Malik's own troubles seemed not worth worrying about.

Sally began describing her case, trying to flatten her voice so the parts that were true sounded as sincere as the parts that weren't. "I received an anonymous tip about six months ago. The caller said I should look into Sam Coyne.

He didn't say why. I did, and I didn't find anything, but I did notice he was a gamer. Like me."

"Shadow World?"

"Right."

"When I didn't run anything about him in the paper, my tipster called back. He said to check out Sam Coyne *inside the game.* So I did."

"You were investigating Coyne's life, *inside a video game?* How would you do that?"

"Same way you'd investigate him out here. Shadow World has records, and sources, and streets and alleyways."

"So what did you find?"

"That Coyne is a killer."

"Inside the game?"

"Right. He kills other players in the game, all female, and in ways remarkably similar to the Wicker Man."

Malik had a bad feeling, the kind he usually had right before he had to fire someone. "Which is sick, but not illegal."

"But then I checked Coyne's killing in the game against the Wicker Man's killings out here."

"And?"

"When Coyne is killing in Shadow World, it's like the Wicker Man doesn't even exist out here. All quiet." This wasn't exactly true, of course, but Sally didn't want to go into Justin's theories explaining the anomalies in his chart.

"Proves nothing."

"True. So I called a cop I know from the Wicker beat, a detective in homicide, and I casually dropped Coyne's name."

"What did he give you?"

"A long, long silence."

"So you still got nothing."

"So I call him every day for two weeks. And he tells me, way off the record, that Coyne is a *person of interest* in the Wicker investigation."

"Along with how many other *interesting persons?*"

"God, I don't know, Stephen. *None* that also turned up in an independent investigation by the city's top newspaper."

"What do you want to do?"

"What do you think? I want to run with the story."

"With what story, Sals?" He moved his hand in the air, typesetting a mock front page. *"Reporter Accuses Man She Has Personal Beef with of Being Infamous Serial Killer."*

"It's a good thing you don't write headlines," she said with a friendly snort. "And I'm not accusing him because he attacked me, he attacked me because I accused him. I want to run with the story that Sam Coyne is a suspect in the Wicker Man killings."

This is a joke, Malik thought. "With all the problems I've got, what makes you think I want to take on the entire partnership of Ginsburg and Addams in a libel suit?"

"It's only libel if I'm wrong about Coyne. And I'm not wrong."

"So you actually think he won't sue?"

"No, I'm betting he will. I'm betting, in the course of the widely publicized civil trial and the ensuing high-profile police investigation, that we'll discover evidence proving he's a killer. The *Tribune* will get credit for capturing one of the most notorious serial murderers in American history, and your job will be saved in the process."

"Sweetheart, if I went along with a stunt like that they'd have my office cleaned out before you could mix strawberries in your morning yogurt."

"It's risky, I know. But risky journalism wins awards." She added, "And saves jobs."

"It'll be the newspaper world's first posthumous rehire," Malik said. "If the *Trib*'s lawyers don't kill me, or that serial killer of yours doesn't slit my throat, my wife will shoot me dead. We're a newspaper, not a clearinghouse for personal vendettas."

"So we're just supposed to sit around and let a killer walk the streets?"

"What killer, Sally? It's like I don't even know you. Bring me evidence. Solid reporting. Show me this guy is who you say he is and not just a big jerk."

"That's what I'm *trying* to do. But he's smart. He might have killed twenty people, and he hasn't left any evidence behind yet. We have to smoke him out. Or smoke out someone close to him who might know the truth."

"Fine. Bring me something besides anonymous sources."

Sally inhaled a lungful of stale, recirculated air. "Coyne tried to break into my house, Stephen. While I was *inside*. There's only one reason why he'd do that: because he suspects I'm on to him."

"I trust your instincts, Sally," Malik said. "Bring me an actual story and I'll print it. But I won't go to press on your theories and cross my fingers they'll be proven true."

At lunch, from her desk, Sally met Justin at the Shadow Billy Goat.

"It was worth a try," Sally said. She didn't tell him she knew he'd been regenerated from one of Sam Coyne's cells—*almost like a plant clipping*, Sally thought in her most cynical moments. Justin would be horrified if he knew she'd found out, and after her confrontation with Coyne (which she had described to him minus that most important detail), her sudden change of heart on Justin's Wicker Man theory needed no explanation.

"Yep," Justin said.

"We've got to catch Coyne in the act, somehow. In real life this time. I think it's the only way."

"I graduate in a couple weeks," Justin said. "I'll have some time after that. Maybe stake him out for real. I'm getting my license this summer, too."

Barwick said, "You're graduating? I had no idea. Congratulations. Where are you going to school next year?"

"I'm not. Taking a year off. My grades and SATs are good enough to get me in just about anywhere I want. But I'm too young for college."

"What are you going to do?"

"Read," Justin said. "The stuff I want to read. Not the books they give you in school. Maybe go see my dad."

Sally tried to remember those late-night conversations through the computer and across the car seat outside Coyne's Shadow apartment. "In New Mexico, right?"

"Right. Spend some time thinking about who I am. Who I'm supposed to be. What I'm supposed to do. I need to pursue that. This other stuff— school—gets in the way."

"What? You mean, like, *find yourself*?" She couldn't disguise a laugh.

"Something like that."

"I don't know that we're *supposed* to do anything, Justin. Except be."

"Maybe *you're* not," he said.

Barwick couldn't tell if the remark was meant to be insulting or if it was just self-absorbed. She decided generously on the latter.

Back in his office, with a day's worth of stories and assignments to approve, Malik began looking up everything he could on Samuel Coyne of Ginsburg and Addams. He found pictures of the man in a tux at charity dinners, and some for-the-record denials on behalf of his clients in the business page archives. He looked a little bit like a handsome asshole. Not at all like a killer. But then, what's a killer look like before you know he's killed? Coyne didn't look like a murderer, but that didn't mean he wasn't one. Only that Malik had been unconvinced.

The Wicker Man, he thought. *Is there any way she could be right?*

— 84 —

Alone at home, Martha opened a bottle of expensive Cabernet she'd grown tired of saving. She poured wine into a deep glass up to the widest part of the bowl and let it sit on the kitchen table until the surface became still, staring into and through it as if it were a ruby crystal ball. Finding no answers there, she grabbed the glass by the stem, painted the back of her tongue with the Cab, and closed her eyes.

Justin was out. For the third time this week. Some nights he didn't come home. There were things she knew, things she suspected, things she feared, and almost nothing she could talk about with him.

It was after nine o'clock and he could be anywhere. He didn't have a car and his bike was still here, but his friends—what friends he had—were older and most had their own cars, fast cars with poor safety ratings. Plus, there were enough places to find trouble within a few minutes' walk. The least of which was not the home of Dr. Davis Moore, just six suburban blocks away.

Her things had been disappearing. Jewelry and cash from her bedroom. Never-used silver from the dining room. Gasoline from the car. Decaying boxes from the attic packed with cut-glass bowls and not-very-valuable art. She could never tell when he had taken stuff, or prove it, or even be confident enough in his guilt to confront him. Or maybe she was confident but too frightened. Frightened of what he might do. Might do to her if she accused him.

When at school or out at night God knows where, he always locked his bedroom door. When she and Terry had moved in, before Justin was even born, the previous owner had handed them a set of keys. Every doorknob in the house had a cheap lock in the knob, installed there by the paranoid old man who had built the place, she explained. They never used the keys, but kept them in a kitchen drawer just in case someone locked themselves out of a room by accident (which was easy to do if you pushed and twisted the knob just right when closing the door behind you). Justin had taken the key to his room about four months ago and now used it every day.

Every night after he left she wandered down the hall past his room on the way to hers and checked to see if it might be open. She told herself even if she ever found it unlocked she would never go inside, but she never got a chance to test that kind of discipline. Every time Martha set her hand on the knob it felt welded in place.

Martha frequently asked him to let her in to clean, but every time she asked, Justin added another task to his routine. He changed his own sheets every week now, or almost. He washed his windows inside and out every two weeks. He dusted. Once he even unhooked the drapes and piled them in the hall to be dry cleaned. All to prove there was no need for her to be in there. Ever.

This night the doorknob turned. Martha didn't consider the promise she'd made to herself. She didn't hesitate.

The bed was unmade. Drawers hung open from bureaus. Dirty laundry spilled from the closet. The air was sour and a remaindered odor stung her nose, becoming more intense when she neared the bed. A rounded pile of garbage topped the trash can like a snow cone and then multiplied into free-standing piles around the room. Martha stepped through it slowly and reluctantly, like she was wading through a basement flooded with sewage to reach the fuse box.

This was all recent. He had given her a glimpse of his room from the hall about a month ago, an eyeball inspection he had allowed in order to get her off his back. It had appeared spotless. How he could have made a mess this big in such a short time, Martha had no idea.

She wanted to open a window, but thought better of leaving evidence she had been here. Just look for it and get out, she told herself. She wasn't sure what *it* was, except that it was anything she didn't want to find.

If Martha Finn had been an overly suspicious woman, and Lord knows by this stage in her life she had reason to be, something would have struck her as staged about the whole thing. The unlocked door. The filthy room. The ease with which she was able to find *it*, sitting on top of his nightstand, the Baggie even open. Translucent yellow rocks spilling onto the dark grain of the table-top like hard candy. A curious collection of homemade devices. She could only imagine the manner in which they had been used, in combination with a lighter and spoon. But used they were. She didn't touch them.

She shut the door as she left, leaving it unlocked, the way she'd found it, walked to her room, and cried.

— 85 —

When he joined the force, the hardest thing for Ambrose to get used to was the discomfiting juxtaposition of violence and food. The disgusting details of this job never let up, even for meals.

As he did many mornings, Ambrose stared at the cinder-block wall, mulling over the Wicker Man case and eating a roach-coach egg-and-sausage biscuit. He was frustrated. Frustrated that he knew little more about Suspect M, the Candlestick Maker, than he did the week that tip had come in. The task force didn't have the resources to put a citizen on round-the-clock surveillance based only on the whim of a single lieutenant, and his men didn't share his certainty with regard to this suspect. Plus, the guy was a moderately prominent figure in the city. Not a household name, but a frequent guest at charity auctions and balls. He no doubt had lots of friends—probably even a few on LaSalle Street. These people could make life for Ambrose extremely difficult if the Candlestick Maker knew he was being watched.

I could do it myself, Ambrose thought. *I could chase him down on my own time.* He thought about Clint Eastwood movies. Dirty Harry. A cop who could operate outside procedure because his instincts were always right. What else did Ambrose have to do with his spare time? Nothing, when his kids weren't visiting. And he had to shake things up. This couldn't go on indefinitely. The next time there was a body, the terrorized people of Chicago weren't going to tolerate a cute speech and a shrug from the leader of the Wicker Man task force. No, he was going back on the street. Solve this case himself. Some reporter would probably write a book about it. *The Candlestick Maker* would make a good title for a true-crime book. The idea seemed smarter to him the more he thought about it.

Looking up through the window in his office door, he could see activity in the squad room. Cops were on the phone. Other cops were running for their cars. Ambrose had turned the ringer off his phone so he could think, and now it blinked at him furiously. He watched Detective DuPree stop himself on the way to the door and reverse directions. DuPree opened the door to Ambrose's office and said between breaths:

"Lieutenant. We got a witness."

— **86** —

Malik spent most of most days in the conference room, meeting with management, meeting with department editors, meeting with his staff. The sight of gray paint, the sound of squeaky chairs, the smell of people sweating in unventilated rooms was usually enough to make him drowsy as soon as the door closed behind him. Not today.

"I got the gist on TV," Malik said to the three reporters who worked the Wicker Man beat. "But tell me anyway."

Sally said, "Five o'clock this morning. Woman walking her dog along Division near the expressway. Sees a man in a hooded sweatshirt standing over a body in the alley. She said he was *hovering* over it. He had a towel in his hand—"

"It was raining, yes?"

Lynn Bellingham said, "It had been storming earlier, but by the time the woman took her dog out, the rain had subsided a bit."

"What else?"

"Man in sweatshirt hears her coming, looks at her briefly, then runs off. She holds her dog back. Struggles over to the body. Sees the dead girl. Calls police on her cell. The body was both strangled and stabbed. Sexual assault. Posed. It has all the earmarks."

"The victim?"

"Prostitute, apparently. They haven't released her name if they know it."

"And the best news?"

"Blood besides the victim's, *and* semen. Cops are guessing the dog walker interrupted his cleanup. That and the rain let up."

"Good golly."

"Torriero, the police spokesman, was practically giddy."

"Suspects?"

"The witness didn't get a good look except to say the attacker was white. But Ambrose himself came out to say they'd be running the DNA against the database and hoped to have a suspect by the end of the week. Put himself right on the line and said it."

"All right," Malik said. "Give me the cops' side straight, get me an interview with the witness, and give me a feature on Teddy Ambrose. He's been on the Wicker Man from the beginning. And I want good pics of the cops working the crime scene. Not that blurry, unframed bullshit we got last time."

Roles were assigned and accepted. Reporters dispersed. Sally remained.

"What?" Malik asked.

She shut the door. "We're going to miss it."

"Miss what?"

"The exclusive."

"Tell me."

"Why do you think Ambrose is putting his ass on the line, promising a suspect in three days?"

Malik turned a chair around in front of him and sat in it wrong way out, resting his forearms across the backrest. "Because he's been on this case for too many years and he's a little overenthusiastic. Also, the conventional wisdom has to be that this guy's been picked up for a felony before, and his DNA would be in the system."

"No," Barwick said. "He's putting his ass on the line because they already have a suspect and they're just waiting for the DNA to confirm it."

Malik understood. "Your stalker."

"Right."

"That's a leap," Malik said. "Ambrose is getting a lot of pressure to name a suspect, and that statement takes the heat off him for a few days and puts it on his detectives. It's political arm-twisting. The odds that this asshole's in the database just makes it a good gamble for him."

Sally's hand disappeared into her hair. "Stephen, this is the way it's going to happen. On Friday, or possibly Thursday if they don't want the best get of their careers stuck in Saturday's paper, the police are going to announce that Sam Coyne is their suspect in this latest killing. They won't mention the Wicker Man, but it will be obvious to everyone because the cops don't hold press conferences every time they find a dead hooker. If he hasn't fled the country, they'll arrest him, but they won't charge him because Coyne's DNA isn't in the system. He's never been arrested in his life. I checked. They'll take his blood, and when it matches, they'll try to connect him to the other murders."

"If you say so."

"But we know Coyne's the guy *right now*. And we're the only ones who know it. We should run it in tomorrow's paper. If we wait for the cops to announce it, the *Trib*'ll be just another white ass in the weekend gang bang."

A few weeks ago, Malik had reconsidered his opinion that Sally Barwick had potential to be an excellent reporter. Now he was reconsidering again. Sally had potential to be a *great* reporter. A great reporter is aggressive, ambitious, and takes huge personal risks. She had that in her, and he didn't. That was why Malik himself had been only a decent reporter, and why he was a failure as an editor besides.

"Say we run it. What's your story?"

"That an ongoing *Tribune* investigation of the Wicker Man murders had been pointing toward Sam Coyne for several weeks. That an analysis of his gaming patterns had revealed a correlation between his copycat activities in the game and the real-life murders. That a police source confirmed Coyne had been on the investigators' short list for some time, and that once DNA tests come back, there is a high probability they will confirm Coyne is their killer."

"I thought you said they didn't have Coyne's DNA."

She shrugged. "They'll subpoena him, ask him to submit to a blood test, and if he refuses, they'll know they have their man. Besides, there are plenty of places to get a person's DNA. Coffee cups, a hairbrush. They'll make a match. I'd just rather do it first."

"How good is your source?" Malik watched her body language. Sally crossed her arms and bowed her head. He tried to recall a seminar he'd taken on body language. *What does that mean again?*

Barwick looked up, right into his eyes. "Good. But he stays anonymous. I can't even say how high up he is."

"Just tell *me*, then."

"No."

"You don't tell me, there's no story."

"No offense, Stephen, but you're getting heat from a lot of different sides. I'll go to jail to protect this source, but I don't want *you* to have to make that choice, as well."

"That's my job, Sally."

"Coyne is the guy. Trust me. When his blood turns out to be a match, no one's going to ask who my source is."

Malik considered what she was offering. The biggest media fish of the year. Every newscast and wire service and paper in the country would lead with the words "The *Chicago Tribune* is reporting today . . ." If Barwick were wrong, his disgrace would only be marginally worse than it was already. If she were right, it didn't matter what they did to him. Hell, he could march upstairs and quit five minutes after the cops made the arrest. He'd be a newspaper legend.

"How sure are you about this?"

"I'm *sure*," Sally said. "I've got the most to lose here, Stephen. And I think we'd both agree you have as much to gain as I do."

Malik stood up and walked to the phone. He punched three buttons. "Don. Get the staff together. Everybody. Now."

— 87 —

A long, hot day at the district. Three meals delivered. Kids tucked in over the phone. Overtime adding up on a dozen officers' time sheets, and no one from higher up complaining. Ambrose was going to sit at his desk until the lab came back with a folder thick with colored squiggles. Then he planned to go home while the techs ran the squiggles through the computer until they had a match. If the DNA wasn't in the system, they'd move on to their top three suspects—the Butcher, the Baker, the Candlestick Maker. In a few hours, Ambrose knew, his gut was going to be proven right.

All three were on tight surveillance tonight, along with two other men favored by separate detectives working the case. Ambrose almost hoped that once word was out they had testable DNA, the Candlestick Maker would start running. Not likely, though. Smug asshole would probably stay right where he's at, daring the cops to arrest him.

Footsteps. A sudden increase in the volume of background noise.

"Lou," Detective Rozas said, using the familiar term for lieutenant. "The television. Channel five. News."

Ambrose hurried out to the squad room. A half dozen cops were kneeling and stretching around a portable television. Another dozen stood around the perimeter listening. Ambrose pushed his way inside the circle.

"The *Chicago Tribune* is reporting in tomorrow's paper that police finally have a suspect in the Wicker Man killings, and plan to make an arrest in the next forty-eight hours. Julie Becker has the report."

The scene cut to a woman standing on Division Street near the latest crime scene. She was attractive and serious-looking.

"Diane, in a page-one exclusive tomorrow morning, the *Tribune* is reporting the results of a long investigation into the Wicker Man killings. An investigation they claim has led to a suspect. Although their investigation is incomplete, *Tribune* officials say information that police were preparing to arrest the man forced their decision to run the story tomorrow.

"The suspect's name, according to the *Tribune,* is Samuel Nathan Coyne, of Chicago. Coyne is a partner at the prestigious Michigan Avenue law firm of Ginsburg and Addams. Representatives of that firm are not commenting tonight, nor is Samuel Coyne responding to the rumor himself. Calls to the office of the police commissioner were not returned, although this story just broke in the last few minutes. We should repeat, of course, that no arrests have yet been made in this case."

Multiple phones rang throughout the squad room. The greenest cops ran off to answer them.

The anchorwoman reacted to an off-camera cue. "Julie, tell us more about events that led to a break in the case."

"Diane, the break came early this morning when a witness walking her dog found the body of Deirdre Thorson, of Chicago. According to police, this witness also saw an individual fleeing the scene. Unlike with previous victims of the so-called Wicker Man, blood and semen were found on the body in quantities large enough to test for DNA. Police assume that the killer was interrupted before he could finish cleaning up."

"Julie, what makes police so certain this is a victim of the Wicker Man and not just a random killing?"

"That's a good question, Diane. Police have not revealed all the details to us, but it was clear in a press conference this morning that confidence is very high this is their man. Quoting anonymous sources within the department, the *Tribune* is saying tonight that if Coyne can be connected through DNA to Thorson's murder, he'll be arrested on that charge alone. Presumably, detectives will then try to string together pieces of evidence that connect him to the killings of some twenty young women in Chicago over the past six years."

Another intro by the anchorwoman and then footage of Ambrose at this morning's press conference. Ambrose pressed the volume button until the sound was muted. His hands rolled into fists, his skin pale but becoming flush, he turned to face his squad.

"I want to know two things," Ambrose yelled. "Number one: which one of you assholes is talking to the goddamn newspaper?" The cops looked suspiciously at one another. A few looked down at their own feet. The mood had gone from jubilant to tense just that fast.

Ambrose scowled. "And number two: who the *fuck* is *Samuel Coyne?*"

— 88 —

His phone had been ringing for several hours, but Sam didn't answer. He was inside the game, leaning on a surfboard bolted to aluminum legs and refashioned as a table at a tropical theme bar called Caymans. He was sharing drinks with three women, judging them, deciding among them.

They were Alyssa, Emmylou, and Robey. The last was a redhead who had downloaded the new software, and she was perfectly rendered. When she turned he could see the waves and strands of her thick hair fall away and come together in a natural bounce. Her eyelashes were like fans over her irises. When she spoke he could see her tongue move against her white teeth. If he knew how to read lips, he figured he'd be able to read hers.

However, he really didn't care what she was saying just now. The girls had been steering the conversation to real-world topics, and that always put him out of the mood. He hated it when people treated Shadow World like a chat room. What happens in the real world should have no impact here. In the game we shouldn't even know who the real president is, or what stocks are outperforming, or what baseball teams are in first place. We have our own president. Our own stock market. Our own baseball teams. He'd been trying to tune them out, waiting for the conversation to hit upon more local topics, but it was difficult.

"Robey and Alyssa, did you see the news?" Emmylou said. "I guess the police are going to arrest him tomorrow. Maybe even tonight."

"Emmylou, that's such a relief," Robey said. "You know there hasn't been a single day since I was seventeen when I haven't thought about him, or been scared of him . . ."

"I can't believe they just said his name on the television like that," Alyssa said. "If I were him, I'd be headed for May-hee-ko."

"Alyssa, I'm sure they have cops all over his house," Robey said. "Actually, they probably arrested him as soon as his name went out on the news."

Interrupting, only because it was better than being bored, Sam said, "Robey, who are we talking about?"

Alyssa laughed. "Sam, what have you been, in-game all day? The Wicker Man, silly. They know who he is. They're going to arrest him anytime."

"His name's Sam, like you," Emmylou said. "Sam Coyne." She giggled. "I'd ask your last name, just to be safe, but I figure the Wicker Man wouldn't be wasting his time playing computer games with the police knocking down his door."

What the hell?

Knock. Knock. Knock.

This can't be happening.

Through his apartment door: "Mr. Coyne? This is the police. Please open up."

Sam left the computer and quickly dialed Bob Ginsburg at home.

"I've been trying to call you for hours," Bob said.

"They're outside in the hall, Bob! For Chrissakes!"

"Mr. Coyne? We have the building manager with us. He's going to open the door. Please lie down on the floor and put your hands above your head where we can see them."

"What's this about, Sam?"

"I don't know, Bob. Jesus Christ. Send somebody to meet me."

"Where are they taking you?"

"I don't have the slightest idea."

Dead-bolt click. Door slamming against drywall.

"Down! Down! Down! Down! Get on the floor now!"

In Shadow World, as Alyssa, Emmylou, and Robey continued to discuss the exciting developments in the Wicker Man case, Sam's silent avatar ferried a pint glass between the table and his lips with a repetitive, mechanical motion.

— 89 —

She couldn't admit it to anyone in the newsroom, but she was nervous. Extremely nervous. Allies asked if she was worried, and she shook her head and laughed. The Web site famous for the "Malik Watch" had started posting odds that by naming Sam Coyne, the previously unknown reporter, Sally Barwick, had torpedoed her own career and possibly brought down a handful of *Trib* executives with her. Already, just since the news had come down, a hundred of her colleagues had placed their bets, with the trend running two to one against her.

Sam Coyne had agreed to a blood test.

Shortly after the news broke on TV, police had asked Barwick in for questioning. Accompanied by a *Tribune* lawyer, she refused to reveal her source in the department but briefed them with all the information that would be in the piece, including Coyne's attacks in Shadow World, the correlation between Coyne's murders in the game and the Wicker Man murders, and Coyne's attempted assault at her home. She was still at the station when they brought Coyne in: four cops, no handcuffs, and three attorneys (including Bob Ginsburg, the *Trib* lawyer pointed out). Sally hid behind a Coke machine until they disappeared into an interrogation room.

They questioned Coyne for three hours and released him after he agreed to a blood test. Sally's stomach wrung itself like a wet towel when she heard that. She had been certain his lawyers would fight any request that might incriminate him. Now, at two o'clock the following afternoon, it appeared possible, even probable, she would be proved wrong about Coyne in a matter of hours—one of the fastest undoings of a promising career in journalism history.

Malik hadn't been seen in the newsroom all day. *This was surely it,* the whispers said. *The Sam Coyne stunt was the last straw. What was he thinking? What was Barwick thinking? We all knew she was a little off her rocker—she had no life outside the* Tribune *except in that crazy computer game—but no one had thought her capable of a suicidal stunt like this. Was somebody setting her up with bad information? Someone who had a beef with Coyne? Was she being played by someone who'd been slammed by Ginsburg and Addams in court? Research recent cases involving Sam Coyne—especially the ones where G&A acted as plaintiff's attorney—and start with the biggest verdicts and work down. We'll need all this when Coyne passes that blood test and we print the retraction next week. The new managing editor will be glad to have the diligence done in advance. Heck, the new editor might even be one of us . . .* Such was the way rumors spread.

Rumors spread so fast, in fact, that an Iowa company specializing in the distribution of agricultural products, a company that had lost a hundred-million-dollar copyright infringement lawsuit last year with Sam Coyne leading the litigation for their competitor, issued a press release denying they had anything to do with the accusations against Coyne. No one had even asked them.

Rumors cut the other way too. Web sites were papered with unconfirmed and unsourced tales of Coyne's promiscuity and kinky bedroom practices.

Sally called Justin on a real phone, her free hand on the cradle in case his mother answered. He was home.

"I just wanted to talk to somebody," she whispered. "I have a bad feeling about this."

"It's going to be okay."

"It's starting to look like we were wrong."

"We aren't wrong."

"But what if he didn't kill Deirdre Thorson? What if that was a copycat and he's giving up his blood because he knows he didn't do it?"

"If his blood doesn't match, that's *all* it will prove."

"Except that my career is over. And I'm going to be named in a trillion-dollar lawsuit. And probably go to jail for contempt or something because I don't really have a source in the police department, but they won't believe me when I tell them the truth."

"You're worrying about things that haven't even happened yet."

"But they *will,* Justin. Don't you see what's going on? He agreed to the blood test. Why would he do it if he knew he was guilty?"

"Lots of reasons. Maybe he's a split personality and doesn't remember."

"Oh, come on."

"Or maybe he's going to challenge the DNA evidence," Justin said. "It hasn't been done much lately, but I've read about a bunch of cases going all the way back to O.J. where accused killers have gotten off by claiming the evidence was tainted. Or the testing not a hundred percent accurate. His lawyer will even say in court, *Why would my client have freely given the police evidence he knew would incriminate him?* Juries are too smart for that these days, but he might try if it was his only hope."

"God, I feel sick." Sally tapped her keyboard, searching the wire to see if any news was breaking on the case. On the far side of the room, Barwick heard a murmur and the swishy, squeaky sound of people standing up from their seats. Stephen Malik walked into the newsroom, stony and purposeful. Attempts by reporters to read his expression couldn't have been more obvious if his face were Braille and they were assaulting it with their fingers. Malik passed Sally's cubicle and didn't pause but wiggled his fingers just under her sight line, and she hung up the phone and followed him into his office as the definitive rumor began its path around Trib Tower. Malik was fired and Barwick's going with him. By the time it reached the tenth floor, the story described how Malik had already been escorted from his office by armed guards.

But by then the truth had entered the system, as well. In a whisper.

"Did they fire you?" Barwick asked in his office.

"They started to," he said in a voice that was hoarse and tired and disappointed. "They started to tell me I had been irresponsible. That the checks and balances we have in place here at the paper should have stopped your story on Coyne before the press. That by circumventing those checks and balances I had betrayed their trust, or betrayed the duties with which I had been entrusted, or betrayed the board of trustees. Something about trust and the betrayal of it, anyway."

Sally urged him with her eyes to get on with it. Did she still have a job?

"And they said this whole Coyne thing was just one event in a series of unfortunate ones, and they were disappointed, and they had given me every chance but they had no choice, and it wasn't personal, and that some financial arrangements could be made with respect to my contract, and if I had even moderate savings tucked away somewhere, a pension, IRA, et cetera, that I could live a very comfortable retirement, which is what they assumed I wanted because a man my age wouldn't be able to find another job after such a high-profile scandal, no matter how they couched it for the press. Also, that I should retain counsel in preparation for the inevitable civil suit."

"God, I'm so sorry, Stephen," Sally said, the beginning of a good cry stinging her nose.

"And then they started in on you. How you would take much of the fall, but you were still young and talented and could no doubt recover from this. There might even be a confessional-type book in it for you."

"So we're both cooked," she said, a little relieved it was over, oddly.

"Curiously, no," he said.

"What do you mean?"

"Because as they were making that speech, word came in. Coyne failed the DNA test."

"Oh my God. It was him?" she whispered, certain she would cry now.

"It was him." Malik was laughing. "You should have seen the sons of bitches. If they weren't sitting on fine brown leather, I swear I could have seen each of them shit his pants."

"Holy God!" Sally spun around his desk and hugged him. "I'm so happy for you. Happy for me, but mostly happy for you."

"Barwick," he said, pushing her to a distance where they could see each other's faces. "I gotta ask . . . Why do you sound so surprised?"

— 90 —

Midwesterners are so used to complaining about the weather, they do it even on the pleasant days, Davis observed. If it drops to the low seventies with an evening breeze in August, they'll call it "chilly" and pack a jacket. Three days in a row without rain will have them worried about their lawns. A mild February surely portends the brutal, sweltering summer to come.

They are also sanguine about bad weather, however, even when it arrives at inopportune times. Between pews on an overcast wedding day, you will hear expert testimony from guests that flat sunlight filtered through dense clouds will eliminate shadows and produce the best pictures.

It was raining on Northwood East's graduation day—a slow, small-caliber assault throughout the morning, interrupted by periods of downpour that sent pedestrians running for cover as if the heavy drops were directed by snipers. The ceremony was moved inside to the big gym, which had neither enough seats nor enough fresh air for students, parents, and extended family. Faculty organizers said they wanted to keep it short this year, but they had no plan for doing so. The principal, the valedictorian, and the commencement speaker, a Northwood East grad who had been an actor on Broadway and a late cast addition to a handful of dying sitcoms, each privately decided the time wouldn't be excised from their own speech.

Six months ago Justin's teachers thought he had a chance to be valedictorian. Not a *good* chance—Mary Seebohm was a dedicated student who'd already been accepted to Harvard, and Justin's dedication, even when he was interested in a subject, was sporadic. Still, he was the wonder kid—clearly the smartest in the school—and when the final semester began, faculty lounge speculation noted that Justin might have a shot if he managed straight A's across his AP schedule and if Mary Seebohm slipped in advanced calculus, a worry she confided to her gossipy guidance counselor, Mrs. Sykes.

Neither of those things happened. Mary Seebohm coasted through calc as easily as her other classes, and Justin's grades, a direct result of his sudden and jarring indifference to schoolwork, devolved into C's and B-minuses. Drugs, they guessed in the teacher's lounge. They'd all seen it a million times before.

Justin finished fifteenth in his class, which would have been good enough for an excellent private school if he'd applied to one. He didn't apply to any schools at all. "I'm taking a year off," he told his guidance counselor. This will end badly, his teachers agreed.

The morning of graduation, Davis told Joan he wanted to go to the ceremony.

"What good could possibly come of that?" Joan asked him.

"None," Davis said.

"Then I'm going, too," she said.

Joan and Davis watched from the open swinging doors of the gym foyer with the bored stepfathers and the chain smokers. Few people recognized him, and strangers who did could no longer make a connection between him and the long-forgotten nastiness with Martha Finn and her son. "We're just here to congratulate Ned and Ella's boy," Davis said to the one couple—former patients—who asked. He was glad they didn't ask who Ned and Ella were.

The students, in blue robes and mortarboards, sat alphabetically in long rows of folding chairs. Their parents pressed against one another in the bleachers like tennis balls in vacuum canisters. Championship sports banners from years past stood rigid above their heads, only occasionally turning a corner like a dolphin's flipper to let past a breath from an exhaling air vent. Clothes dampened by the rain outside stayed damp. Coughs and sneezes echoed skyward. Between the south exit and the auxiliary gym—the wrestling room, as it was called—lines formed outside bathrooms while savvier parents ducked into the locker rooms.

"Today is a very special day for all of us," Mary Seebohm began unpromisingly. "It marks the end of our high school careers. For some, it marks the end of our academic careers. For many, it marks the end of our athletic careers. For each one of us, it also marks the beginning of our freedom.

"For eighteen years, give or take, we have been human beings without choices. Sure, we made little decisions—what color to paint our room, what instrument to pursue in band, whether to try out for cheerleader or pom-pom squad, quiz bowl or debate, whether to run for student council, or to take metal shop instead of wood shop. But when it came to the most important aspects of our lives, we had no choices. Today that changes.

"Seated in this footba—I mean basketball gym are one thousand one hundred and twelve individual destinies. Each of us has the potential to make a difference. To be heard. To help our fellow man, or to hurt him. To achieve great things, or to vanish into obscurity. To be graceful, courageous, uninhibited, powerful, merciful, caring, cruel, callous, artistic, creative, productive, promiscuous"—cheers—"mischievous, inspiring, beneficent, intimidating, loving, cautious, fearful, dominant, truthful, fair, generous, law-abiding, kind. We will never have more choices, and thus more freedom, than we do right now. Every day between now and the day we die is a day with fewer choices than the one before it. And so I implore you, my fellow graduates of Northwood East, my friends, my classmates: choose wisely."

Mary continued. Davis checked his watch. Seven minutes. Ten minutes. His clothes stuck to him in uncomfortable places. The man just behind him and to his right exhaled through his nose in quick whistles. Davis took a step forward. The line to the men's bathroom had grown by a dozen in just the last few minutes as parents heard nothing from Mary that sounded like a summation. Davis thought about a visit to the urinal himself. He even thought about taking Joan's hand and suggesting they leave. She didn't want to be here, anyway.

Martha Finn appeared in the foyer through a parting curtain of bodies, her eyes at maximum aperture, her skin tight and angry over her skinny jaw. She looked old, and Davis wondered how many years it had been since he'd last seen her. Not that many. She should see a doctor. Even her intense rage couldn't account for the unhealthy pallor on her face.

"Dr. Moore," she whispered tersely. Her eyes directed him to the glass-and-metal doors leading outside. He nodded and followed her, putting a hand on Joan's arm, telling her to stay put. He'd be back. It will be all right.

Outside, under a narrow asphalt roof over the entrance, rain pelting the concrete just a few yards away, Martha hugged her own arms and said, "I know you've been seeing my son." She was trembling as if a combustion engine inside her were both powering her speech and keeping her anger in check.

"He came to see me," Davis admitted. "After you told him he was a clone. We've done nothing but talk."

"Since you've been meeting him, he's changed. Did you know he's been doing drugs?"

Davis started. "Drugs? That's crazy," he said. "There's no way."

Unconvinced, Martha said, "Have you been giving him drugs?"

"Of course not."

"Have you tried to make him stop?"

"Mrs. Finn, I assure you, I have no idea what you're talking about. Justin isn't doing drugs." As he said it, however, he wondered. She seemed so certain. Had she caught him? As close as he felt to Justin, how well did he actually know him? How much time had they really spent together? *Would I know if Justin were on drugs?* He answered himself. *Yes. Yes, I would.*

"I don't know what to do," she said. "I'm so scared. Scared of him. Scared of what he might do. To himself. To me. To somebody else." She looked Davis in the eyes. "And there's nothing I can do or say. How can he be so sure of himself when I'm so insecure?"

Davis said he was sorry. It was wrong to have met with Justin behind her back. He didn't make excuses. He didn't try to explain why he and Justin had been meeting. Why they had been sneaking around. To his surprise, she accepted that small concession with a nod and then opened the door and disappeared into the foyer, making her way back to the gym.

"That was weird," Joan said when he returned. "What did she want?"

"An apology," Davis said. "Let's get out of here."

"Are you okay?" she asked. Davis dipped his head in a way that resembled a nod.

They stepped out to an open area of the foyer to put on their jackets. A girl, perhaps five years old, in a pink dress, with sun-blond hair, approached them from the direction of the gym. "Excuse me," she said.

"Yes?"

"That boy asked me to give this to you." She handed Davis a program from the commencement.

"What boy?" Joan asked. The girl shrugged.

Davis opened the folded booklet. Scribbled in black pen: *415 Saint Paul Rd. 11:00. Tonight.*

— 91 —

"Thanks for coming," Justin said. "This might be the closest we get to a celebration." He threw his arms in the air. "Congratulations! We got the bastard."

The spring surf licked the beach on the other side of the dunes. Across a hundred yards on either side of them, couples made out on blankets thrown over the wet sand at irregular intervals. Muffled shouting over a muffled stereo marked the epicenter of the graduation party at 415 Saint Paul Road, just steps from the water. It was unclear to Davis if it was being supervised by freethinking adults or if there were still parents so apathetic and stupid they would leave town the weekend of their kid's graduation and expect him not to turn their home into a three-million-dollar frat house.

Davis said, "Should I be celebrating, Justin? Tell me."

"Of course you should. Coyne's been arrested and, according to the papers, already convicted. Quote: *The trial, it seems, is almost a formality.*"

"What happened to your theory?"

"What do you mean?" Justin smiled in the manner of a comedian waiting for his audience to get his last joke.

"You said that when Coyne kills in Shadow World, he doesn't feel the urge to kill as the Wicker Man. Didn't Coyne just murder someone in the game a few weeks ago? The night he attacked Sally?"

"It's an inexact science." Justin smirked.

"It's bullshit," Davis said. "Your whole Wicker Man/Shadow World theory is bullshit." He turned and pressed his shoe into the damp spring sand. His footprint made a detailed impression, outlining every tread and recess in his sole.

"I know what you did," Davis said, and as he said it he knew the accusation could not be undone. That it would change things between them. The significance was not in the truth of the statement, and Davis would admit he had no evidence to support it. Indeed, before the idea occurred to him he never would have thought Justin capable of such a thing. Sure, he had read Justin's psych reports, and once worried over missing dogs in the Finns' neighborhood, and he and Joan had held endless discussions about what Justin might one day become (in her office and, more recently, across the low valley where their pillows met). Even so, they had never considered it anything but a remote possibility. Davis had never entertained the notion, not for a moment, that their darkest fears had become real.

But now he knew it to be true. The moment Martha Finn told Davis she suspected Justin was taking drugs, he began to accept it. Mothers know things about their sons. Justin wasn't taking drugs, but there was something else profoundly wrong with him.

From the day Justin knocked on his door, he and the boy had been connected by a priori truths, not facts in evidence. It was true that Sam Coyne had killed Davis's daughter. It also must be true that Coyne had killed others, in numbers impossible to figure. For the past year he and Justin had kept these awful truths between them, and their inability to share them with the world had felt like a penance to Davis. For being a selfish person. A bad husband and a mediocre father. Unmasking AK's killer had once been something like his religion, but he became resigned to life as a monk, with silence in service of the truth being its own reward. The final secret he shared with Anna Kat would be the face and the name of her killer.

He hadn't counted on Justin, however. The evangelist, determined to bring the word to the people at any cost.

"I was going to tell you," Justin said.

"Bullshit," Davis said again.

"Seriously. I considered that you might be happier if I didn't. But I was going to tell you. Because we're not done."

"No, no, Justin," Davis said. "We're done. The only question is, how are we going to make things right?"

Justin laughed and shook his head. "You don't think things are right? The man who killed your daughter is going to prison, probably for the rest of his life. Not for Anna Kat's murder but—"

"Not even for a murder he committed."

Justin climbed halfway up the dune and looked toward the lake, which he could make out in the darkness only by the tiny white foam of the soft breaks. "You know how we talked once that it might be possible for one self to exist simultaneously in two bodies? I felt him. When I was killing that girl, I felt Coyne. I understood him. I knew why he had to do it. Why the Wicker Man comes out. I understood what it means to have an urge beyond your control. To be a puppet in the hands of compulsion. I felt bad for her. I did. But once I started—I mean, there was this rush. Stopping it would have been like—like stopping an orgasm."

Davis felt sick. He crouched in some tall grass.

"I'm sorry," Justin said. "I know that's hard for you to hear in those terms. But don't you want to know everything? I don't know why Coyne picked Anna Kat, but once he did, she had to die. It was inevitable, like an accident. Like a bolt of lightning. There was nothing either of them could have done to stop it. I thought you'd find that comforting."

Davis couldn't even conceive of the concept. "We have to—we have to go to the police."

Justin slid back down the dune. "Now? What will that do? Set Coyne free? Put him back on the street? Put *you* in prison, probably for the rest of your life? Where's the justice in that? For you? For AK? For your wife? For the parents of the dozens of people Sam Coyne has killed and will kill in the future if we set him free? Because I'm telling you. I felt it. He won't stop."

"Where's the justice for Deirdre Thorson? What about her? What about her parents?"

Justin sniffed. "That's why I said we aren't done." He had a glaze on his eyes, like Vaseline. "Dr. Moore, the reason I know Sam Coyne won't stop killing is because now that I've killed, neither will I." Justin picked up a handful of packed sand and crumbled through his fingers as he explained. And when he was done, Davis knew it would happen just as the boy said.

Justin at Seventeen

— 92 —

Writing is the pursuit of truth, Barwick supposed, but the whole truth was outside her purview. Big Rob had preached that, and it applied to journalism as well as investigation. Both disciplines were about identifying facts that will lead to understanding, and withholding facts that will lead to confusion. She remembered a conversation she once had with a war correspondent just returned from front lines two continents away. "I could have filed a story every day about the good things that were happening there," he said. "About the schools that were opening and the hospitals being rebuilt and the valleys being repopulated. About women in Parliament and the growing economy and the long-term hope of a new nation. I could have filed a story every day that would have painted a real rosy picture, and it all would have been one hundred percent true. But to my eyes, things *weren't* going well, so I served the truth by focusing on the car bombings and the assassinations and the political corruption and the religious feuds. *That* was the real story, and it was my obligation to tell it even at the expense of lesser truths. Hell, in fifteen column inches you couldn't tell the *whole* truth about a lost kitten."

Over afternoon sandwiches and white wine, on a broad mahogany deck alongside the Ohio River, Sally answered questions from a mousy young reporter from the *Cincinnati Inquirer*. Sally's just-published book, *In the Sights of the Wicker Man: The Unmasking of America's Most Feared Serial Killer*, sat on the table between their dishes.

"Why do you think he did it?" asked the reporter, whose name was Alice. "Why do you think Sam Coyne killed?"

"I don't know," Barwick said. "Compulsion, I guess. But he was rational, too. He took the time both to pose the bodies and to cover up his crimes, and when he came after me it was only because I threatened to expose him.

296

He didn't become a killer because he was desperate. He became desperate because he had so much to lose by getting caught."

"That's one of the most compelling things about your book," Alice said. "Coyne led so many different lives—respectable lawyer, loyal son, sex addict—and those were just the ones he lived *publicly*..."

"Right."

"...and then he was a sexual predator, a murderer, and most of these lives he replicated one way or another inside Shadow World."

Sally said, "That was the fascinating thing for me in writing this story. As a Shadow World True-to-Lifer, I was very aware of the ways in which we all lead multiple lives. I think for Sam Coyne this became a pathology."

Alice smiled. "And what are *your* other lives like?"

"Well, in at least one of them, I have a boyfriend," joked Sally, thinking of both dreamy Eric Lundquist and precocious Shadow Justin. "No, seriously, one goal of a True-to-Lifer is to have no secrets. Or no secrets from yourself, anyway."

Eyebrow raised, Alice said, "So on this book tour, will you be revealing the identity of the Conductor? Maybe here in this interview?" She chuckled hopefully.

"The Conductor" was Sally's name in the book for her mysterious police informant, called that because of his insistence on meeting her aboard a tourist trolley that circulated through downtown.

"No, no," Sally said, reaching for her wine. "I promised I'd never do that."

Barwick suspected there were many cops who knew the Conductor was a fiction. They would never say so, however, as they would also have to admit that Sam Coyne had never been one of their suspects. It was better for Ambrose and the superintendent and the mayor to say nothing and have the public assume they had been hot on Coyne's trail when the story broke. If Barwick didn't want to reveal her nonexistent source, that was just fine with City Hall.

Nowhere in the book was the name Justin Finn.

Before Justin had moved out west to spend time with his father, he and Sally met in Shadow World one last time to make certain they could keep each other's secrets.

"You're going to be okay, living with this? The way it played out?" Shadow Justin asked. They were sitting on a short wall along North Avenue Beach, watching fit and young avatars play volleyball.

Sally said, "Sometimes you need to perpetuate a lie to preserve the truth, like burning trees to save the forest, or hunting deer to save the herd. Sam Coyne killed Dierdre Thorson. He is the Wicker Man. That's not a lie. If people knew about you, it would muddy the waters, make the truth of that statement unclear. Coyne's lawyers would say that if two people have the Wicker Man's DNA, that casts doubt on their client's guilt." She watched real-looking waves break around a handful of swimming avatars. "But you and I know only one of those two people is a killer."

Shadow Justin nodded.

They stood up to leave but lingered on the sand for a moment. Sally pulled him to her, the face of Justin's avatar so close it filled her screen. They kissed clumsily—she doubted he had ever kissed a Shadow World girl—and they walked away, Justin to the north, to the suburbs, and Sally back into the city.

The Cincinnati sun ducked from behind a white cloud and quickly warmed Sally's dark cheeks. The after-work crowd was arriving, and as the volume of background noise increased, drinks and appetizers appeared by the trayful from behind the bar.

Alice said, "Forgive this question, I'm not a gamer. What is Shadow Sally Barwick doing just this moment? Is she sitting here with some version of me? In some version of this restaurant?"

"She really is in Shadow Cincinnati," Sally said. "She's also promoting a book about Sam Coyne: *The Shadow Chicago Thrill Killer.*"

Shielding her eyes from the sun's glare, Barwick was momentarily envious of her on-screen alter ego, who had undoubtedly written a book with fewer fictions than Sally was capable of writing in real life.

— 93 —

Decades of irregular stains had turned the thin gold carpet six different shades of pistachio. The place smelled something horrible, too. Given the nature of what must have taken place between mostly illicit lovers in this room (and other rooms like it at the Lawrence & Lake Shore Mayflower Motel), Davis would have been surprised to hear the windows had ever been cracked open or the thick gold curtains ever drawn. Who knows why Justin chose this neighborhood? It was one of hundreds in the city where they could walk anonymously in the street, and one of dozens where the neighbors wouldn't raise an eyebrow or a ruckus if they noticed a teenaged boy and a middle-aged man entering the same motel room an hour apart.

An opened pack of cigarettes and a lighter and a leather belt and an emptied syringe were arranged carefully around a Coke can (cut in two, with the bottom of it blackened and turned upside down) on a small, round table. Justin was flat in bed, covered with a sheet, watching an old sitcom on television. One of the characters had a catchphrase—*"That's my Jimmy!"*—which he blurted out in a shrill Southern frequency that tickled Davis's brain as it decayed against his eardrums.

"One last party?" Davis said, pointing to the syringe. He was careful not to touch it, conscious of everything in the room he laid hands on. He would wipe it all down when it was over, but that wasn't a license to be careless.

Justin rolled onto his left side and pulled the sheet up to his neck. He looked like he'd either been jarred awake or hadn't been sleeping at all. "The cops will tell my mom it was an overdose. I left my room at my dad's place looking like a crack house. She'll think I ran away because of drugs. That will be better for her. Better for you."

Davis sighed. "So, last year. Your mother told me you were doing drugs. She thought I was giving them to you. But you weren't really buying drugs at all, were you?"

"Oh, I was buying them," Justin said. "I put them all over my room. Everywhere but in my arm. I mean, I tried it once, but I didn't have time for that crap. Too much to do." He added, "Too little time."

Davis set a blue duffel down on the corner of the bed and began emptying its contents—thick plastic bags the size of large burritos and filled with clear liquid; more rubber tubes; a rectangular metal contraption, shaped like a small coatrack, with a heavy base, hooks along the top, and three crude levers at the bottom that looked like little teeter-totters.

"Is that it?" Justin said, leaning forward, asking a dumb question because he knew Davis would be glad for it, glad for the attempt at conversation, which had been so hard over the last few days and was especially hard now.

Welded together by Davis himself, the machine was unsophisticated. The bags hung from the hooks and were attached to the rubber tubes with valves, which were attached to the levers. The tubes converged at another valve and ended with an intravenous needle, which would be inserted into a vein in Justin's right forearm. Around Justin's left wrist, Davis would affix a plastic strap attached to a wire. With his left hand, Justin would start the process by pressing the yellow lever, beginning an IV saline drip. When he was ready, he'd press the green lever for thiopental. Within a few minutes, he would be lost in a deep coma. When he fell asleep, his arm would drop below the side of the bed and the weight of it would activate the third, red lever, sending him a lethal dose of potassium chloride, the same chemical the state of Illinois, after his appeals had expired, would order into the veins of Sam Coyne.

The trial had been long but unsuspenseful. The case against Coyne had been solid, especially with regard to Deirdre Thorson's murder. The prosecution cherry-picked four of the Wicker Man murders and convicted him on those, as well, based on the similarities in the crime scenes and Coyne's inability to provide alibis years after the fact. Dozens of women testified to the ways Coyne associated violence and sex. Several came forward after his arrest to say Coyne had attempted to assault them. One of those women had been Martha Finn.

The defense tried to cast doubt on the DNA evidence, insisting their client hadn't been anywhere near North and the Kennedy that night. He'd been playing a video game, alone in his apartment, and Shadow World records showed, in fact, that he had been logged on at the time. To the prosecution, however, this looked like premeditation. An attempt to establish an alibi before the fact.

DNA, they said, didn't lie.

When Lieutenant Ambrose took the stand he was grilled by the defense about Armand Gutierrez, the original suspect in the Wicker Man case. He was also asked about Suspect M, the Candlestick Maker: a wealthy commodities broker named Francis Caleb Stasio. *Isn't it true, Lieutenant, that right up until the very hour your men burst into Sam Coyne's apartment and brought him in shackles to Area Five headquarters for questioning, you believed with all your heart Francis Stasio was the Wicker Man?*

Ambrose had to admit that Stasio had been his best suspect before the murder of Deirdre Thorson. He wasn't asked what changed his mind.

And didn't Mr. Stasio leave the country shortly after the arrest of Mr. Coyne? Ambrose said Mr. Stasio was free to travel wherever he wanted.

Sally Barwick took the stand as well. *Isn't it true, Ms. Barwick, that you had a personal dispute with the defendant? That you have not named your alleged "source" within the police department? That you have received an advance worth several hundred thousand dollars for a book about the Wicker Man case?*

Sally admitted it all, but the judge refused to compel her to give up her sources. As the prosecution pointed out in chambers, the DNA proved Ms. Barwick's allegations. The identity of the person who initially provided her with the tip was irrelevant.

Coyne's attorneys (there were five of them) brought out the details of almost a dozen murders in Chicago, Aurora, Milwaukee, and Madison, each having been committed since Coyne had been arrested and denied bail. The judge also permitted expert witnesses to testify to the facts of six killings that had taken place in Seattle while Coyne was in custody. "Maybe the Wicker Man has moved on to Seattle," one of Coyne's attorneys said in his closing argument. "Maybe he has taken the opportunity provided by my client's arrest to flee the country. Maybe he's still here in Chicago. I don't know for certain. What I do know for certain is that it is reasonable for you to doubt that Sam Coyne is the Wicker Man." Prosecutors dismissed the more recent murders as copycats. Once all the details of the Wicker Man case had become public, Ted Ambrose explained, specifically the way the bodies had been arranged by the killer postmortem, similarities between the crime scenes became irrelevant.

As the jury deliberated, prosecutors offered a surprise deal. If Coyne would plead guilty to the murder of Deirdre Thorson—the one count where the evidence was rock-solid—they'd drop the other charges, and the death penalty with them. Sam's lawyers begged him to take it. They had danced around the DNA evidence, tried to confuse the jury with probabilities and statistics, but no one on the defense team believed they'd been convincing. Every year it became harder to fool a jury about DNA. With genetic therapy leading to miracle cures, and cloned children filling out youth soccer rosters, people understood the concept now. DNA didn't lie.

"But it *is* lying," Sam insisted during courthouse press conferences. "I wasn't there. I didn't kill Deirdre Thorson, or any of those girls." Observers and television pundits agreed that Coyne sounded sincere.

Nevertheless, after six days, the jury found Coyne guilty of four counts of first-degree murder and sentenced him to die by lethal injection.

In the motel room, Justin kicked the sheet away and sat cross-legged on the bed. His chest and his feet were bare. His jeans were unbuttoned, revealing just the thin, logoed waistband of his white briefs. He examined the machine as Davis assembled it.

"Yellow, green, then red," he said. "Hello, old bean, you're dead."

Davis removed the phone and the digital alarm clock and the heavy lamp from the nightstand. Watching Justin on the sidelines of his field of vision, Davis tried to reconcile Justin's relaxed and indifferent pose with what the boy was about to do. Last night, awake in bed next to slumbering Joan, and again in the car on the way here, he had rehearsed a speech designed to talk Justin out of this. This isn't necessary, he would tell him. Of course, he knew Justin would say the fact that it's unnecessary is also what makes it right. And Davis recognized that although he could not want this for Justin, he selfishly wanted Justin to want it for himself.

Davis sat on the hard mattress with his back to Justin. "If you want to make it look like an overdose, then why don't you just overdose?"

"Overdosing is hard. It's like killing yourself with a hammer." The boy laughed into Davis's back and his mildewed breath stung through Davis's cotton shirt. "You still haven't figured it out. You still don't know why I need to do this, and yet you're still here. That's you. Loyal. Reliable. Just like a real dad. Just the way I want it."

"It's *not* the way I want it," Davis said. "Explain it to me. Convince me this is what you want."

Justin put his hand on Davis's shoulder and spun him gently onto the mattress so his polished black wing tips rested on the starchy pillowcases and he propped his weight awkwardly on his arms at the foot of the bed. They were facing each other now in a way that, to Davis, felt inappropriately casual. Executions should have a formality to them, he thought. A formality befitting their finality.

"I don't want to commit suicide," Justin said. "There's no justice when a bad man goes out on his own terms. Deirdre Thorson needs someone to avenge her. Just as AK did."

"But Justin, these *are* your terms," Davis said, dodging the opportunity to tell Justin he wasn't a bad man. "I'm here because you asked me to be. As much as I hate what you've become, if you changed your mind right now, I'd pack all this up and leave." That was true. What he'd do next, he had no idea.

Justin said, "I have to do this. And I need *you* to do it because *you* want me dead."

"It's not true."

"Yeah, it is." Justin picked up the IV attached to Davis's death machine and pressed the capped point of it into his palm, stopping himself before he broke the skin. "We caught Coyne. He'll get a needle in his arm, even if it's not anytime soon. But you're angry and you're sad at the lengths I had to go to, to get him. Measures you were unwilling to take. And now I'm a liability to you. I am evidence of your crime, your seventeen-year-old crime, in the same way that I was evidence of Coyne's. The only way you can put all this behind you, all the pain from the last twenty years, is if I'm dead. And the only way Deirdre Thorson can have justice is if somebody kills me. Somebody who wants me dead."

"You don't have to die. You could go to prison."

"Would it have been good enough for Anna Kat if Coyne got thirty-five to life?" Davis didn't answer. "Ten years from now the state'd just put a needle in my arm, anyway, with a lot less dignity and a lot more agony and a lot more shame for my mom. Not to mention that they'd put you in prison with me. That ain't right." With a finger he touched the metal skeleton and its poisonous plastic organs. "Set up this scary death thingy and everyone gets what they want. Everyone gets what they deserve."

"Not me," Davis said softly, putting his feet on the floor again.

"But you don't have to be in a hurry," Justin said. Davis expelled a quiet laugh.

They talked for another hour. About books. About philosophy. About the chemicals in the plastic bags and what they did. How long it would be between the time he fell asleep and the time his heart stopped, and how long after his heart stopped before he was dead.

"If they do an autopsy they'll catch this," Davis warned, his conscience still pushing him halfheartedly to act as if he cared. "They'll know it wasn't heroin."

"Doubtful," Justin said. "Cook County Coroner is way understaffed. They hardly do autopsies anymore—like maybe one in ten corpses that come through. Cause of death is almost always declared on the scene. I read it in *Time* magazine. If it looks like an overdose, if it smells like an overdose—" He reached into a backpack on the other side of the bed and pulled out a small bag of white powder and a pocketknife. He opened the knife and sliced the bag open, spilling it onto the polyester flowered-print bedspread.

"I guess I've never seen heroin before," Davis said. It sounded almost like a confession. "I thought I had but I hadn't. Not like that, anyway. They showed it to us in med school but it wasn't so, so *white*."

Running his fingers in a tight pattern through it, Justin said, "Ninety-eight percent pure. This shit'll kill ya."

"Where'd you get it?"

"Around. Another of those things you shouldn't know," Justin said. "Hand me all that stuff over there."

Davis dug into his own bag and pulled on a pair of rubber gloves. Then he grabbed the spoon and the lighter and the leather strap and the can bottom and the syringe and a distended cigarette filter, and he took them to Justin. Justin tossed them on top of the spilled heroin and bounced gently on the mattress a few times so the tableau would appear less arranged. He took a sip of water from the nightstand and spilled the rest on the sheet and on the floor next to the bed, tossing the plastic cup after it. There wasn't enough of the powder to cause a cloud, but Davis waved his arm around in front of his face and wished he'd brought a surgical mask.

"Let's do this now," Justin said. He put his head back on the pillow and dropped his arms to his sides.

The tubes and the valves and the salt water and the poison, all connected to Justin's heart through a narrow needle in a blue vein. Davis tightened Justin's belt around his forearm to help him find a way in, and he swabbed the area with a cotton ball soaked in alcohol. Looking at his young, pale skin, Davis wondered if anyone would believe Justin was an addict. That this was an OD. Maybe they would if they tasted the white powder on the bed and realized his stuff was too strong. Stronger than he knew, they'd conclude. But who would sell a kid like him pure heroin? What would be the point? (And yet, in truth, somebody had.) Still, any cop with a second thought in his head would see right through this, he was certain. There was no stopping it, though. Nothing to do but finish it. He thought about something Justin had once told him about the illusion of free will and realized that he, Davis, made the choice to be here twenty years ago, when he first held Sam Coyne's DNA in his hands. When he didn't destroy it along with that first evil notion.

"All right, then," Davis said.

"It's the right thing," Justin said again, and Davis was embarrassed that the boy should be comforting him.

There was no eulogy. No good-bye. No sentimental exchange. No meaningful looks. No expressions of gratitude or understanding or love. No paternal speech. No acknowledgment of debt. No outward acceptance of their roles. Davis inserted the IV into Justin's right arm and attached the plastic strap to his left wrist, and Justin reached underneath the tube running across his body and pressed the yellow lever. The saline drip began.

"Now what?"

"When you're ready, push the green one. Just keep your left arm out over the side of the bed, next to the machine. When you fall asleep, your arm will drop and the red lever will flip, and that will be it. Just don't drop your arm before then."

"What happens if I drop my arm early?"

"It will be a lot more painful," Davis said in his even, practiced bedside tone. "But don't worry about that. I'm watching you. You can start the thiopental whenever you're ready."

"Nuh-uh," Justin said. "You have to do it."

"Justin . . ."

"You have to. Push the green one."

"I don't want to kill you."

"You have to do it."

"No, I don't."

"If you don't, I'm going to stop it." Justin lifted up his right arm and tensed it, like he was about to yank it free from the IV.

Davis said, "Then go ahead. Stop it. You've read a lot of books, Justin, absorbed a lot of abstract knowledge, but this doesn't balance any cosmic scales, no matter what you think. The woman you killed has a family—a mother and father and brothers and sisters—and they'll never know how their little girl died. They'll never be able to look into the eyes of the person who killed her and try to understand why it happened. If you want to give them justice, then you should come clean with what you did—with what *we* did. Throw the whole sick story out there in the open and let people gape at the perversity of it. When they lock the two of us up, *that* will be something like a comeuppance."

Davis stood, a pain like heartburn in his chest. Justin stared up at him, nothing in his expression hinting at a reply. Davis rushed into the bathroom and knelt before the toilet. If he wasn't for certain going to throw up before, the feel of the slick, unclean linoleum triggered a gag reflex inside him and he hacked a tablespoon of stomach acid into the bowl. He sat there a moment, delaying his return by wiping down the floor and the outside of the bowl with a wet towel, wondering if the effort to remove any traces of his presence might cause suspicious zones of cleanliness in a room as dirty as this one. He flushed and wondered if Justin might have pushed the green lever in his absence and asked himself if he wished that were true, then walked back into the motel room before admitting to the answer.

Justin was still awake, staring at the ceiling.

"They can't, but you can," Justin said.

"What?" Davis returned to his seat at the side of Justin's bed.

"Look into the eyes of the man who killed your daughter and try to understand why it happened."

"That's bullshit."

"No, it's not." Justin picked up his head and turned it awkwardly in Davis's direction. "Dr. Moore, when I killed that woman, *I was him.* I felt what Coyne felt when he put his hands around Anna Kat's neck and squeezed the breath out of her. I felt powerful. Like nothing I imagined. I can't get that from any drug. From any book. There was nothing abstract about it. I felt *good.* I felt *invincible.* And I didn't feel any remorse. No sadness for her. No empathy. Nothing for the people she loved and left behind. The only difference between Coyne and me is I know it's wrong to feel nothing for other people, and that's barely a difference at all. Deirdre Thorson's parents *won't* be able to look into the eyes of the man who killed their daughter, but you can look into the eyes of the man who killed yours. These are his eyes. Exactly his eyes, and now they've seen what he saw. And how many times over the last twenty years did you think about looking into these eyes, about being this close, not in a courtroom, or through jailhouse glass, but alone with these eyes in a room like this one so you could make them see just for once that they aren't always in control?" Justin waited a moment for Davis to respond, but he didn't. Davis stared. His expression was inscrutable beyond sadness. They looked at each other, neither one moving or talking or even breathing, it seemed.

Then Justin's right arm began to feel warm.

The heat radiated out from the needle under his skin and burned beneath his flesh, up toward his shoulder and down toward his fingertips. Justin turned slowly to look at his arm, certain it would be aflame. He couldn't move it. It was like a heavy, fiery log attached to his body. The top of his head was numb. It felt as if all his blond hairs were standing on the ends of their itchy follicles. He drew a labored breath, but his lungs were rewarded little for it. He turned again, not to look at Davis, but to look at the machine.

The green lever had been flipped. Davis had pressed it while Justin was talking.

Justin's face puckered. There was nothing for him to do. His left arm was suspended over the edge of the bed and if he could keep it elevated, keep it from falling, keep it from releasing the red lever and the gusher of potassium chloride it held back, he could survive.

But he knew that he couldn't.

Davis saw shock in Justin's face, the recognition that the undoable had been done to him. Even as the thiopental relaxed the muscles in his cheeks and around his eyes, there was still enough involuntary response to react to the horror of what was happening. Justin struggled to turn his head again, and when he met Davis's gaze he forced a crazy, euphoric smile, as if helplessness were a drug to him—like killing, a nonreplicable high.

When it was done, Davis returned every item he came with to the blue duffel bag, crossed each one off a list he had written on a piece of paper folded down to about three inches square, and stuffed the list in his shirt pocket so he'd remember to destroy it later. He wiped down the chairs and the tables and the doorknobs and even Justin's wrist, which he had held momentarily when looking at the veins in the boy's arms, before he had snapped on his gloves.

He put on a baseball cap and sunglasses, not much of a disguise but, like the SPF 15 he rubbed on in the sun, it was *something*. When he was home he would destroy everything he wore today—his clothes, his hat, even his boots—in case someone tried to match fiber evidence he'd left behind. He had shed parts of him here, certainly, hairs and skin and traces of vomit in the bathroom, but he hoped they would be lost among the detritus of previous occupants, poor housekeeping being as effective a cover as antiseptic. And who knows, maybe Justin was right. Maybe the cops didn't look too hard when the answer seemed so obvious at the scene. He hoped so. They hadn't looked too hard in Northwood twenty years ago when faced with the death of a girl the same age.

No one below seemed to notice as he traversed the second-story concrete walkway, and no one peeked from behind the thick gold curtains or the identical aqua doors as he peeled the surgical gloves away from his hands and stuffed them into his bag. His car was in a self-park garage a few blocks away.

Going back to the hours he'd spent with cadavers in medical school, Davis had always felt a kind of comfort in corpses, their lifelessness a sign that we are more than a sum of our organs and tissue and blood. More than cells in some magical combination. It seemed apparent to him that whatever it is that makes us human individuals is absent in a corpse, and according to the laws of conservation must still be present somewhere else. That was the closest thing he still had to metaphysical religion, but he believed it sincerely.

As he stared at Justin's freshly dead body, moments before he walked out the door, the old rule didn't seem to apply. Justin seemed as lifelike as ever, his left arm nearly touching the floor, his head cocked off the pillow, drool pooling in the corner of his mouth. Whether Justin was still inside or had never been there to begin with, he couldn't know. Justin promised Davis he'd feel exhilarated for taking a life, but he didn't. Even now, he felt worse for having conceived Justin than he did for killing him, and he thought that feeling curious. Not right. Unless maybe creating Justin and destroying him were the beginning and the end of the same act, and the destroying had just been easier.

He didn't feel nothing, though, and per Justin's caution he knew that was a good sign.

Instead of nothing he felt relief.

— 94 —

The white sign ran the length of Harold Devereaux's front porch, with vinyl letters pressed on in black:

Soldiers for Christ / Hands of God Picnic Social

A half dozen men and women sat in chairs or stood against the wood siding, using the sign to shield their eyes from the late-morning sun. Twenty or so children played about, some on the swing set, some out in the old barn, a few in the house, where they were stepped over and patted by elders with paper plates full of watermelon and hot dogs and cold pasta salad. A band played under a yawning oak tree—guitar, bass, keys, and drums in an incompetent punk formation both too old and too young for this crowd. Their lyrics were political and radically conservative, antigovernment, anti-immigrant, and, of course, anti-cloning. Hardly anyone was paying attention.

In the yard behind the house a man in a clerical collar sat at a bleached picnic table and gestured crazily as he spoke, his hands shooting out from his body like yo-yo tricks, always coming back to rest on the redwood tabletop before flinging themselves again to make this or that point. He was Reverend Garner McGill, the founder and "chief executive minister" of Soldiers for Christ, a nationwide organization that claimed more than 250,000 members (although to qualify for membership all one had to do was agree to receive the free Soldiers for Christ newsletter six times a year). Fifty of the more devoted members of the organization had come down for a weekend of joint meetings with the smaller and lesser-known Hands of God, a summit Harold had conceived and arranged himself. The purpose was social first and strategic second, Harold said, although privately he worried the Hands of God had lost direction since Mickey's retirement, and he thought perhaps a merger of the two groups might revitalize the HoG and radicalize the SFC, changing both for the better.

The Soldiers for Christ was the country's best-known religious anti-cloning group. Reverend McGill was known and despised in every fertility clinic in the nation. He had friends on Capitol Hill and had even spent the night in the White House during a previous administration. His sermons could fill revival tents for a month or basketball arenas for a week. More and more he chose the latter.

The Hands of God, however, remained obscure, occasionally mailing press releases about clinics and research facilities with especially heinous practices (according to them) or statements concerning the status of anti-cloning legislation in Washington. They claimed about forty members in their Ohio church, and had a mailing list of some five thousand. Because of threatening letters bearing its name, the government labeled the Hands of God a suspected terrorist organization, although the group officially denied having anything to do with terror and the feds had never pressed charges. Five of the thirteen founding members were here, the others having passed away or moved on. They didn't talk about their real work. Not in public.

Harold Devereaux's farm wasn't public.

"How many on the list are his?" Reverend McGill was saying to Harold, who sat across from him. "I mean really. I always figured Byron Bonavita was an urban myth or something. He never had any affiliation with *us*, and I never met anyone who knew him. I think the feds always knew he was dead and kept pinning the killings on Bonavita because it was less embarrassing to say they couldn't find him than admit they didn't even know the real fellow's name." Words spilled out of McGill in a high-pitched Georgia drawl, but his laugh was loud and low and rhythmic, like Santa, only *heh! heh! heh!* instead of *ho! ho! ho!*

Harold wiped his hands low on his cream-colored wide-collared silk shirt, on the hips, where the sweat and the grit wouldn't show so much. He was listening but his eyes scanned the yard behind McGill in a slow sweep. People had broken up into fours and fives on chairs or stumps or other temporary seating. He knew most of these people through the Web site and chat rooms and virtual anti-cloning meetings conducted in Shadow World. He knew only a handful of them by their faces, however.

Mickey the Gerund had his fingers two knuckles into the mulch around the tall decorative grasses at the corner of Harold's main house. He hadn't been much of a gardener when he was young, but in all those years on the road, driving past miles of wilderness and irrigated pasture and landscaped yards and potted medians, fertilizer and seedlings became part of his fantasy life. He began watching gardening shows on the motel televisions and reading up on shrubs and flowers and trees and grasses and dirt. Since retiring, he spent most of his time about the grounds of the Hands of God church, tending to the lawn and the beds of tulips and the small plot of vegetables. The other members of the church thought he deserved a quiet retirement, and they enjoyed the fresh vegetables and the respectable appearance that Mickey's labors afforded.

This afternoon at Harold's, Mickey was sifting through the gardens trying to deduce what brand of plant food Harold used to such great effect in hot weather. He knew if he asked, Harold wouldn't know. Harold had a landscaper, no doubt, and the landscaper was hired by Harold's pretty wife. Mickey was also digging with his hands in order to look occupied. He really didn't want a bunch of strangers asking him about his days on the road. Mickey may have longed for a garden in those days, but never human contact. He had been a traveling monk, a man alone with God, and he still believed that other people were only obstacles standing between him and the Lord.

"Hey, Mickey!" Harold shouted. "Come here! I want you to meet someone!"

Exhaling, Mickey stood slowly and turned to see what horror Harold had planned for him. An overweight Baptist grandma from Arkansas who'd baked him purple-frosted Jesus cookies? A teenaged HoG wannabe who would burst into tears if his mommy gave him two cross words but who was convinced that it was his destiny to execute gynecologists? Evangelical parents who wanted him to lay his hands on their colicky tot? He'd met all of those just since he'd arrived last night. If this many people knew him by sight, he considered it a miracle he wasn't sitting on death row.

As he drew closer he saw it was Garner McGill. He knew the man, though they had never met face-to-face. McGill was the anti-cloning generalissimo who cheered the Hands of God from the sidelines but who, despite calling himself a "soldier," didn't have the balls to tell his quarter million followers what was *really* required to be a member of God's army. *You'll never hear Reverend McGill say you can't fight evil with petitions and bullhorns,* Mickey often said at private meetings back in Ohio. *God's enemies will be defeated at the end of a gun and McGill knows it, but he doesn't want the rifle in his own hands.*

"Have you two met?" Harold asked. "Reverend McGill? Mickey Fanning?" They shook.

"This is a *pleasure*, a real pleasure," McGill said. "Mr. Fanning, I don't have to tell you how important your personal ministry has been to the cause of righteous men. The Lord smiles upon your work, and He celebrates your sacrifice in the service of your faith."

Mickey nodded. *What a load of crap.* "Reverend," he said. He sat down next to Harold and in his periphery he could see other Soldiers for Christ wandering over. He scooted to his right, hogging the rest of the bench so no one could claim a seat on either side of him.

Harold said, "The reverend and I were just talking about the list."

"Yuh," Mickey said, grabbing a potato chip between two fingers and plunging it deep into the dip, nearly to the tips of his soiled fingers.

"The reverend was wondering—and to tell you the truth, I started to wonder, myself—exactly how many of those red lines were yours."

Mickey shrugged. "Lots of them. Almost all of them, I suppose, one way or another."

"All of them?" Reverend McGill said. "Not really."

"You got a copy with you?" Mickey asked.

Harold did, in his pocket. He unfolded it, six pages stapled together, and he set it in the middle of the table. Eight or nine Soldiers for Christ surrounded the picnic table, none daring to squeeze in on the bench, and leaned in to get a look at the infamous list. They'd all seen it on the Internet, but here they were sharing it with three legendary figures of the anti-cloning movement: Reverend McGill, Harold Devereaux, and Mickey Fanning. They'd all heard stories about Mickey's dedication and coldness of heart, about how he'd circumcised himself with a razor blade and a bottle of aspirin, about how he'd killed dozens of doctors and scientists. They just weren't sure which or how many of these tales they should believe.

From behind his ear Mickey produced a pencil, which he had used to dig about in Harold's garden. He wiped soil from the lead in the margins of the first page and began putting marks next to the names.

Heads leaned forward all around as Mickey methodically checked off the names of dead and retired doctors. Dr. Andrea Ali, Dr. Jim Baggio, Dr. Phillip Byner, Dr. Thomas Curry . . . In places, he claimed eight or nine in a row before skipping one with the tip of his lead. On more than one of those streaks, a lanky bearded kid, no more than twenty, whispered a "Whoa. Dude."

When he turned the last page over he had marked 87 names without a word. He flipped the list right side up and pushed it to the center of the table. The gathering of Christ's soldiers burst into chatter. Mickey slapped the back of his neck and examined his palm. Three bloody mosquitoes had been flattened there with one blow.

"Let me see that," Harold said, pulling the list toward him with a skeptical chuckle. He turned the first page. "Here. What about this one? You claim Jon Kucza was one of yours. Jon Kucza died of a heart attack."

"Nicotine overdose," Mickey corrected. "I slipped it into his coffee grounds. He was already on the patch. Never tasted it."

Harold tilted his head to show he was impressed, but continued to pore over the list. "Geoffrey Gahala. He died in a hiking accident."

"He was hiking all right," Mickey said. "It was no accident, though." The soldiers whistled and clapped.

Reverend McGill held up a hand. "I can't say I know whether to believe you, Mr. Fanning. What would be the point of killing any of these doctors and making it look like an accident? What deterrence value does that action have?"

Mickey had both of his palms down on the table, and he was staring at his filthy hands. "Who said it was only about deterrence?"

"Obviously, the taking of lives such as these must be justified by the greater good," McGill said. "Don't misunderstand me, Mickey, you have performed miracles for the movement through your *public* displays of protest. But I don't understand why you would allow any doctors to die without sending a message to the general population about the evils of the cloning profession. What about the greater good?"

Mickey looked up from his hands, not at the reverend, but at Harold. "Sometimes the greater good is just a dead doctor. Those men and women offended God, and now they're dead. Perhaps that's as good as it gets."

While his followers turned to McGill for a response, Harold found another name of interest. "Lookit here. Davis Moore," he said. "Moore quit his practice but he still stumps for the pro-cloners. I saw him on the news less than a month ago."

"You're the one who drew a line through his name," Mickey said. "I just claimed his retirement as my own. Count it as half a victory."

"That's fair," Harold said. "But he hung it up years and years after you shot him. How can you look me in the eyes and take the credit for that? Seriously. There could have been any number of reasons he gave up being a doctor."

Mickey stuck his jaw out and smiled over the underbite in a manner that gave Reverend McGill a slow chill. "Some take longer than others," he admitted. "And let's just say that I did more than shoot Dr. Moore in the shoulder." No one reacted, so Mickey continued. "Some things you mean to do, some things you don't, and *everything* you do has unintended consequences."

Leaning his large frame so far back he had to hook a foot around one of the table legs to keep from falling over, Harold said, "What are you goin' on about, Mickey?"

Without looking up, Mickey said, "To be honest, I don't think the reverend wants to hear it."

The soldiers grumbled. McGill's presence was forcing a premature end to a good story, and they planned on walking away from the famous Mickey Fanning with a good story at the very least. The reverend was losing a popularity contest among his own flock. He started face-saving measures. "Mickey, you're among friends here. I assure you that nothing you can say will shock me. There has been no greater supporter of your work than the Soldiers for Christ. Of course we maintain a certain—veneer—to remain palatable to the suits in Washington as well as plain folks in Peoria. But we understand this is a war. Whatever tactics you have used in pursuit of your many accomplishments are no doubt justified. You have earned that much respect and more, in my opinion." The soldiers muttered their agreement. The bearded kid patted Mickey on the back, to Mickey's irritation. Harold was gratified to hear the reverend coming around to more radical, forward thinking.

"I shot Davis Moore about twenty years ago, from sixty-five yards," Mickey said. "I missed by two inches and he survived. A year or so later I was driving back through Chicago and decided to have another go at him. It was a cold, cold winter and I didn't have time to set up all the necessary precautions for a proper—uh, *elimination*—so I decided to try something a little different. A tactic that didn't work that night, but which has served me well in the years since.

"Moore's daughter was working in a clothing store. Two hours before closing, I walked in and hid in one of the dressing rooms. While I was in there, I took out a piece of paper and I wrote her a note." Mickey removed from his pocket a worn and smudged piece of paper, creased into quarters. He unfolded it carefully, as if it were a fragile page from an ancient manuscript. "This very one, in fact." The reverend adjusted his glasses to examine it closely. In black and red inks Mickey had drawn a crude but anatomically accurate heart, a coiled snake, a pair of hands (one pointing to the heavens), and the initials HoG. The names of six doctors were written in black and crossed out with a red pen. Last on the list, but not crossed out, was the name "Dr. Davis Moore." Finally, in block letters, was a Bible verse everyone at the table recognized:

SEE! THE MAN HAS BECOME LIKE ONE OF US, KNOWING WHAT IS GOOD AND WHAT IS BAD! THEREFORE, HE MUST NOT BE ALLOWED TO PUT OUT HIS HAND TO TAKE FRUIT FROM THE TREE OF LIFE, AND THUS EAT OF IT AND LIVE FOREVER.

All the words were in black ink except for HE MUST NOT BE ALLOWED TO . . . LIVE, which was in red.

Mickey said, "I planned to give this to Moore's daughter, Anna, when the store thinned out toward closing—"

"Anna Kat," Harold corrected. Mickey stared at him. "Her name was Anna Katherine. They called her Anna Kat."

In the ensuing pause Reverend McGill took a loud sip of root beer while Mickey fixed a displeased stare on Harold Devereaux. Harold squinted unapologetically in reply and Mickey continued. "While I was writing this, Anna—Anna *Katherine*—snuck into the changing room next to me with a boy I guessed was about her age. Sixteen or seventeen. I never saw his face and they couldn't have known I was there. I listened as they sniggered and shushed one another, and I could see their clothes fall to the floor in the space between our stalls. I picked my legs up off the floor to be certain they wouldn't see me and I sat very still as the boy pushed himself inside the Moore girl, their bodies slapping together with great violence. Occasionally they would slam loudly into the wall and I could hear him hitting her—slapping her, pinching her—and she responded each time with a muffled but ecstatic purr. So young and so self-loathing, it was everything I could do not to retch.

"When they had finished with one another, they dressed and the boy left the changing room first. I remember her saying good-bye in a hush, and I remember he didn't reply. A minute or two later she returned to the sales floor, although I assume the boy was long gone by then. I got the impression these trysts were a naughty secret between them.

"I waited another half hour and then put on my gloves. I didn't want there to be a lot of customers in the store and the place seemed quiet. I soon found out why. A storm had passed through and Anna Katherine had closed up for the night. Sent everyone home. She and I were alone. As you can imagine, I startled her a piece when I walked out of the dressing room, and in her face I could see thoughts occurring one after another. Foremost in her mind was the worry that I had heard her fornicating. I walked very close to her and she took a step back, but was trapped against the counter in the center of the store. My mouth was inches from the top of her head. I held up the note and I said, *Your father might be innocent in the eyes of the law, but he still has to answer to the Hands of God.* I put the note on the counter and I walked quickly to the door. The whole encounter lasted seconds. She couldn't have picked me out of a two-man lineup.

"But I hadn't counted on the door being locked.

"Before I could find the dead bolt, she kicked me hard in the back of my knee. I went down to the floor. She screamed, 'You shot my father, didn't you, you sonofabitch!' I spun around and slapped her across the face. She fell backward and I started again for the door, but she said, 'I know what you look like, asshole,' and she reached for the phone. Before she could dial three numbers I smacked it out of her hand and I grabbed her arm and put my fingers around her neck, forcing her to the ground in the middle of the island where they keep the registers. As she went down, I felt her arm snap. She was too scared to cry out, so she just cried. I knelt beside her so we couldn't be seen from the street, but the snow was coming down fast now and there weren't many people out. We crouched there for minutes probably, my grip just tight enough to keep her from fighting. She had seen me well enough by now, and if the FBI showed her a picture of Byron Bonavita, she'd be able to tell them I wasn't him. My best cover would be blown. The entire Hands of God operation would be compromised. I looked into her eyes and this time I saw more rage than fear. And here, Reverend, is where we come to both the unintended consequences, as well as the greater good. I made a choice—not a choice, really, but a necessary decision—and I squeezed her throat shut until she stopped breathing, and then I kept it shut for a few minutes more.

"Once she was unconscious, I tore open her blouse. I knew she had just been with this fellow, and I thought I could make it look like rape. Fortunately, the boy had done most of my work for me. She had marks on her breasts where his hands had squeezed her too tight. I cut open her jeans, and there were marks on her thighs and on her ass where he had slapped and punched and pinched her. I checked to make sure she was dead, retrieved the note from the counter, and I walked out into the street, where the blizzard covered the boot tracks behind me."

Three of the children raced around the corner of the house where Mickey had been digging earlier. One trailed the other two, pumping a multicolored water pistol that wasn't shaped anything like a gun, but nevertheless boasted a range of twenty or thirty feet. In the quiet around the picnic table, you could hear the water spitting out the end of the pinhole barrel.

"A child," the reverend said finally. "My God, a child."

"Unintended consequences. The greater good," Mickey said. "By all accounts, Moore became obsessed with his daughter's murder. His wife eventually committed suicide with a handful of pills. Another man was killed in some crazy accident involving Moore in Oklahoma or Nebraska someplace. The wheels were coming off his chassis. He finally had enough. He quit.

"This is the part of your work that you have refused to see, Reverend. This is what happens on the front lines of war. That night in the store, with my hand on the Moore girl's throat, I could have backed away. If I had, my entire mission, my entire twenty-year mission, would have been compromised before it began. There would have been no pressure on the cloners and the experimenters, the Frankensteins and Mengeles of modern science. There would have been no fear. No surrender. You wouldn't be sitting here, preparing your speech, waiting for the coming day when you can claim victory on the cable news networks.

"Over the years there have been other times when so-called innocents died at my hand. These were people who got in the way. Collateral damage, the U.S. military calls it. But the Lord never again asked me to make a decision like the one I made that night in Chicago. I believe the Lord tested me that day, the way He tested Abraham. Only, the Lord never stopped my hand because the Lord knew what was to occur in the wake of that girl's death. For Him, the all-knowing, there are no unintended consequences; there is *only* the greater good.

"You looked horrified when I described to you the death of Anna Katherine Moore, and you should have. It was a horrible thing. She was a pretty girl, with much promise, no doubt. She had dreams and plans and people who loved her. I took all of that away with a squeeze of this hand. You should know, then, that it did not make me glad to do it. The boy she had sex with that night took pleasure in her pain, but I did not. Nor did I take pleasure in the deaths of any of the doctors on Harold Devereaux's list. I killed because I was called upon to kill by God, and despite that holy mission, every murder I committed under its charter was a sin. I fully expect to be sent to hell for them without the ultimate gift of God's grace. If he condemns me to hellfire, I will accept that mission without anger, because there is honor in doing as He bids, even if what He wishes for you is eternal suffering and everlasting shame.

"As for you, Reverend McGill, you have rejoiced in my acts, and yet you feel that you have not sinned because it was not you who pulled the triggers, who set the bombs, who crushed the Moore girl's larynx. But it is God who has called all of us to this task." Mickey clutched the list in his right hand and collapsed it into his fist. "I did not choose to kill Dr. Ali, or Dr. Denby, or Dr. Friedman, I was put to the task, as you were put to yours. I have given my whole life to it. I have sacrificed for the sake of mankind, so that His will may be done. I don't know why I was chosen, but I think it's entirely possible that the Lord does not send innocents to hell for the sake of the *greater good*, but rather chooses sinners, like me, and asks them to commit sins on His behalf.

"You see, the Lord expresses himself in paradoxes. Do you know what a paradox is, Reverend McGill? A paradox is both itself and its opposite at the same time. By definition it can exist only by the will of God. I believe the modern-day saints and the modern-day martyrs are examples of these paradoxes. Because in the war you and I are fighting, the war against contemporary secularism, you won't find the saints sitting at the right hand of God. You will find the true saint, the true martyr, in the depths of hell. Because he will have given not just his life for the good of his fellow man, but he will have sacrificed his eternal soul."

By the time Mickey had finished, the entire grown-up faction of the Soldiers for Christ/Hands of God picnic social had gathered around the redwood table, probably sixty people in all, and even the ones who had come late, even the ones who had heard only the end, even the ones who had arrived for the end but who couldn't make out the intent of Mickey's low, measured tones, realized something significant had happened. The worst gossips among them had their mouths stunned shut, and whispered inquiries about the event that just happened were repelled with hostile glares. Harold Devereaux stared at a black knot in the center plank of the table. Away from them, the children sat in a wide circle and played a game—*duck, duck, duck, duck, duck, duck, GOOSE!* Mickey the Gerund had said everything he was going to say for the evening, and everything he felt he might say for very long while.

Reverend McGill, unable to cry aloud, put his head in his hands and squeezed his palms against his eyelids, hoping to stop anything inside him from leaking out.

— 95 —

Cheap cardboard boxes in the old basement blue room were stacked to the ceiling along two adjacent walls. Files and papers and binders and tapes and discs. Witness statements, police reports, autopsy findings, crime scene photos. They still had more to box up, lots more, and Joan, in cuffed blue jeans and a white sleeveless shirt, surveyed the remains and had a hard time believing it had all fit in this room. Twenty years of wondering and waiting, puzzling and praying were recorded on these pages, and just like that Davis was throwing it all away.

"It's over," he told her the night Sam Coyne was delivered to death row in orange prison scrubs and chains that shackled his wrists to his waist and his ankles to each other. "I want it all out."

Joan walked over to the chair where he was sitting and creased herself into his lap. "Do you mean it? All of it?"

He wrapped his old and freckled arms around her like a safety bar on a carnival ride. "All of it," he said. "Every page, every index card, every crackpot theory I scribbled on a memo pad, every computer sketch, every staple, every paper clip, I want it out on the curb. I'll call somebody to haul it away."

"To burn it?"

"Yes!" he said. "To burn it!"

They would pack it up together and it would take an entire weekend, not that the weekends were that different from the weekdays anymore, or wouldn't be when all the bad memories were turned to char and ash and her husband was one hundred percent hers. She would retire too, in the fall, after her patients had the chance to find new doctors. And though, at forty-nine, every month seemed shorter than the last one, the autumn seemed ages away, as far away as summer seemed to a ten-year-old at Christmas. Joan passed the time by dreaming up ways they could use the room once it was emptied.

"An art studio," she said. "We could take up painting together."

"I like it," he said.

"Or an exercise room."

"We walk."

"But in the winter..."

"That's true."

"We could buy a pool table."

He laughed. "I've never seen you shoot pool."

"You could teach me."

"I used to be good..."

"That's what I've heard."

"...in med school."

"So prove it," she said.

He also ordered her to haul away his family files, the one ton or so of paper and cardboard and old photographs that connected him to Will Denny and Anna Kat and everyone else on his family tree. "Call the historical society," he said. "The Newberry Library. The Mormons. Maybe they'll want it. I don't care anymore. Don't need it anymore." Joan was delighted.

A dozen times in the last few months she had marveled out loud at the word "trial," saying how apt it was, not just for the defendant but for everyone with a relationship to the Coyne case. The detectives seemed to age on the stand. The state's attorney lost thirty pounds, and the papers speculated that the beef-eating people of the state of Illinois might balk now at electing someone so thin and sickly to be their governor. Joan was nauseated every morning, the ordeal being as close to a pregnancy as she would have, and at the end of gestation her discomfort would be over, and a life—twin lives, actually, Davis's and hers—would be born again.

She filled a box to overflowing and forced the flaps shut, knowing her work didn't have to be pretty. The boxes with handles were for the convenience of burly hired men who would come to cart it all away on Monday. What a wonder of a day that will be! How big this room will look, empty except for possibilities!

Joan assembled a new box and taped its bottom and reached for a file drawer to empty into it. These documents were old, nearly as old as Anna Kat's murder, yellowed and torn into tabs where pages had protruded at the top and their edges had been slammed and buffeted by the opening and closing of the drawer. Between them Davis had slipped data discs written in ancient formats, and she wondered if you could even find a computer to read them anymore. She tossed a half dozen into the box and they landed with a dull, plastic splat.

From the back of the drawer Joan retrieved a brown folder belted shut with a stale rubber band. The contents were pristine. Barely handled. *I wonder if Davis even looked at these,* she thought. They appeared to be witness statements from Anna Kat's friends, taken by the police in the days and weeks after her murder, and every one of a dozen was bound on the left margin with black wire, like a school report. Scanning the interviews, Joan understood why Davis might not have read them. They were emotional, devastating, punctuated with sentimental reminiscences and long tangents about trips the girls had taken with AK, or funny things she had said, or selfless acts she'd performed on their behalf. Little of it seemed pertinent to the investigation, and all of it would have been tough for him to read.

One would have been more difficult than the rest.

It stood out because of a note attached to the cover with brittle tape. It was scribbled from one detective to another:

Ken—
This kid's alibi checks out—he was with his parents at the time of the girl's death. Keep this info from the Moores for now. No reason to put them through it. If we get a suspect, I'll deal with it then.
Mike

Joan looked around the room. Davis had gone upstairs for something. She had been half listening when he told her what. "Honey, have you seen this?" she called to him.

She heard his footsteps maneuver to the top of the stairs. "Seen what?"

"This thing," she said, distracted now, turning the first page and seeing, as a tremor of horror moved through her torso, as a spasm of bad feeling shook sweat from her pores, that what she held in her hands was an interview with seventeen-year-old Sam Coyne.

"Down in a minute," she heard him say.

Joan began to read, absorbing just a few lines at a time before she was compelled to turn the page.

ML: Several people saw you at the Gap the day Anna Katherine was
    killed.

SC: Yeah, I was there.

ML: Were you having a relationship with her?

SC: What, like officially?

ML: Yeah. Officially.

SC: We were just messing around. Just sex and stuff. It was no big deal.

ML: Did you have intercourse with her that day?

SC: Yeah. In one of the dressing rooms.

ML: And then?

SC: And then I went home.

Another page:

SC: She was a freak. I guess I am too. We had fun. But we kept it a
    secret.

ML: Why?

SC: I don't know. It wasn't anything exclusive. I see other girls. She's got
    this boyfriend, Dan. He was *sort of* her boyfriend but she wasn't
    really into him. She had a dangerous side he didn't understand.
    Anyway, we didn't want people talking. I was seeing other girls and
    I think she was embarrassed.

ML: Embarrassed?

SC: I think she wished she could be the kind of person who didn't want
    to be with a guy like me. But she *did* want to be with me. We did it
    all the time: in school, at her house, at my house, at work. The more
    dangerous, the better. She just didn't want anyone else to know.

And another:

ML: Did you see anyone else in the Gap that day?

SC: There were lots of people.

ML: No one suspicious?

SC: Nah.

ML: No one who looked like they didn't belong there?

SC: I guess I'm not sure what that means, but no.

    Joan closed the report. She had a vision of Davis's eyes when he read it. Of
the tears. The blindness. The anger. The phone call to the police. *You knew all
along there hadn't been a rape! You never told me!* The original detectives all retired
now. The cheap boxes unpacked. The file cabinets filled and reorganized. A

new computer at the desk, one with more power and speed. Late nights reassessing all the evidence with fresh and wizened eyes. Wondering how he could have missed this. What else he could have missed. The guilt. The sleepless nights. The new passion. The fury. The madness. Rededicating his life to the capture of a new nameless, faceless killer. A killer still out there. A killer still laughing, still pleasuring himself twenty years later with thoughts of the day he killed Davis Moore's little girl. Vengeance. Coldness. And Justin. Poor Justin. His sad life for nothing. A boy who never should have been born again into this world. Who was miserable because of it, right up until the day he died of an overdose. How to cope with that? The responsibility. The culpability. And not just Justin, but Jackie. His first wife. Troubled Jackie. Hadn't her husband's obsession pushed Jackie beyond her limits? His obsession and this goddamn conspiracy, which Joan had once been a part of? Hadn't it driven Jackie to her death? And wasn't Joan at fault, too? Hadn't she covered for Davis? Abetted him? Loved him? Flown to Brixton with him? And Phil Canella? Dead for nothing. For a mistake. An assumption. A misunderstanding. A file, a single file among thousands, unread. Davis's feet on the stairs.

Davis's feet on the stairs.

Joan shuffled Sam Coyne's statement into the middle of the stack and tossed the whole lot into the open box. *Coyne was still a killer, wasn't he, even if he hadn't killed AK? He killed Deirdre Thorson and those other girls.* She piled another layer of paper on top without investigating its provenance, covering the lost witness statements like thin frosting over a cake.

Davis appeared in the doorway with a glass of pale pulpy liquid for each of them, garnished with wedges of fresh lemon. "Have I seen what?"

"Nothing," Joan said. She took the lemonade. He smiled at her. He sighed.

"What a mess," Davis said.

And his wife, who loved him dearly, entombed the contents of each box with long strips of brown tape.

ACKNOWLEDGMENTS

Many thanks to:

Everyone who read this book in manuscript form, including Scott Tallarida, Jim Coudal, Dennis Mahoney, Dr. Jon Svahn, and Kevin Fry, as well as Ann and Mike, Pete and Shari, and Tom and Patty. Reading a person's unpolished novel is about as much fun as painting his house and takes almost as much time to do. Every thoughtful reading of that first draft is reflected in some way on these pages.

Simon Lipskar and Dan Lazar at Writers House. In our first conversation I told Simon he would never have a client who knew less about publishing than me. He hasn't told me I was wrong.

Jordan Pavlin and Emily Owens Molanphy at Knopf. Jordan understood this book better than anyone and improved it by magnitudes with a few strokes of a pen. Best of all, she let me believe that each upgrade was my idea.

John Warner, who for the last five years has been ridiculously generous with his time, talent, advice, patience, and friendship. Dave Eggers, John Aboud, Michael Colton, Daniel Radosh, Michael Rosen, Rosecrans Baldwin, Andrew Womack, Pete Fornatale, and John Hodgman, who each provided me opportunities I had not yet earned. Everyone at Coudal Partners—Jim, Susan Everett, Bryan Bedell, Kristin Albert, Dave Reidy, Anthony Vitigliano, and Michele Seiler—for picking up the slack while I was away, allegedly writing a book. Bert Zaczek, who, alone among my many lawyer-friends, was willing to take me as a client.

My friends Pat Brennan and Jim Poulsom of Hubbard Street Studios. Jon Langford of the Mekons for the use of his terrific song "Last Night on Earth," but also for more than twenty-five years of amazing, twisted, lovely music.

Nick Alicino and Rick McBrien, who never could have known what they meant to me. Bob Schmuhl and Walt Collins, who believed I could be a writer many years before I did.

And most of all my parents, Bill and Loretta, who, forty-five years ago, with an infant and a toddler, left a sensible life in the Midwest for a much less sensible one in New York City, teaching their children that a gamble in pursuit of something you love is hardly a gamble at all.

ABOUT THE AUTHOR

Kevin Guilfoile's fiction has been published in *McSweeney's*. He lives in the Chicago area with his wife and son. *Cast of Shadows* is his first novel.

A NOTE ON THE TYPE

This book was set in Janson, a typeface long thought to have been made by the Dutchman Anton Janson, who was a practicing typefounder in Leipzig during the years 1668–1687. However, it has been conclusively demonstrated that these types are actually the work of Nicholas Kis (1650–1702), a Hungarian, who most probably learned his trade from the master Dutch typefounder Dirk Voskens. The type is an excellent example of the influential and sturdy Dutch types that prevailed in England up to the time William Caslon (1692–1766) developed his own incomparable designs from them.

Composed by Creative Graphics, Allentown, Pennsylvania

Printed and bound by Berryville Graphics, Berryville, Virginia

Designed by Robert C. Olsson